LEGENDARY

LH NICOLE

Book One of the Legendary Saga

OMNIFIC PUBLISHING
LOS ANGELES

Omnific Publishing
1901 Avenue of the Stars, 2nd floor
Los Angeles, CA 90067
www.omnificpublishing.com

First Omnific eBook edition, February 2014
First Omnific trade paperback edition, February 2014

The characters and events in this book are fictitious.
Any similarity to real persons, living or dead,
is coincidental and not intended by the author.

Library of Congress Cataloguing-in-Publication Data

Nicole, LH.
Legendary / LH Nicole – 1st ed.
ISBN: 978-1-623421-03-8
1. Fantasy — Fiction. 2. Fantasy— Arthurian.
3. Young Adult — Fiction. 4. Romance — Fiction. I. Title

10 9 8 7 6 5 4 3 2 1

Cover Design by Micha Stone and Amy Brokaw
Interior Book Design by Coreen Montagna

Printed in the United States of America

This book is for everyone who loves a good tale of bravery, loyalty, and love.

And it is for the Lady Knights of my Round Table who have supported me so much, in every way, since I began this project.

I love you all.

PROLOGUE

Bleeding, bruised, and all but dead, Merlin stepped from a swirling portal into the magical realm of Avalon. Behind him, his brother knights and friends, Sir Galahad and Sir Lancelot, carried a dying King Arthur between them.

"Lady Titania, queen of the Fae and ruler of Avalon, I beg your help," Merlin cried out. "All the realms stand in mortal danger, and we have no hope of victory without you."

The men stood silent as Merlin's voice reverberated through the valley. Wind rushed around them, sending leaves and fallen petals aloft in front of the knights.

A beautiful, regal woman appeared in the churning greenery. "I have heard your call, my dear Merlin."

With a pop, the wind died, dropping the foliage to the ground at the queen's feet. Her copper hair fell in long curls, framing a face which looked as soft as flower petals, though Merlin knew there was nothing soft about her. The Fae queen was unpredictable and dangerous when tested. She stood as tall as the knights, her body a perfect hourglass shape with the top half covered by a tight, shimmering gold bodice. Her skirt hung from her hips and flared loosely around bare feet, which were decorated with Fae jewels and silver anklets.

Still supporting King Arthur and suffering from their own painful wounds, the knights bowed to the queen of Avalon. Merlin dropped to one knee before her. "My lady, I have trapped Mordrid in a void between the realms, but I cannot kill him. Only someone of the

Pendragon line can wield Excalibur and end his evil for good, but Arthur is the last of that bloodline." Merlin looked up at the queen, trying to contain his rage. "If Mordrid is allowed to continue unchecked, he will soon break free of his prison and destroy our realms."

Titania studied him for what felt like an endless moment. Her cold, glittering emerald eyes betrayed no emotion, but Merlin knew she understood all that was at stake. Glancing back at King Arthur, she saw the wounds in his side, the blood pooling at his feet as he slowly bled to death. Arthur's loyal knights did not fare much better—their jaws were clenched tightly against their pain and their bodies shook as the power of Avalon flowed over their wounds.

"And what would you have me do, Druid? Did not my lord give you an army to fight alongside you?"

"Yes, my lady." Sir Galahad spoke for the first time, his voice labored and thin as he held back a groan of agony. "But Mordrid's treachery knows no bounds. He delayed the arrival of the army long enough to drive his magic blade into our king." The knight's voice cracked, his eyes cast downward in shame.

Titania scoffed at the knight. "But your king is a great strategist. Surely, he would have planned for such an event."

Sir Lancelot answered before the others could. "It does not matter how it happened! Mordrid is still a threat to everything *all of us* love, including your realms."

"Please, my lady," Merlin begged. "Save Arthur. My magic is all but exhausted and I no longer have the strength to save him." He rose, meeting her calculating gaze.

Titania glided forward, stopping before King Arthur. She placed a long, elegant finger beneath his chin and lifted his face to hers.

Arthur's vision was so blurred that he could barely make out the figure in front of him. A cool breeze washed over his face, clearing his vision and causing the pain that had been gripping his body to vanish.

"Arthur Pendragon." The Fae queen addressed him in a silky voice.

Arthur peered into eyes of the deepest green.

"Do you want to live, Arthur Pendragon? To save the realms, to regain your life and find your happiness, will you do what is asked of you? If I save you, will you rise up and do what must be done to stop Mordrid and his evil?"

Arthur's intense gaze did not waver. "Yes, my lady. I swear on my life I will not rest until Mordrid's dead body lies at my feet." He would do anything to avenge his kingdom and his fallen brothers.

Titania ran her fingers over Arthur's cheek, gazing at him with a look akin to pleasure. "I have always had a fondness for you, dear king." She stepped away and gave her attention to Arthur's company. "Your king has given his word. Are the three of you willing to do the same?"

"Yes, my lady. You have our oath," they said together, their faces shining with pride and determination.

Queen Titania smiled, triumphant. "Prepare yourselves."

The Fae queen threw her arms above her head, and the valley was consumed with the potency of her magic. Galahad and Lancelot covered their eyes against the force, curling their bodies to shield their king. Merlin held himself still—he could not show any more weakness to Queen Titania.

When the magic subsided, they found themselves in a chamber hidden deep in the mountains of Avalon. In the center of the chamber was a stone bed, lit from above by a small opening in the mountain's wall.

"Do you have the Grail of Power?" Titania asked Merlin.

Arthur's Druid reached under his cloak and pulled the coveted Grail free, handing it to her.

"Lay Arthur on the stone," she commanded. Lancelot and Galahad carefully placed their king on the stone bed, stepping back as the Fae queen lowered the cup to catch several drops of Arthur's blood. "Each of you must add your own blood to the Grail."

Lancelot exchanged a guarded look with his friends. Galahad nodded to his brother-in-arms, pulling a dagger from his belt. The knight slashed a new wound in his palm, squeezing a few drops of blood into the golden, jeweled cup. Taking the dagger, Lancelot cut a matching wound, adding his blood, which was followed by Merlin's. Facing Titania, the three men wore expressions of determination and hope, along with ones of guilt and regret.

Titania pricked her finger, adding a drop of her own enchanted blood, and whispered ancient, binding words. She then tilted the Grail over her open palm. The blood poured out, transforming before their eyes into a glittering ruby.

As Merlin studied his king and friend lying helpless and as pale as moonlight, guilt choked him. His fellow knights felt the same sense of failure. If they had foreseen Mordrid's curse, their king would not have been on the verge of death and they would not have had to retreat to Avalon.

As they looked down at Arthur, the ruby rose from Titania's palm and hovered above the king.

"Arthur Pendragon, you are the once and future king. I command you to sleep until the one who is destined to awaken you seeks you out and calls for your aid."

The blood ruby consumed Arthur's consciousness, slowly darkening everything in the king's sight. He wanted to reassure his loyal knights and friends, but all he could see and feel and hear was Queen Titania. Her mighty emerald eyes demanded his acceptance, and he found he could not fight her power. The ruby returned to Titania's hand as she stepped away from the shrine.

Galahad and Lancelot relaxed as Titania moved away from their king, but the calm did not last long.

The queen fixed her gaze on them. "I have done what you asked and saved your king's life, but now you three must accept the cost. Never again may you reenter the mortal world without Arthur by your side. Your lives are now bound to his, and you will only be freed after his quest is complete." Titania's commanding voice was as hard as diamonds as she examined the knights. Sir Galahad was drowning in his guilt; Sir Lancelot was struggling to balance his desire to defend his king with his wish to rejoin his wife. Merlin's eyes were downcast, his fists white from tension, his shoulders shaking as he tried to rein in his anger at the woman who had betrayed them—the witch, Morgana LeFay.

"I warn you now, break your vows to me, to your king, fail in the tasks set before you, and you will pay a dire price."

"We will not falter," Sir Galahad swore.

"See that you do not." Titania smiled, calling on her magic to hide her from the knights' view.

"My queen, what have you done now?" Titania's husband, Oberon, king of Avalon, materialized at her side, visible only to her eyes.

Tempering her voice, the Fae queen answered, "I could not stand by and let Mordrid go unchallenged, my lord." If her plan was to flourish, it would take centuries, but Oberon could not know her intentions. Her husband was a master deceiver, the only one to ever challenge her own skills of deceit.

He stepped in front of Titania. "You know my laws. Directly interfering with mortal affairs is forbidden," he thundered.

"Yet you gave them an army, my husband." Her eyebrow rose, almost mocking her king.

"I am king of Avalon. It is for me alone to decide *if* or *how* we influence the mortal realm."

Titania bowed low. "My apologies, my king," she said, her voice honey-smooth and placating.

"You know the laws of Avalon and the consequences of your actions. You are no exception to them."

Indeed, she did know what her punishment would be for her interference, but it was a small price to pay for what it would accomplish. She would be banished to the mortal realm until Oberon saw fit for her to return. There would be much work for her to do during her banishment.

Queen Titania rose to her full height, her chin held high, and met her husband's unwavering gaze. "Indeed, my lord." She turned from him and looked at the knights. "But you must agree that their story—and what is to come—will make a tale worthy of legend."

King Oberon studied his queen silently before vanishing from the cave.

"So it begins." The queen departed for the mortal realm, a cunning smirk on her lips, satisfaction bright on her face.

I

It has weakened! For the first time in centuries I can feel the barrier thinning. She must be there — my escape — my queen. I am so close to having my revenge! I can feel her. Her strength is unbelievable, a siren's call. Her emerald eyes have haunted me since the first time I saw her. She will be mine! My Destined One!

Mordrid

Aliana Fagan's eyes snapped open the instant the voices stopped. "Not again," she moaned, pushing up onto her elbow to look at her bedside clock only to see that it wasn't even five in the morning yet. "Why can I never sleep past dumb o'clock in the morning?" the eighteen-year-old asked her empty room, turning to glance out her bedroom window.

This was the third night in a row that this strange dream had plagued her. Then again, compared to the tragic, fiery nightmare that had haunted her for the past two years, this new one was like a fairy tale.

She'd dreamed that she had been in a thick forest, wandering on an unfamiliar path, being pulled toward something she didn't understand. The path had led to a huge, beautiful lake and a hidden cave covered with hanging vines and small white flowers. A woman's beguiling voice, mingled with deeper, pain-ridden voices, called to her. Beseeching her to come to them, begging for her help.

Knowing she wasn't going to get any more sleep, Aliana threw off her comforter and padded down the hall of her family's London flat where she now lived, and started up her father's old computer. Her current home had been in her family—or rather her *adoptive* family—for three generations. Her eyes fell on the framed picture by the computer. It was an old photo of her with her parents at the beach behind their house in South Carolina.

She looked away from the happy photo and pulled up her father's digital files about Avalon and his studies into the King Arthur mythoi. She couldn't explain why, but each time she woke from the new dream, her first thoughts went to the legendary story.

Aliana's father—adoptive father, she reminded herself—had been a renowned anthropologist and, for the last decade of his life, a well-respected history professor. His life's mission had been to uncover the truth of King Arthur and Camelot, as well as Avalon's possible roots in the real world.

The hidden cave from her dream invaded her thoughts again. What was beyond that wall of ivy and flowers? If it was real, like a small voice in her head insisted that it was, maybe she was close to finding Avalon! Just the thought sent excitement racing through her body. Uncovering the truth behind Avalon was a dream and passion she had shared with her father all of her life.

Even though the wound from her parents' concealment of her adoption was a constant ache, she couldn't deny that they had loved her just as much as they had loved each other. Growing up surrounded by that love had made dating difficult, because she would always compare what she had with the boys she dated to what her parents had with each other. And after the last guy she had cared for had left her heartbroken after nearly raping her, she'd made a promise: she wouldn't let another guy get so close to her again unless she felt the same love from and for him that her parents had for each other.

But having someone love you won't stop them from lying to you, she thought bitterly. She shoved her resentment aside to focus on figuring out the dream, and started a search for wooded areas and forests that would correlate with her father's studies. *If* the dream was reality—the woods, the lake, the cave—then the answer might be in this research.

Aliana poured over the files, her excitement and passion for the legends flaring bright again. Her father had tons of files and research about King Arthur and his Knights of the Round Table, the Druid Merlin, and the evil Morgana and Mordrid. But her father was the only one who spelled it like that though—Mor*drid*. When she had asked about it, he'd shown her a copy of an aged parchment he and his old mentor had discovered in the eighties. The battered scrap referenced Arthur and Mor*drid,* and next to the villain's name had been an ancient symbol many believed represented wizard or sorcerer. Her papa may not be around to finish his work, but maybe she could do it for both of them. It was seven o'clock by the time she'd made a solid plan, showered, and changed.

Her eyes dropped to the phone lying on her dresser as its alarm went off. It was her reminder about lunch with Wade Edrick and Owen Nyhart, her best friend and newfound cousin, respectively.

"Son of a biscuit!" She couldn't meet with them today. She needed to follow through with her plan. The need to search for the lake, and the hidden cave, and those strange voices was a compulsion she couldn't ignore.

Knowing her cousin would already be awake for his daily swim, Aliana called him to cancel.

"Well, isn't this a fantastic surprise," Owen said. "Now what reason could my absolutely smashing cousin have for calling me this early in the morning?"

Aliana laughed at Owen's exaggerated British charm. "Morning to you too! Listen, I need to talk to you about something."

Owen groaned. "Blimey, in the month and a half since we met, you've said those exact words to me three times, and they always precede you canceling our engagements."

Aliana sighed. "I'm sorry." She had meant to tell him about her dream and what she was going to search for. He knew about her love of Camelot and her *slight* obsession with King Arthur and the Knights of the Round Table. But maybe it was a good thing he had interrupted her—if she'd told him she was going exploring in a heavily wooded area by herself because of a dream, he'd call her totally *potty* and make sure she was locked away.

Heck, she was ready to lock herself away, but she couldn't fight the overwhelming desire to try to find those voices and that hidden cave.

"I got a call from a magazine and they want me to get some pictures of the English countryside." Aliana chewed her lip, a nervous habit of hers. She didn't like lying to Owen.

They had only known each other for six weeks, but the bond they had forged seemed to stretch back much longer than that. Like her, Owen had no family left. Aliana had come to London over a month ago to find her real mother, but had found him instead. Since then, they had been nearly inseparable. He had even told her several nights ago that he had always felt like he'd been missing a part of himself and that since her arrival, she'd helped to fill that gap. He also shared her enthusiasm for Arthurian legend and she often thought that he'd have made an amazing Knight of the Round Table if he had lived in Camelot.

She and Owen shared dark brown curly hair, bright green deep-set eyes, and a fair complexion. Aliana stood at five feet eight inches, tall for a girl, and her cousin was just under six feet, more bulk than trim, not that he wasn't in great shape. Owen loved to swim and it showed. Aliana had always been on the chubby side as a child, but in the last few years since she'd taken up nature and travel photography, she'd gotten herself into better shape, out of necessity as much as desire. Climbing mountains, traveling through jungles, and diving in deep waters required a certain level of fitness.

"Aliana, did you hear anything I just said?" Owen's thick British accent snapped her out of her thoughts.

"Um…"

He sighed again. "All right, we can reschedule, but please take care out there! And ring me when you're on your way back. Maybe we can have dinner together instead."

After assuring him she'd be okay, they said their goodbyes, and she packed up the last of her camera gear—tripod, several lenses, a speed flash, and a remote trigger. She thought about the only other guy in her life she cared about. Wade. He and his sister, Lacy, were two of her closest friends, more like her own siblings, really. Their parents had been best friends so they had spent a lot of time together while growing up.

Wade and Lacy had come to London a week after Aliana had first arrived when Lacy had scored a study-abroad internship with a posh party-planning firm in London — it was her way of technically putting off starting college. Lacy was perfect for the job, and Wade, being the protective big brother that he was, had insisted on going with her. Luckily for Wade, there was a Kung-Fu master in London with whom he'd been wanting to study, so he had a justifiable reason to go other than just looking out for Lacy and Aliana. But they were missing one member of their "musketeer band" — their other best friend, Dawn Anson. Aliana wished again that her absentee almost-sister was with them. Fortunately, Wade and Lacy had hit it off with Owen pretty quickly.

Aliana was still thinking about her "family" when she finally reached the large forest just a couple of hours from her flat.

Well, this all looks *singularly like my dream,* she thought as she made her way through the tall trees, being sure to keep track of her progress in the small notebook she always carried. She wasn't sure why she'd chosen the path she did, but the pull to follow it had been undeniable, and with each step and turn she took, her hope of finding Avalon grew and grew.

"But…why does England have to have so much damn mist?" she mumbled.

Pausing to check her GPS, Aliana pulled out a small notebook and marked her spot on the map she'd made. After an unfortunate incident in the mountains of China not long ago, she'd become paranoid about getting lost when traveling by herself. Fortunately, she wasn't likely to run across anything more dangerous than a snake in these woods.

"Then again, considering how much I hate snakes, that could still be pretty bad." Tucking the notebook back into her pack, she reconsidered for a moment. The path she'd chosen had become nothing more than a dirt trail that the forest was trying to reclaim. She'd already tripped over two roots and gotten tangled in the foliage.

Worse still, fog had started rolling through several yards back, and the deeper she went, the thicker it became. Suppressing a slight shiver, she pulled her scarf tighter around her neck and kept walking.

She stopped to rest a little later, set her camera and pack on a nearby stone, and took a drink of water from her bottle. She pulled her nearly waist-length hair into a high ponytail and went deeper into the forest.

Finally, the fog broke, and Aliana turned on her camera. Just because the mist was annoying didn't mean it couldn't provide great ambiance for a picture. As it thinned, a path appeared between a wall of rock and a boulder that was almost completely covered in glittering green moss.

The fog rolled and swirled gently over the path, playfully lapping at the sides of the rock wall and boulder. Pushing through the underbrush, Aliana set her tripod and focused on the wall of rock. It wasn't until she gazed through the viewfinder that she saw it—a hanging vine with a single white flower.

The sunlight broke through the trees, shining rays of light across the bloom. Automatically, her finger depressed the shutter button, capturing the shot, but she couldn't breathe. The flower looked just as it had in her dream. Detaching her camera, she haphazardly shoved the tripod back into her pack before hurrying over.

The bloom was a white water lily with a pink stamen.

"That's not right." She studied it more closely. "Water lilies have yellow centers and they definitely don't grow on hanging vines." She stopped before touching the silky petals. What if she was losing her mind and just seeing things? Would the bloom vanish if she tried to touch it?

"This is crazy! I'm scared to touch a flower." With a huff, she reached out, brushing the silky petals. A soft, bubbly current trickled through her. Her jaw dropped, and her body went numb. Pink lights sparkled around her, disappearing into her skin as quickly as they'd come. A pressure settled lightly in her chest.

Aliana studied the bloom for a moment before making a more detailed inspection of the area around her. Rays of sunlight now broke through the forest, lighting the trees, leaves, and patches of moss. When the light hit the fog, still lazily swirling about, it sparkled like diamonds. The beauty was beyond picture perfect, but it was more than that. It was like there was a power opening her eyes, allowing her to see in greater detail and more vibrant colors than ever before.

"If this is a dream, I'm going to be ticked," she mumbled.

She glanced back to the flower hanging against the rock, hearing the voices from her dream again. But a small, lingering doubt plagued her. *How* could any of this truly be real? Maybe her mind was lying to her, like her parents had.

Photography was the one thing that would never lie to her. A raw photo couldn't hide anything from her; it was pure and untainted. An exact replica of what she saw. And sometimes it even revealed what she hadn't seen on her own. Everyone loved to tease her that she lived through her camera. It went *everywhere* with her.

A sheer sense of joy and excitement engulfed her as she took in the beauty around her. The trees were covered in lush, green leaves, and ivy climbed their trunks. Small blooms hung from random branches, scenting the air with a mix of delicate floral and morning dew.

Even if she had wanted to, Aliana couldn't turn back now. She was meant to be here, to find the cave covered in vines and flowers. Walking past the boulder and small flower, keeping her camera at the ready, Aliana continued on her path. She hesitated when she came to a split in the trail, but the little pink lights appeared, guiding her way, and without another thought, she continued.

She wasn't sure how long she'd been walking, but with every passing turn and hill, excitement quickened her pace. She had to be getting close to whatever was pulling at her. After a yard or two, Aliana came to yet another hill. Turning to snap a couple pictures of the path behind her, she caught a noise in the distance — *a waterfall!*

She sprinted up the hill and was shocked by what she found. There, ten meters in front of her, was a lake larger than most football fields being fed by a waterfall more stunning than any she'd ever seen. The falling water glittered like gems in the sunlight, creating a mist that spread out over the lake.

Coming to the water's edge, she kneeled down, skimming her fingers across the glistening surface. The water was refreshingly chilled even with the sun shining down on it. She stood up, examining the lake. The waterfall wasn't very high, and it poured over an expanse of slate protruding from the sides of a short cliff. There, she saw them — deep green vines with white blooms swaying in the breeze created by the falling water, covering the entrance to a cave.

"No freaking way!" She quickly made her way around the edge of the lake toward the cave. "It's real." Excited giggles tickled the back of her throat and her heart raced. *This is exactly what was in my dream!*

But by the time she reached her destination, doubt began to plague her. Absently chewing on her lip, she let her camera hang by her side while she studied the vines for a few moments. Picking up her camera, she snapped several pictures of the cave, and then checked her view finder; it couldn't deceive her. Her hands trembled as she looked through the pictures. Everything was there. It was real.

She took a step forward, then another. Reaching out a shaking hand, she brushed aside the veil of vines. The only light penetrating the darkness of the cave came from behind her.

"Stop being such a sissy, Li!" she scolded herself. Before she could change her mind, she reached into her pack and pulled out several pieces of rope. Gathering the vines, she tied them back like curtains, letting the sun's light shine freely into the hollow.

Grabbing her pack, she made her way into the deep cave. After a few turns, the light she'd let through was almost gone, bringing old fears surging to life. Keeping a tight hold on her emotions, she pulled out her cell phone, praying it still had a flashlight app. After what seemed like endless moments, the app activated and her phone lit the cave. Holding the shining beacon in front of her, she carefully made her way through the cave, making sure to watch where she stepped.

"Please don't let any beasties be living in here," she prayed. She flashed the beam from her phone onto the walls and floor, paranoid and searching for any kind of creature hiding in the dark.

Something scraped against the wall off to the left. She spun around, her light carefully held in front of her. It was only a mouse. She let out a breath as the creature gave a squeak and ran away from the light.

Laughing at her own foolishness, she resumed her trek. She walked for another ten minutes until she saw light ahead. She clicked off her cell and headed toward the light at a faster pace, finally reaching the exit. Wildflowers and rich grass stretched from the cave's opening all the way to the forests, which continued to the foot of the snow-kissed mountains hiding this amazing oasis from prying eyes.

Immediately, she picked up her camera and started capturing the scenery around her. Walking further into the valley, she saw a pond off to her left. Next to it was a white and blue tent that looked like it was made of creamy silk. It reminded her of something from *Arabian Nights*.

Uncertain what to do, she gazed at the pond. It wasn't very large, but its bright blue waters looked clean and refreshing. She backed up and took several shots of the tent and pond, picturing a beautiful woman lounging here, waiting for her beloved to join her. Moving closer to the pond, she set aside her pack and ran her fingers across the water. Ripples expanded out from where her hand touched the surface. As the tiny waves drew closer to the center of the pond, bubbles began to burst from beneath the water.

Biting back a yelp, she jerked her hand away from the pond and stood. A moment later, a small patch of blue appeared beneath the waves, pushing its way out of the water.

Not a patch, she realized — *hair!*

A woman rose from beneath the pond's surface, her tresses flowing elegantly around her heart-shaped face. Her skin was as pale as snow, and her almond-shaped eyes were as blue as the depths of the ocean and surrounded by thick, coal black lashes. Her dress was the palest of blue, draping off her shoulders and hips in perfect Grecian style. Strips of silk laced with pearls formed sleeves, and she wore a long, beaded sash around her waist.

The beautiful woman floated above the water, studying Aliana as carefully as Aliana was studying her.

"So, the Destined One has found her way home." Her voice was like twinkling bells, soft and feminine. She dipped into a curtsy. "Welcome to Avalon. It is a great joy to see you and to know that you will soon awaken the sleeping king. I am most eager to gaze upon and converse with him again."

"Who…who are you?" Aliana asked.

The woman giggled a bell-like laugh. "I am Deidre, a Water Nymph. My clan has guarded the watery gates of Avalon since the beginning." She glided toward Aliana, sighing when her feet settled on the lush grass.

Aliana's thoughts turned to the Arthurian mythoi, trying to determine who she was talking to, and she recalled one of the most well-known characters of the legends. Could she really be standing right in front of her? Talking to her? "The Lady of the Lake," she murmured, her cheeks flushing.

"Indeed." Deidre giggled again and gracefully made her way to the tent. "Come sit, Destined One."

Still reeling, Aliana followed her into the tent, which was lined with soft, silky pillows, and sat on an overly large, cream-colored cushion. "My name is Aliana Fagan." She stretched her hand out to the Nymph, but Deidre merely stared at it.

Embarrassed, Aliana pulled back and looked through the tent opening at the valley. She saw so many kinds of trees and plants she didn't recognize. Focusing her gaze further out, she saw the mountains with their peaks shrouded in fluffy, white clouds. Something out there was calling to her.

"What is wrong, young one?" Deidre asked, her wide eyes curious.

"Nothing. Sorry. This is all just a little freak-out worthy. Why are you calling me 'Destined One'?"

"Your coming has been foretold for centuries. Only the Destined One can wake the sleeping king."

"Sleeping king? What king?"

The Water Nymph's mouth opened wide as if to form a vowel sound, but Aliana cut her off.

"Do *not* say King Arthur!"

The Nymph smiled brightly. "Very well. I won't, but that does not change the truth."

"Okay, now I know this is all just some kind of crazy dream." Aliana shifted her legs, preparing to stand, but Deidre stilled her when she reached over to pat her arm, like a mother placating a child. The Nymph's hand was as cold and smooth as the water, and Aliana couldn't deny that the sensation was real.

"Centuries ago, a prophecy was made, foretelling of the Destined One. She will come at the world's greatest hour of need to awaken King Arthur and help return him and his knights to their rightful power and glory."

"You can't be serious! I'm a photographer, not a Knight of the Round Table. I can't awaken King Arthur. I wouldn't even know how or where to start!"

Deidre reached her hand toward Aliana's forgotten bag. Little bubbles opened the flap, lifting out her notebook and placing it upon Aliana's lap.

"I will show you the first part of your journey." The notebook opened, and the Nymph's eyes flashed white as she held her hand over the blank pages, whispering words in a language Aliana didn't understand. Droplets of silvery water splashed onto the page before absorbing and spreading out.

The water turned to black ink, beginning to outline a map. Aliana's outrage about the damaged pages vanished, her eyes going wide as the ink grew thicker, showing the Lady of the Lake's valley surrounded by forests and mountains. A path formed, leading away from the mountains and through the forest, across to the next page. The path collided with what appeared to be the ruins of a tower near the banks of a stream. Part of Aliana finally started to accept that this was real. Magic did exist and so did Avalon! *I wish you could see this, Papa.*

"You must travel to the ruins of the Sidhe, then find and free both Loyalty and Magic before you can find the king."

"I don't understand—loyalty and magic? How am I supposed to free a virtue and something I didn't know existed till now?"

"You must trust yourself!" Deidre chided softly. "You have found your way here, guided by the magic inside of you. This is your destiny. You cannot fight it. No one can."

Aliana sighed and looked down at the completed map.

"Once you free them, Magic and Loyalty will guide you to the king. But I must warn you, if the Sidhe or any others on the side of darkness discover you before you reach the king's resting place, you will not make it back to your world. You must take many precautions to protect yourself."

"How am I supposed to do that?" Aliana asked, getting to her feet. "I'm still not even sure this is actually happening!" Her heart feared the truth, whatever it may be.

"Avalon is as genuine as your world, I assure you. Your arrival here is the beginning of the fulfillment of the prophecy."

"How is it possible that this is all here but my father was never able to find it after all his research? With all our technology, that lake on the other side of the cave must be on a map somewhere!"

The Nymph giggled again. "Dear Aliana, only those who possess magic or have proven themselves worthy have the ability to find Avalon without help. All of your world's technology is void of magic and life. It stands no chance of ever leading to the discovery of the mystical lands that share this planet."

Aliana turned her head away, biting the inside of her cheek and giving herself a mental slap. *Why me? I'm not anything special.* "I'm sorry, Deidre, but you've got the wrong girl." She snatched up her stuff and threw her pack over her shoulder before taking a few steps toward the cave, the map still in hand.

"And where will you go?" the Nymph asked, stopping Aliana's march. "The moment you crossed over into Avalon, *you* signaled the start of the prophecy. You will never outrun your destiny. If you try, the consequences will be dire."

Aliana turned back to the blue-haired woman, trying to figure out what to believe.

"Are you willing to let your self-doubt doom King Arthur and his men?"

The Nymph's words burned at something in Aliana's heart. There was no way she could accept that all of this was real, but…what if it was? After all of her father's research, their grand adventure to find Avalon and Camelot, could she really just walk away, never knowing if what Deidre said was true?

With a deep sigh, Aliana asked, "Sidhe? I've read about them. They're supposed to be some pretty nasty, dark fairy-like creatures or spirits, right?" Real or not, if Aliana was going to take this quest further, she needed to get as much information as possible.

"Yes, and they are more dangerous than you can imagine. Humans are far more susceptible to their dark magic than other creatures are. Once caught in their trap, no one can escape, not even you." Deidre's voice was solemn and troubled.

Aliana shivered at the Nymph's warning. "So how do I avoid getting caught?"

"The Sidhe rest during the day. Their power wanes with the rays of the sun, but at night, it reaches its zenith. Your only hope of getting into the ruins and back out again is to do so while the sun is still high in the sky."

Deidre pointed to Aliana's new map. "I will warn you that you must follow the path shown here. The Sidhe are not the only creatures that pose a great danger to you. As long as you do not stray from this path, you will be protected. Leave it, and I cannot guarantee your safe travel."

"What else do I have to fear here?" Aliana was an accomplished traveler and had spent a lot of time in dangerous parts of the world both with her parents and on her own. She glanced down at the map and brushed her fingers across it.

"Avalon has many children. She is full of creatures that are born of magic and do not take kindly to humans. Some, like the Sidhe, are not on the side of goodness."

"Is there anything else you can tell me? Like *what* these other creatures are or what exactly *Loyalty and Magic* are?"

"I can only guide your way to your first task. We all have our parts to play in this. What is to come is something you must discover on your own. That is the law of Avalon."

Aliana quirked an eyebrow and gave a small snort of annoyance. "Law of Avalon? Of course! Why wouldn't a magical land have its own crazy law against giving me the information I'll need to protect myself?"

Deidre smiled. "But I have, sweet Aliana. I have set you a safe path. From there, you will find your own ways to protect yourself."

Heaving a sigh, Aliana returned a small smile before nodding. "I'm sorry. I don't mean to seem rude or ungrateful for your help. This is just a lot to take in."

The Nymph nodded, seeming to understand. "You can do this. You are the Destined One, after all." She gazed up at the sky. "You must go now if you are to reach the ruins of the keep before midday. You cannot linger in one place too long or you'll risk being found by the wrong forces."

"I understand," Aliana said, dropping her eyes.

The Water Nymph glided to Aliana, placing a cold hand on her shoulder. "May the grace of Avalon go with you, sweet Aliana. I will be waiting here for your return and that of the king."

After Aliana nodded her thanks, Deidre walked to the pond, stepping across its surface. She turned to look at Aliana. With another curtsy, the Lady of the Lake sank back into the pond from whence she had come.

2

The call of Avalon's magic shook me from my slumber. The Destined one must have found Avalon. I will search out Sabine, as she will need to make everything ready for the king. But how will I find them? Titania's magic has forbidden my return to the forests. I'll have to find another way. Soon Arthur will be restored, and so will my powers.

— Merlin

Looking down at the map again, Aliana noticed a small red spark on it. "Very handy—a magical GPS."

She made her way across the meadow to the opening in the forest. Loneliness rose within her, adding to her unease and frustration. *Papa would know what to do, what to expect.* Fighting sudden tears, she set out at a brisk pace, peering past thick clusters of leaves and tall, thin tree trunks. According to the map, she was heading northeast in the part of the forest labeled Red Wind. She hoped that referred to a kind of tree or something rather than some magical beastie that would want to eat her for lunch.

She quickened her pace, keeping her camera in her hands to capture the area around her. A new series of photos was already forming in her mind. Suddenly, a clump of bushes off to the left started to shake. She heard little whimpers coming from the shrubs, and it sounded like a small animal was hurt.

Aliana knew she needed to keep moving—the sun was rising higher and higher and she still had a long way to go. But could she really leave behind an animal that may need help? She went to the bushes and kneeled down, carefully brushing the leaves aside. Caught at the foot of one of the bushes was a small, gray and black fox-like creature, its small paw tangled in the roots. The animal looked up at her with big, black, frightened eyes.

"Aw, you poor thing," she cooed softly. "It's okay. I'll help you."

Trying not to spook the little creature, Aliana gently grasped the rough wood wrapped around its paw, pulling it away until the fox-like critter gave a small yelp, breaking free and springing to its feet. Releasing the branches, Aliana walked around the bush, leaving her pack on the path and inching closer to the curious animal as it carefully watched her. The little thing sat back on his haunches like a dog begging for a treat. Its gray fur was fluffy and long, reminding her of a Pomeranian. Except this creature had three long, bushy tails, each tipped with the same patches of black that covered its paws, muzzle, eyes, and the tips of its long, curved ears.

"Aren't you the cutest thing?" she said, trying to keep it distracted as she lifted her camera and aimed it.

When she pressed the shutter button, the little creature started and jumped back, eyeing the camera before turning and disappearing into the trees. Shaking her head, she checked the image.

"Not possible!" she gasped.

The creature in her photo wasn't the adorable animal that had just been in front of her. The thing in the picture had glowing red eyes and small, sharp fangs lining the rim of its mouth. The fur was spiky and clumped together, and deadly sharp claws poked out from the paw that had been only inches from Aliana's hand. The little monster looked like it was ready to pounce through the camera screen and take a bite out of her.

Confused, Aliana studied the trees, trying to see if the thing was still there, but she saw nothing. Getting up, she looked back only to realize that she was now several feet from the protected path she had been warned to not leave.

"Not good." She slung her camera over her shoulder and scooped up her bag, hoping she hadn't broken whatever protection the path provided. Shuddering, she picked up her pace until she reached the path.

She walked another mile before she heard whinnying and the unmistakable sound of hooves hitting the ground. Baffled, she looked in the direction of the sound but made sure she didn't move from the path. Her jaw dropped. There, becoming visible through the trees, was a tan-colored horse with a white mane that matched its large, feathered wings.

"A Pegasus!" Forgetting everything else, Aliana made her way to the creature, fascinated and excited to try to get photos of the mythical animal. Before the Pegasus moved away, she brought up her camera, taking several pictures of the beast half hidden in the trees.

Its head bobbed, as it tossed its beautiful mane and whinnied again. Aliana peered into the animal's intelligent, brown eyes and moved closer, stretching out her hand and gently brushing the silky soft fur on its nose.

"Beautiful," she whispered. The creature was taller than any horse she had ever seen, and its strong wings stretched from its shoulders to past its tail.

The Pegasus nudged her hands with its head, asking for more attention. Laughing, she stroked the creature's nose and rubbed its neck. The large animal huffed at her before moving back.

"Don't go," Aliana pleaded, stepping forward to keep her hand on its neck. "I won't hurt you." She followed it as it continued backing away, until she remembered — "The path!" She spun around, seeing only trees. "No! How could I be so *stupid?*"

Flustered, she turned back to the Pegasus. "This is your fault you know." More than a little afraid, she stepped closer to the beautiful creature. "It shouldn't be that hard to find my way back. I just have to go back the way we came."

The creature stilled, its ears twitching. Something whistled by Aliana's head, followed by a loud *thunk*. Whatever it was had hit the tree next to her. Aliana's hair fell from its high ponytail before cascading down her back and around her face.

Frozen where she stood, she saw an arrow with black feathers stuck in the tree, still vibrating from the force of its hit. Her hair band and a thin pile of her hair lay at her feet. The Pegasus reared up on its hind legs, wings flaring as it cried in fright.

Grunting shouts came from their left, getting louder and closer. Another arrow shot from the trees, this time missing them completely. Aliana jolted into action. "Run!" she cried, pushing at the Pegasus.

"Get it! Get it! Don't let the beast get away," a voice commanded in a pig-like squeal.

"Come on, girl!" Aliana shouted, winding her way through the trees. The Pegasus stayed close, keeping her large body between Aliana and the grunting creatures. Another whistling sound passed right behind them, the bolt hitting another tree.

"We gotta keep going!" She darted to the left, trying to put more trees between them and their pursuers.

"Stop!" a new voice shouted, this one deep and melodic.

Heart pounding in her ears, Aliana couldn't help but obey the command that had come from the distance. She looked around frantically, keeping her hand pressed to the Pegasus, ready to take off running again when she could figure out a safe direction.

"You have no right to stop us!" the piggy voice grunted.

"You have trespassed in the Red Wind forests. You are not welcome here." Though deep and melodic, the new voice pulsed with danger. "Go back to your caves where you belong. This forest is not yours to hunt."

Outraged squeals rang through the forest, and rushed footfalls became quieter as the hunters apparently ran away.

Pressing close to the Pegasus, Aliana hoped that whoever had chased those things off wasn't coming for her next. Groping blindly in her pack, she grabbed the journal. But there was no little red star or any other sign of her location on the map to guide her to the safe path. She stepped away from the surprisingly calm Pegasus, looking around, trying to find something that would help her find the way back.

"Halt!" The sound of the deep, dangerously melodious order came from behind her. The Pegasus's wings flared slightly as it lifted and dropped its front hooves. Annoyed by her own fear, Aliana took a deep breath, hiding her fright away and squaring her shoulders. She turned to face whatever or whoever was behind her.

There stood a man only a few inches taller than her, dressed in gold and black. He had a regal air about him, with pale, cream-colored skin, a long lean face, and silver eyes. A curved, wickedly sharp sword hung at his waist. In his hand, he had a long wooden bow, and strapped to his back was a quiver full of arrows. He was like a character out of *Robin Hood* or *The Lord of the Rings*.

His hair was pin straight and black, falling to just past his shoulders. Aliana saw the top part of a pointed ear poking out from the dark curtain of hair. His enchanting beauty made her pretty sure that he was an Elf, and she felt some reassurance—Elves were the good guys, right? After all, he did just save her from whatever those things were.

"Who are you? What are you doing in this forest?" he asked.

"I'm lost," she explained, hoping she was right to trust him. "I was following the path The Lady of the Lake told me to take when I saw this Pegasus, and then we were chased and shot at by those things you scared off." Her nerves were too short to censor her thoughts. "I can't find where I am on my map either, and I need to find a safe place for this Pegasus."

The Elf studied her, and Aliana wondered what he must see. *Probably a fool with crazy hair,* she thought to herself, just now remembering that she had lost her hair tie and nearly her head. She ran her free hand through the windblown locks, trying to get them in some semblance of neatness.

The Elf looked from her to the Pegasus. Her troublesome companion started whinnying again, bobbing its head up and down before gently pushing at her shoulder, trying to move her closer to the Elf. He nodded at the Pegasus as if he understood what it was saying.

Returning his attention to Aliana and bowing his head slightly, he said, "Forgive my harsh tone. These forests are not safe for travelers, especially your kind."

"My kind?" Aliana narrowed her eyes, wondering if he was slighting her because she was human.

He nodded. "The Pegasus told me she accidently pulled you from your path just before you were found by the Goblins. She says you protected her, and for that I will show you the way back to the path you are meant to be taking."

Grateful, but still wary of the Elf, Aliana showed him her map. He glanced at it briefly.

"We are close to the path, but we must move swiftly. These woods become more dangerous as the day goes on." He turned and started walking.

Aliana looked at the Pegasus, then quickly caught up to her guide. "What were those things? And how did you show up at just the right time?"

"Red Wind forest is one of our territories, our home. We Elves keep watch and protect all the creatures of the forest from those filthy Goblins, the Sidhe, and all others who would seek to do harm."

"Wait, you said Goblins, as in the short, mischievous, creepy-bad-magic kind of creatures that love to hoard gold?"

The Elf gave her a lopsided smile. "I have never heard them described in such a manner before, but yes, those are the creatures I am referring to. But they are not like the stories you humans tell. They are dangerous and deadly creatures. Their lust for magic and gold is what drives them." The Elf's face turned dark and angry. "They will swear fealty to whoever will give them what they desire. They swore allegiance to dark magic during the great battle of Avalon." Amazed, Aliana paid rapt attention. "They remain loyal to it to this day. Far too many times the Goblins and others have killed the animals to use in their magic rites."

"That's horrible!" Aliana gasped, looking at her Pegasus friend, who was still beside her. Gently, she rubbed the soft neck.

The Elf regarded Aliana out of the corner of his eye. "The Pegasus possesses great magic not unlike the Unicorns. Take the magic of a Pegasus, and you gain their ability to fly and run at incredible speeds."

"No way! I'm glad those Goblins didn't get her." Aliana sighed, remembering the foxy creature from earlier. She opened her mouth to ask about it, but the Elf interrupted her.

"What is your name?" he asked.

"Aliana Fagan, and I'm sorry again for wandering into your forest, but I'm glad I got to meet this Pegasus." Gazing sideways at the Elf, she watched for any sign of recognition. If the Lady of the Lake was right, others in Avalon must know who she was. But if the Elf had heard of her, he gave no sign.

He stopped walking, and using his longbow, he pushed aside a tall bush, revealing Aliana's path.

She smiled. Turning to the Pegasus, she stroked her nose before kissing the creature goodbye. "Stay away from those Goblins." The Pegasus snorted before nudging its head against her.

The Elf offered his hand to Aliana, helping her step over the thick roots of the bush and onto the path before following.

"You never told me your name," Aliana said. "I'd like to thank the person who helped me."

"I am correct in assuming you are the Destined One, am I not, Aliana Fagan?"

Aliana nodded, unsure what he would do.

"Your coming has been foretold for many centuries. We've been expecting you. Elves are on the side of good and light. To have the world consumed by darkness would destroy us."

Aliana let out the breath she was holding and smiled at him.

"My name is J'alel. I will tell my people of your arrival. The Elves will stand beside the king again when he calls us. But heed my warning—do not stray from this path again or its protection will be lost to you. There are few of us who patrol these woods and many creatures that would seek to stop you from fulfilling the prophecy."

Assuring J'alel that she wouldn't leave the path again, she smiled and said goodbye. The Elf stepped back into the forest, and Aliana headed down the path, pulling out her map. Her red star was back, and she was surprised and delighted to find that she was only twenty yards or so from reaching the end of the forest path. "Hell of a detour."

J'alel's warnings were heavy in her mind as she stowed the book and her camera into her pack and jogged toward the forest's edge. She wasn't going to let herself get distracted again, no matter what. The sun was high in the sky, but beyond the midpoint which meant it was past noon, and she was behind schedule. Finally, she entered the Valley of the Sidhe. The map showed that her destination was just over the next hill. Scaling the mound, she took in the sight of the ruined keep. It was covered with char marks and dead vines. Large piles of rubble still lay where they had fallen during battle. She looked around to see if anyone was keeping watch, but she saw no living thing.

"Creepy and probably not a good sign," Aliana mumbled. She saw the remains of a wall just a few yards away to her right. "Guess that's as good a place as any to stow my pack while I free *Magic and Loyalty*." Moving aside a chunk of stone, she hid her things in a small gap before rearranging the stone the way it had been.

As quietly as possible, she crept closer to the rounded wall of the tower, making sure to stay low. She examined the burn marks running along the jagged stone wall of the structure. Clearly the keep had been attacked by fire, but what had thrown it? Flying horses, Unicorns, Goblins, and cute-then-creepy fox-like creatures existed here. Who was to say a Dragon hadn't done that damage?

"You don't have time for this," she told herself. But her curiosity was too great. Her camera was still in her pack, so she pulled out her phone instead and took a few pictures of the marred stone so she could study it later when she was home.

She sobered at the thought. *I have to get home first, and to do that I need to stop getting distracted!* With renewed purpose, she moved toward the front of the keep, counting her blessings that she had yet to find any real threats. As she rounded the front of the tower, she came upon a large, open courtyard rimmed with stone slabs of various sizes. Each one was held up by chunks of rock. Some of the stones bore scorch marks similar to the ones on the keep, and others were covered with tiny trails of brown. In the center of the courtyard was a stone altar large enough that a person could lie atop its surface. But, unlike the keep, all of these stacked stones were smooth and polished, like marble. There were nine slabs altogether, each one with engravings that Aliana didn't recognize. The slab at the center didn't seem to fit with the others. It was almost completely covered with reddish-brown stains. Looking closer, she saw that some of whatever it was that had made those stains had run over to trickle in thin lines down several of the supporting stones.

Oh boy, Aliana thought. Like with other ruins she had seen on digs with her father, this altar was probably the most important thing to those who inhabited the place. Still not seeing any sign of life, she left the shelter of the wall, carefully making her way closer to the outer rim of the courtyard. From there she could see the arched entrance to the keep. It was flanked by short walls.

To get inside she would have to walk right out into the open where anything keeping watch would easily discover her. She hunched, crawling under one of the stone tables to hide while she figured out her next move.

It was then that she saw it—poking out from beneath a bench that had been turned onto its side was a leg! It was burnt orange in color with black splotches, the tattered remains of what appeared to be an animal-skin boot partially covering it.

Cold shivers shot down Aliana's spine as she crawled oh-so-carefully across the dry grass to get a better glimpse. Peeking around the upturned stone, Aliana found a sleeping monster with greasy black hair and a grotesque body covered by a tattered animal-skin shirt and pants that Tarzan would have been proud of.

She wanted to scream and run but quickly covered her mouth before she could. Her chest tightened as she tried to breathe past her cold terror, but she couldn't manage more than a hyperventilating gasp. This horrible monster must be the Sidhe that Deidre had warned her about.

Its body was bulky like that of an out-of-shape quarterback. His harsh face bore a wide, flat nose and a cruel mouth filled with pointed teeth. He had big arms with large hands tipped by pointed nails that were stained black like the spots covering its whole body. Lying just inches from the sausage-like hand was a twisted dagger tipped with dried blood.

She tried to back away, but lost her balance, falling flat onto her backside. Scrambling backward, she collided with a large stone. Eyes wide, she scanned the area, praying that there weren't any other beasts around, but her luck seemed to have run out. It was as if her eyes had been covered with a film before, blinding her to the presence of the Sidhe. Now she saw that there wasn't just one—there were a dozen other bodies poking out from behind the scattered stones.

Biting her lips to keep from screaming, she scrambled to her feet, frantically looking toward the keep's entrance. There were no Sidhe bodies blocking her way. *Thank God!* In her panic, she wanted to make a mad dash for the pointed archway, but she forced herself to take a deep breath and move carefully and quietly through the courtyard to avoid waking the monsters.

Finally making it to the planked entryway, she glanced back at the courtyard. None of them had awoken, but she couldn't help thinking, *It'll be a miracle if I get out of this alive.*

3

Hidden from her sight, I watch the girl. Is it really true — this common, mortal girl is the one who will restore the Golden King? I am not sure she will even survive the Sidhe. The Pegasus, still by my side, huffs at me, pawing its hooves. Clearly the creature disagrees with me. We will have to wait and see.

J'alel

Aliana glanced around the inside of the keep, not surprised that it was as damaged as the outside. Piles of small rocks and dust littered the stone floor. A set of stairs wound up and around a thick pillar in the middle. The large, curved room was bare of furnishings and decorations save the torches lining its walls.

As she circled the stairs, she saw that not only were there steps leading upward, another set also descended. The outer edges of both sets of the winding stairs were crumbled and cracked, as if some kind of railing had been violently torn away.

"Somehow going up seems like a bad idea," she whispered, hoping the sound of her voice could help brush aside the dead air and calm her racing heart.

The light from the torches only penetrated so far through the gloom of the wide lower stairs. They looked stable enough, but the darkness had panic rising in her chest again. She imagined the walls closing her in, trying to trap her below in the dark forever. Shivering, she decided to risk the upper stairs.

Slowly climbing several steps, she kept as close to the inside edge as she could, avoiding the cracked stone pieces. On the last few steps, the stones had started to scrape and shift against each other. Heart in her throat, she climbed to the next step. The one behind her crumbled away, leaving only a stump of stone attached to the pillar. Gently, she tapped the next step with her foot. Nothing happened, so she stepped onto it, and just as she did, it disintegrated. Throwing out her hands, she just barely caught the edge of the next step and dangled above the floor twelve feet below her.

With all the strength she could muster, she tried to pull herself up, but she felt her grip slip. Struggling to hold on, she heard another crack sound from under her fingers and her heart shook. But she couldn't let her fear rule her. From this distance, she could hit the ground without getting hurt *too* badly, but once there, she'd have to be quick to get away from any crumbling stones that might rain down.

Letting go of the step, she held her breath and bent her legs, bracing for impact with the floor. She hit the ground harder than she had expected, and the air rushed from her lungs. Her legs buckled, her foot rolling over a small chunk of littered stone. Using her momentum, she tucked her body and rolled to the side. Rough stone scratched against her arm. Her abused hands grabbed at the floor as she rose to her knees, bracing her feet against the ground.

"Son of a biscuit." Looking around, she expected to see the Sidhe surrounding her, awakened by the sound of her fall, but none came.

Panting, she glanced up to where she had been. Too many steps had fallen away and there was no way she was going to be able to go up now. She wiped the sweat from her brow with the back of her shaking hand, breathing through the adrenaline rush. Her palms and fingers were red and raw. Dust and dirt covered her arms, and a thin stream of blood trickled past her elbow.

Untying her cotton scarf, she dabbed at the blood. The cut wasn't deep, but it was long. She hissed as she pressed the cloth against the cut but gritted her teeth and wrapped the wound tight. Then she pushed up from the floor, grabbing her cell, grateful it hadn't been damaged when it had slid from her pocket after the fall.

"Guess the only choice now is down." Shoring up her courage, she turned on the flashlight app and carefully made her way down the first few steps.

The light from her cell phone lit the narrow stairwell enough for her to see a landing and a door a few steps below. Thankful to have made it safely down the first flight of stairs, she stepped onto the landing and held up her light, studying the heavy, chipped wooden door. Gripping its rusted brass handle, Aliana tried twisting, but it wouldn't give way. She pushed at the door, then pulled, but it refused to open.

Sighing, she peered down the next flight of steps, hoping to see another landing, but all she saw were dark stairs. *Why does everything have to be so dark? I mean, these things are magical! Why don't they have magic little balls of light in here?* She scowled. *Suck it up, girl!* As long as her cell phone didn't go out, she'd be all right.

She made it to another landing with another door, and like the first, it refused to open. She continued down the stairs, surprised that the panic she had felt was slowly ebbing away. At the third level down, there were two doors, one on each side of the stairs, including a small one that led into the pillar. She tried the bigger one, which was in the same disrepair as the others, and like those before, it refused to open for her.

The door in the pillar was less damaged, but it also *felt* different from the others. Wondering what kind of room would be in the middle of a pillar, Aliana lifted the ringed door handle and was surprised when it turned for her. As the door opened inward, a wave of hot air hit her. Its scent reminded her of a hot spring she'd visited with her mother years earlier.

Sticking her head inside, she saw that the room was small and round, lit by several old-fashioned lamps hanging from the walls. She slipped into the room, quietly closing the door behind her and sliding the lock into place. Resting her suddenly heavy forehead against the rough wood, she closed her eyes and took a breath as the last of the adrenaline in her system burned off.

Her eyes shot open again as a deep, rumbling growl came from behind her. *Please God, No!* She slowly turned around, her numb fingers gripping the door handle tightly, ready to flee from the room if she had to. Hanging from the ceiling was an ornate cage of gold and bronze with twisting bars and small glowing stones. The cage was partially covered by a piece of cloth so tattered that looked like a good wind would completely destroy it.

She didn't know what could be in the cage, and she was way too morbidly curious to not find out. Stiffly, she reached up, grabbing a corner of the fabric and yanking it away from the cage.

"Oh my stars!" she breathed, shocked but amazingly unafraid. Trapped in the cage was a real, live Dragon!

Aliana gazed at the small, marbled Dragon that watched her from the dangling cage. This creature was nothing like the monsters she had imagined as a child—no bulky body or spiked tail. Instead it had a long, snake-like body and large, clawed feet. Its thin wings flared slightly, showing leathery skin riddled with veins of silver. But its head was the most fascinating part—elongated and angular, topped with short, pointed horns and covered with more veins of silver. Its mouth hung slightly open, giving her a glimpse of sharp teeth. The little creature's ears pointed out to the sides as if straining to hear something.

Staring back at her were eyes as clear and purple as amethyst jewels. She should have been terrified, but somehow, she knew this Dragon meant no harm to her. Pulling out her cell phone, she snapped a picture of it. Unlike the little fox thing, this creature looked the same in the image as it did in real life. The Dragon was real!

"Hello." Aliana waved, half expecting the Dragon to answer. "Avalon has certainly proven to be full of surprises, so why wouldn't a Dragon talk?"

The Dragon just stared back at her, as if waiting to see what her next move would be.

"I guess you can't talk, huh? Oh well." She didn't disguise her disappointment. *How amazing would a talking Dragon be?* "Judging by that big ol' lock on your cage, I'm guessing you aren't in there by choice." She inched closer and examined the ornate lock. "This doesn't look like any lock I've seen, but there's a hole for a key." She glanced around the room before turning back to the Dragon.

Now that she was a mere foot from the cage, the creature seemed larger than it had before. She realized that there was some kind of power radiating from it, like a warm buzz she could feel brushing her skin inside and out. It comforted her.

"Where is that key?" she murmured. The Dragon held her gaze for a moment then flicked its head to the side before glancing back at

Aliana. "Over there?" Arching her eyebrow, she made her way to the table along the wall. It was cluttered with sheets of paper and scrolls.

She searched the desk but couldn't find anything that might open the lock. Another low growl had Aliana jumping in shock, knocking her knee into the table and sending everything scattering to the floor. Wheeling around, she glared at the Dragon. "What the heck was that for?" she demanded in a low voice, her Southern accent slipping out. "I'm trying to help you and you go scaring the life out of me!"

The Dragon's head tilted to the side, watching her for a moment. Aliana could have sworn the creature was smirking at her. Then it nodded down to the floor.

Glaring at the magical creature, she took its hint and crouched, starting to go through the papers again. Picking up one of the fallen scrolls, she noticed a pin dangling from the leather cord that held it shut. A closer glance revealed a twisting gold knot at the top and a bent tip.

She looked back at the Dragon and held up the scroll. The creature nodded its head once. "Well I guess it's worth a try. You might not be able to speak, but at least it seems you can understand me."

Yanking the key off the cord, she threw the scroll onto the table and grabbed the cage lock. Hot sparks erupted from the metal and zapped her fingers. "Shoot!" Aliana cradled her hand, checking for signs of a burn. "Great. How the heck am I going to get that thing open if I can't even touch it?"

Glancing around again, she saw a pair of thick leather gloves hanging on a peg next to the door. Putting them on, she took a deep breath. The lock sparked again when she grabbed it, but her hands were safe. She jammed the key into the lock, twisting and juggling until it fell open in her hand a few seconds later. Looking at the Dragon, she saw its eyes light from within as it stared at the lock.

"You're not going to jump out of there and fry me are ya?" Maybe the Dragon had been locked up for a reason. So why wasn't she scared of this creature? Any person in her right mind should be scared. It growled softly again, its tail twitching like a cat's did right before it pounced. The Dragon lifted its gaze to her. "Fine, but if you try to fry me, I won't be held responsible for my actions." Her warning sounded hollow even to her ears. What could she possibly hope to do against even a small Dragon?

After dropping the lock and gloves, Aliana opened the cage door, and the Dragon shot out to freedom, the strength of its wings knocking the door from her hands. Gray and silver wings filled her sight as she watched the creature zoom around the room before landing on top of its former prison. Its long body wrapped around the top of the cage, its face coming to eye level with Aliana. Transfixed, she stared at the little thing. It was so beautiful with its wings flared and purple eyes glowing with power.

"So you are the Destined One? You're taller than I thought you would be."

"You talk?" Aliana snapped from her stupor.

She was startled by the gravelly laugh that came from the Dragon. "The magic that held me in that cage trapped me in many ways." Its voice was ageless and deep and distinctly male.

"You called me 'the Destined One'—just like Deidre and J'alel did. So the Lady of the Lake was telling the truth about that."

She didn't think she would get used to being called that, though.

The corner of the Dragon's mouth turned up in a smile. "What else did our Lady tell you, Destined One?"

"First off, my name is Aliana, and the Lady of the Lake only told me that I was destined to awaken King Arthur." Rolling her eyes, she shook her head. "Honestly, I'm not sure she had all her marbles in place. If nobody else can wake him, how am I supposed to?"

The Dragon growled softly. "Typical of a Nymph. They never tell you what you need to know."

"What do you mean?" She gazed at the creature, crossing her arms over her chest.

"Only the Destined One will be able to bear the power needed to awaken the fallen king." Before she could ask one of the dozens of questions in her head, the Dragon answered one of them. "My name is Daggerhorne. My role is to serve as guide and protector to the Destined One. There will be many challenges which you cannot hope to complete on your own."

She felt her chest tighten. Doubts screamed at her. Yet, despite that, something felt *right* about this. For the first time since her parents' deaths, the wound inside her heart felt smaller. She remembered what her father had always told her: *"Never give in to fear, little star. Accept whatever comes. The important thing is meeting it with courage and giving it everything you've got."*

Letting out a breath, she gathered her courage and said, "Okay, so with your help, I'm supposed to awaken King Arthur, reunite him with his knights—who all died hundreds of years ago, by the way—and restore them to their former glory. Have I missed anything?"

"Sarcasm is not becoming, my lady."

"Sorry, but right now that's about all I've got." Her father had always told her that she had the explosive spark of a star inside of her and that was what made her the spitfire her mother had always called her.

"Did you really think I was going to 'fry you' for freeing me?" The Dragon laughed.

Aliana arched her eyebrow. "You're the first Dragon I've met. How was I to know you'd be so friendly?"

Shaking his head, he continued, "Did the Lady of the Lake tell you anything else?"

"Yeah, she gave me a magic map showing me the way here. I am meant to find *Loyalty and Magic*." The Dragon nodded and stayed silent, causing Aliana to tap her foot impatiently. "I'm gonna guess you're what I'm supposed to find. Does that mean you know how to get to Arthur?"

"You're half right. I'm Magic, but you're still missing Loyalty. Without him, we will not find the hidden entrance to King Arthur's hollow."

"Him? There's another creature imprisoned here?"

Daggerhorne chuckled. "Sir Galahad is not a creature. He was the most loyal of Arthur's knights, trapped here by the Sidhe hundreds of years ago."

Hundreds of years? How could a man survive imprisonment for so long?

"I have heard the Sidhe talking of a warrior trapped below the keep. I believe we'll find him if we go down the stairs just outside this room." Aliana didn't like the thought of traveling deeper into the Sidhe's home, but there was no way she could leave a man imprisoned, whether or not he was the one who could lead them to King Arthur.

"We need to go quickly," Daggerhorne warned. "Moonrise is fast coming, and we need to be gone from this place before then." He jumped from the cage, landing on her shoulder. His claws dug softly into her skin as he twisted his warm body around her neck like a necklace, but she could barely feel his weight.

She pulled out her cell phone and stepped out of the room and onto the landing, carefully checking that they were alone. By some miracle, her battery was still fully charged. *Let's just hope it stays that way. I doubt I'm going to find a magical charger here.*

"Someone should tell these Sidhe it's not smart to keep things in such disrepair," she whispered as they descended.

"This keep once belonged to the Elves, but the Sidhe seized it in battle shortly after Camelot fell. The Sidhe were Mordrid's closest allies. They took what they wanted and drove the remaining Elves far from here."

Aliana knew that according to legend, Mordrid was King Arthur's archenemy and an incredibly evil person. With every step she took, shivers ran down her spine. She shouldn't be here, but how could she turn back? A man had been trapped for hundreds of years, and now she had the chance to free him.

Pushing the fear aside, she quickened her pace. The sooner they found him, the sooner they could leave. Reaching the last step at the bottom of the tower, she saw three different halls branching away from the base of the stairs. Mercifully, the area was lit with several torches, so she shut off her cell phone and grabbed one.

"Which way do we take?" she whispered.

Daggerhorne leaped from her shoulder, landing on silent claws. Raising his head, he sniffed the air. "This way."

Aliana followed him through dank hallways before she saw a small opening cleverly hidden in the wall. Without pausing, she and Daggerhorne ducked into the room it opened to. The cold air was stale, sending more shivers of dread rushing down her spine.

Leave! her mind screamed, but she paid no attention.

In the center of the room was a tall, thick block of solid amber crystal. Moving the torch closer, she saw that the crystal glowed softly with its own magic. At the heart of the amber was a man.

"Is that Galahad?" Her voice trembled, horrified. "What have they done to him?"

She held the torch higher, trying to get a better view of the trapped warrior. He looked like he was ready to destroy anyone foolish enough to try to take him on. *He must have been trapped during a fight.* It was hard to see any real detail, but she could see he was tall and broad. He would have been fierce and formidable on a battlefield.

"He guarded the entrance to Arthur's hollow. The Sidhe were desperate to find it, so they lured Galahad away and into a trap. But the knight was prepared and fought them off. They realized they wouldn't be able to defeat him, so they did what they had to."

Aliana glared at Daggerhorne. "You sound like you *approve* of what they did."

"Not at all, my lady. But my kin have been hunted to near extinction by humans, especially Uther Pendragon." His voice was pained. "As have the Sidhe and all bearers of magic." Daggerhorne looked up into Aliana's eyes. "Humans have always sought to destroy what they do not understand. Or they plot to use those who hold the power of magic for their own selfish gain."

"Then why did Arthur have a sorcerer in his court as one of his most trusted advisors?"

"Arthur Pendragon was not like his father or like any other man in that time. He believed that magic was not something to fear and that those who wielded the power should have as much freedom as any other man."

"Well, at least that sounds like the King Arthur of legend, but how do you know this, Daggerhorne? Surely you weren't around back then."

"My kind live for hundreds of years, longer if we are surrounded by magic. I am far older than you think."

Aliana shook her head. "I don't want to know, Dagg."

"Dagg?" The little Dragon gazed skeptically at her.

"No offense, but you have a long name." She shrugged, turning back to Galahad.

"So this is Lancelot's son, the warrior who found the Holy Grail and was renowned for his chastity and purity," she mused aloud, stepping to the amber and brushing her fingers across the rough surface that hid his face.

Dagg gave a small snort of disgust. "You humans. You can't keep track of your history. Lancelot was his cousin twice removed. And none of the knights were chaste."

Aliana's eyes widened. "I think I'm processing a little too much right now, so let's just free Galahad and get out of here. Then we can deal with your history lessons."

"Very well," he said, circling the stone. "Sir Galahad has been trapped for far too many centuries. It is time we give him back his freedom."

"I totally agree, but *how* are we supposed to free him?"

"To free the man trapped in time, you must possess a weapon wielded by him, burnished by the flames of magic."

"Flame of magic? Where is his sword?"

Frustrated, she ran her hand through her hair as she finally drew her attention away from the trapped man and looked at the room. The walls were lined with dozens of swords, knives, maces, and battle-axes—displayed like trophies. She studied all of them closely, but only one stood out to her. Hanging above a battered, green shield bearing naught but a painted sword was a warrior's broadsword. The design was simple steel and leather, but the cross guard was engraved with Celtic markings.

"Is that his?" She picked up Daggerhorne to let him see the sword better.

"That is the sword of Galahad." Daggerhorne spread his wings and jumped from her hands, digging his claws into the brick, clawing his way to the sword.

"Okay, so we have his sword, but can you tell if it's been burnished by magic? If it hasn't, how do we free him? We can't sneak out of here, get the magic we need, and sneak back in without being caught by the Sidhe."

Daggerhorne chuckled again as he turned his head to her. "My lady, I am a Dragon born of magic. *I* can burnish the sword, but once the flames consume the blade, you will have little time before the magic burns out."

She was supposed to wield a sword covered in fire? Aliana turned and looked at Galahad again, wondering if he realized what was happening around him. She prayed not. How could a person stay sane like that? No matter what the risks, she couldn't give up just because she might get hurt. A glimmer of hope burned a little brighter in her chest.

"Do it," she told the Dragon. "We can't leave him trapped in there a moment longer. No one deserves that kind of punishment."

4

The Destined One surprises me. Aliana is so youthful, so brave, but also vulnerable. Her heart is broken and aching with loneliness. Shame washes over me. I am supposed to be her protector. If I had not spent two centuries locked in a cage, maybe I could have prevented whatever she has suffered! How can she do all she must when self-doubt and sadness rule her?

— Daggerhorne

Aliana stowed her torch in one of the empty holders along the wall and watched Daggerhorne's purple eyes flash bright with magic. He drew a breath, and she felt the energy in the room sizzle against her skin, rushing to do Dagg's bidding. Fire roared from his mouth, but it didn't look like normal fire—single stars of magic lit each separate flame as they licked their way up from the pommel to the tip of the sword.

"Now!" Daggerhorne commanded. "Take up Galahad's sword and free him."

With both hands, she grabbed the sword and whirled around to face the amber. The magic fire fizzled and popped against her skin, sending waves of prickles surging up her arms, but she ignored it. Closing her eyes, she drew in her breath as she raised the blade high over her head. With all her strength, she brought the sword down, cutting into the solid formation.

The opposing magics collided, and the shock from the blow left her arms shaking, her hands unable to keep their grip. Opening her eyes, she saw that the sword had cut into the edge of the block, but other than that, the amber seemed unaffected. Furious with herself for failing, she tried to pull the sword free for another try, but the flames melted into the stone, disappearing completely.

"What did I do wrong?" She let go, stumbling back a step. Before she could ask Daggerhorne to burnish the sword again, a crack echoed around the room. Small fissures in the amber formed where the sword was lodged, spreading like a spider's web deeper and deeper into the stone. Chunks started to fall, disintegrating, leaving no evidence of the amber's existence.

Aliana was shocked when she got her first good look at Galahad. He was breathtakingly handsome. His features were Roman in shape, and his wavy hair was light brown, but the paleness of his skin spoke of his northern heritage. His jaw was strong and clean-shaven, his mouth was set into a firm line, and his eyes were closed.

The last of the amber fell away, revealing a powerful body, honed by years of fighting and training. Over his hand and wrist was a thick cuff of silver, decorated with a Dragon taking flight — the Pendragon seal. Here before her was a Knight of the Round Table, Camelot's protector and loyal servant to King Arthur.

Dazed, her body moved closer to his, as if of its own accord, and her hand stretched out to brush against the cold silver of the cuff, tracing over the back of his strangely warm hand. The moment her skin touched his, a spark shot from her heart down her arm and to their connected hands. His eyes snapped open, finding hers immediately. Aliana's world tilted. His eyes were a shockingly clear shade of blue — and they were focused on her! She was drawn into his captivating gaze, and a band clicked into place around her heart.

Barely able to breathe, she was drawn even closer to him, her hand reaching up to rest lightly against his chest. His muscles tightened and shifted under her touch. Before she realized it, his hands shot up, capturing hers and pinning them behind her back. He held her prisoner in his iron grip, though his breathing was shallow and rapid.

Her legs gave out, and she sank to her knees. Galahad followed her down, preventing any chance of escape. "Who are you?" His demanding voice was cracked and dry from disuse.

Aliana tried to answer, but she couldn't form any words.

"Who *are* you?" His voice was deeper and stronger now. "What are you doing here?" His face was inches from hers, and his eyes were a mix of confusion and cold anger as they searched hers.

She forced words past her terrified lips. "I…I'm Aliana Fagan."

Galahad's grip tightened, and pain shot through her arm, the gash from her injury on the stairs throbbing. "Please let me go," she whispered. Terrified by his sternness, she tried to twist her arm free, but he was too strong. "I mean you no harm. I—I just want to help."

"You forget yourself, Knight of Pendragon!"

Galahad's eyes turned to meet Daggerhorne's.

"You are bound by Arthur Pendragon's code of honor, yet you would attack the woman brave enough to free you from your imprisonment and restore the king to this world?"

Galahad's eyes closed, and he was finally able to take a deep breath. His eyes returned to Aliana's, the cold anger burning away. Taking another breath, his eyes never left hers as he pulled her to her feet. He held her ever so gently until she had her balance back.

The knight towered over her; she just barely reached his broad shoulders. Backing away, she studied him, rubbing her sore arms and checking to see if she was bleeding through her makeshift bandage. Galahad seemed to take up all the available space in the small room. When she'd touched him, he had been solid muscle. A dangerous kind of strength rolled off of him, scaring and comforting her at the same time.

Galahad turned to Daggerhorne, looking away from Aliana. His face contorted, like he was confused. Though she was still upset by his actions, she couldn't help but feel bad for him.

"Lord Daggerhorne, what are you doing here?" There was a strange cadence to Galahad's deep, soft voice with a long drawl on As and Es.

"*We* are here to free you from the Sidhe and get to Arthur's hollow so we may awaken him. But I find myself worried that you will be unable to lead us there. You have clearly forgotten everything you stand for if you would take such action against a woman." Daggerhorne's power warmed the air as he narrowed his eyes on Galahad.

Taken aback by the Dragon's harshness, Aliana glanced away from Galahad and glared at Dagg. "Stop! He's been trapped for centuries, and he doesn't know me from a Sidhe."

"Lord Daggerhorne is right, my lady," Galahad said, facing her again, surprise in his expression. "There was no excuse for me to hurt you the way I did, no matter the situation. I beg your forgiveness for my actions."

His Carolina-blue eyes were clear and focused, the confusion from moments ago banished and replaced with a calm confidence.

"Apology accepted." She smiled softly, holding out her hand. "It's nice to meet you."

Galahad smiled back, looking way hotter than should be allowed for a guy who'd been frozen in amber for centuries. His hand closed around hers, strong and sure. He gave her a small bow, bringing her hand to his lips and brushing a gentle kiss across the top. The newly formed band around her heart tightened, and her stomach felt like it had filled with dozens of popping bubbles.

"It is an honor to meet you, Lady Aliana. I am Sir Galahad, first knight of Camelot and loyal servant to Arthur Pendragon."

Wow was the only thought she could process as she stood numb to everything but his hand holding hers.

Galahad scanned the room that had served as his prison. No traces of the petrified amber remained. The only sign of where he had been was his sword lying discarded on the ground. His brow furrowed. "How did you free me?"

"Your sword," Aliana answered. "Dagg burnished it. It broke the amber trapping you."

She watched Galahad bend down to pick up his weapon, taking in the grace of his movements and the air of power that clung to him.

After an appraising glance at his sword, the knight straightened and turned back to them. "We need to go."

Dagg nodded. "The Sidhe will soon notice that their enchantment has been broken. We need to be far from here when that happens."

Aliana grabbed the torch and headed toward the opening that led back into the hallway.

Before she could leave, Galahad placed a warm hand on her shoulder, pulling her back. "I go first," he told her. When she narrowed her eyes at him, he added, "It's safer, and I have a weapon."

Aliana wasn't used to following anyone, except maybe her father. She opened her mouth to fire a smart comment, but Daggerhorne's soft growl stopped her.

"He's right, my lady." Stretching up, the Dragon wrapped himself across her shoulders again.

Considering that she was deep inside the lair of an enemy she knew very little about, she decided that following wasn't such a bad idea. "Okay, but we need to stop by the stream behind the keep so I can get my pack. All my stuff is in there."

Nodding, Galahad surveyed the hall before motioning for Aliana and Dagg to follow. He kept his sword at the ready and his eyes watchful. They made it to the stairs unchallenged, but Galahad's posture remained tense.

"Watch out for the steps," Aliana warned in a low voice. She pushed the torch to the side, showing him the crumbling stairs.

"Leave the torch," he warned. "The light will attract unwanted attention."

Aliana started to panic. She couldn't do this in the dark. Her fear of being trapped became so great that it threatened to crush her. "Galahad, it's completely dark up those stairs. We need to be able to see!"

"We can't take the torch. It will take too long to extinguish if we need to hide from the Sidhe," Galahad explained softly, carefully studying her expression. "How did you get down here?"

Wanting to hit herself for letting her fear overwhelm her, she pulled out her cell phone, clicking on the flashlight. Smiling at the look of amazement on Galahad's face, she explained to him that if needed, she could click it off in an instant and they would be hidden. His wonder made him seem so youthful, and she realized that he couldn't have been older than his mid-twenties when he was trapped.

"What kind of magic is this?" he asked Daggerhorne.

Aliana answered, "It's not magic. It's technology. You'll get used to it."

Placing the torch back in the holder she had taken it from, she followed Galahad up the stairs, being sure to keep the light directed at the steps.

"We need to go faster," she whispered. "Those things were sleeping when I got in here, but that was a while ago, and they could be awake by now."

Looking back, Galahad hesitated, then nodded and continued. When they reached the floor where Aliana had found Daggerhorne, she gently grabbed Galahad's elbow, whispering, "We're three flights away from the main floor. We have to be sure the Sidhe aren't around."

Without a pause, Galahad took command. "Lord Daggerhorne, when we get to the top you will check to see if it is safe for our exit."

Dagg nodded from his perch on Aliana's shoulder. Even more focused than before, Galahad continued to lead the way. His boots made almost no sound as he climbed the steps, unlike Aliana, who felt like she was making enough noise to raise the dead. *Or the Sidhe.*

She rested her hand against the knight's back, pinching a small piece of his leather tunic, trying to stay close to him. He made her feel safe. He looked over his shoulder, his eyes scrunched together, questioning whether she was okay. With a shy smile, Aliana shrugged her shoulders.

Reaching the first landing, she saw the door that had been locked earlier hanging open. Tugging on his tunic, she pointed to the door. He nodded, raising his sword. Gripping his tunic tighter Aliana clicked off her phone's light. She was scared, but Galahad's closeness and the faint light coming from the room helped her keep from panicking. Dagg's warm leather-like wing brushed gently against her shoulder, reminding her that he was here for her too.

Placing a finger to his frowning lips, Galahad motioned for silence. Climbing the last few steps to the landing, the knight gently moved Aliana behind him, covering her as they stepped past the door. Once past it, he held his sword ready, his face set in hard lines, and motioned for Aliana to stay put while he checked the room.

Nodding once, Aliana stroked Daggerhorne's scaled body like she would a cat's, trying to calm herself. She watched Galahad nudge the door further open with his sword and disappear into the room. She waited to hear the sounds of a fight, but everything remained dead quiet.

Galahad reappeared after a minute, took her hand, and pulled her into the room. He shut the door quietly, sliding the wooden lock into place as she studied the large room. Wooden benches were covered with decorated masks and piles of richly-colored fabric. Pegs stuck out from the walls, holding dark cloaks. The masks were various sizes and shapes, some large enough to cover a person's face while others were just large enough to surround a person's eyes.

"Do you think we should grab some of these?" she asked Galahad quietly. "If those things are awake, maybe we can disguise ourselves." Thinking of how disgusting the Sidhe were, she wasn't thrilled about wearing something that belonged to them, but it would be worth it if it protected them.

Galahad considered her suggestion for a moment, then nodded. "I agree. Since the door was opened, it would be safe to assume the Sidhe are also wearing them."

Leaving Galahad to pick their cloaks, Aliana walked over to the table of masks. They were all beautiful in an eerie sort of way. "Why do the Sidhe have these?" She ran her fingers over one of them but couldn't tell what they were made from. They appeared hard and stiff, but the material was soft to her touch.

As he sorted through cloaks, Galahad said, "I cannot be sure. The only creatures I know of that would wear such masks are the Elves. I cannot imagine what purpose the Sidhe would have for them."

Thinking these had once belonged to the Elves made them seem less eerie and more beautiful, but if the Sidhe had had them since taking over the keep, God only knew what they could've used them for.

"The Sidhe are cousins of sorts to the Elves," Dagg explained, jumping from her shoulder down to the table. "Their rituals are as much the same as they are different. You are right to think these masks will help us escape. Tonight are the full moon rites, and these disguises will hide the fact that you are human."

Aliana picked a simple black and gold mask for Galahad. Next to it was a deep green, leafy mask with swirls of dark purple and pointed edges.

"We need to hurry." Galahad now stood directly behind her, and Aliana swallowed, surprised by his nearness. Looking over her shoulder, she saw Galahad hold up a heavy, green cloak.

"For you, my lady." His hands were warm as he placed the cloak over her shoulders, resting them there a moment longer than needed. Biting her lip, Aliana took the cords from his calloused fingers. Tying the cloak securely, she took a small breath, inhaling Galahad's wintery scent. He smelled like crisp air before a heavy snowfall, with a hint of warm spices. She felt a sense of disappointment when he stepped back to don his own cloak.

Instead of obscuring his large body, his ebony cape emphasized the width of his shoulders and strong arms. She held out the mask she had chosen for him, and he took it, the corner of his full lips turning up in a smile.

He would be a good kisser…What am I thinking? Aliana quickly spun around before her blush could give her thoughts away.

She peered at Dagg, still sitting on the table, surrounded by masks. The Dragon's eyes crinkled at the edges with laughter, his large mouth turned up on the sides as he smirked knowingly. Why did Galahad have to be so hot? *Stop that line of thinking right now!* Aliana knew herself—she always fell too hard, too fast.

She dropped her mask on Dagg's smug face and twisted her hair, tucking it into her hood. The Dragon chuckled as she picked the mask back up and tied it around her head. It molded perfectly to her face, as if it had been made just for her. Hoping that the mask and low lighting would hide her blush, she turned toward Galahad.

With the cloak and mask, together with the sword sheathed at his waist, Galahad looked like a dark knight ready to infiltrate another's castle so he could sweep a beautiful maiden away into the night. He glanced over and caught Aliana staring at him.

Embarrassed all over again, she fixed her eyes on the door before saying, "We should go. Deidre said to not stay in one place too long."

He came over to stand just in front of her and brushed escaped locks of her hair off her shoulders, tucking them into the hood of her cloak. He watched her intently as he raised her hood up into place. "There. Now you are ready."

Hoping Galahad couldn't see her furious blush in the low light of the room, she broke eye contact and went back over to the table to pick up Dagg. The Dragon chuckled in her ear as he settled over her shoulders again, tucked inside the oversized hood.

"Shut it, Dagg," she whispered furiously to him. "There's nothing for you to laugh at."

"If you say so," he said, his Dragon's breath warm against her ear. Aliana turned back to Galahad, watching him lift his own hood before unsheathing his sword and unlocking the door.

She needed to focus on the Sidhe and the danger, not on ogling the hot knight. Pulling out her cell phone, she was about to click on the light, but Galahad's hand on top of hers stopped her.

"No need," he whispered. "There is enough light from up top. We will not need your *technology*." The way he said "technology" made it sound like a bad word.

Annoyed, Aliana peered around his shoulder into the hall. It was better lit than before, but it was still dark enough to have her hands and neck sweating. *I can do this!* she told herself reluctantly, putting her phone back into her pocket.

As they ascended the final flight of stairs, she stayed close to Galahad. Before they reached the top, just out of view from the main floor, his arm went out to hold her back. "Lord Daggerhorne." He nodded to her Dragon.

Dagg jumped from her shoulder, his wings flaring out as he landed soundlessly on the stone stairs. The little Dragon paused at the top step, sniffing the air before poking his head up and vanishing to the floor above.

Anxious, Aliana tapped her index finger silently against her thigh. The tapping became a drum, beating in time with her heart, gradually speeding up. The drumming calmed her nerves. In her mind, she could hear deep horns joining the dark, primal beat and a woman singing unknown words in a sultry, smooth voice.

Dagg reappeared before them, and Aliana stopped tapping her finger, but the melody remained in her mind. The Dragon said the ground floor of the keep itself was empty of life. "But we are too late. The Sidhe are awake and have already started their ceremonial rites in the courtyard. We must use extreme caution. The magic surrounding us is strong."

"What do you mean?" Aliana asked softly, scooting just a little bit closer to Galahad, a random wish to dance with him popping into her head.

"The Sidhe are able to put a person into a trance-like state in which they become their slaves," Galahad said darkly. He turned to her, circling his free hand around her neck, gently tipping her face up to his. "The only way to escape their pull is to focus on something else. Focus hard enough that you can block the influence of their magic." His blue eyes pierced her. She forgot all about the dark music, focusing on the twisting knots in her stomach. "Do you understand, my lady?" he asked softly, his eyes searching hers before wandering down her face.

"Yes," she whispered, wishing she knew what he was thinking as he examined her.

Galahad took a deep breath, straightening, and pulled his hand from her neck, his fingers trailing lightly over her skin.

"I will lead the way," Dagg said, breaking Aliana's attention on Galahad. The little Dragon was smirking at her again.

Still twisted in knots from Galahad's touch, she followed behind the guys, wrapping her cloak tightly around herself, hoping that would help block out the Sidhe's magic. When she tried to focus on something, as Galahad had suggested, it was his amazingly clear blue eyes, strong square jaw, full lips, and warm and soothing presence that her mind fixated on.

Enough! I shouldn't be thinking about him like that. I shouldn't want to be so close to him. Think about…photography!

Instead it was the music from just moments ago she thought of, recalling the dark melody and crooning voice. She crept to the archway, pressing tightly to the side as Galahad peered around the wall to see if the way was clear.

Speaking so softly that she could barely hear him, he said, "We need to jump over the side of the wall, just on the other side of this arch. From there, we can make our way around to the back and retreat into the forest."

"Okay," she said, trying to keep the dark melody foremost in her mind rather than Galahad. The music was louder now, sounding as if the pounding bass was only a few yards away. Swaying with the music, she followed Galahad under the arch, not wanting to be far from him. She chanced a quick look at the courtyard, wondering if the music taking over her mind was coming from there.

Small fires created a path from the keep and surrounded the courtyard. The sinking sun's orange and gold glow played against the stone tables, dancing across the white, flowing dresses of five women as they twirled around the altar. Two of the women had pale blond hair, and the other three were brunettes. Flowers and small beads were woven through their hair.

Transfixed, Aliana peered through the flames that separated her from the dancers, meeting the brown eyes of one of the blondes. The blonde smiled, closing her eyes in pleasure. Two men dressed only in white drawstring pants danced alongside the women, seemingly bound in the same thrall.

5

*The Destined One looks so young, innocent even. But the
shadows in her mesmerizing eyes speak of pain, loss, and fear.
Fear of me, yet she still fought me with a courage I have not
seen from many females. The moment I felt her soft touch,
something inside me broke. All I want to do is possess this
girl. It is a need I cannot seem to fight, yet I know I
must—my memories are still piecing things together, and I
haven't forgotten that my first duty is to my king.*

~Galahad

A Sidhe covered in a brown cloak approached the striking blonde.
Playfully, the woman pulled back his hood, revealing a large
mask with short stubby horns. It covered all but his mouth. Dozens
of creatures, which looked nothing like what Aliana had seen sleeping in the courtyard earlier that day, watched the dancers. They were
dark and ethereal, dressed in thick wool jackets and brown leather
pants. Their long, raven-colored hair seemed to absorb the light of
the setting sun. Seven of them stood at the center of the courtyard,
wearing heavy cloaks and masks like the ones she and Galahad wore.
Several other Sidhe appeared to be female, dressed in layers of dark-
colored material with thick ropes of bright silver and gold woven up

their arms and across their torsos. Some wore eye masks that tied around their heads while others used masks held up by carved wands, but their beauty was unmistakable.

Most of the Sidhe swayed together in large groups while a few split off, moving and gliding sensually in pairs. But none, save the ones wearing cloaks, touched the people in white.

"My lady," Aliana heard a growling voice call to her. She glanced around the courtyard, trying to see who had called her. Something sharp scratched her hand, and she gasped, momentarily distracted from the Sidhe. "Do not listen to them! *We must leave now!*" Daggerhorne hissed. He'd slipped out from beneath her hood and now hovered by her side.

She pulled herself up so she was sitting on the edge of the wall. Swinging her legs over, she peered at Galahad, whose mask highlighted his bright, blue eyes—she wanted to get lost in them as she danced with the knight around the fire. He reached up, grabbing her about the waist, and pulled her down to him.

Biting back a gasp, she stared up at him, absorbed in his warm eyes and even warmer embrace. Slowly, she brought her arms up, wrapping them around his neck, feeling the soft skin and silky hair under her fingers. "We should go dance with them," she whispered, a small smile on her lips.

"Lady Aliana, focus on me," he ordered her harshly.

"Oh believe me, I am! There are other people out there with the Sidhe. They're not being hurt. We should join them." She felt intoxicated by him and the music. She just wanted to go into the courtyard and dance with Galahad.

She looked away from him and back at the dancers. They were now surrounded by all of the Sidhe. The creatures that had been wearing cloaks earlier had shed them and were now only in animal skin pants, held about their waists by thick, gold ropes. Two female Sidhe wore black, glossy scraps of cloth that barely covered their nearly flat chests. Tiny coins hung from their short skirts, jingling as they moved.

The Sidhe with the horned mask lifted his blonde dancing partner onto the altar so that she was kneeling. He joined her as the other disrobed Sidhe took their claimed humans into their arms, grinding and sliding against them while they watched the couple on the altar.

The flames surrounding the courtyard flared high as the last rays of the setting sun fell prey to the darkness of night. The Sidhe on the altar ran his fingers through the woman's corn-colored locks before tugging her head back. His free hand ran down her face and over her exposed neck to her shoulder, which he gripped tightly as he lowered his mouth to her neck.

"*Aliana!*" Galahad whispered fiercely into her ear, but she couldn't turn away from the scene. How she wished she were out there with them, with Galahad, dancing around the fire.

Galahad's rough hand grabbed her chin, forcing her eyes back to his. "Focus on me, Aliana." She blinked several times, trying to clear her mind, but her body started to shake. The need to be with the Sidhe fought violently with her desire to be close to Galahad.

With an unhappy growl, Galahad's hand splayed against her back pulling her tighter against his body. His other hand slid into her hood, threading through her hair. Closing the distance between them, he crushed his lips against Aliana's in a kiss that demanded her full attention.

A wave of heat tore through her body. The band around her heart gave a hard tug. The kiss was passionate and frenzied, his lips warm and hard against her softer ones. Everything else faded away except for the two of them, and the slow fire inside her, building, burning away everything that tried to come between them.

All too soon, Galahad pulled away. Aliana opened her eyes and smiled up at him. His hand trailed down her neck then back up and cupped her cheek. He took a deep breath, keeping his baby blues glued to her. Slowly, he let his hand drop from her cheek and rest at her waist.

Being sure to keep his arm around her waist, he reached down to pick up the sword he'd apparently dropped. She felt weightless against him and had no will of her own, so when he pulled her away from the courtyard, she went without a fight. Dagg flew beside them.

"Where did you hide your bag?" Galahad demanded, and Aliana felt the tension in his body. Even though they were several yards away from the keep, he was still on high alert. "Where, Aliana?"

She scrunched her brows together, trying to remember. Her eyes darted up and down the stream before settling on the closest piece of ruined wall. "Um, over there...I think." She pointed to a small pile of stones.

Galahad nodded at Daggerhorne, and the Dragon zoomed off toward the stones as Aliana looked around, confused. It felt like she was waking up from a dream. She had just been in the keep. How had she gotten here? "Galahad, what's going on?" Feeling his arm tighten around her waist, she remembered him pulling her from the wall, trying to get her away from the Sidhe. She remembered his fierce eyes and the kiss he'd claimed as he'd broken her free from the spell of the beating music.

Gasping, she pulled out of Galahad's arms, heat rushing up her neck to her cheeks. Galahad had kissed her!

And it was amazing. Her memories of the stolen moment flashed in her mind. No one had ever kissed her like that—none of her exes had ever been that passionate. But why had he been? They'd known each other for five minutes, why…how could he kiss her like that and mean it? Her elation from seconds earlier vanished as her practical side took over.

Galahad let her pull away, though his face darkened, and he stayed close. Dagg returned, flying up to her with the straps of her bag hanging from his claws. Gripping the bag tightly, she kneeled, opening it for no other reason than her need to do something that didn't involve Galahad. But the knight grabbed her hand, pulling her up and toward the trees.

"We need to reach the safety of the forest. The Sidhe will not enter there, and then you can get whatever you need." He sounded angry and determined, and his grip on her wrist was unbreakable. His long legs ate up the ground so quickly that she almost had to jog to keep up with him.

"Galahad, slow down," she pleaded, tugging at his grip.

His eyes stared straight ahead, his sword at the ready, but he shortened his stride. Relieved, Aliana was able to move next to him, but he still didn't look at her.

Maybe he's upset he had to kiss me. In the stories, Galahad was celebrated for his purity. It was the whole reason he had succeeded in retrieving the Grail. But Dagg had also said that none of the knights were chaste. So maybe he was angry because she was stupid enough to have gotten caught in the Sidhe's magic.

But distance is a good thing, she reminded herself. *I need to keep my space and not get so wrapped up in him. After all, he's only with me now because I freed him and have to awaken King Arthur. He'll be gone just as soon as he doesn't need me anymore.*

Aliana hated that realization, but it was better to keep her expectations realistic from the start. If she wasn't careful, she might let him get too close. *And I know what happens then—they get bored of my traveling and my desire to wait before having sex, so they cheat on me with my art models or try to rape...No, don't go there!*

To say Aliana didn't trust her judgment of men was an understatement. Her friend Wade would be laughing at her if he could hear her thoughts right now. Any time she went off on a tirade about guys, he would shake his head and tell her she was being ridiculous. "Just wait," he'd said the last time. "You're gonna meet the perfect guy and then I'm gonna get to give you a big fat *I told ya so.*"

Rolling her eyes, she'd replied, "That's not happening any time soon, bud. My perfect guy doesn't exist outside of my dreams." Wade had just laughed before they'd resumed her martial arts training.

Daggerhorne glided above their heads, constantly circling to make sure no Sidhe pursued them. "We can stop for a moment once we're in the woods," Dagg said, flying low.

Aliana's *was* tired. Her muscles were sore and shaky, and it felt like all the energy had been drained from her body. Yet some kind of power still hummed in her chest.

"There used to be a small clearing not far from the border," Galahad said. "Perhaps we can use it if it's still there."

Just before they reached the trees, the three of them were violently shoved forward and slammed to the cold ground. A pulse of searing pain cut through Aliana. Her already sore muscles screamed as she sucked in a breath, trying to roll onto her side. She bit back a whimper as she accidently rolled onto her injured arm.

"What the hell was that?" Her voice was thin and labored.

"Magic," Daggerhorne replied, already back in the air, his gaze fixed on the fiery courtyard. Piercing screams ripped through the quiet and Aliana covered her ears, trying to block out the utter terror in the voices. The screams ceased as quickly as they had begun.

Aliana looked up to see Galahad kneeling over her. "Are you all right?" One of his hands rested at her side while the other slid under her head. He gently pulled her up.

She gripped a fistful of Galahad's tunic and stared up at the keep, tears swimming in her eyes. "Please tell me those screams weren't from those poor people back there." The people they had left behind.

He dropped his eyes from hers, nodding.

That could have been me! A tear slid down her cheek.

Galahad carefully pulled Aliana back to her feet. She wasn't able to meet his eyes and continued staring back at the keep, feeling her heart break with shame, anger, and guilt. She ripped the mask from her face and pulled frantically at the ties of her heavy cloak, throwing both onto the ground. Galahad pulled off his cloak and mask as well, dropping them next to hers.

He didn't offer her empty words of comfort, somehow knowing that was not what she needed. He gently brushed away her tears with his knuckles and laced his fingers through hers. He just stood there, silently lending her his strength, letting her take whatever comfort she could from that.

Her body on autopilot, she followed Galahad through the dark forest. He had saved her from the Sidhe's magic, but they had left those other people without even attempting to free them. Since leaving the keep, Dagg hadn't crawled onto her shoulders again, but now he hovered close. Aliana was determined to get control of her emotions before they found a place to rest. The small corner of her mind she used as an emotional hidey-hole was the perfect place to push the guilt until she could deal with it.

Galahad led her past more moss-covered trees before stepping into a small clearing littered with fallen tree trunks, clusters of large, flat stones, and rounded boulders. The opening provided a beautiful view of the star-studded sky. A crescent moon lit their resting space. Noticing that the trees were filled with large, shiny, green and red apples, Aliana suddenly realized how hungry she was.

Galahad pulled her over to the closest cluster of rocks, embedding his sword in the ground and guiding her to sit on a flat, stone surface. He kneeled next to her and took her pack from her hands. "Do you have anything to clean and re-bandage your wound?" He pulled back the flap.

Panicked, Aliana snatched her bag, or tried to. "Give me that!" But Galahad refused to let it go. For a moment, they played a silent game of tug-of-war, their angry gazes warring with each other. "I can take care of it myself! I don't like people rifling through my stuff." A girl had to have some privacy, after all.

"My lady, I am just trying to help you."

Aliana couldn't tell if he was offended or confused by her refusal.

She shook her head. "Thank you, but I can handle it." Everything was spinning out of control, and she felt like she was losing her ability to take care of herself. There were so many things she didn't know or understand about Avalon, and the thought of having to totally rely on someone else to get her through this was…unsettling.

Galahad narrowed his eyes, reaching out and tugging at the cloth around her arm.

"I said no, Galahad!"

"You can't clean it properly on your own. Let me help you," he growled at her in frustration. Aliana narrowed her eyes at him, trying to pull away again.

"Lady Aliana, please let *me* see to your wound." Dagg's voice was calm with an air of authority that reminded her of her father's when he was dealing with one of his students. "The magic of Avalon can sometimes have ill effects on humans."

She huffed, feeling like a scolded child. "I wasn't trying to be difficult, but I don't need people to do everything for me, either." She narrowed her eyes on Galahad as she reached into her pack with her good arm and pulled out a bottle of water and her first-aid kit.

"You seem disturbingly well prepared, Aliana," Dagg said as he examined the first-aid supplies.

"Yeah, well, you live and learn. Get caught once without it, you make sure it doesn't happen again." Dagg gave her a questioning look, but she avoided responding to it both because she didn't want to relive her first trip without her family, and also because Galahad would probably focus on her bad decision.

The knight didn't say anything as he watched Aliana open the water bottle and place it and the bandages next to him. Taking advantage of her cooperation, he unwrapped the soiled cloth from her arm. She bit the inside of her cheek — the fibers of the scarf had bonded with the dried blood and pulled roughly at her skin.

For all of his irritation with her, Galahad's touch was extremely gentle. He took great care washing away the dried blood while Dagg watched silently from his perch on Galahad's arm, his purple eyes missing nothing. As the mess around her wound cleared, she saw that the cut had already mostly closed. All that was left was a thin scab.

"That's not right," she said. "That cut was deep and much wider than this." She poked at the red skin, but even the pain from earlier was almost gone.

"Interesting," she heard Dagg mumble to himself. "Avalon's magic does not normally act in such ways with human blood."

"What do you mean?" she asked while Galahad poured more water down her arm, washing away the last of the dried blood.

"You're fortunate," Galahad interrupted before Dagg could answer. "I remember the first time I came to Avalon. I had wounds all over me, and the magic felt like it was trying to burn away my blood. Had Avalon's magic not been tempered, I am not sure how long I could have endured the pain."

Aliana frowned. "That's strange. It hurt at first, but after a while the pain lessened. Honestly, I had forgotten all about it until that blast of magic hit us." She dropped her eyes. "What happened to them? What did the Sidhe do to those people, and how did they get here?"

Dagg jumped from Galahad's arm, circling around them in the air as he told Aliana what she wanted to know. "The Sidhe lure mortals here and use their human spirits to strengthen their powers and make them less vulnerable to the sun's light. Sidhe magic is dulled by the sun's rays and thus they become weak or tired. Humans thrive in sunlight. The problem with stealing the spirit of a human is that it does not last very long—no more than two moon cycles—so they have to constantly find new humans to drain."

Aliana thought for a moment. "So it's the same thing as stealing a Pegasus's magic to gain their ability to fly?"

"How do you know about that?" Dagg asked, a worried kind of curiosity in his voice.

"I saw a Pegasus earlier. I followed it into the woods, but we were attacked by some Goblins." She ran a hand through her hair, thinking about the whistling arrow that had almost done her in.

"What? You were wandering in these forests by yourself, unprotected?" Galahad's jaw clenched tight.

"And why shouldn't I? Despite what you may think of me, I *can* take care of myself. I've been traveling on my own for a while now, and it's not like I had another choice." Just because she'd nearly gotten trapped in the Sidhe's web didn't mean she was helpless. Wade and her father had made sure she was very capable of defending herself.

"Oh really." Galahad tightened his grip on her arm, reminding both of them how easily she could be hurt. "Is that why you have this wound—because you know how to take care of yourself so well?"

"Get your hand off me!" Aliana wrenched out of his grip. "For your information, my arm got cut while I was trying to find *you* back in that damned keep when the stairs crumbled right underneath me!" She poked her finger into his chest.

"Enough, both of you!" Dagg commanded, flying between them. "This is getting us nowhere. We all need to rest for a few minutes and get some food in us."

Jaw locked tight, Galahad kept his eyes on Aliana when he said, "Very well, but then I want to know exactly what has happened to you since you arrived here in Avalon."

"Why would I tell you when all you're going to do is snarl and glare at me?"

"And when are you going to understand that I am concerned for your safety?" Galahad gripped her chin, forcing her eyes to his. "You are the key to awakening the king and reuniting the knights so we can defeat Mordrid! Your life is important and cannot be placed in danger so easily." His face was mere inches from hers; his breath teased her lips, and his blue eyes darkened. His gaze flickered from hers for a moment, dropping lower, then back up to her eyes.

Aliana looked away, pulling from his grip. So she was right—she was only a burden to him. Closing her eyes, she pushed back her disappointment and focused on calming her racing heart.

"Lady Aliana," he said softly. "Please understand that you are important. Only you can break our curse."

Unable to bear his nearness, she got up from the rock and walked a few feet away. She crossed her arms, staring up at the starry sky.

"My lady?" Galahad placed a gentle hand on her shoulder. "Do you understand?"

Putting on a smile, she turned to him, simultaneously pulling away from his touch. "I get it Galahad. You need me to fulfill this prophecy." Her voice was calmer and softer than it had been seconds ago. "I don't intentionally place myself in bad situations. I did the best I could with what I was told by the Lady of the Lake."

"Tell me, please, what has happened since your arrival here in Avalon? I need a better understanding of what you know and what you have seen."

Aliana walked past him, taking a seat on a small stone, away from the one still covered with her first-aid supplies. Galahad followed and sat on a rock directly across from her.

"I came through a cave by a lake in my world…" She paused for a moment. "Wow, it sounds really weird saying that."

Galahad raised an eyebrow.

"Sorry, this is all new to me and very strange."

"I understand. I felt much the same when I came here with King Arthur."

Aliana leaned forward, resting her elbows on her knees. "I grew up listening to all the different stories about King Arthur and the Knights of the Round Table. I feel like I know all of you already. But what happened to everyone? Why are you here? And when did you live in Camelot?"

Galahad chuckled, as if amused by her eagerness. "In time, my lady. First I need to hear what has occurred since you've been here."

She told him about meeting Deidre and what the Nymph had said she was supposed to do. She described the little creature she had freed from the bush and meeting the Pegasus. Galahad's jaw tightened when she told him about the Goblins, though she purposely left out the part about the arrow almost taking her head off. The knight listened, taking everything in silently.

"I thought they were going to get us until J'alel stepped in. He made me nervous at first, but then the Pegasus seemed to talk to him, and he helped me get back on to the path. He said he knew of the story of the Destined One and that the Elves would stand by King Arthur again if he called on them."

"That is good to know." Galahad relaxed slightly. "The Elves are strong warriors and their magic has helped us on more than one occasion. You said there was a creature that was not what it appeared to be. Can you show me the image you captured of it?"

Nodding, Aliana got up, grabbing her camera from her bag. Turning, she almost ran into Galahad, who was now right behind her.

She stepped back against one of the stones. "Geesh you move like a ninja."

He scrunched his eyebrows. "What is a…ninja?"

"Uhh…never mind." She turned on her camera as Galahad moved to stand directly behind her and peer over her shoulder.

"Is this more of your technology, my lady?"

For a moment, his closeness made it difficult for Aliana to speak.

6

*Wade and I are eating lunch alone since Aliana's off on
another of her adventures. Wade isn't the type of person
I normally associate with. He's brash, American,
loud-mouthed, American, a comedian, and still
American. In spite of that, I like him. Maybe because
he and I are total opposites or because he understands
loyalty. I'm glad Aliana has him in her life.*

—Owen

Acutely aware of the heat rolling off Galahad, Aliana cleared her throat and leaned forward, putting a little more space between them. "This is a digital camera. They're designed to capture an image in real life so you can preserve the memory."

"Like a mosaic or a fresco?"

"Exactly. Only it's an instant, perfect recreation. I like to think that it catches a heartbeat of time." She gave him a big smile, looking between the camera and him. "The great thing about photography is that I can create something that tells a story with only a glance. I sell a lot of my pictures. That's what I do to make money. I find and create images that inspire people and draw them into the beauty of what I see." That was the part she loved best about her art.

"Does your father or husband not see to your needs?"

"No, my parents are dead and I'm not married. I take care of myself and I do it quite well." Aliana leveled a stern look at Galahad. "Things are much different now. Women have their independence, even if they have families and husbands."

"I meant no disrespect," Galahad insisted, holding his hands up. "The world now must be much changed from the one I knew."

"Sorry." Aliana offered him a small smile, not sure if she was more sorry for rushing to judgment or because she realized how much they wouldn't fit together. "Here's the picture of the creature." She held the view screen up to him.

Galahad's eyes opened wide. "It looks so real."

"Like I said." Aliana beamed at the way he studied the picture as if it was the most important thing he'd ever seen.

He frowned and handed the camera back to her. "You are sure this image is true?"

"Yes, but the creature that I saw with my own eyes was cute with nice fur, adorable black eyes, and definitely no fangs. It did have three tales like in the image, though."

"That is a TreTale, but this one has been tainted by evil magic."

Fear skittered down Aliana's spine. "Why would someone do that? And why didn't it look like that to my eye?"

"As you learned earlier, these forests are protected, but they hide many a great prize. Sorcerers have been known to spell a creature of the forest so that they may find a target without entering the forest. Once the spelled creature finds what it is searching for, the magic allows them to lead their master to the prey." His frown deepened. "Even if the prey has moved on to a new place."

Aliana bit her lip, her nerves rattled by this more sinister angle to the creature. She hoped it hadn't been sent to find her Pegasus friend.

"What do you think Dagg?" she asked as she slid her camera strap over her shoulder, but no answer came. She scanned the area, trying to find the little Dragon but didn't see him. "Dagg? Where do you think he went?"

"I do not know, but we cannot move on without him." Galahad glanced at the apple trees. For a moment, there was a look of such need on his face that it hurt Aliana to see it. *He literally hasn't eaten in ages.*

Galahad nodded toward the trees. "Those are the apples of Avalon. Eating one is enough to fill a person's stomach for half a day. Would you like to try one?"

Aliana considered the apples then shifted her eyes to Galahad. "Sure, I haven't eaten since this morning."

Galahad moved quickly to the trees and plucked two very large apples. Talk about temptation! Ripe, juicy apples and an honest-to-God-drop-dead-gorgeous knight in shining armor. Aliana couldn't help smiling as he made his way back with two perfect apples. Why did he have to look like the charming and brave fictional hero?

"Here, my lady." His fingers brushed across her palm as he placed the fruit into her waiting hand. Whatever magic he had used to free her from the Sidhe came rushing back, and she couldn't turn away from him. With sheer force of will, she took a step back. The moment she did, her head cleared and a nervous giggle escaped her throat.

"Thanks." She took a bite, and sweet, tangy flavor burst in her mouth. "Wow!" she said after swallowing her first bite. "This is fantastic!"

Galahad smiled as he took a bite of his apple. Aliana watched, fascinated, as he devoured half the large fruit in three bites. His eyes met hers for a moment before she glanced away, taking another bite. Before she could embarrass herself any further, she started packing her medical supplies away while she finished her apple. She didn't have to look to know that Galahad was right behind her. She heard him pull his sword from the ground and re-sheath it.

"May I ask you a question?" he asked. Aliana placed the apple core on the ground as she gazed up at him and nodded. "Can your camera capture a human's image in the same way?" His eyes sparkled with curiosity.

She knew she shouldn't, but she really wanted a picture of Galahad. "Yes, let me show you." She pulled the camera off her shoulder and stood, adjusting the settings for night time and pointed the camera at him.

"Stop, my lady!" he ordered.

She did, confused by the sudden change in his demeanor. "What's wrong?"

Galahad remained silent and it dawned on her — when photography had first been invented, many cultures thought that it would take a part of a person's soul. Though that was long after his time, he might think the same. He was probably afraid it would take a part of him.

"Galahad, I won't deny that a picture takes a fragment of a person, but it's not what you're thinking. Can I show you? Please." She used her big kitten eyes on him. She wanted him to understand the thing she loved the most—and he would be amazing in her photos.

He let out a small sigh, slowly nodding his head. Aliana bit back a smile as she snapped a few frames, making sure to capture his beautiful eyes.

"All done," she announced. "Now, did that hurt?"

The corners of Galahad's mouth turned up in a smile. "May I see them?"

"Take a look."

She handed him the camera, and Galahad's body froze as he studied the picture of himself. At first, his eyebrows pinched together, then his eyes widened. He seemed confused for a second before his features smoothed into a flat expression, like he had shut down his emotions.

He hasn't seen himself in several hundred years. It must be a shock. Aliana moved closer to him, placing her hands on his, still holding her camera. She hoped she could help calm whatever intense emotions she suspected he was hiding.

"Are you okay? It must be a bit shocking at first, seeing yourself that way, but it's a really good thing. I promise."

He remained silent, glancing at her hands on his. He cleared his throat before saying, "Queen Titania would most likely enjoy having you capture her image this way."

Aliana felt her jaw go slack. "Queen Titania, as in queen of the Fae? As in Shakespeare's *A Midsummer Night's Dream*, Queen Titania? Wait, does that mean Oberon exists?"

Galahad nodded, smiling at Aliana's stunned expression. "I do not know this Shakespeare, but I assume you have heard of Queen Titania, then?" he said, trying to hide his amusement.

"Of course I know of her. Everyone does!" Aliana paused for a moment, her lips twitching at the corners. "Did you just try to be funny, Galahad?" Unbelievable! One minute he was being a domineering he-man and the next he was cracking dry jokes.

"I do not know what you're talking about, my lady." His face was serious, but his blue eyes twinkled with mirth.

"You are full of surprises, Sir Galahad." Aliana smiled, letting go of her disappointment from earlier and accepting that they could perhaps become friends.

"If you two are done, I've brought someone to see you."

Aliana's head snapped around to see Dagg wearing a big grin. The Dragon flew out from the trees, and behind him was J'alel, in all his elven glory—his sword hung at his side, his longbow strung across his back, and his black hair lifting with the breeze.

"J'alel!" Aliana smiled brightly. "What are you doing here?"

"I've been patrolling close to the keep. I wanted to see if you were truly the Destined One. I see now that you must be." J'alel looked from her to Galahad. The Elf focused his narrowed gaze over Galahad like he was sizing up an opponent. Likewise, Galahad had been watching every move J'alel had made since stepping out of the woods.

"J'alel, this is Sir Galahad. Galahad, this is J'alel."

Galahad extended his arm to J'alel, and without hesitation, the Elf gripped the knight's forearm—a warrior's greeting now lost in history.

"My grandfather told me much about you, Lord Knight," J'alel said. "He wished he had been there for you when the Sidhe attacked."

"You look just like him," Galahad said. "S'han was a good Elf. He helped us greatly when we first came to Avalon. Does he still live?"

"Alas, he passed to the light five cycles ago. But he did make his wishes clear to me: if you were to be freed in my time, I am to help you in your quest to protect the sleeping king."

"We would be glad of any help you can provide. And I already owe you great thanks for saving Lady Aliana from the Goblins earlier."

J'alel looked at her, and Aliana arched her eyebrow. Why were they carrying on a conversation like she wasn't there? "It was indeed my pleasure." The Elf smiled. "And I have another who wanted to see you." He turned toward the woods, whistling.

Galahad stepped close to Aliana. He was tense again, his hand resting on his sword. He and the Elf had seemed to get along well just moments ago, so she didn't understand why Galahad wouldn't trust him.

Before she could think any more on it, she saw her Pegasus emerge from the trees. "No way!" She giggled, running over the creature. "Hey, girl." The flying horse gave a happy whinny, butting her head into Aliana's hands, demanding to be petted. Aliana laughed and stroked the soft, tan pelt. "I'm glad to see you too…Belle." She thought the name suited her new friend. "She's beautiful, isn't she? I'm so glad you saved her from those Goblins, J'alel." Her smile faded for a moment. "After seeing what the Sidhe did, I can only imagine what would've happened to Belle."

J'alel bowed his head to Aliana. "I am glad I came across *both* of you. Belle, as you are calling her, has stayed with me this whole time. She has been just as worried about you as I have been."

"As much as I've enjoyed this conversation," Dagg said, interrupting the trio, "we should pack a few of these apples and start making our way to King Arthur's hollow."

"How far are we from him, Sir Galahad?" Aliana asked.

"A day's walk, perhaps." He looked from her to the Pegasus pressed close to her side. "However, if your friend wouldn't mind giving us a ride, we could be there before the moon reaches its peak."

Aliana stiffened as Belle tossed her head, flaring her wings wide. "You mean we would have her run us there?" Aliana asked, hoping she had misunderstood their intent. But she was rarely that lucky.

"No, I mean she could fly us," Galahad stated.

Aliana gulped and felt herself turn a few shades of green. "Are you trying to be funny again?"

Galahad grinned devilishly. "You brave the Red Wind forest and the Sidhe's tower by yourself, yet now you are frightened of flying on a Pegasus?" He crossed his arms over his broad chest before stepping closer to her. Aliana now stood surrounded by all four of her strange companions.

"I am not *frightened*." Okay, so that one was a lie. "But I couldn't fall hundreds of feet to the ground in the forest or the keep."

"No, you just got trapped by the Sidhe's magic and fell from crumbling stairs," Galahad pointed out.

Aliana opened her mouth to defend herself, but J'alel spoke up first. "And, if I may add, you nearly had a Goblin's arrow shot through you and your friend here."

Aliana glanced between the two men, jaw tightening. So what if she'd had a few issues earlier? "You're telling me that riding a flying horse with no saddle or reins never ended badly?"

"You seem to forget that I will be with you. Do you not trust me to protect you?" Galahad's eyes bored into hers. "The issue is settled." He looked past her to the Pegasus.

Belle rubbed the side of her head along Aliana's shoulder, trying to give comfort. Aliana stared up at the bright moon that lit their entire surroundings. *Lord save me from the arrogance of men!* "Fine. But when I fall to my death, don't say I didn't warn you." She turned her back to the two smug men, muttering to herself about arrogant males.

A hand gripped her elbow, jerking her back around and into a hard chest. Stunned, she gazed up into Galahad's fiery blue eyes. "I will see to your safety, my lady. Do not doubt that."

Unable to speak, Aliana nodded her answer.

J'alel cleared his throat. "Belle says she will gladly assist you in any way she can."

Aliana broke away from Galahad, blushing as she met the Elf's amused eyes. She pursed her lips in annoyance at him.

"So how am I supposed to get up there without a saddle? In case the two of you haven't noticed, Belle here is, like, twice the size of any normal horse."

The Pegasus kneeled down on the ground with her wings flared so Aliana wouldn't step on them. "Guess that answers that," she muttered to herself. Even lying on the ground, Belle came up to her waist. As she was preparing to throw her leg over the large creature, a pair of strong hands gripped her about the waist and easily lifted her onto the animal.

Belle's muscles shifted under her silky pelt as she rose to stand. With a small squeak, Aliana grabbed onto the snow-white mane, holding so tightly her fingers started to ache. She glanced at the three guys who were all watching her. Daggerhorne chuckled while J'alel smiled luminously. Galahad was the worst, staring at her with a smirk on his lips.

She blushed, beyond embarrassed, as she awkwardly adjusted her seat. "I hope y'all enjoyed that. Can we go now?" At least she'd be able to enjoy watching Galahad struggle to get onto Belle's back.

As if reading her thoughts, Galahad placed his hands on the Pegasus and pulled himself up, swinging his leg behind her as easily as if he were floating. He settled himself flush against Aliana from his chest all the way to her thighs. Calm as ever, he enclosed her in his arms, wrapping one around her waist and grabbing a handful of Belle's mane with his other hand.

"This seems like a really bad idea." Her heart beat so strongly that she was afraid Galahad would hear it.

With a chuckle, the knight turned back to J'alel. "We will send word to you after we awaken the king, but in the meantime, Aliana told me of a TreTale that has been cursed with dark magic. Can you track it and find out what its master was after?"

J'alel, who had been absently stroking Belle's neck, looked shocked. "Do you fear it was searching for the Destined One?"

Galahad nodded as Aliana shook her head wearily.

"Guys, I had just gotten to Avalon. How could anyone even know to look for me?"

J'alel nodded to Galahad. "I will see to it. I hope to have an answer for you when you return."

"Thank you," Galahad said.

"Fine, just go ahead and ignore my opinions." Aliana fumed.

Dagg landed on Belle's head, shaking his head. "It would be unwise to not investigate, Aliana."

She sighed. She just couldn't catch a break with these guys!

"We need to go." Galahad tightened his grip on her waist, kicking his heels into Belle's flanks and causing the Pegasus to rear up.

Aliana shrieked, tightening her death grip on the mane in her hands. Belle took two leaping steps, flapping her large wings and lifting into the night sky.

Aliana squeezed her eyes shut, trying to bury herself against Galahad. Her breath came in gasps as the cool air whipped over her face.

"I will not let anything happen to you," Galahad whispered into her ear.

Still terrified, she cracked one eye open and saw a beautiful star-studded sky. The mountains in the distance, covered with thick trees, and a rushing river below all glowed in the moon's silver light. The shining crescent was the largest she had ever seen. It seemed so close, like she could just reach out and touch it.

Laughing, Aliana realized that she had relaxed, even loosened her grip on Belle. "This is all so beautiful!" She wished that the world would stand still so she could live in this moment for the rest of time.

Dagg flew close to them, his Dragonish smirk firmly in place. "I hope this means there will be no more screaming." Aliana stuck out her tongue at him, noticing he was carrying her pack in his claws.

"I guess you're our new pack mule," she teased, looking over her shoulder at Galahad. "What do you think? It suits him, doesn't it?" She wiggled her eyebrows.

"It would be a shame if I dropped this, Lady Aliana," Dagg retorted, his smirk sufficiently dimmed.

"Do it and I might decide to clip your wings," Aliana shot back, thrilled to have someone to tease.

Dagg laid a Dragon claw over his heart, dramatically faking a wound. "That is simply mean."

Grinning, Aliana leaned back against Galahad and admired the striking landscape before her. "I'm sorry I reacted so badly."

"I understand your fear." Galahad's arm tightened briefly around her waist. "But please trust that I will never do anything to place you in danger."

Aliana took a deep breath, letting her eyes wander. Even with the wind whipping around them, Galahad's wintery scent was the only thing she could smell. "It kinda feels like we are the only people in the world...like we own the night."

Galahad leaned closer, his lightly whiskered cheek resting against the side of her face. "I am pleased you are happy, Aliana."

Her heart melted. That was the first time he had used just her name without adding "Lady." The sound of it coming from his lips was almost hypnotic.

They stayed silent for several minutes until Galahad spoke again, his head still pressing against her cheek. "Do you see those cliffs over there?" Aliana nodded. "The magic surrounding the king's hollow will not let us any closer. We will have to land between those cliffs and walk the rest of the way."

"Sounds like fun," Aliana said reluctantly. Hadn't she already done enough hiking for the day? She studied the canyon ridges. It was hard to see clearly, even with the moonlight, but it looked like strange piles of boulders lined the entire rim almost as a sort of barrier against anything approaching from the woods. Galahad held her tightly as Belle swooped down toward the canyon, landing more gracefully than Aliana would've thought possible on such rocky terrain.

Galahad leaned into her, swinging his leg back and dismounting oh so perfectly before holding his hands out for Aliana.

"Umm, shouldn't you go see if the area is clear or something?" She tried to sound casual, but really she didn't want him to laugh at her while she attempted to get off Belle.

"I scouted from the air. We are perfectly alone here," he assured her. Aliana stalled, trying to think of some other way to distract him, but he grew impatient. "We need to hurry. The sooner we awaken the king, the sooner we can get back to the Lady of the Lake and fulfill the prophecy."

Aliana waved him off. "Lecture, lecture, that's all you do."

Galahad's jaw tightened as he continued to stare at her.

"Fine," she huffed. Leaning back, she carefully slid her leg over Belle, making a point to ignore Galahad, but he had other ideas. Like earlier, he grabbed Aliana about the waist, lowering her to the ground, tucking her close to his body the whole way.

Blushing, she glanced down and stepped away, bumping into Belle. The Pegasus tilted her head as if to say "excuse you."

"Thanks for bringing us here, Belle." Aliana ran her hands over her soft feathers before petting her neck.

Galahad placed a warm hand on the small of Aliana's back, ushering her forward. With a final bray, Belle trotted away and leaped back into the night sky.

"We must be careful through here," Dagg warned, circling Aliana. "The magic guarding this pass is stronger than any I have felt in a very long time."

"Perhaps Queen Titania added another layer of protection after I was captured. Guarding this pass was one of our duties."

Aliana looked at Galahad, confused. "Our? I thought you were the only one here with Arthur."

For a moment his face went blank, his eyes lost focus, and for a brief second, Aliana saw great sorrow in those eyes. "No."

Aliana's stomach dropped at the despair and pain in that one word. Something terrible must have happened to hurt him so badly.

"Stay close," he told her, his face still blank. He led the way with Dagg flying at Aliana's side. Something didn't feel right about this place. It was like she could feel the cold fingers of danger trying to worm their way inside of her.

"Stay close to me," Galahad reminded her again.

Her knight was several feet ahead of her already and Dagg was quickly catching up to him. She kept a careful eye on the jagged pieces of rock beneath her, afraid they might shift or that she might slip and break her ankle. That would just suck. Looking up, she saw that Galahad was even farther away than before, but he didn't seem to notice. She took another step forward, slipping and knocking into the stone wall with a painful gasp. "Son of a monkey!"

"Lady Aliana, are you all right?" Galahad glanced back, and his eyes widened as if just now realizing how far apart they were.

Something banged against the cliff wall, rolling down the ledge. Aliana watched, terrified, as a boulder the size of a yoga ball crashed directly in front of Galahad and Dagg.

"Run, my lady!" Galahad yelled as two more boulders came crashing down. He was forced to jump back to keep from getting crushed. Aliana cried out as another huge rock shattered behind her, sending shards flying like shrapnel. She threw her arms over her head, frozen with fear.

7

*She is going to get killed! The magic barring my path
to her is too strong. I will never be able to penetrate it.
Only four beings in Avalon have enough power to create
this kind of barrier. If any of them have set against us,
we are doomed. Curse this magic! She is my charge.
I have to protect her!*

— Daggerhorne

"Move, Aliana!" Dagg ordered as boulders, large and small, continued to fall, blocking a very pissed off Galahad from coming to her aid. Recovering from her shock, Aliana took several running steps but was forced to the cliff wall again as another boulder flew over her head.

She chanced a glance up. A large rock sailed over the ledge like it had been tossed. She took two leaping steps forward before the boulder landed where she had been standing. Another crashed sounded to the side of her. Stifling a cry, she covered her face. More shards of rocks scratched her arms, some cutting deep enough to draw blood.

Looking up again, Aliana realized why that last boulder had missed—she was under a slab of stone protruding from the cliff wall.

"Lady Aliana, you must make your way to me! Something is blocking me from getting back to you!" Galahad shouted, his voice hard and biting.

"We have bigger problems than that. Something is throwing those rocks from above!" she shouted.

He and Dagg both looked up. The Dragon shot up like a bullet toward the canyon top, but before he was more than halfway up, he was smacked down into Galahad, knocking them both farther away.

"Galahad! Dagg!" Aliana ran out from beneath her hiding spot as three more rocks came crashing down.

"Worry about yourself, not us!" Dagg ordered.

Heart pounding, she peered upward and saw a very large boulder heading straight for her. Acting on instinct, Aliana leaped forward, landing on her knees and barely getting out of the stone's path before it hit the canyon floor. She pushed herself up, running to get under another jutting piece of slate.

"Aliana, be careful!" Galahad growled.

"Stop barking orders at me! I can't think with you distracting me!"

She heard Galahad yell and watched him slam against the invisible barrier. A stream of purple Dragon fire arched into the air, directed at a boulder falling straight toward Aliana, but even Dagg's magic couldn't penetrate magical wall. She was on her own.

Safely hidden, Aliana took several deep breaths. She poked her head out from under her protective cover, and studied the cliff walls. She noted more pieces of rock sticking out along the cliff wall, and an idea struck her. If she could make it to the other coverings, she could get out in one piece, but she would need to move fast and not take another wrong step. Her heart pounded in her ears, adrenaline shooting through her limbs like wild fire.

Aliana looked at the guys again, frightened that the falling rocks would hurt them, but they both just watched her, seemingly in no danger at all. The boulders were only falling around her. How had they gotten separated in the first place? Galahad was much too careful to have allowed that to happen. *Could something else be influencing us?* One minute she'd been within arm's reach of him, and the next he'd been yards away from her. Something about this wasn't right.

Taking another breath, she listened, tuning out the commands that Galahad continued to shout. Two rocks hit the ground. Twenty seconds later, another three dropped. Next, a single, large boulder came down, followed closely by another. She waited, listening and counting. The rocks were falling in a consistent pattern, almost like the beat of a dance.

She waited for the next two to fall before taking off for the next cover. She chanced another peek up, angling closer to the wall and throwing her arms over her head as the next three rocks hit the ground. Using the time gap that followed, she made it under the next protective covering just as another rock struck behind her. She was close to the canyon mouth and to Galahad, who watched her very carefully.

Keeping her mind on the task in front of her, she waited for the next time gap. She stuck to her pattern, making it to the next slate covering without a problem. All she had to do was make it to one more ledge, and then sprint the rest of the way to safety.

Choking on rock dust, she ran forward, arriving unharmed at the last stone cover. That had been the easy part. She peeked up at the cliff's edge before looking back to Galahad and Dagg. The open span to them was longer than the distance between the outcrops had been, but if the falling rocks kept to their pattern, she could make it — and then hope that she'd be able to penetrate the barrier that her protectors couldn't.

Waiting for the right gap, she ran as hard as she could, dodging the tumbling rocks and their shrapnel as she went. *Almost there!* Her foot slid out from under her, and she fell hard onto her knees.

"Aliana!" Galahad cried as rocks crashed around her. Furiously, he pounded at the invisible wall.

Pulling herself to her feet, she made another dash toward him, chancing a glance up, and abruptly pulled back, swerving close to the wall and narrowly missing another falling rock. What would happen if she couldn't get through the invisible wall? What could she do then? *Besides get squashed like a bug in this disaster zone canyon*, she thought. But she had to chance it.

Rushing forward, she reached out her hand, amazed when Galahad grabbed it as if there was no barrier at all. He yanked her into his arms, launching them both away from the crashing rocks and toward the canyon opening. She held onto him as tightly as she could, and they flew through the air. He landed hard on his back, grunting. Aliana sprawled on top of him. When her heart stopped racing, she lifted her head from his chest, meeting his shocking blue eyes.

"Thank you," she whispered.

Galahad ran his fingers through her hair, pushing the dark curtain away from her face as his eyes flicked over her, checking to make sure she was okay. She erupted in panicky giggles. She'd actually done it! She'd survived the rockslide of doom all on her own! Pride filled her. *Take that!*

Galahad frowned. "I do not think this is a laughing matter. You could have been killed before we even got to the king!" His eyes blazed, and Aliana felt herself getting lost in him again as sparks shot through her body. There was something exhilarating but also strangely calming about her body's automatic reaction to him.

"This magic was not here before. I am sorry you were put in such danger," he said.

Aliana smiled gently at him. "I'm just glad we made it through there in one piece." Galahad frowned but the intensity in his burning gaze died down. "It's not your fault, Galahad. You've been gone from here for centuries, so it actually makes sense that someone added extra protection."

Galahad opened his mouth to say something but Dagg spoke first.

"We are now one step closer to the king," the Dragon said, bringing their attention away from one another, "and we need to move quickly. Who knows what else stands between us and our goal."

Galahad and Aliana got to their feet, and Dagg settled on her shoulder. She gazed back at the canyon pass, which was now completely still. "I'm not sure why, but for some reason, I get the feeling I'm being tested."

Galahad nodded somberly, watching Aliana rub her hand over her chest as she tried to banish the persistent tightness she felt there. "Are you injured, my lady?"

"I'm still out of breath," she lied, not wanting to alarm him. They needed to move on, and having Galahad worry about her health was only going to delay them further.

Galahad scowled but moved forward, leading them to the entrance of King Arthur's hollow. As they walked, the adrenaline rush ebbed from Aliana's system, but the tightness in her chest increased to a sharp pressure. She gripped her pack tightly to her chest to disguise the fact that she was trying to ease the irritation. The pressure wasn't painful, but taking a deep breath was becoming difficult.

Thinking back, she realized that the pressure had never really gone away since she'd first entered this strange land. She had just chalked it up to nerves before, but now she wasn't so sure and debated whether she should say something to Dagg and Galahad. Her Dragon guardian might know what was causing it and how to fix it. But what if they thought her weak for it? Or worse, what if they focused more on her than getting to King Arthur? No, it was better to keep it to herself for now.

"Around this next turn lies the hidden entrance to King Arthur's hollow," Galahad said.

Aliana quickened her pace, eager to see what she imagined would be an amazing sight. Rounding the corner, she stood dumbfounded. In her imagination, she'd envisioned a grand, tiered entrance lined with intricate engravings and beautiful designs, something regal and magnificent befitting for a king. But what was before her was nothing like she had expected. A steep dirt trail with steps formed by protruding roots led upward to a simple but perfect circle carved into the mountainside. Plants and moss grew wild on the curved cliff that surrounded the opening, covering everything so thoroughly that there was more green than gray. Aliana looked to Galahad with confusion, surprise, and delight.

"Quite a sight," Dagg said.

Galahad held his hand out to Aliana, and she didn't hesitate to take it, letting him lead her up the steps. Dagg flew ahead, circling the entrance. As she drew closer, Aliana saw that the opening was lined with smooth, gray stones covered in strange, flowing, druid-like markings.

"This is unbelievably cool!" She ran her fingers across the smooth symbols, taking in as much detail as she could. Her father would have loved deciphering these mystery drawings. Reaching into her pack, she grabbed her camera and took dozens of pictures of the entrance and the surrounding area.

"Those markings were put here by Merlin as protection against all but those of us who swore to protect our king." The sadness crept back into Galahad's face.

Aliana took his hand, giving it a gentle squeeze in hopes of returning some of the comfort he had given to her earlier. His eyes met hers and Aliana felt herself blush. She pulled her hand from his, and her curiosity was piqued when she saw disappointment in the set of his mouth.

"What about me?" she asked. "Will Dagg and I be able to get in?"

Galahad smiled at her. "You are the Destined One. I do not believe any magic could keep you out."

Biting her cheek, Aliana nodded. "Well, let's do this before I lose my nerve or come to my senses."

Galahad studied her. "Odd. I did not think you one to back away from as easy a task as entering a cave, my lady."

How dare he? Her offended eyes met his, and she saw mirth dancing in his blue depths. One corner of his mouth turned up.

"That was not nice, Sir Galahad." Shaking her head, she marched past him and walked through the cave entrance.

If she had been on the outside, she would have seen the markings around the entrance flare to life, shining so brightly that Galahad and Dagg were momentarily blinded.

"Lady Aliana," Dagg called. "We cannot get through."

Aliana twisted around to face them. "What do you mean you can't get through?"

"Come see for yourself, my lady." Galahad's voice was calm, but his face set in anger.

Unbelieving, Aliana strode back to the entrance and reached her hand toward Dagg, planning to drag the silver devil into the cave by his tail—there was no way she could do this alone—but her hand hit a cold wall. "What in the name of all that's holy?" She placed both hands against the barrier, looking up and down, side to side, trying to find some kind of lever or something that would rid them of this nuisance.

"Your friends will not find a way in, young one," a woman's raspy voice said from behind her.

Aliana snapped around toward the voice. Standing in the shadows was a small figure wrapped in a dusty, brown cloak. The garment swung in tattered pieces around the woman's feet as she walked toward Aliana, but the woman's head remained hidden beneath a deep hood.

"Who are you?" Aliana and Galahad demanded at the same time.

The lady cackled. "My dear, you did not think that you would simply walk in and awaken him, did you?" She stepped closer. "You have done well with the first two tests, but there is one more you must pass to prove yourself worthy of claiming the title of the Destined One." Her aged smoky, sultry voice scraped over Aliana's skin.

"What do you mean *test?* Are you responsible for that disaster zone back there?" Aliana could almost feel the old woman's cold smile.

"That *disaster zone* as you call it was to test your wit and ability to think under dire circumstances. There are still tasks ahead that require both. Your first test was to find the courage to face the unknown and free the lord knight and your guardian. King Arthur's champion cannot lack the traits he had in abundance."

Aliana wanted to roll her eyes, but she wouldn't put it past this lady to do something terrible to her for it. Again, she studied the old woman. There was something terrible about her but also something... *familiar.*

"Why can't Galahad and Daggerhorne be with me? They don't need to stay locked outside!"

The shrouded woman cackled again. "Only the Destined One can awaken the king. She *alone* must prove herself worthy."

Aliana glared at the woman for a moment, and then sighed, turning back toward her two companions. With a sad smile, she placed her palm on the cold barrier opposite Galahad's palm, wishing she could touch him again. She knew she shouldn't want that, because once she awakened Arthur, there would be no need for her knight to stay with her.

"Well, look at it this way," she said, "once I do this, at least you won't have to worry about saving me from any more death traps or magical creatures." She laughed weakly. "And you'll have your king back."

"You are more than just a means to awaken my king," he said with absolute confidence. "Do you think that I could let you walk away from us?"

Aliana's heart jumped, and she hoped she wasn't imagining the emotions in his words and in his eyes.

"Do not be so worried, Lady Aliana," Daggerhorne said, breaking their moment. "You were born for this. You are more than capable of passing the final test."

She nodded with a tight smile, appreciating the Dragon's confidence in her, but disappointed to be reminded that she was only needed for this purpose. Then she turned and joined the old woman.

"My lady," Galahad called out as she moved away from him. Aliana hesitated but then looked back, meeting his eyes. He didn't say anything, but his eyes and the hand he still had resting against the barrier said plenty.

The old woman cleared her throat.

"Be safe," Galahad finally said. Aliana smiled, then turned again, nodding for the woman to lead the way.

Aliana followed the old woman for several steps before finally asking the question burning in her mind. "Who are you? And why are *you* here to give me this test?"

The woman cackled. "I have been destined to give your final test since the covenant was first struck."

"I don't understand. What covenant? And what does this prophecy I keep hearing about actually say?"

"Knowledge is learned when it needs to be, not when we wish for it to be given. People of your world have forgotten that and grow arrogant in their quest to know everything."

Aliana opened her mouth to reply, but her voice failed. The cave was getting darker with every step. She forced herself to take calming breaths, made more difficult by the intense pressure in her chest. Trying for nonchalant, she patted the pockets of her jeans, looking for her cell phone, but she didn't feel it. Her heart leaped; where had she left it? Her breath came quicker, and her hands curled into fists, her nails biting harshly at her skin. "Breathe," she hissed, trying to fight back the traumatic childhood memory that threatened to drown her.

"Are you all right, child?"

Aliana's head snapped up, staring at the woman who now stood only a foot from her. The fading light from the entrance shined into the hood and onto the woman's face. For the first time, Aliana got a clear look at her mystery guide. The woman's heart-shaped face had been wizened by long years of life. Wispy, golden orange ringlets framed her high cheekbones, plump lips, and emerald eyes sprinkled with silver.

"Where are we going?" Aliana's voice cracked.

The woman's eyes bored into hers. Under the soul-penetrating gaze, the memory Aliana had been trying to block surfaced. She'd been a frightened child, trapped in an ancient chamber, her foot pinned under a large piece of rock that had fallen when she'd tumbled through the sinkhole above. Dust and cobwebs had choked her as she'd cried out for her daddy. She'd screamed when something unseen skittered across her arm. For almost an hour, she had remained trapped in the dark room with only a small ray of light to give her any hope. Her teary eyes had frantically shot back and forth, trying to see into the darkness. But there had been nothing but a cold emptiness, a room forgotten in time, a hidden monster that wanted to consume her.

Gasping, Aliana stumbled back. Her hands shook and her knees threatened to give out. She squeezed her eyes shut, trying to block out the horrible memory. Her father had eventually come to save her. He hadn't left her trapped in the darkness.

Aliana had become stronger over the years, and she refused to let fear rule her life! Sucking in air, she found her strength again and stood straight. She couldn't let this woman see her as weak and unable to face her demons.

The woman's eyes lit with approval, and a small smile graced her lips. She stepped back into the darkness. For a heartbeat, Aliana thought she was alone again. But before the panic could resurface, torches sprang to life with a whooshing sound, lighting their path.

Aliana followed the woman down the corridor, taking in every detail she could. The cave walls had been covered with elegant, beautiful drawings. Standing side-to-side, eight valiant knights formed a line facing a small army of thirty or more black-armored knights. "What are these drawings?" Aliana asked, fascinated by the ancient art.

"You have searched a long time to know the truth of Camelot and its king, but the truth may not be what you wish it to be," the woman answered cryptically.

"No disrespect," Aliana said, glancing back at the woman, "but I have just found out that Dragons, Elves, Nymphs, and Goblins are real. I had to save a legendary knight, escape those crazy Sidhe, and I've been told I have to *awaken* one of the most famous men in history. I've kinda accepted that everything I thought I knew about Camelot and King Arthur is nothing close to the truth."

"You have spirit, girl. That is good. You will need every ounce of it *and* all the courage you can muster to do what is needed of you." The woman looked past Aliana to the drawing on the walls. "This shows the Fae's account of Arthur and his men during their last battle with the evil Mordrid." The woman held out her aged hand. Colored sparks of magic burned under her skin before they jumped to life, circling tightly in her palm. The old woman blew a gentle breath. Aliana watched, transfixed as the magic sailed from her fingers to the drawings, giving them life before her eyes.

The valiant knights fearlessly charged the black knights' line. They cut and slashed at their enemies quickly, breaking the enemy's formation. With their armor, it was impossible to distinguish between King Arthur's eight men except for the different emblems on their shields. Aliana watched as, one by one, they slew their enemies only to be surrounded by more and more.

"The Knights of the Round Table were feared by all the realms. Their individual strength was unmatched, and together, nothing but the strongest magic and trickery could defeat them," the woman explained.

Walking along the wall, Aliana followed the knights' progress. Leading the charge was a knight carrying an elaborate shield bearing a golden Dragon. At his back was another man holding a simple circle shield bearing only the image of a sword. The two fought in perfect synchronization as they defeated a whole battalion of black knights. Not far from them was another of their friends. His shield was covered by three intertwining rings. This knight plus a fourth with a burning sun on his shield joined the first two as they raced off to fight an unseen enemy.

The four remaining men continued to battle the growing number of black knights. No matter how many they cut down, more enemy knights continued to come at them. But the four Knights of the Round Table never faltered. They stood their ground and fought the evil knights as they advanced, not letting a single one pass to follow their friends.

"So few against so many…" Aliana breathed. "Who are those black knights?"

"They are tortured souls called from the underworld and given armored bodies that are bound to the one who called them. Mordrid knew he could not defeat Arthur without magic and deceit, so his ally, the sorceress Morgana le Fay, conjured the army to serve him. When a black knight was cut down, another would take its place. Morgana used all her power, along with that stolen from the fire birds, to create their hellacious army. The tortured souls would not rest and could not be fully defeated until either their purpose was fulfilled or their master destroyed."

Aliana gasped as she watched the first of Arthur's knights die. She swore she could hear the outraged cries of the other knights. One by one, she watched Arthur's men fall, feeling each death like the cut of a knife against her own heart until the last of the four fell to the ground.

From the surrounding forest carved into the wall came an army of perfect soldiers armed with swords and bows, their numbers as great as those of the black knights. This new army pushed the black knights back, holding them at bay.

"Why didn't they fight with the knights from the start?" Aliana cried.

"Mordrid had sent the Sidhe army to delay the Fae, giving his black knights time to fulfill their evil purpose." The woman's voice was calm and indifferent, like she was talking about the weather and not the lives of men who mattered.

8

Fury twists through my gut. I loathe this magic keeping me from my king's side and from Lady Aliana. Watching her in that canyon — helpless to aid her — was torture. And now I am again unable to protect her and see that my king, my friend, is indeed safe. If this old woman is who Lord Daggerhorne and I think she is, Lady Aliana could be in even more danger than before. I swear I will not allow this again!

Galahad

Aliana looked past the fallen knights in the wall drawings to follow the other four men farther down. Three of them were busy cutting through more black knights and smaller creatures that seemed to be a hybrid version of a troll and a pig. Behind the line of enemies stood a lone, dark figure. He watched the carnage with a sinister smile on his lips. *That has to be Mordrid!*

The fourth of Arthur's knights had sheathed his sword and was throwing balls of liquid fire at the enemy. Bolts of lightning struck down several of the evil creatures, leaving only ash behind. The lightning strikes created an opening for the man bearing the gold and red Dragon shield.

"Merlin and King Arthur! That has to be them." Aliana moved her attention to the knight with the sword-covered shield as he ruthlessly cut down enemy knights and Goblin-like creatures. His moves were confident, fierce, and powerful, fueled by cold determination.

"Galahad," Aliana breathed his name. She watched him take a blow from one of the black knights. "No!" But he didn't fall. He used his shield to simultaneously knock the sword from the black knight's hand and cut off the knight's head. Aliana looked away from the merciless kill and found the last of Arthur's men. He was quick, striking the enemies and getting out of their range before they could strike back. She studied his shield, hoping to piece together the identity of the last knight. *Maybe Lancelot?*

She looked to King Arthur, who now fought furiously with Mordrid. They seemed to be evenly matched, exchanging blows one after the other until Arthur finally knocked the sword from Mordrid's hand. Moving quickly, Arthur had Mordrid on his back, Excalibur pointed at his throat. Aliana let out her breath. *He got him!*

Mordrid shot a blast of magic toward Arthur, forcing him to stumble back. The sorcerer got to his feet, throwing wave after wave of magic. Arthur deflected the magic with his shield, but the strikes were so rapid he couldn't get in a counter-attack. He finally found an opening, cutting at Mordrid, but the evil sorcerer was no longer there. Arthur swung around, quickly finding his enemy and slashing his sword, but Mordrid disappeared a second time. Aliana's heart pounded as she searched along with Arthur for the sorcerer. Suddenly, he reappeared behind Arthur, driving a dagger deep into the king's side.

Aliana's eyes misted as she watched Mordrid withdraw the blade only to plunge it in again and again before he let Arthur's body fall to the ground. Galahad and the unidentified knight rushed to the king's side. With a raging cry, the mystery knight charged at Mordrid but was thrown back by another strike of magic. Galahad lunged to attack but didn't get the chance because Merlin trapped Mordrid in a ring of roaring fire as he called down more lightning. Mordrid shielded himself, but he was unable to break away from the fire's grip. Frantically, the sorcerer sent his power at the flame, but his dark magic was consumed, the fire blazing higher and closing in around him.

Mordrid made one last attempt at freedom. A large, dark cloud formed overhead, bearing down toward the trapped wizard, but Merlin's magic proved faster. He let loose a blast that collided violently with Mordrid's cloud. Aliana shielded her eyes against the light that shot out from the wall, bathing the cave with a blinding glare.

When the light faded, she looked back at the drawings. Mordrid was gone. Galahad and the mystery knight supported Arthur's limp body as Merlin opened a swirling, silver portal. With a glance back to the battlefield and their fallen comrades, the four entered the portal and disappeared from sight.

"What happened?" Aliana demanded. "How was Arthur still alive? Who was that other knight?"

"Merlin, Sir Galahad, and Sir Lancelot brought King Arthur to Avalon. The king was on the brink of death. Merlin was sure that though he had stopped Mordrid, the sorcerer was not defeated. Only Excalibur can kill Mordrid, and only a Pendragon can wield it. To defeat Mordrid, they needed Arthur alive. They brought him here to Avalon hoping to find salvation, and they did so at Queen Titania's hands. But everything has a price."

Aliana's heart pounded loudly in her chest, threatening to break free. "Why does that not sound good?"

"Queen Titania saved Arthur's life, placing him in his enchanted sleep. Those who brought him had to swear to guard the king in a hidden resting place until the Destined One came to awaken him. Their lives are bound to King Arthur until the quest is complete." The woman's shadowed gaze bored into Aliana as she spoke her next words.

"Before the darkest hour strikes, the Destined One shall come forth.
Avalon's lost daughter must thrice and alone prove her worth,
Then can she fully possess the power to awaken the king.
It shall become her destiny to reunite the Round Table,
Unearth and reclaim their lost relics,
Become the key to undoing the evil Mordrid has wrought.
Only with her can the once and future king prevail."

"You can't be serious!"

"You wanted to know what has been foretold, and now you have what you desired. Does this knowledge now displease you?"

Aliana bit her tongue before she said something to upset this undoubtedly dangerous woman. But how the heck was she supposed to help save the world against Mordrid? And why hadn't Deidre or Dagg told her this little tidbit? *Probably because I would've left.* But this was too much to try to process right now. She needed to focus on something easier first.

"If Merlin and Lancelot all made the same vow as Galahad, where are they? Why aren't they here with us?" A cold gust blew through the cave, howling as it passed.

For the first time, the woman's voice rose in anger. "All four men entered the bargain of their own free will. They made their choices knowing the cost if they broke their vows."

Dread nipped at Aliana. Was it possible that Merlin and Lancelot had *abandoned* King Arthur? "But they all lost so much," she whispered, gazing back at the now motionless drawings.

"Merlin and Lancelot chose to follow other paths. They left Arthur's side, abandoning Galahad in order to return to the mortal world. They had to pay the price for their betrayal."

"And what about Galahad?" Her voice wobbled. "What did he do to deserve imprisonment by the Sidhe?"

"He failed to stop them, and he failed to protect the Grail of Power. Magic always has a cost."

Aliana let out a frustrated cry. "Of course. Is that another part of your stupid *Law of Avalon?* Does your *law* say that brave men have to suffer such tragedies?" She glared at the woman who seemed to care so little for the suffering of others.

"You have known your own losses, your own tragedy." The woman's honey voice drew Aliana back.

With a flick of the mystery woman's wrist, the cave plunged into darkness. Aliana bit back a cry, determined to not give in to the cruel woman's trick. After an endless moment of darkness, new light flowed into the cave from above. Aliana looked up, finding a small window cut into the side of the mountain. Beams of light fell, shining upon a stone shrine on the other side of the cave.

"How…" Aliana's voice drifted. Lying upon the cold, ivy-covered stone was the man she had been dreaming about since she was six years old — King Arthur.

"Now begins your final test, child."

Aliana blinked as the mystery woman returned to her side, forcing her gaze from the king. "Are you going to tell me who you are first?"

"You wish to be beside the king," the woman stated, completely ignoring Aliana's question. "But to do that you must first cross the bottomless grotto."

Aliana followed the woman's gaze to a thin bridge of stone which stretched across the cave to Arthur.

"Doesn't look too hard," she said, swallowing. She stepped onto the bridge, peering into the darkness below. There was no bottom in sight, and the only thing she could hear was the faint, constant howl of stale, cold air. Before she lost her nerve, she raised her gaze to Arthur, moving further onto the walkway. The ground shook beneath her feet, and she scrambled backward and off of the bridge, falling onto her butt. The bridge's center crumbled, leaving a large gap in the walkway. All that was left of the bridge at Arthur's end was a small nub of rock jutting out. She couldn't even hear any sign that the fallen rocks had hit the bottom of the chasm.

"How am I supposed to get across now?"

"I'd think that would be obvious."

Aliana pushed up from the ground, slapping away the dirt on her jeans and glaring at the old woman. "You can't seriously tell me that I have to jump across that gap. Who do you think I am? Indiana Jones with my trusty little whip and bad taste in hats?"

"There is always another option, my dear."

"I thought so."

"You can take what I am willing to offer and walk away from all of this." The woman's smoky voice made Aliana uncertain. "What if I could give you what your heart craves the most? What if I told you I could give you back your parents? What if you all could be a family again?"

Aliana's soul trembled at that bombshell. She wanted her parents back more than anything else she could ever remember wanting in her life. She wanted it more than she had ever wanted to find Avalon. It wouldn't matter anymore that they'd lied to her about her real parents. She could ask them about it herself, get the answers to all the questions that had been haunting her.

"You can't bring back the dead," she whispered, fearing to hope.

"No, only the Underlord can restore a life. But I can turn back time, save your parents from their fiery death." The woman circled her hand, creating a ring of mist. Aliana watched as her parents' faces filled the empty space. They were side by side, her father's arm wrapped around her mother's shoulder, both holding out a hand to her. Their smiles made her heart swell in happiness.

"Oh, my sweet girl," her mother said. "I have missed you so much."

"We've both missed you, little star," her father said. "Please come back to us. We love you so much."

"Mama, Papa," Aliana whispered, raising her hand to touch them as tears stung her eyes. Her fingers met her mother's, feeling the gentleness flowing from her touch, but the image shimmered and disappeared.

Aliana's frantic, tear-filled eyes found the mystery woman. "Bring them back!"

"Are you choosing them, then? Choosing your parents over the path set before you?"

Aliana hesitated. She looked back as her parents' image returned. The image had changed. She was in their arms, hugging them as they stood on the beach, bathed in the setting sun. They sat down at their picnic table, laughing and enjoying dinner together, like they always had during their summers at home in South Carolina.

She smiled, prepared to tell the woman to return her to her family, but a thought stopped her. What would become of all the people and creatures she'd met since entering Avalon? The Sidhe had already killed seven humans. Belle was nearly a Goblin sacrifice, and that poor little TreTale had been poisoned. What about Deidre and J'alel? They had shown such faith in her. A band tightened around her heart as she felt Galahad's worry for her and his hope of being reunited with his king. The veil of bliss faded as she remembered all that had happened in just one day and thought of the knight and Dragon who were counting on her.

"No one would think less of you for choosing your family," the woman's voice whispered in her ear. "Merlin chose to abandon the king and return to the mortal realm. Even the noble Lancelot turned his back on Arthur and Galahad for his beloved Guinevere."

"What will happen to King Arthur, Galahad, and Dagg if I choose my parents? Can I come back to awaken the king after I have my parents back?"

The woman's head tilted slightly, her smile cold. "You will have no memory of any of this if you choose to return. By choosing your family, you give up the right to claim the title of the Destined One, and things will return to the way they were before you arrived."

"What about Mordrid? Will he still be a danger?"

"You will be happy with your family."

Aliana looked at her parents again. They'd always taught her to stand up for what she felt was right, no matter how hard that might be or how much it might hurt. If she turned her back on Galahad and Dagg, they would go back to being trapped by the Sidhe, and Arthur would continue to sleep. Their lives and so many more would suffer because of her selfish desire. Aliana looked away from her parents' smiling faces and over to the sleeping king.

She couldn't do it. She couldn't sentence them to an eternity of imprisonment.

"No," she whispered, brushing away her tears and raising her chin. "I won't abandon Galahad and Arthur. My parents wouldn't want that." What little of her heart remained whole shattered to pieces. But she couldn't make any other choice.

The woman's smile turned friendly for the first time. "Then all you must do is make your way to the king. Your final test is a test of your faith. You must believe in yourself and the decision you've made. Once you cross that bridge, you will claim your destiny."

"Faith…right." Aliana rolled her still wet eyes. "Have faith that I'm not going to fall to my death and let down the world at the same time. No pressure there."

Sighing, she took one step onto the bridge. It was barely wide enough for her to stand with her feet side by side. When nothing happened, she took another step, then another, until she stood just a few feet from the gap. It seemed like maybe four yards to the other side. If she got a running start, she might be able to make the jump.

Backing up, Aliana took a breath. "Have faith," she reminded herself. Rocking back and forth, she steeled her nerves. "One…two…three!" She took off, focusing only on Arthur and reaching the other side. Her foot hit the crumbled ledge, and she pushed herself forward, soaring over the gap. A faint trail of glittering pink light guided her path across the abyss. As the other side got closer and closer, she felt herself start to fall. For a brief second she thought she wouldn't make it, but the pink lights gave her faith.

She hit the ground hard, her own momentum sending her rolling as her arms twisted and scraped against the hard earth. She finally stopped, hitting a rock and knocking what little breath she had left from her lungs. With her heart thudding hard in her chest, she glanced up, trying to get her heartbeat under control.

The old woman glided across the now re-formed bridge. "You have done well, child."

Aliana blinked, forcing her vision to clear and the room to stop spinning, but she couldn't stop the ringing in her head.

"You have passed the third and final test to prove your worth of the title Destined One." The smoky voice was filled with joy.

The buzzing in Aliana's head grew louder, and words ran through her mind so quickly that she couldn't understand most of them. "What's happening to me?" she gasped. Her chest grew tighter. Something inside of her was rising to the surface, trying to escape. She tried to keep from panicking, but she didn't know what was happening or if she could control it.

"Only the Destined One has the strength to harness a spell strong enough to free King Arthur. The power has been growing inside of you since you first entered the forest surrounding Avalon's gate."

Sweat trickled down Aliana's cheeks as she fought to hold the power within her. Struggling, she made it to her feet. Her grip on the rock in front her was the only thing keeping her from falling back down. She studied the man lying on the ivy-covered altar. The magic bounded as words started to string together in her mind. Gritting her teeth, she pushed away from the stone and made her way to the king, ignoring the strange woman only a few feet from her.

The legendary king didn't look anything like she thought he would. He appeared young, like Galahad. His thick, chocolate-colored hair swept across his forehead. Even lying there asleep he radiated a power and strength that had probably made men tremble before him. His skin was pale and smooth over his square jaw, and his nose looked like it may have been broken once or twice. He was as tall as Galahad, easily over six feet, and in great shape for a guy who'd been asleep for hundreds of years. His armor and clothes were untouched by either time or the dampness of the cave. There was nothing to show that he'd been mortally wounded when he'd arrived here.

Aliana sat next to Arthur on the altar and leaned over him. Gently, she brushed the dark locks from his brow, lowering her lips to inches above his. She focused on the power flowing within her, gathering the forming words and whirls of magic. Somehow, she knew exactly what to do.

"Arthur Pendragon, our once and future king, your time has come. Your people need you once again to rise up and fight for them." The power drew her closer to him so that her lips nearly touched his. "Hear my voice; come to me." Then her lips met his as she breathed out the final words.

The power burst forth from her. Aliana closed her eyes, surrendering to the magic flowing from her lips to Arthur's, breathing life back into his hard body. When the last wisps of power flowed from her, she pulled back, breaking away from his full, firm mouth. Slowly, she opened her eyes, watching the color return to his face. She ran her fingers over her lips in awe, still feeling his mouth on hers. The power flowing between them wove a tangled web and somehow, a small piece of her heart healed itself.

Arthur drew in the first breath he'd taken in almost fifteen hundred years.

It was then that she realized what she had just done. She had just *kissed* King Arthur! Before the shock of her actions could set in, the king's eyes opened. In that moment, all she saw was a rich gold bursting in his eyes. They were such a clear brown, they seemed to glow. Nothing could have torn her eyes from his, and for an endless moment, King Arthur looked at her with pure exhilaration and joy, his beautiful lips turned up in a smile.

He raised his hand, brushing his fingertips gently across her lips before his large hand cupped her cheek. The gentle warmth flowing from his hand had Aliana sighing as she leaned into his touch and smiled back softly.

"It is you," he whispered, his voice weak.

"Lady Aliana," Galahad's voice called to her.

She jerked away, shocked out of the spell's fading power by the worry in Galahad's voice. Arthur's brow furrowed, his eyes questioning hers, but Galahad and Dagg were across the bridge before either of them could say another word.

Aliana slid off the altar as Arthur pushed himself up. Her vision blurred, and she gripped the stone tightly, trying to keep from collapsing. After taking a deep breath, her head stopped spinning and her vision cleared. *Thank the stars!* She wouldn't make a fool of herself in front of a king, after all.

Galahad stood a few feet away, awe and shock clear in his blue eyes as he met his king's gaze for the first time in over a millennium. Galahad unsheathed his sword, placing the tip into the earth, and kneeled before King Arthur. Aliana moved back, giving Arthur room to stand. She couldn't hide her surprise when he got to his feet with ease, as if he'd never been enchanted in the first place.

King Arthur gazed down at his knight and smiled. "Sir Galahad, my old friend."

"My king, it is good to have you with us again." The knight looked up. "Once again, I offer you my sword and my loyalty as a Knight of the Round Table, and as your friend."

Arthur placed a hand on Galahad's shoulder. "Rise, brother, you know you do not need to bow before me." Standing, Galahad re-sheathed his sword, and the two men embraced each other, laughing.

Dagg, who had been watching everything in silence, landed next to Aliana's hands on the altar. King Arthur studied the silver Dragon for a moment before glancing at Aliana.

"It is good to finally meet you, King Arthur. I am Daggerhorne, guardian to the Destined One." Dagg bowed his head.

"Sire," Galahad said, stepping forward, seeming the happiest he'd been since Aliana had freed him. "May I introduce the Lady Aliana Fagan?"

"Hello," Aliana said, amazed at how steady her voice sounded while her insides were a mess of emotions pulling her in so many directions. Her eyes drifted back and forth between the two men towering over her. She let go of the stone, determined that her legs would hold her. And they did, but only for a moment.

Galahad was suddenly at her side, his arm around her waist, supporting her. Grateful, Aliana leaned into him, breathing in the wintery scent that she was becoming so fond of.

"It is a pleasure to meet you, my lady." Arthur's accented voice rumbled as he bowed to her. "I am eternally in your debt for awakening me."

"No problem. Glad I could help." She stifled a nervous giggle.

"It is good to see you moving about again, great king." The mystery woman stepped out from the shadows. With a grand flourish, she threw off her brown cloak, revealing her true form.

Dangerously beautiful.

That was the only way Aliana could describe her. She was taller now, with long, wavy, copper locks and skin as pale as a china doll. She was dressed in an elegant green bodice with sheer gold sleeves.

Her matching green skirt hugged her hips and was slit on both sides. Queen Titania's emerald eyes matched her dress, and her pink lips smiled like she knew all the secrets of the world. Next to her, Aliana felt like a complete disaster with her clothes torn and caked with dirt. Her hair was probably a total rat's nest.

"Queen Titania." King Arthur bowed deeply to her. Galahad bowed his head to the Fae queen, but stood straight and kept his arm tight around Aliana.

"The first undertaking is complete, but now I fear the true challenges lie before you all." Titania studied each of them carefully, seeming to take note of Galahad's arms supporting Aliana and the way Arthur stood slightly in front of the pair. The queen smirked.

Aliana didn't like that look in her eyes. She leaned in closer to Galahad, grateful for his calming presence.

"What must we do next, your Majesty?" Arthur asked.

"Follow the prophecy. The Destined One is the key. She will guide you to your next task." Her hard gaze met Arthur's, then moved on to Galahad's and Daggerhorne's before meeting Aliana's. The queen's eyes softened just a bit. "There is great danger ahead for all of you but especially for the Destined One. Mordrid will know that she is the key. You know the lengths to which he is willing to go in order to win. You all must guard Aliana well; keep her from harm."

"We'll protect her no matter the cost," Arthur vowed, his voice fierce.

"She will be protected at all times," Galahad swore as he gazed down at his charge.

Aliana reddened, turning to Dagg, surprised the Dragon had been so silent. Her green eyes met his purple ones, and he nodded at her.

"No one will be safer, my queen," Dagg assured her. "But we must get to the mortal realm soon. There is still much to be done, and I am sure Aliana is ready to go home."

The queen moved past Arthur and stood in front of Aliana, who straightened as much as her aching body would allow. Titania tucked a stray lock of Aliana's milk chocolate hair behind her ear as she smiled, almost fondly, at the young woman. "You have done well, young one. You are truly worthy of your destiny." With those words, the Fae queen stepped back. "I will send you all back to the Lady of the Lake. Aliana knows the way to the mortal realm from there."

Galahad, Arthur, and Dagg all bowed to Queen Titania one last time. The beautiful queen held out her hand again, and the same magic she had used earlier sprang to life, circling them. Its warmth seeped into Aliana's aching muscles as her head started to spin. She tried fighting it, but the magic was too strong. She looked up, barely able to see Galahad's worried eyes. She glanced in Arthur's direction, meeting his anxious, golden brown gaze before darkness consumed her.

Queen Titania's parting words whispered in her head: "Until we meet again."

9

Her eyes, those sparkling emeralds, had been my only companion since the Fae queen cast her spell on me. Her voice, her laugh mesmerized me. I wanted to draw her in close, to feel her lips on mine. Her sweet taste is still on my lips. Yet a memory — a ghost — is holding me back.

— Arthur

Aliana looked at the carnage around her. Abandoned pieces of scorched black armor littered the ground alongside mutilated and dying gray monsters. The sounds of battle raged around her. Loud crashes of thunder roared through the air, and swords clashed as men and monsters struggled for supremacy. The scent of death and blood surrounded her as more black knights fell to their enemies.

She watched, horrified, as the story Titania had told her now played out in gruesome, vivid detail. The four brave knights fell to the swords and pointed spears of the monstrous black knights. Aliana cried out, wishing she could do something as the knights died in pain and violence. But she was totally helpless.

She looked away from the dead men and toward King Arthur, Galahad, and the men she now recognized as Lancelot and Merlin. King Arthur and Galahad fought back to back, and they were a devastating team. *Lancelot battled alongside them, his raven hair plastered to his head by sweat, his pale green eyes burning with fury. Next to him the golden-eyed Druid incinerated beastly Goblins and zombie knights, all of it just as the Fae drawings had shown her—except this time Arthur and his knights didn't wear helmets. She could see the fury that burned in their eyes.*

The sinister warlock sneered, blocking the fireballs Merlin threw at him. "You are weak, Merlin. Neither your king nor your Druid powers, can stop me!" *His voice was shrill with glee.* "Or did you fail to learn that lesson after Morgana's death? All the realms will bow to me, and those foolish enough to resist will die slowly while I claim ultimate power."

This guy is nuts! Aliana felt her fear all the way to her bones. *The sick delight in Mordrid's black eyes made her feel nauseated.*

Merlin threw aside his sun shield and called down lightning to burn the minions to ash, creating an opening.

"Galahad, Lancelot, hold them back," *the king ordered, charging forward, sword held high. He shot through the opening and caught Mordrid by surprise, knocking the warlock's shield from his hand. Mordrid struck back, his magic giving him the ability to strike as hard and as fast as the warrior king.*

"You never learn, Arthur, and that will be your death." *Mordrid slashed his sword down on Arthur.*

Arthur parried Mordrid's strike, nearly ripping the blade from his hand. "Excalibur and I disagree. All your treachery will have been for naught!" *he roared, disarming the villain and cutting a gaping wound into the sorcerer's arm.* "Your dark magic cannot heal Excalibur's bite."

Mordrid fought back, but Arthur pinned him down with Excalibur pressed hard against his throat. "It ends now, warlock." *Arthur prepared to drive his blade down upon Mordrid, but he disappeared.*

"Coward!" *Arthur bellowed in rage.* "Fight me like a man!" *He swung around, searching for Mordrid. The king struck again as the sorcerer reappeared, but again Excalibur cut though empty space.*

As quickly as Mordrid had disappeared, he re-materialized behind the king, wrapping a thin arm around Arthur's throat, plunging a dagger through the side of his armor. Breath rushed out of Arthur's lungs. Aliana felt the blade burning as it cut through his flesh.

"You'll never kill me, Arthur," *Mordrid said into the king's ear. He pulled the dagger from Arthur's side, then stabbed again.* "You don't have the power."

Aliana felt the fire that rushed through Arthur's veins, burning him from the inside out.

"Arthur!" she cried.

Galahad, Lancelot, and Merlin all looked to their king, but Mordrid's black gaze jumped to Aliana's, trapping her in his power. She felt his fascination and surprise. His lips pulled up into a snarling smile as he studied her through red and black eyes.

With his evil smile fixed on her, the evil magician withdrew his dagger, plunging it into King Arthur's side one last time. "Die, Arthur, knowing that I will rule all the realms with my chosen queen by my side."

"No!" Aliana's cries mixed with Galahad's and Lancelot's as Mordrid pulled the dagger free, letting Arthur's body fall to the ground.

"Lady Aliana." She felt Mordrid's cold touch on her skin as he breathed her name. He took a step toward her, his tongue licking his twisted lips.

Aliana's eyes were wide with terror as Mordrid advanced. "Please, no," she whimpered, still frozen in the same spot she had been in since entering this strange vision.

Lancelot charged at Mordrid, but he sent the knight flying back with a flick of his hand. Before the evil sorcerer could get to Aliana, fire surrounded him, exploding outward, consuming everything.

"Aliana." Cool winds wrapped around her as the fire raced toward her. "Wake up."

Her emerald eyes shot open as sharp claws shook her awake. Daggerhorne's anxious face was the first she saw. Taking a breath, she looked past the Dragon, confused, to see Galahad, Arthur, and Deidre.

Am I still dreaming? I must be. There's no way all of this really happened! She closed her eyes, trying to wake herself up, and lifted her lids, expecting to see her bedroom walls, but all she saw were the worried faces of people she had only ever dreamed of.

"What is wrong, my lady? Why were you screaming?" Arthur's soft voice washed over her. Galahad's worried blue eyes asked her the same question. Both men's reactions felt strangely intimate.

"Is this real?" she asked, sitting up on soft silken pillows and blankets.

The men looked at each other, their mouths pressed into tight frowns, but the blue-haired Nymph smiled. "This is all very much real, Destined One." She turned to the men. "Perhaps we should step back and give Lady Aliana some space to compose herself." Deidre moved away, her ice blue gaze pulling the men reluctantly out of the tent with her.

Aliana lay back down, still half believing this was all a dream. Dagg's warm, scaly body snuggled against her arm.

"You cannot keep disbelieving, Aliana. You have accomplished more in a day than most people do in their lifetimes, and you have been brave and fearless through it all."

Aliana scoffed but couldn't stop her smile as she sat up again, stretching. "Why don't I hurt anymore, Dagg?" she asked, remembering her screaming muscles and aching bruises and cuts. Then she thought of the sensation during her dream—the fire burning her from the inside. *Is that what Arthur had to suffer through?* She looked down at her clothes to find them whole and clean again. Even her favorite hiking boots looked polished and brand new.

"Queen Titania's magic healed you when she transported us here. When you awoke King Arthur, most of your energy was drained. Using magic always has a cost, and holding in so much power for so long exhausted your body."

Aliana bit her lip. "Will I have to do something like that again? I felt like I could just go to sleep and never wake up."

"I hope not, my lady, but we can build up your magical tolerance with training."

Aliana groaned and buried her face in her hands. "I already have martial arts training, now I have to do this too?" She knew she was whining, but hey, she had just pulled off several miracles, according to Dagg—she deserved a moment of self-pity.

The Dragon laughed and tendrils of smoke curled from his nose. Aliana peered through the tent opening and watched Galahad and Arthur talk with the petite and animated Deidre, who couldn't seem to keep from touching Arthur at every opportunity. For a moment, jealousy sparked in Aliana's chest, but then she peeked at Galahad and her heart fluttered. She dropped her eyes before she could get caught staring.

"My lady, are you all right?" Dagg asked.

Aliana looked up, plastering a smile on her face. "Yeah, I'm sorry, just got lost for a moment." She turned back toward the trio next to the moonlit lake. Arthur's golden brown eyes caught hers over Galahad's shoulder for a brief moment before Deidre pulled his attention away again.

"You know your feelings are apparent on your face," Dagg teased her gently. "You are drawn to both men and confused by it."

Aliana felt her cheeks heat up. "It's not that." Dagg appeared unconvinced. "It's just that I feel like I know them. Ever since I was a kid I've dreamed about meeting them. I've read everything about the Arthurian legends. I know most of the stories by heart. I've even done a photo series about it. Coincidently, it was my first big success as an artist. But realizing how much magic plays into their story is just a challenge to believe. I never *really* thought magic was real until now."

"I can understand. Though the Sidhe kept me trapped for many years, I spent much time in the mortal realm before that. Mortals have lost their belief in magic and what they can't see. But you'll get used to it."

Grateful for his attempt at comfort, Aliana scooped up the Dragon and scratched him under his chin, causing him to growl in pleasure. She laughed as she got to her feet. "Thanks for taking care of my bag. You're my perfect pack mule." She grabbed her bag and headed out of the tent, giggling at Dagg's sour expression.

She met Galahad and Arthur's confused gazes as she approached. "Thank you for your help, Deidre. I don't think I would have gotten as far as I did without that map."

Deidre giggled her bell laugh. "I could have done no less, my lady." She curtseyed. "But before you go, I have something for King Arthur." The Nymph turned away and walked into the shallow water. Arthur and Galahad shared a raised eyebrow of amusement, and Galahad shrugged his broad shoulders.

The water around Deidre's feet bubbled, and tiny drops of water floated up, carrying with them a long, curved sword sheathed in a black leather case. Amazed and thrilled, Aliana stepped between the two men, a delighted smile on her face as Deidre took the sword and turned back to them.

"J'alel brought this to me earlier. He said the fire Elves forged it especially for King Arthur to use until he can once again reclaim Excalibur." Deidre held the sword in her hands, presenting it to the king.

Walking into the water, Arthur kneeled before her, taking the sword from her hands. Aliana smiled brightly, watching another classic piece of legend happen before her eyes. She looked up at Galahad, so excited she wanted to start jumping up and down like a child. She blushed as she realized he'd been watching her instead of Arthur. She glanced away, embarrassed.

Why does that keep happening?

"Thank you, my lady. I humbly accept such a rare and precious gift." Arthur rose to stand in front of Deidre. "But I thought you would have Excalibur."

"Alas, great king, I do not. And to defeat Mordrid, you will have to search it out and claim it once more."

"Do you know where it rests?" Arthur asked.

Deidre shook her head. "The prophecy speaks of the Destined One helping you in your search to reclaim what is yours."

"Unearth and reclaim their lost relics," Aliana quoted, remembering the daunting words.

Arthur frowned, coming out of the water to stand by her. "I have yet to hear any of this," he said, fastening the new sword about his waist.

Deidre nodded reassuringly, and Aliana explained, "Just before my final test, Queen Titania told me the prophecy, but a lot of it doesn't make sense:

"Before the darkest hour strikes, the Destined One shall come forth.
Avalon's lost daughter must thrice and alone prove her worth,
Then can she fully possess the power to awaken the king.
It shall become her destiny to reunite the Round Table,
Unearth and reclaim their lost relics,
Become the key to undoing the evil Mordrid has wrought.
Only with her can the once and future king prevail."

She surprised herself by being able to recall Titania's ominous words so well.

Arthur crossed his arms over his chest, one finger thoughtfully tapping his chin.

Galahad's deep voice rumbled. "We know Lady Aliana is the Destined One and the 'thrice and alone prove her worth' refers to the tests she had to undergo today."

"Courage, wits, and faith," Aliana murmured, suppressing a shiver. She wouldn't want to go through those tests again.

"Most of it makes sense if you think it through," Arthur said. "Our next task is to find the knights, then go after Excalibur and the Grail of Power. Lady Aliana is the key, as the queen said."

Aliana let out a breath. Apparently she had more to do than she first thought. "So where do we start searching for Lancelot and Merlin and the other knights?"

"The mortal realm," Galahad said, his voice heavy. "That is where Lancelot and Merlin went."

"But they went there hundreds of years ago. There's no way they would still be al —" Dagg's clawed paw tightened on Aliana's shoulder cutting her off.

"We will return to the mortal realm," King Arthur decided.

Deidre nodded, approval written across her beautiful face. "Good luck to you, Destined One," she said to Aliana, then turned her flirty blue gaze to Arthur. "And to you, great king." She ran a finger down Arthur's strong arm.

Aliana glanced away to see Galahad with a knowing smirk on his lips. She nudged him, her eyes asking what was so funny. The knight shook his head, still smirking.

"Thank you, my lady," Arthur said as he and Galahad both bowed to the Water Nymph. Deidre curtseyed again but peered at Aliana and winked one beautiful, ice blue eye as she began to sink back below the water.

"Thanks again, Deidre. I hope we get to see you sometime soon!" Aliana called out right before the Nymph fully submerged. As she fished her journal and GPS out of her bag, it hit her that she was really going home. Finally. She'd been gone way too long.

Not even bothering to ask, Galahad took Aliana's pack for her. She wanted to protest, but his light blue eyes met hers with a raised eyebrow, daring her to argue.

It's not worth it, girl, she told herself. With Dagg perched on her shoulder, she led them through the soft grass and lovely flowers toward the cave opening. Stepping into the total darkness, Aliana swallowed her fear and grabbed her cell phone. Before she could turn on the flashlight, Dagg jumped from her shoulder, hovering in front of them.

"Allow me." The silver Dragon's purple eyes glowed as he summoned a small iridescent ball of light to illuminate the cave. Grateful and more relieved than she wanted to admit, Aliana patted the Dragon's head when he reclaimed his position on her shoulder.

"How long until we reach the other side, my lady?" Arthur asked as they made their way through the twisting tunnel.

"Um, maybe fifteen, twenty minutes." She turned to face her companions. "And, though I appreciate it, please don't call me *my lady*. I'm just plain old Aliana, and I am certainly no lady." She looked both men in the eyes, hoping they would understand.

"We will call you whatever you wish my…Aliana," Arthur replied for both of them.

Still facing them, she walked backward. "I don't want to seem too eager, but I've been dying to ask you guys some questions."

Neither man told her to turn around, but they both moved in closer and Arthur's eyes flicked anxiously from her to the space behind her when he said, "You have but to ask."

"Well, I guess my first question has to be—when did all of this happen? What year was it when you ruled Camelot?"

"My father was crowned king in the year of our lord five hundred and sixty-five. Our family was one of the last of the Roman lineage to have ruled the lands. Our realm was split into six separate kingdoms. Camelot was the largest and strongest of them all."

"Wow! Okay, that fits with the lesser known stories of Camelot. Now for the next million questions." She hadn't told them about her dream or what Titania had told her before Arthur awoke. She wanted to hear their side of the story first. There was more to it than what she'd been told; she just knew it.

"What happened to the Knights of the Round Table, and what were their names?"

Galahad's lips drew tight, his square jaw becoming even more defined in his angry silence.

"There were eight of us," Arthur said, his brown eyes shining as he remembered his loyal friends. "Galahad and myself, Gawain, Percival, Owaine, Leyon, Lancelot, and Merlin." Arthur's brow furrowed. "But as to what happened to them, I am not sure. My memories of that day are still unclear."

"Percival, Owaine, Leyon, and Gawain all fell fighting the black knights, while the rest of us fought Mordrid and his guards," Galahad answered solemnly.

Just like it had been in her dream and Titania's story.

"Wait, Merlin was a knight? I thought he was your advisor." Aliana's brow scrunched.

"No, Merlin sat at the Round Table as a knight. His skills with a sword were not the strongest, but his magic made him more dangerous than most in the five other kingdoms," Arthur said with a slight smile.

Just another piece of the legends that was wrong. God, this was so confusing. Everything Aliana thought she knew about Arthur and his men was probably going to change. But would it be for the better?

"I know that Mordrid mortally wounded you, Arthur, and that after trapping him, Merlin brought you and the others to Avalon." She cast a worried glance at Galahad. She didn't want to upset him, but she had to know. "What happened after you made the deal with Queen Titania? Where are Lancelot and Merlin?"

Arthur looked to Galahad with sad brown eyes.

Has Galahad already told Arthur what happened? Aliana felt hurt for a moment but then reality struck her. Of course he would tell Arthur. He couldn't keep something like that from his king. *Just people he doesn't trust.*

Galahad opened his mouth to answer, but froze as he stared past Aliana in awe. They had already reached the cave entrance to the mortal world. Her rope still held the vines to the side, allowing the early evening glow to spill into the cave as it lit the clear lake just outside. Aliana sighed softly, seeing the rainbow created by the fall's mist.

"We're home," she said, momentarily putting her curiosity aside.

Dagg jumped from her shoulder, soaring in the air, diving through the waterfall. Aliana giggled as she walked out of the cave, grateful to smell the clean, crisp lake air. She turned with a large smile on her face, expecting the guys to be right behind her, but they'd stayed just inside the entrance, caught up in the scenery before them. Their eyes were a little wider, their jaws slightly slack.

"You two all right?" she asked as she walked back over to them.

Galahad was the first to snap out of his stupor. "Yes, my la… Aliana." His voice was soft. "Returning to our world was something I was not sure would ever happen." He smiled softly.

Aliana could only imagine what that must feel like. He and Arthur had had their home ripped from them and were thrown into a strange, new land. Squaring her shoulders, She took the king's and the knight's hands in hers, slowly pulling them from the cave and back to into their world, their home. Familiar sparks rolled up her arm from Galahad's touch.

Arthur smiled, studying the area in silence. Galahad inhaled the fresh air. "Avalon is a wondrous place, but nothing can best the smell of the forest," he said as he lifted and kissed Aliana's hand. "I never thanked you for freeing me and now you have brought us home. Thank you." He stepped closer, gently squeezing her hand.

Aliana beamed, returning his smile, and looked to Arthur. When he raised her hand to his own lips, she realized neither of them had yet released her. Her heart skipped a few beats as butterflies danced in her stomach.

"I too owe you a great many thanks, Aliana. You have done so much for us already, and I know there is so much more that is still to come." Arthur's thumb traced over the knuckles where his soft lips had just been.

Galahad's blue eyes darkened when they landed on her and Arthur's joined hands. Clearing her throat, Aliana stepped back, pulling away from both men. *I am in so much trouble!* "Don't thank me yet. Wait till we get into the city. You might not be so grateful when you see how much things have changed in fifteen hundred years."

Identical worried frowns and furrowed brows appeared on their faces.

10

I nearly ran off the road when the block in my mind shattered. I knew as soon as I woke that everything was going to change. The Destined One is finally here! King Arthur will be restored, my brothers returned to me. But how am I going to face them after abandoning the king? My beautiful Guinevere's worried eyes still haunt me every day. I will find her again. Surely the Destined One will see her returned to me. She must.

Lancelot

Snorting a laugh, Aliana turned on her GPS. "No way!"

"What's wrong?" Dagg asked, landing on her shoulder and gazing at the small device.

"This says I've only been in Avalon for seven hours." She looked at Galahad, dumbfounded. "The moon was just starting to set when we were with Deidre!"

"Time passes differently in Avalon. Sometimes it is faster than the mortal world, other times it is slower," Dagg explained.

She checked her cell phone and confirmed that her GPS was right. "That's trippy. At least Owen won't be going too crazy, yet."

"Who is Owen?" Galahad and Arthur demanded.

"Owen is the whole reason I'm still in England."

Shadows stole across their faces, and Galahad said, "You said you were not married."

Aliana shook her head. "Oh, for heaven's sake, what's wrong with you two? Owen's my cousin."

Neither man's expression changed, and then it hit her. "Oh, gross! That's so last century—we don't marry our cousins anymore!" Arthur and Galahad reddened slightly with embarrassment, but the shadows lifted from their expressions. Arching an eyebrow, Aliana turned to Dagg, who was grinning like a fool. "Let's go, guys."

Arthur and Galahad flanked Aliana as she led them through the trees, away from Avalon.

"If you don't mind, Galahad, I'd like it if you could finish telling us what happened." She half expected him to refuse or to change the subject, but he surprised her.

"After Titania sealed the bargain, Merlin laid magical barriers and traps while Lancelot and I set physical traps and made friends with the Elves and other races who lived in the forest. Years passed as we guarded the hollow and the Grail. Merlin was the first to notice that we had stopped aging. He believed that was because the oath bound our lives to Arthur's, and that so as long as his enemy Mordrid was alive and our quest incomplete, we would not age."

Aliana's gaze snapped up from her map. "How old were all of you when you made the oath?"

"I had just celebrated my twenty-first anniversary before Mordrid's attack," Arthur answered. "Galahad is only a year behind me."

"You…you can't…you've got to be kidding me!" Aliana sputtered. She'd noted their youthful appearance but hadn't realized they were only slightly older than her.

Arthur and Galahad both looked at her, confused, and she started to think their faces were going to get permanently stuck that way. Hers probably would too if they threw any more curve balls at her.

"What do you mean by 'kidding you'?" Galahad asked.

"Pulling my chain, joshing me, joking."

"No, Aliana, we are serious. How old are you?" Arthur asked.

"I just turned eighteen." Sighing, she pushed her shock aside. "Okay, so now that I am sufficiently surprised, hit me with the rest of your story."

"We would not hit you, Aliana," Galahad said, looking appalled.

"Oh my stars, this is going to be harder than I thought," she muttered. "It's an expression. It means 'please continue with your story.'"

Arthur nodded to Galahad, who said, "Several years after arriving, the Fae brought us news about Camelot. Our home was being divided amongst the other kingdoms. Everything we'd fought so hard to protect was gone, but we took what comfort we could in the knowledge that it wasn't at Mordrid's and Morgana's hands. We carried on for years until S'han came to us one day with news that Morgana was alive and had been seen in one of the Druid villages. He said she had as much power as ever."

"You didn't tell me that, Galahad." Arthur scowled.

"Forgive me, sire." Galahad frowned, his eyes growing darker as he explained to Aliana, "Merlin killed Morgana before our final battle. We all watched him pull his sword from her dead body."

"He did?" Aliana gasped in horror and disbelief, stumbling over her own feet, but Galahad's hand steadied her. "Most of the legends say Morgana and three other priestesses took Arthur to Avalon to be healed. In others, she just kind of fades away. But *all* of the stories say she reconciled with Arthur before the end."

For the first time, Arthur's calm façade broke. Fierce anger swept across his strong face. "She betrayed us to Mordrid. She murdered hundreds of innocents, destroyed villages, and wreaked havoc on peoples' lives." Rage colored his words. "There was nothing she could have done to ever make me forgive her."

Galahad's fists balled tightly at his side, like he wanted to strike something or someone. "According to Merlin, a person's magic dies when they do and she should not have been alive. We never thought we would hear of her again, so after we got the news, Merlin left Avalon to search her out. If she had as much power as we believed she did, she could have freed Mordrid from his prison."

Aliana nodded. She understood why Merlin had left, but something didn't feel quite right. "Wasn't his leaving considered a betrayal by Titania?" she asked. "Why would he have risked it?"

"Merlin believed that since Morgana threatened Arthur's return, his actions would not betray the oath. Several years later, when Merlin still hadn't returned, Lancelot left. He said he wanted to search Merlin out, to make sure Morgana had not killed him."

Aliana bit the inside of her cheek and they walked in silence for a few minutes as she struggled with the story. Something was missing. Titania had given a different reason for Lancelot's departure from Avalon — Guinevere!

"Look, I'm trying to be sensitive here, but…what about Guinevere?" Her worried eyes studied Arthur. "In all the stories, she was married to you, Arthur, but had a secret love affair with Lancelot. In some of the stories that betrayal even leads to your downfall." She braced for the anger that was sure to follow.

All three of her companions chuckled. "Guinevere was betrothed to me when we were very young," Arthur explained. "But she had fallen in love with Lancelot and I agreed to break the betrothal so they could wed."

"So there was no secret affair? She didn't come between you and Lancelot?" Arthur shook his head. Sighing, Aliana remembered something Dagg had mentioned earlier. *This should be good for a laugh.* Glancing at Galahad, she said, "You should know, all our stories say you were Lancelot's son."

Both men burst into laughter. It was hypnotizing to watch, seeing such tough warriors relax. It made them seem younger and even more swoon worthy. *It should be been illegal.*

Biting her lip, Aliana looked down at her GPS before asking her next question, expecting the answer to be pretty ugly. "Then what happened to Guinevere?"

The mood changed, their laughter fading. Arthur's voice dropped lower as he said, "Guinevere disappeared just after we thought Morgana was killed. She was riding to Camelot with a group of knights when they were attacked. All were slaughtered, their bodies mutilated and strung up as a warning. But we were never able to find her body."

"I am so sorry, Arthur." Aliana laid a comforting hand on his strong arm. "You still cared for her even though she was in love with Lancelot." She could feel it. She turned to Galahad. "That's why Lancelot really left isn't it? To find her…or at least her body."

He nodded once, and said, "Lancelot refused to believe she was dead." The knight's heavy, blue eyes looked off into space. "He grew mad with his belief that she was still out there and that Mordrid might have her. He said he was leaving Avalon for Merlin, but yes, I believe he also wanted to try to find Guinevere."

"Even though so much time had passed in the mortal world?" Aliana couldn't imagine loving someone that much, but her father would have done the same for her mother in that situation. Nothing would have stopped him from finding his wife. Her heart dropped realizing what she needed to find out next. "He and Merlin both knew they would be punished for leaving, but what about you, Galahad? Why were you punished with imprisonment? I know what Titania told me, but I want to hear it from you."

Galahad's handsome face could have been carved from stone as his next words pushed through his clenched teeth. "What did she tell you?"

"She said you were trapped by the Sidhe and that you lost the Grail of Power." Aliana didn't want to repeat the rest of Titania's words for fear she'd upset him more.

"After Lancelot and Merlin left, guarding both the Grail and Arthur fell to me. Somehow, a small gargoyle got past Merlin's barriers and my traps and stole the Grail." Galahad met Arthur's gaze with his chin held high. "I set new traps after realizing the flaw in the protection, and then I left the hollow to get the Grail back, trusting that the magic and the new traps would be enough to protect you, sire."

Arthur nodded but didn't say anything. Galahad looked away into the forest, continuing. "I was led into the Sidhe's trap. They took me back to that tower, intending to force me to reveal the location of the hidden hollow, but Lord Daggerhorne found me and we tried to escape. I was fighting my way out when they trapped me in that amber stone. We were all so arrogant, thinking that we were justified in our reasons to abandon our duty."

Galahad stepped ahead of them, turning to face his king. "I beg your forgiveness for my failure, sire. I should have stopped them from leaving. I offer you no excuse for my failings. I only hope that you will give me a chance to atone for my mistakes."

In the time that she had known him, Galahad had never been so open, so exposed, so unconfident in himself or his actions. Seeing him humble himself in front of Arthur, the band around her heart cracked.

Arthur shook his head. "Galahad, you take too much on yourself. Titania's twisted way of thinking is not mine. Lancelot and Merlin made their own decisions. It is not a reflection upon you. And the Sidhe are masters of trickery. No one, not even you, could face them alone and prevail." Arthur placed his hands on Galahad's shoulders. "I do not blame you for anything! We will retrieve the Grail and find a way to reunite the knights. We will defeat Mordrid and reclaim everything we have lost."

Galahad nodded, relief in his small smile. But his gaze dropped to the forest floor as Aliana took up her place at his side. *I think he's afraid his friends may be dead.* Slipping her GPS into her pocket, she took Galahad's hand. "Come on, let's get going so we can get back to the city and figure out our next move."

His deep blue eyes stared at their connected hands before jumping to her face. Confidence slowly returned to his smile, and she released his hand, looking to Arthur, who watched them with a guarded gaze.

They walked in heavy silence for a few moments before Dagg broke it. "How are we going to find the others?"

Aliana held back a sigh. She had hoped to avoid this part of the conversation until they'd reached her flat. She was mentally exhausted and feeling a bit defeated—so much had changed, and so much of what she thought she knew was wrong. "Four of them died and we don't know what happened to Lancelot and Merlin after they left. How could either of them still be alive?" she asked.

"Queen Titania bound our lives to the king's," Galahad said. "We have to believe they still live."

Arthur placed a hand on Galahad's shoulder. "We'll find Merlin and Lancelot. I know they are out there. I believe all of our brothers are. The Fae queen had many ends in sight when she helped us."

Dagg jumped from Aliana's shoulder. "You should tell us more about the modern world, Aliana. There are many things we are going to need to know."

This was a topic she could handle. For the next hour, she filled them in. They marveled at her stories about all the new places and countries that had been discovered and were amazed that she was from a faraway place called South Carolina. She explained to them modern governments and technology. Arthur seemed to catch on quickly, surprising Aliana with his almost instant understanding of the changes.

"Wait till you see how people travel now! Cars, planes, trains. It's all so wonderful and so much faster than riding horses."

"You do not seem to have a fondness for riding horses." Galahad's words were teasing.

Heat pooled in Aliana's stomach and flowed to her cheeks as she thought of their flight together on Belle. "Yeah, well, I agree with Sherlock Holmes' sentiments—they are hazardous at both ends and cunning in the middle."

They all broke out laughing. Aliana was happy that she could get their minds away from their tragedies. In that moment, she decided that she was going to do everything she could to show both men how much happiness and beauty the modern world had to offer. They had been so young to carry so much responsibility! She was determined that they would experience fun and play, even while they fulfilled the prophecy.

More than halfway through the forest, Aliana felt a ping of uneasiness slide down her spine. She looked at the surrounding trees, but didn't see anything that might be a threat. Dagg shifted on her shoulder, feeling her tension. "What is wrong?" he rumbled into her ear.

Arthur and Galahad stopped, hands on their swords, as they corralled her between them. Their trained eyes saw what she hadn't. "Stay behind us," Galahad ordered, his eyes still searching the trees as he handed Aliana her pack. She held the bag loosely in her hand, ready to ditch it if she had to.

"Do you see them, Galahad?" Arthur's voice was quiet.

"I count three on my side, sire."

"I have three over here." Both men drew their swords.

The sound of the blades cutting the air sent chills down Aliana's spine. Dagg leaped from her shoulder, his gray wings carrying him soundlessly through the air as her warriors took up their attack positions. She was scared. Not only of what was out there, but because the forest surrounding them didn't leave much room to move if this turned into a battle.

"Whatever you do, do not leave our side," Arthur cautioned.

Six towering creatures melted out from the shadows of the forest. They surrounded the trio on two sides, their long, sharp swords held in front of them. Their black armor was dented and scratched as if they had seen too many battles, too much death. Hatred and evil rolled off them in waves, making the air thick. But what terrified Aliana the most was the total darkness behind the helmets where there should have been eyes.

The black knights were even more terrifying in person than they had been in her dream. The one standing in front of Arthur took a step forward. A horrific red glow lit its helmet from within. Aliana's blood halted as the black knight's choppy, metallic voice rang out. "So the Destined One has finally come forth." Its hellish, red gaze fixed on her. Her hands trembled worse than they had when she'd been trapped in that forgotten room, but she took a deep breath, trying to think past the fear.

"Mordrid," Galahad snarled, his eyes furious as he studied the enemies surrounding them.

Dagg circled them from above, waiting to attack, his amethyst eyes burning bright.

"Very good, Galahad, nice to know your time with the Sidhe hasn't dulled your memory," Mordrid's voice taunted through the monstrous black knight.

Neither Galahad nor Arthur answered. The black knights shifted closer. From above her came a loud, angry growl from Dagg, surprising Aliana.

"Hand over the Destined One and we can all be on our way," Mordrid said.

"That will never happen, demon." Arthur raised his new sword.

"You will give her——"

Dagg let loose streams of Dragon fire, cutting off the evil knight. Arthur and Galahad sprang forward with thunderous battle cries. Everything happened so quickly after that, and Aliana had a hard time keeping up. Galahad battled his opponents back, thrusting and slashing as the demons tried to get past him. Two of them charged Galahad, creating a small opening for the third to slip by. Aliana dropped her bag, shifting on the balls of her feet, ready to put all her martial arts training to use. But she didn't have to. Dagg rained down more fire, blocking the thing's path as Galahad stepped forward and cleaved the black monster's head clean off. The helmet soared through the air, knocking into a nearby tree.

Aliana gagged as the putrid smell of decomposing flesh filled the air. The armor fell to the ground in pieces, like a marionette cut from its wires.

Arthur fought off two more black knights as the leader held back. He was studying them, Aliana realized, looking for their weaknesses.

Arthur fought with a combination of efficient, quick parries and hard blows, confusing the black knights. He cut off the sword arm of the nearest knight, and the empty armor fell uselessly to the ground.

The leader stepped in, drawing Arthur's attention from the mutilated creature. Dagg swooped down, spitting purple balls of magic at the leader while Aliana watched the maimed knight retrieve his sword. As soon as he grabbed it, the knight charged through the small opening his fall had created—heading straight for her.

Reacting on instinct, Aliana jumped back, turning and taking off running. Adrenaline surged as she ducked around a large tree, trying to circle back to her protectors, but the knight cut her off and Aliana realized now what a huge mistake she had made.

The utter silence of the knight frightened her as much as his sword did, but she pushed fear aside, determined to get away. The demon rushed forward, his blade swinging in a wide arc. Aliana bent backward as the sword cut through the air, swinging inches above her arched body. The knight stumbled from his own momentum, and Aliana straightened, taking off toward Galahad. She skidded to a halt, nearly knocking into the one-armed knight, who had somehow gotten ahead of her.

The beast attacked, and the only thing she could do was dodge and weave, avoiding the blade that was very much intended to cut her into pieces. Her heart pounded, her breath choppy and heaving, and she wasn't sure how long she could keep this up.

A strategy formed as she ducked another blow. If she didn't time this just right, she was done for. Stepping in line with the remaining arm just as the knight brought the sword down, Aliana launched into a back flip, kicking her feet into the monster's forearm. The force from the unconventional and unexpected blow knocked the blade from his hand, sending it clattering to the ground. Landing in a crouch, Aliana kicked her foot out, sweeping the black knight's legs from under him and sending the monster tumbling to the ground.

She sprang up, sprinting past the fallen knight and back toward her friends, but the cold, armored hand grabbed her ankle, pulling her off her feet. Wildly, she kicked at her captor, desperate to break free. She grabbed a rock the size of her fist and threw it at the knight, loosening his iron grip enough for her to kick free. She scrambled back, colliding with a tree. She was trapped. The knight was back on his feet, sword raised high, ready to deliver the final blow. She squeezed her eyes shut and felt sweat trickle down her face. *This can't be it!*

At the sound of metal clashing with metal, Aliana's eyes snapped open. Another sword had blocked the black knight's blade from striking her down. The second sword parried the knight's, and with one swift stroke, the black knight's helmet rolled to the ground with the empty armor falling seconds after.

Eyes wide, Aliana stared up at her dark-haired rescuer.

"Forgive my interference, but it looked like you needed a hand." Pale green eyes met hers as the tall, olive-skinned warrior offered her his hand. He'd been in her dream!

Barely aware of it, she took his hand and pulled herself to her feet. "You're Lancelot! But how?" Her mouth hung open in shock. She was beginning to realize that the dream had actually been a very real vision.

Smirking, he placed two fingers under her chin, clicking her mouth closed. "We need to rejoin the king, my lady." With Aliana's hand still gripped in his, Lancelot pulled her toward Arthur and Galahad. A giant of a man with spiky, blond hair fell in on her other side.

Arthur and Galahad stood back to back, surrounded on all sides, but they fought on while Dagg dive-bombed the enemies with magic attacks.

"Perhaps we should even the odds," Lancelot said to his large friend. The behemoth struck the nearest black knight from behind, knocking it aside, as Lancelot dragged Aliana into the small space between Arthur and Galahad.

"Lancelot, Percival!" Galahad spared a quick look of surprise when the black knights he was fighting fell back a few steps.

Aliana's warriors moved together like they had never been separated. The four closed ranks around her, and Dagg circled closely above.

"They do not touch Aliana," Arthur ordered. As one, the four men attacked. Three of the four remaining black knights fell to rotting pieces at their feet.

"This isn't over! I will have her one way or the other!" Mordrid cried as Arthur cut the head from the last standing black knight.

"Are you all right?" Galahad asked, turning to Aliana and sheathing his sword.

She nodded, grateful that the cool breeze was sweeping away the odor of decay left behind by the rotting demons. Lancelot was exactly like she remembered from her dream, shorter than his three friends but still a few inches taller than her. Unlike Galahad and Arthur, Lancelot had a lean build and compact strength. His thin lips turned up in a smile as he bowed to his king.

"Sire, words cannot say how happy I am to see you." His voice had a smooth, cultured, British accent.

"I am relieved you are here with us, my friend." Arthur placed his hands on Lancelot's shoulders, smiling.

Lancelot hugged Arthur like a lost brother before motioning his giant blond-haired friend closer. "Sire, may I present Percy Wincott, Sir Percival reborn."

Percival stepped forward, bowing to Arthur. "Though I don't have my memories of the past, I am happy to serve you in any way I can." His Southern accent was smooth, like his quiet voice and whiskey-colored eyes.

"Wait a second…" Aliana stepped away from Galahad, amazed. "You're American! How is that possible?"

Percy hit her with a mega-watt, country-boy smile and a shrug of his broad swimmer's shoulders. "Not really sure, but I am pleased to meet you." He held out his hand.

She returned the smile, shaking his offered hand. "I'm Aliana Fagan, nice to have another Southerner in the pack." She felt the strength in Percy's grip, but his hand was gentle with hers.

Arthur pulled Percy's attention from Aliana. "How is it you do not have your memories, yet you are acquainted with Lancelot, Percy?"

He straightened and let out a sigh. "That's a long story for another time, your Majesty. And it might be best if we got moving to a safer location."

Galahad's jaw clenched and he slid burning eyes onto Aliana. "Why did you leave our side when we told you to stay with us?"

"I'm sorry, but that thing was coming right at me!"

Dagg came to rest on her shoulder while Arthur and the other two men surrounded her. Gone was the easy mood from moments ago.

"We would have handled it," Arthur reprimanded her gently. "You put your life at risk. If Lancelot had not shown up when he did, you would have been taken prisoner or worse, killed."

Aliana scoffed, rolling her eyes and throwing her hands into the air. She pushed past the arrogant men.

"Did you guys not see that I actually managed to fight off that nasty thing—without a weapon—by myself?" She turned to Lancelot, hoping to get some support.

"Yet you still almost met the business end of a sword," Lancelot said, his heavy British accent making his words seem harsher. "You did, however, have some nice moves and you kept your head instead of panicking."

"Either way, Aliana," Galahad said, "next time we tell you to stay beside us, make sure you do."

"Okay, I know it wasn't my best decision, but I reacted. I know in a fight I'm the weaker person, and I was trained to get the hell out if I'm in a bad situation." She glared at all of them, daring them to tell her she'd done the wrong thing. Her decision might not have been the smartest, but it wasn't the wrong one either. One thing was for sure, she was getting tired of these guys always assuming they knew best and that she couldn't defend herself. Her fists balled, shaking with anger and waning adrenaline, as she bent down to retrieve her pack.

"What's done is done," the little Dragon said after Aliana had straightened. "Arguing will get us nowhere. We need to get out of these woods and to a safe place."

The four men exchanged a look but nodded in agreement.

II

Hot damn! When Lance told me about the Destined One, I sure as hell never expected her to be like this! As cool as she is, I'm even more stoked to meet the king and Sir Galahad. They feel so familiar, like Lancelot did when I met him. But I'm nervous. How can I possibly be what they need me to be when I don't remember anything? I'll just have to prove to them that they can rely on me.

— Percy

"How did you get here this morning?" Lancelot asked Aliana.

"I drove. My car is parked near the south entrance."

"The green Mini Cooper?" Lancelot asked.

Warily, Aliana nodded. "How did you know?"

"I've watched these forests for decades. I know when people come and go," Lancelot answered, barely bothering to favor her with a glance.

"Yeah, that's not a weird thing to say." She stopped and looked at him. "What are you, like, double-oh creepy?"

Percy chuckled as Lancelot glared.

Clearing his throat, Arthur laid a hand on Aliana's shoulder. "We need to keep going."

"All righty then, this isn't going to be awkward at all." Aliana shook her head, leading the party to the real world. Even though she knew she risked having Galahad and the others gang up on her again, she asked the question that had been nagging at the back of her mind. "I thought Mordrid was still trapped in whatever prison Merlin sent him to. How was he able to summon those black knights and—" she shivered involuntarily "—talk to us through one of them?"

The knights exchanged looks, their brows creased with worry. Arthur turned his eyes to Dagg and asked, "Is it possible that Mordrid has escaped?"

Rubbing his chin with his claw, Dagg answered, "It is impossible to say for sure. Merlin cast the spell to trap him, so only he would know for certain if Mordrid has escaped, but…"

"But what?" Aliana asked when the Dragon hesitated.

"His black knights seemed very weak. I suspect they would've been much harder to kill if he was free. And he would have surely sent more than six."

Everyone took in the Dragon's words quietly, and a silence followed. Percy was the first to speak again. "Since we have no way of knowing for sure if he's gotten free, all we can do is hope for the best and be ready for the worst. At least till we find Merlin and get the answers."

Arthur nodded with a small, approving smile on his lips. Lancelot took over the conversation, giving Arthur and Galahad tips on how to assimilate to the modern world. Aliana took the opportunity to ask Percy, "How does the whole being reborn thing work?"

"Not really sure. The only explanation Lance and I've come up with is that Titania somehow knew when we would be needed, so her prophecy made sure we would be here when that happened."

Aliana nodded, trying to piece together this new information with everything else she'd learned. Something about Lancelot didn't feel quite right to her. There was too much about his story that was unknown. Her gut warned her to be careful how much trust she put in him until she knew more. She desperately wanted to ask Dagg what else he knew about the knight, but she couldn't do it in front of the guys. Besides, the little Dragon had curled around her neck ten minutes earlier and was currently having a nap.

She almost sighed in relief when she spotted her green Mini. Smiling, she fished her keys from her bag. Looking up, she saw a large, black SUV parked a few yards from her small car.

"I'm guessing that's yours," she said over her shoulder to Lancelot.

"Yes. Sire, I have clothes for both you and Galahad to change into." He stepped to his car and pulled the tailgate open.

"Clothes?" Arthur asked, his eyes roving over Lancelot and Percival's outfits.

"Yes. I'm afraid what you're wearing now would draw too much attention."

"Right, well, while you guys do that, I need to call my cousin and let him know I'm alive." Aliana turned from the guys as they all disappeared behind the SUV. *Things are going to get very interesting,* Aliana thought as she dialed Owen's cell.

He answered after the first ring. "Where are you?" His voice was tight, his accent thicker than normal. "You all right? What the bloody hell took you so long to ring me?"

"I'm fine, Owen. I just got back to my car." How the hell was she going to explain all of this to him?

"You said you were going to ring me this afternoon."

"Sorry, I got a bit side-tracked." She glanced at the SUV that hid her new friends and smirked at the understatement.

Owen let out a sigh. "I'm just relieved you're okay. How soon until you're back home?"

Aliana meant to answer, but her eyes drifted to Galahad as he stepped into view. The handsome knight wore nothing but a pair of faded jeans.

"Oh Mama," she crooned, forgetting everything but the well-sculpted knight before her. His shoulders were wide and strong, his chest covered with a light dusting of dark hair that tapered off above a set of abs most men would kill for. She knew he was powerful, but seeing him like this, he just seemed like so much *more.*

"Aliana, can you hear me?"

She swallowed. "Um…" Was someone talking to her?

"Aliana!"

She snapped her eyes away from Galahad. "Sorry, what were you saying?" Her face warmed while butterflies tilted her stomach side to side.

"I asked how long until you will be back in London." His worry seemed to be quickly turning to annoyance.

Closing her eyes, she shook her head, trying to clear away the vision of Galahad half naked—an impossible task. "I'm getting ready to leave now, so you can stop worrying. I'm afraid I'll have to skip dinner tonight, but I'll call you soon. Bye." She hung up, not letting her cousin respond.

She knew she shouldn't, but she stole another peak at Galahad. Her phone nearly fell from her hand. Arthur stepped beside him with his back to her, saying something that had Galahad cracking a slow smile as he pulled on a dark green T-shirt. Aliana's eyes drifted to Arthur. The muscles and faint scars on his back and shoulders rippled as he pulled a crimson shirt over his head. It clung to him like a second skin, covering his golden body. Aliana's eyes drifted lower. The dark jeans he wore shaped his backside as if they had been made just for him. She had seen plenty of hot guys before, but none of them held a candle to these warriors.

"Dear God above." The phone slipped from her hand. Shocked back to reality, she fumbled, barely managing to grab the device before it hit the ground.

Galahad's eyes found hers and he smiled like the Cheshire cat. Aliana spun around, trying to cool her suddenly burning cheeks. *Damn my pale skin! I'm probably red as a tomato.*

She sucked in a breath and turned, watching the guys approach. Lancelot was the shortest, just less than six feet, while Percy stood inches taller than even Galahad. Percy wasn't what you'd call classically good looking, but there was a quirky kind of cuteness to his long face and large smile. In contrast, Lancelot's olive skin and unusually pale eyes gave him an air of mystery. That mystery was what made her slightly worried.

Clearing her dry throat, Aliana said, "Well, you two seem more the part in those clothes." She reached out, pulling away a loose string hanging from Galahad's sleeve.

Before he could say anything, Lancelot spoke. "Aliana, you will join us in my car while Percy follows in yours."

She shook her head. The cheek of this guy! "Sorry, cowboy, nobody but me drives my car."

"We don't have time for this," he said. "There is still great danger for you."

She rolled her eyes, hands on her hips. "Then why don't one or two of you join me in my car?"

The four big guys looked between her and the very tiny Mini like she had lost her mind. It wasn't really that she had a problem with people driving her car. Her problem was the way these guys kept telling her what to do, treating her like she had no mind of her own and expecting her to jump at their decree.

"I do not know about these things," Galahad said. "But I am not sure how *you* manage to get in that tiny box, much less any one of us."

The others chuckled while Aliana bit back a frustrated growl, but this Southern girl wasn't done yet. With a sweet-as-pie smile, she stepped closer to the guys, her hands hanging loosely at her side. Percy was the only one with the good sense to give any hint of being nervous.

"You know, I think you're right." She stared up into Galahad's blue eyes and pointed her finger at each of the knights. "Not a single one of your tough-guy, know-it-all egos would even come close to fitting through the door." With a huff, she tossed her keys to a stunned Percy, swinging her bag over her shoulder as she pushed past them and turned to lean against the black SUV. "Well, are you guys gonna get a move on or just stand there all day looking like the Lost Boys?"

Lancelot was the first to recover, ushering a confused Galahad and an unbelieving Arthur to the car. Aliana hid her smirk as they climbed in, and Dagg chuckled in her ear.

"And how long have you been awake?" she asked the Dragon.

"Longer then I'm sure you wish I was."

Aliana slid into the back seat next to Galahad while Arthur frowned and climbed into the front. She gazed out the tinted window, giggling as she watched Percy fold himself into her car. It really was too small for him.

She looked up, meeting Arthur's golden gaze in the side mirror. The king offered her a small smile before he turned confused eyes toward his seat belt. Aliana glanced at Galahad, who wasn't doing any better.

"Here let me." Taking the buckle from Galahad's hand, she clicked him in. Lancelot started the engine, causing the other two ancient knights to jump. Aliana hid her snigger behind her hand while Dagg jumped onto the center of the dashboard.

"So, Lancelot, how are you still alive?" Aliana asked as they started the long drive back to the city. When he didn't answer, she tried again. "You and Percy look younger than Arthur and Galahad. How is that?"

"I'll be happy to explain once we reach my home, but first there is still much that King Arthur and Galahad need to know before we get to London."

"Why don't we go to my place first?" she suggested, not liking the idea of being in a stranger's house.

"My home will be the safest place. It is well protected and hard to find, even with magic."

"I'm not saying we all shack up at my place. I'm saying, at the very least, I need to get some of my things before I go to your house for a sleepover." His arrogance pushed her buttons. "Besides, I need to talk to my cousin and my friend Wade; I have to tell them what's going on. They may be able to help."

"Absolutely not!" Lancelot shouted.

"I can't keep this from them! They'll never just let me disappear with strangers."

Galahad frowned at Lancelot, and Arthur studied the raven-haired knight with questioning eyes.

"Why do you think your friend and cousin could help?" Galahad asked.

"I'm not really sure why," she admitted. "I just do."

Lancelot studied her in the rearview mirror, and then Arthur said, "I think we can take the time to give Aliana what she wants, Lancelot. She has done much for us already. We cannot deny her these comforts."

Lancelot nodded at Arthur's decree.

I guess it's good to be the king, Aliana thought as Lancelot quickly changed the subject.

Two hours later, the group pulled up to the gate in front of Aliana's flat. The building was old-world beautiful and situated on the bank of the Thames River in an exclusive neighborhood. An impressive address didn't matter to her or her parents, but they all loved the home Aliana's grandparents had bought after World War II. Aliana gave Lancelot the gate code, and Percy followed them in.

Aliana slid out of the car, grateful for the chance to stretch her tight muscles, while Lancelot went around back and pulled out the sword belts.

"Are those really necessary? I promise there aren't any evil creatures waiting for us in my flat."

"A warrior never goes anywhere without his weapon," Arthur said.

Deciding to let that comment go, she watched Percy twist his large body out of her car, muttering curses as he finally got free. He tossed the keys to Aliana like they were evil and fixed a dark glare on Lancelot.

"Next time you get to drive the clown car across the country, and I'll drive the grown-ups' car."

"Hey now." Aliana tried to sound offended, but her giggles gave her away.

"I told you I'd get even, Percy," Lancelot said, shrugging.

Still giggling, Aliana led them to the elevator, curious to see how Arthur and Galahad would handle their first elevator ride. The five of them piled into the tiny lift, taking up most of the space as Aliana turned her house key in the lock and hit the button for the top floor.

"Why the key, Aliana?" Arthur asked, fascinated by the machine pulling them smoothly up into the building.

"My mom's parents bought the top floor of the building decades ago and converted the entire space into a four-bedroom apartment. No one can get up to the top level unless they have a key."

"Then your parents were nobility?" Galahad questioned.

"Were?" Arthur asked before she could answer.

Aliana's eyes dropped. "My parents died two years ago." She refused to look up, not wanting to see the pity she was sure would be in their expressions, or worse, encourage any more questions. "To answer you, Galahad, no, my parents weren't nobility. My mother's family came from old money here in London. My father was one of the leading historians and archaeologists in the world, and my mom was a popular actress and dancer. She insisted we keep this place after my grandparents died, even though we lived mostly in Charleston."

The elevator dinged, and the door slid open before anyone could ask more questions. She escaped the suddenly suffocating confines only to nearly run into a tall man with buzzed brown hair and tense green eyes. He stood with his hands tucked into his jean pockets.

"Owen!" Aliana's heart leaped happily as her cousin pulled her into a rough hug. "What are you doing here?" For the first time since waking up from her dream that morning, she relaxed, sinking into his familiar and comforting embrace.

"I was going mental worrying about you." His soft voice sounded almost hurt. "Who are they?" He scrutinized the four men filing out of the elevator, and his eyes hardened when he saw the swords in their hands. He stepped around Aliana. "Why do they have swords?"

She laid her hand on his shoulder, trying to figure out what to say.

"Owaine?" Arthur stepped forward, but Lancelot's hand stopped the king.

Owen scowled. "Sorry, mate, you have the wrong guy." He stopped Aliana as she tried to get around him.

"Perhaps we should all go inside and discuss this." Lancelot stepped forward, but Owen met him half way.

"I don't think so, mate." Owen's eyes landed on the silver Dragon perched on Lancelot's shoulder. Startled, he grabbed Aliana's arm, ordering her to get into the flat.

"Owen, it's okay." She took her cousin's hand in hers. "Dagg isn't going to hurt anyone, and I invited all of them here." Aliana watched the way Galahad and Arthur looked Owen over, not with untrusting glares but with veiled curiosity. The two exchanged a quick glance.

Aliana looked at Owen again. Hadn't Arthur said one of his knights was named Owaine? Aliana gripped her cousin's hand tighter. "I'll explain everything inside." And she was going to make sure Arthur explained why he'd called Owen *Owaine*.

Eyes still fixed on Dagg, Owen nodded, circling an arm around his cousin's shoulders. Once inside, Aliana disappeared into the kitchen while the guys took in her home. She hoped they would be too distracted to notice her disappearance because she was desperate to get some space and gather her thoughts. She'd hoped to have a day or two to get her story together before she brought her cousin into this. *Oh no! What's Wade going to do? There's no way Owen won't tell him!* Suddenly, it all became too much. Panic had her heart racing. She was about to start hyperventilating.

"Aliana." Dagg landed on the black marble counter. She peered into his glowing purple eyes, and a wave of warm energy flowed through her body, calming her.

"How did you do that?"

"I have many talents." The little Dragon smirked. "The others are waiting on you. If we don't get in there soon, I fear your cousin is going to do something drastic."

"Owen is so protective."

"He's also considering throwing Lancelot out of the window."

Aliana shored up her courage and walked back into her favorite room in the entire flat. The family room had overstuffed black chairs and couches, a killer entertainment center, and creamy white walls. She and her parents had made a tradition of curling up together on the couch and watching movies or TV each night. Off to one side was her father's desk and bookshelf, still filled with his research books and prized artifacts. But what made this room so special to her were the dozen pictures decorating the walls. Her parents had insisted that all of the art be hers—pictures she had taken of her mother dancing, places she had traveled to with her father, and many others.

Owen stood facing her new friends, staring them all down, his arms crossed over his thick chest.

"I guess introductions are in order." She stepped next to Owen, looping her arm through his. "Owen, this may seem hard to believe, but this guy—" Aliana pointed to Arthur "—is King Arthur. Next to him are Sir Galahad, Percy—who happens to be Sir Percival reincarnated—and, finally, Lancelot. Guys, this is my cousin, Owen Nyhart."

The four men nodded, murmuring a polite greeting.

"And what about that?" Owen pointed to the Dragon on the coffee table.

"*He* is Daggerhorne…my Dragon guardian."

Owen's eyes narrowed as he looked between her and the silver creature. Blowing out a breath, he plopped down onto the loveseat, pulling Aliana with him. "Okay, pleasantries have been exchanged. Now will you please tell me what the bloody hell is going on? Are these guys the reason you were so late getting back?"

"You do not speak to Aliana like that," Galahad threatened, glaring at Owen.

"Who are you to tell me how to talk to my cousin?" Owen demanded, jumping up, ready to go at it with Galahad. All the guys were tense and watchful.

"Whoa. Down, boys. There's no need to fight." Aliana stepped between Owen and Galahad, placing a hand on each of their chests. Neither man stepped back. "Both of you sit down…*now!*"

With a final sneer, they finally backed up a step. Aliana sighed, relieved, but wondering why they had to be such asses.

Arthur placed a hand on Galahad's shoulder, pulling the blue-eyed knight back. "Please forgive us, Aliana. Why don't we all sit down and talk like civilized people."

Lancelot, Percy, and Galahad all sat on the large couch while Arthur got comfortable in the lounge chair. Aliana took a seat next to her hothead cousin on the love seat, tucking her legs underneath her.

"Owen, I should start this by telling you that this is going to be hard to believe, but everything we're going to tell you is the truth," Dagg said from the coffee table.

"Brilliant! It talks too!" Owen snapped.

Aliana glowered at her cousin, feeling very protective of her Dragon. "Yes, *he* talks. Now shut it and listen."

Owen appeared understandably skeptical, but he didn't say anything.

"My name is Daggerhorne, and I am guardian to the Destined One, Aliana. It has been prophesied that she will help King Arthur and his reunited knights stop Mordrid and Morgana from destroying all of the realms."

Owen's eyes grew large and unbelieving as he raked his gaze over everyone in the room. "Aliana, are you sure this is real?"

"I know it's hard to believe," she said slowly. "I'm still struggling to believe it too, but Owen, *I was in Avalon today!*"

I2

When Aliana stepped out of the lift she seemed different — more alive. But then I saw the guys with her and my world went barmy. I know them somehow. My gut tells me they're important to me. But their swords and their crazy stories make me question my gut for the first time in a while. Seriously, a talking Dragon? What trouble has my cousin gotten into now?

Owen

Owen gulped and nodded for Dagg to continue, but Lancelot took over for the Dragon. "You, Owen, are a reincarnation of Sir Owaine, a Knight of Camelot and a member of the Round Table."

Aliana bit back her gasp of surprise as she felt her eyes grow to the size of saucers. *OMG, Owen's a knight!*

Lancelot continued, "Percy and I are like you, reincarnations of our former selves. Only I have my memories intact, while the two of you do not."

"And why is that, Lancelot?" Aliana piped up, hoping to finally get one of her questions answered.

"We will get to that," he said, dismissing her again.

Owen looked across the table to Galahad. "So, are you a supposed reincarnation too?"

"No, I am as I was during the time of Camelot, as is King Arthur."

Owen glanced to Aliana, confusion drawing his mouth tight as he arched a questioning eyebrow.

Lancelot picked up the story. "Arthur and Galahad have been in Avalon since their last battle with Mordrid over fifteen hundred years ago. Merlin, Galahad, and myself brought Arthur to Avalon as he was dying. We made a pact with Titania, queen of the Fae, to save his life, but the price was that we had to remain in Avalon with the king until the Destined One came to free Arthur and bring us back to the mortal realm."

"Except you and Merlin weren't there, Lancelot," Aliana cut in.

Lancelot nodded his head. "We will get to that, but first, please explain to us how you got to Avalon and what happened before you returned."

Sighing, Aliana told them about her adventures in Avalon. She left out the part about the kiss stolen by Galahad. What had happened between her and the knight wasn't something she wanted the others to know. Not until she figured out how to get her feelings for him under control. She did tell them about Titania's offer to turn back time and give her back her old life and her parents.

Every pair of eyes had widened in surprise at that information.

"Thank you." Arthur's words caught her off guard. "You had the chance to live your life and you chose to help us instead. It was an incredibly courageous thing to do."

When Aliana didn't say anything, Galahad took over for her. "When we got back, Lady Deidre had a message for us from J'alel. He'd searched but found no trace of the cursed TreTale, so we do not know who sent it or who it was meant to track." Galahad ran a hand through his brown locks.

"I told you guys you were overreacting," Aliana said, then looked to Lancelot. "Now, how did you and Percy find us while we were being attacked by the black knights?"

Owen's whole body stiffened. "What do you mean you were attacked by black knights?"

"Just that," Arthur told Owen, briefly explaining the demon knights.

Aliana squeezed Owen's arm, visions of the horrible monsters flashing in her mind. The memory of their putrid scent still made her want to gag.

"Because of the prophecy, I could feel when you arrived at the forest of Avalon." Lancelot drew her mind from the darkness. "I have had dreams over the years about the Destined One, but last night was the first time I saw your face, and I could once again see the entrance to Avalon. I knew you were coming. When you woke Arthur, I felt the magic pulsing in my body, as did Percy."

"I felt it as well," Galahad added. "As soon as you freed the king, the barrier fell, allowing Lord Daggerhorne and myself into the cave."

"But how did you find us in the woods?" Aliana asked Lancelot again.

"When I left Avalon, several things changed. I was able to sense magic, or rather, hone in and track it. Over the centuries I have trained myself to recognize different…patterns, if you will. Each one is as unique to the caster as a personality. The dark magic led us to you just in time."

"Why did you never return?" Galahad's deep voice was quiet, his shoulders tense and his gaze fixed on his dark-haired friend.

"I could not find my way back." Lancelot looked past everyone to the photos on the wall. "Titania's punishment for breaking my vow was that I would always remember, but never find the entrance again. And she must've insured I'd be unable to track Merlin's magic, because I've yet to be able to sense his power."

"Was it also Titania who gave you the ability to track magic?" Arthur asked, his eagle-sharp eyes studying Lancelot.

Lancelot cleared his throat. "Not exactly. I believe my ability to sense the magic is because of the pact and the time I spent in Avalon." He looked at both Aliana and Owen. "Magic always has an effect on people. Spend enough time surrounded by it and the magic starts to seep into you."

"But how are you still alive?" Aliana asked softly. "Titania didn't strike me as the kind to let someone break a vow and just punish them with banishment."

"You are very perceptive, Aliana. The Fae queen is ruthless in her punishments." His eyes clouded. "I have lived since the day I returned to the mortal world, but I am not immortal." Lancelot's pale eyes, shadowed with angst, finally met his king's. "I can die, but within a few years I am reborn. In every life, when I start to mature, the memories of every previous life I've lived return to me. Every detail from every life is fresh in my mind. I can't forget *anything*. Every scent, every sight and sound as clear to me as the moment it happened." Aliana wondered if Lancelot realized he was clutching his hands together.

With the truth falling from Lancelot's lips, Aliana saw that there was much more to him than the I-know-what's-best façade he let the world see. If this was Lancelot's punishment, what had Titania done to Merlin?

"So, what will happen to you now that Arthur is back in the mortal world — if you're killed?" Owen broke the sad silence.

"I don't know, but I hope I don't find out any time soon."

"How did you meet Percy?" Aliana asked, pulling his focus back.

"I was visiting London, a little over a year ago," Percy said. "I was here with some teammates for a competition when I ran into Lancelot at a pub."

"I recognized him instantly and introduced myself," Lancelot said, "but I realized he had no memory of me. We talked and he told me that he was about to graduate high school, so I asked him to call me after graduation if he was interested in a job opportunity in London. He called, and I hired him as an assistant at my consulting business. Once we got to know each other better, I told him about who I was, who he was, and our history."

"I didn't believe him at first, but I gave him a chance because it just felt right." Percy smiled at Aliana, his brown eyes sparking. "He showed me all of the artifacts he had from that time, and that night, I swear I had some kind of wonky dream that made me a believer."

Aliana leaned forward, her interest piqued. "What was it?"

"Heck if I remember. I forgot it as soon as I opened my eyes!" Percy shook his head then asked, "How did you find Owen?"

Owen squeezed her hand and gave her an encouraging smile. Aliana took a deep breath, trying to calm her nerves, tightening her grip on his hand.

"I already told you my parents died two years ago. After their deaths, I was going through their files and found two copies of my birth certificate. One with my parents' names and another with the name of a woman I didn't know." Aliana felt the pain rushing to the surface. "I looked through more of the files, and I found an adoption record from a lawyer here in London. It wasn't hard to put two and two together, and I realized I was adopted." Aliana looked past everyone out the window, studying the lights of London.

"Your parents never told you?" Percy asked softly.

Shaking her head, Aliana put on her calm face, trying desperately to hide the sadness and betrayal she felt. "No, I confronted one of my father's closest friends, my godfather, and he told me it was true. I made it my mission to track down the woman on my original birth certificate, but all I found was an address here. So, I got on a plane and went to the address, but it was a cemetery. She had died after giving birth to me." Aliana bit her lip, forcing tears back. Not only had she lost the people who'd raised her, but her birth mother was also dead, all because of her.

"I found Aliana there that day," Owen said. "The woman she had found was my aunt. I had gone to bring flowers to my mother and aunt's graves and ended up bringing Aliana back to my place. We spent the night talking, getting to know each other. Luckily for Aliana, she now has a smashing cousin to look after her."

"Whatever." Aliana couldn't help her watery giggle as Owen hugged her closer. "It's more the other way around. I swear Owen can't do a thing on his own. I don't know how he managed to live to nineteen." Owen retaliated, pinching her in the arm. "Dagg, you're the only one left to explain your side of things."

"My story is far simpler than all of yours, I assure you," the Dragon said. "I was born from the pact. My only purpose is to be your guardian. For centuries I passed through all the realms, forever searching for you and learning everything I could so I could better protect you."

It was quiet for a moment, and Aliana peered up at her cousin. "You're taking all of this pretty well, Owen."

He gave them all a thoughtful once over and glanced at Percy. "How did you feel when Lancelot told you all this?"

Percy grinned boyishly. "I felt like I had found something that had been missing."

Owen nodded. "I've always felt like something was missing from my life too, like big pieces of a puzzle, and now I'm finally finding some of those missing pieces." Owen kissed her head. "It's all because of you, dear cousin."

"I think we have all said enough for tonight." Arthur spoke as Aliana tried to hide her yawn.

"It's nearly midnight. Aliana, do you have enough space for all of us to stay here?" Lancelot asked, as he rose from the couch.

"I thought you wanted us at your place," she said.

Lancelot frowned. "Your home already has its own magical protection, and it's damn strong. If I'm not mistaken, anyone who isn't invited in by you, wouldn't be able to get in here. I haven't felt anything this powerful in decades."

"What?" Aliana frowned, looking around. Everything felt and appeared the same as it always had. "How could that be? I would have known if my parents had magic." She wavered. Would she have known? They had kept her adoption from her; what else had they hidden? The thought struck at her aching heart.

"I don't know how," Lancelot said, "but it's more than strong enough to protect all of us. We won't be in any danger here."

Confused and unsure, Aliana gave the guest room with two beds to Lancelot and Percy, and the second guest room to Galahad. "Owen, I'm afraid you're going to have to sleep on the couch tonight. Arthur, you can have my parents' old room next to mine." It was hard to think of anyone but her parents sleeping there, but if anyone should have their room, it was King Arthur.

Lancelot said, "I have more clothes in the car. I'll go get them while everyone gets settled in." Aliana tossed him the apartment key as he put on his shoes.

After seeing the guys settled in, she leaned against her bedroom door, grateful for the privacy. There was so much that her brain was trying to process. She wasn't sure how she'd managed to keep herself together for this long, and now everything was starting to crash down around her.

"You have a colorful room, Aliana."

Aliana nearly shrieked at Dagg's lazily offered comment. The little Dragon was curled up on an overstuffed, pale green pillow. Her entire room was decorated in light summer colors, the walls painted a pale yellow and covered with prints of her favorite paintings and photographs. A blue and pink comforter lay over her bed, and half a dozen colored throw pillows were strewn across the floor where she had thrown them a few nights ago.

"I have a very bright personality, as you should know. What are you doing in my room, anyway?"

"I'm your guardian. I am to always be at your side to protect you."

"But Lancelot said we were safe here." Aliana desperately wanted to be alone so she could have her impending breakdown without an audience.

"Are you saying you don't enjoy my company?" he teased.

Aliana sighed. She didn't have the energy to fuss with him *and* stay in control of her emotions. "I love your company, but there are ground rules. You vanish while I'm changing clothes, and absolutely no snoring. You snore, you're gone."

"If you insist," he said, smirking.

Nodding, Aliana locked herself in the bathroom. She turned on the shower, wrenching up the temperature to as hot as she could handle. Standing under the falling water, she felt tears spill from her eyes as she choked back a sob. Titania's offer played over and over again in her head. She didn't regret her decision, but seeing her parents again had brought back all the pain and loneliness she'd worked so hard to push away.

"Stop it, Li!" she scolded herself. "They would be proud of you. You're stronger than this." She started to think about Galahad and kissing Arthur. She had saved three lives today, four if she counted Belle. So many of her dreams had come true despite the pain.

She straightened her shoulders, shut off the water, and wrapped herself up in a soft towel, her long hair plastered to her skin. She hated weepy girls who let self-pity rule their lives.

Leaning forward, she wiped the steam from her mirror. She didn't consider herself beautiful. Pretty, yes, but in a normal kind of way. Blotting her hair, she remembered the feel of Galahad's fingers tunneling through her hair as he kissed her. She'd already started to develop strong feelings for him, but what would he possibly see in her? She had a small nose, thin upper lip, and a slightly plump lower lip, "half lips" as she always called them. Her bright green eyes were the only thing she really liked, but she didn't see anything special about herself that could hold the attention of a guy like Galahad.

Shaking her head, she grabbed her brush and walked out of the bathroom, completely forgetting the silver Dragon curled up on her bed.

"That towel doesn't look like it would be comfortable to sleep in."

She shrieked, pulling the towel tighter around her body while Dagg roared with laughter.

"If you were any kind of gentleman you would turn around!"

Still laughing, he stretched a wing to cover his face. "Better?"

Aliana glared at the Dragon, grabbed her pajamas, and stormed back into the bathroom. She changed quickly, brushing through her long, unruly hair and braiding the damp mass. Stepping back into her room, she was slightly annoyed to see Dagg still curled on her pillow with his eyes closed. "And what makes you think you get to sleep on my bed?"

"I'm your guardian. Besides, your pillow is comfortable," he mumbled, half asleep.

Far too exhausted to argue with him, Aliana crawled into bed, praying she'd get more than a few hours of sleep.

Three hours later, she jerked awake, gasping for air. She still felt the fire from her dream blasting her with tiny pieces of exploded metal and wood. Shaking, she glanced over at Dagg, afraid she had woken the very perceptive Dragon. She sighed as she realized he was still asleep.

The nightmare that haunted her was not something she'd ever shared with anyone, not even the people she was closest to. She looked around the room, trying to distract herself, and her eyes landed on a purple dress and mask hanging next to her vanity. She repressed a groan, just now remembering the art gallery auction she was supposed to go to the next night...well, technically tonight. She wanted to cancel. The event was for her mother's charity. She had avoided it for the last two years, but this year, Wade and Lacy had steamrolled her into promising to attend. Both of her friends were active in the charity, even more so after Aliana's parents had died, and she knew they'd never let her out of her promise.

What would she do with all of the guys? She couldn't see them letting her go off by herself. She'd have to take them with her, and maybe that wasn't such a bad thing. It would be a great way to show Arthur and Galahad more about the modern world, the beauty of modern art, and maybe some of her work that was up for auction.

She still sometimes found it hard to believe that she was an accomplished artist at the age of only eighteen. But she'd been surrounded by art while growing up. Her parents had homeschooled her so they could travel for their work, and she often had to keep herself busy, so she'd taken up photography. It was Wade who had first entered her photos into contests, and after winning a few of them, everything just seemed to click.

Sliding out of bed, Aliana tiptoed out the door, past her cousin sleeping on the couch, and into the kitchen. She wasn't going to get any more sleep tonight, so she decided to make breakfast for everyone. Making sure the volume was turned down on her portable speakers, Aliana set her iPod to shuffle and hoped the music would help her drown out the sounds from her nightmare.

And it worked, except her thoughts jumped from her personal torture to trying to wrap her head around everything that'd just happened. *Can Owen really be a knight? It suits him, but...* Her thoughts drifted as she put a tray of biscuits into the oven and hummed along with a Taylor Swift song. It was strange doing something so normal while four ancient knights were sleeping close by—five if she counted Owen. *Can it be coincidence that my long-lost cousin is involved in this quest I've gotten myself into?* She poured a bowl of whipped eggs into a pan. Turning off the heat on the bacon, she picked up the heavy, sizzling pan. As she turned, she saw Galahad in the doorway watching her, his sword at his side.

With a shocked squeak, the pan slipped from her grip, and there was no way she could avoid getting burned. But before the pan fell, Galahad was next to her, his hand closing around hers on the handle of the heavy pan. His sword clanked against the ground where he had been standing only a second ago.

Taking the pan from her hands, he set it down gently on the counter. His bare arms brushed against her and sparks shot through her body like they always did when she touched his skin. Aliana knew her eyes must be huge, and she felt the burn of embarrassment in her cheeks. She was also very aware of how close they were and thought she saw the same kind of awareness in his eyes. But with her boyfriend track record, she wasn't sure she could trust what her eyes saw.

"Galahad...how did you?" She looked over at the sword lying on the ground and back to him. Opening her mouth to speak, she caught the scent of something burning. "Oh no, my eggs!" Pulling away from him, she grabbed the pan from the stovetop and sighed before scraping the burned mass into the garbage.

Peeking out of the corner of her eye she saw Galahad watching her again, his eyes sweeping over the skin left exposed by the thin straps of her black tank top. Aliana fought the urge to straighten her hair and pull down her shirt to cover the slice of pale skin that showed above her long, purple pajama pants.

But she lost the fight. "Sorry, I wasn't expecting anyone to be awake," she said, and his blue eyes rose to her green ones, a half dazed smile on his mouth. "I bet you're not used to this kind of night clothes, huh?" She cleared her throat and ran a hand over her braid.

"No, I am not." His eyes flickered down her body before jerking back up. "But I could get used to them." Aliana grinned. Then he scowled and asked, "You will put on more clothes before the others join us, yes?"

Her eyes narrowed, and she met his question with one of her own. "How long have you been up, and how the heck did you move so damn fast when you grabbed the pan?" Just another odd thing she could add to the huge pile of confusing that had been dumped on her.

"I do not know how I moved so swiftly. But I need to apologize—for something else."

Her brow furrowed. "What?"

"I believe I broke that strange knob on the door to my room."

"What do you mean *broke?*"

Galahad shrugged and went to retrieve his sword. "It ripped off the door when I twisted it," he said, leaning the blade against the island.

"Oh. It must've been loose. I can try to reattach it later."

Galahad leaned on the counter next to her. "I do not think that is possible."

"You've got to be kidding me. After everything we've been through, you don't think I can handle fixing a doorknob?" she asked with an arched brow.

Galahad held up his hands in surrender. "No. That is not what I mean. The knob, as you call it, was...crushed."

"Come again," she said, incredulous. There must be more power in those hands than she'd thought. "I guess that's a problem, isn't it?" Aliana shook her head. "You never answered my original question. Why are you up so early?"

"I heard noise and thought someone had broken in."

"Oh, I'm sorry, I didn't mean to wake you. You can go back to bed. I'll be quieter."

Galahad shook his head, walking over to pick up his sword. "I have done nothing but rest for a very long time. I would rather stay and help you if you need my assistance."

13

I have never felt like this. Everything about this girl fascinates me.
Watching her now, singing and cooking, she's so soft, not the brave
girl who had risked herself to save people she thought only part
of a story. When she got caught up in the Sidhe's magic and tried
to get me to go with her, I panicked. Me, Sir Galahad, notorious
for my calm disposition and ability to remain clearheaded in battles,
had fallen under her spell and reacted without thinking. I don't
regret kissing her; I just wish our first hadn't been to save her life.
Yet I am conflicted — why does my connection to Aliana want
to overshadow my oath and loyalty to my king? I have always
been able to set aside my desire for a woman of my own...before.
— Galahad

"I was just making breakfast," Aliana said, pulling out more eggs. "I'm not sure when everyone will be up, but I know y'all will want breakfast."

"Why are you awake so early, Aliana? We went to sleep but a few hours ago and the sun has not yet started to rise."

She shrugged. "I guess I'm just still trying to process everything." Not a total lie.

"Then what can I do to help?" he asked again.

"Um…" Looking around, she spotted the potatoes that still needed to be cut. "I'm guessing you're pretty handy with a blade, so you can cut the veg for the home fries."

She grabbed a knife and showed him how she wanted the potatoes and peppers cut. She grabbed more eggs, and they worked shoulder to shoulder.

"What are all these foods?" Galahad motioned to the platters and bowls around them.

"I'm making us a nice, Southern breakfast: bacon, eggs, home fries, biscuits, pancakes, and grits."

"Is this something you would make with your parents back at home?"

Aliana's lips pulled into a frown. "Sometimes, on long weekends or a special occasion, but normally I just have a bowl of Cinnamon Toast Crunch. It's a really good cereal, though we can't get it here," she explained when he wrinkled his forehead. "If we get back to my home in the States, I'll let you try some."

"Do you not miss being at home? You said last night that you have been here for a while."

"I haven't really been home much the last couple of years. There's always another place I want to go." She shrugged, hoping he wouldn't pick up on the slight tremor in her voice.

"So, you haven't been home since your parents died," he stated, almost to himself.

"I traveled a lot before..." She was trying to change the subject.

"So you've been traveling alone?" he asked carefully enough that Aliana wondered if he was thinking of their conversation in Avalon.

Her frown faded. "My friend Wade joins me when he can, but mostly I travel for my art, so it's better that I'm on my own."

"You mentioned him earlier. Who is Wade?" Galahad set his knife down and turned toward Aliana with that same intensity he'd had earlier.

"Wade's one of my oldest friends, the closest thing I've ever had to a brother."

Galahad took a small breath, dropping his eyes and resuming his cutting. They finished making breakfast, and then Galahad answered her questions about Camelot, telling her about its past and the kinds of people who lived there. The rising sun brightened the kitchen as Aliana stood over the stove, showing Galahad how to make pancakes. She laughed when he burned his first batch of the fluffy treat and again when he scowled after tasting cheesy grits.

"I understand you like that, Aliana," he said after rinsing his mouth with water, "but I don't think I can eat those again."

"There's plenty of other good food to eat," she assured him, still giggling as she covered the food to keep it warm and started brewing a fresh pot of coffee.

Owen stumbled in, pulling on his Radiohead T-shirt from the night before. He rubbed the sleep from his eyes, grabbing a coffee mug from the cabinet.

"Good morning." Aliana smiled at his sleepy glare. Before Galahad could say anything, she said, "Owen's not a morning person. Best not to talk to him till he's had his first cup of coffee."

"Ali, you need to stop being so bloody cheerful in the mornings!" Owen mumbled, pouring his coffee and taking a sip.

"Don't call me Ali," she said, throwing a piece of strawberry at her smart-ass cousin and nailing him right between the eyes.

Unfazed, he took a bite of a cheddar biscuit. "You Yanks sure do one thing right across the pond. What were you two doing up so early anyway?"

"Couldn't sleep," Aliana and Galahad said together. Owen eyed them, shrugging, and filled his plate before taking a seat. Galahad followed suit, filling his own plate and joining Owen at the table.

Smiling, Aliana went back to drying the last of the dishes.

"Leave that for later," Owen said. "Get your plate and join us. You need to eat if you're going to keep operating on only a few hours of sleep a night. Gotta keep your energy up somehow."

"Geez, Owen, you're as bad as Wade and my friend Dawn. I'm fine, and don't call me Ali or I'll cut off your biscuit and coffee supply."

Galahad looked between them, studying her for a long moment. She glanced down, hoping he wouldn't notice the shadows under her eyes. Setting the last dish aside, she filled a plate for herself and leaned against the countertop as she ate.

A few moments later, Percy, Lancelot, and Arthur walked into the kitchen, smiling broadly. "What smells so good?" Arthur asked.

"Are those grits and home fries I see?" Percy asked. He filled a large plate and bit into a biscuit.

"I thought we could all use a good breakfast." She smiled as Percy finished the biscuit in two bites.

"Thank you," Lancelot said, sitting down next to Arthur, digging into his eggs.

"We should be leaving soon," Lancelot said. "We need to get to my home and make our plans for finding Merlin, Gawain, and Leyon." Lancelot dabbed the corner of his mouth with his napkin.

Aliana hid her smile, imagining him in the eighteenth century—the picture of perfect properness. Her phone chirped from the next room, and Dagg flew into the kitchen, carrying it. "Shut the damn thing off, Aliana! It won't stop making that incessant sound." He dropped it into her open hand.

Shaking her head, she scrolled through all the frantic texts her friend Lacy had sent just this morning. Excusing herself, she dialed her stressed-out friend.

"Lia, thank gawd it's you! I've been worried sick! You were supposed to call me yesterday morning and let me know you got the dress!" Lacy babbled. "Tell me it got to you in one piece. Not that I don't trust my brother, but you know Wade. Please tell me you're still coming!"

"Calm down, Lace. I got the dress and it's beautiful. You really out-did yourself! And, yes, I'm coming. I made you and Wade a promise, so I'll be there." She glanced back at the kitchen and caught Arthur's eye as he grabbed the last of the pancakes.

Lacy sighed heavily over the phone. "Good, now I only have, like, a bazillion more problems to handle before the party tonight."

"Lace, the gallery party is going to go great! You're brilliant at these things. Tonight's going to be epic. I know it."

"Thanks, Lia, I'm just really glad you're going to be there. I haven't seen you in almost a week."

"I know, Lace. Speaking of the party, I'm going to need to add a few guests to my reservation."

Aliana heard her friend's surprised gasp. "Really? Who and how many?"

"Four more plus Owen. It's a long story but I can fill you in later."

"Are these four all men?" Lacy asked slyly. "Are they hot?"

Aliana bit back her giggle, looking back toward the kitchen. She couldn't resist teasing her friend. "I guess," she said nonchalantly.

"Not fair! Okay, I've added them to the list. I expect y'all here at seven p.m. sharp. Any later and I'm calling in the National Guard."

"I think that only works in the States, Lace." Aliana rolled her eyes.

"You above all people should know how persuasive I can be, Lia," Lacy chided, laughing.

"Oh, I remember! The only times I ever got into trouble was whenever you had one of your 'brilliant' ideas."

"Exactly! Okay then, I gotta go. The florist is here. I'll see you at seven sharp." Lacy hung up before Aliana could say goodbye.

Walking back into the kitchen, she found Dagg perched next to her plate, happily eating the last of her breakfast. "Hey, you moocher, get your own food!" Everyone laughed as she swatted the Dragon away. All he left her with was a half-eaten pancake.

"Now that we are all fed, we should be going," Lancelot said, rinsing off his plate and surprising Aliana that he'd be so domestic.

"That's cool," Aliana said, "but there's some place I need to be tonight. Well, actually, we all need to be."

"Oh, right, your mum's fundraising party," Owen said.

"Aliana, it's too dangerous," Lancelot said immediately.

"Relax, Lancelot. The party is at a crowded hotel in the middle of London. No chance of attack there. Besides, this is for my mother, so I have to be there."

"What charity?" Percy cut Lancelot off before he could argue more.

"My mother started a charity over ten years ago to award scholarships for students in need to study all forms of art."

Arthur and Galahad frowned, confused. "I'll explain it later," Percy told them.

"Besides, I already promised my friends I would be there. I won't back out on my promise." She fisted her hands on her hips, squaring off with Lancelot.

The stubborn knight looked over her shoulder to Arthur. Aliana peeked at the king, seeing Arthur nod his head.

Halfheartedly, Lancelot said, "Okay, but we have to be very careful, and you will have one of us with you at all times."

Aliana smiled. "Great, thanks. Owen already has a tux, but we'll need to get some for the four of you, plus masks. It was Lacy's idea to make it a masquerade theme, and she'll flip if it doesn't go right."

"I will handle that," Lancelot said. "Percy and I have tuxes and we can have two more sent over for you and Galahad, Sire." Lancelot and Owen agreed to go get the suits while the others stayed with Aliana.

She glanced at her watch and saw that it was almost eleven a.m. "I need to finish cleaning up, and then I need to start getting ready for the party. Is there anything the three of you want to do in the meantime?"

"We can clean up for you," Galahad offered. "Maybe you could get more sleep before tonight."

"No need, I got plenty of sleep," she lied, hoping Galahad wouldn't push the subject. She didn't need any more fiery dreams today.

He scowled at her, seeming like he wanted to say more, but nodded. Arthur watched their exchange, veiled interest in his golden gaze.

"Maybe Percy can explain some more things to y'all."

"Sure," Percy said quickly. All through breakfast, he'd been glancing between the two legends, clearly anxious to get to know them better. "Lance mentioned several things he wanted to fill you both in on." He seemed to make an effort to sound blasé, but he still looked like a kid about to open presents.

Almost reluctantly, Galahad and Arthur left the kitchen behind Percy. Galahad glanced back to Aliana, and she couldn't stop the flush that spread across her cheeks.

"You shouldn't lie, Aliana," Dagg said when the boys were out of hearing range. "You didn't sleep for more than three hours last night, and you spent most of that tossing and turning."

"You were asleep when I got up, so how would you know?"

"We are connected through the magic of the prophecy. I can feel what you feel when I want to, and you will soon be able to do the same with me when we train you how to use your magic."

Aliana abruptly set down the pot in her hand. "What? I can't…" she started but stopped, remembering everything in Avalon and the power she'd used to awaken Arthur. "I can still use magic?"

"Yes. When we find Merlin, he and I will train you so you can defend yourself with it."

Aliana just stared at him, completely lost for words.

"What's wrong?"

Lying to Dagg clearly wasn't going to do her any good. "I'm still trying to get used to everything, and I'm a little nervous about tonight."

"What about tonight worries you?"

"It's not really worry," Aliana said as she scrubbed the last dish dry. "I…haven't been to one of these parties since my parents died. Tonight will be the first time they're not there with me."

"I understand. Dragons are very loyal to their clans. When one of us is gone, we all feel the loss."

"It must have been horrible to be trapped in that cage for so long." She scratched the little Dragon behind his ears.

"What was harder was not being able to search for you. It has been my only purpose since my creation. If I had been free, perhaps I could have found you sooner."

Aliana couldn't let herself think about what might have been different if he had. "We should go find the guys," she said, putting away the last dish.

"I can hear them in Galahad's room. They are saying something about…a broken door handle," Dagg said, confused.

Aliana left the kitchen with the Dragon on her shoulder and headed toward the guys.

"I don't know how it happened. It came off right in my hand," Galahad said.

"Could it be because of the magic you were trapped in?" Aliana asked, surprising the trio.

Galahad looked up, embarrassed, holding the crushed handle in his hand. Why did she find that so…cute?

"Don't worry, Galahad. I'm not mad about the broken door knob," she assured him. "I'm just trying to figure out this new strength and that burst of speed earlier in the kitchen."

"What?" Arthur asked.

Galahad quickly filled them in.

"Perhaps Aliana is right," Arthur said, stroking his chin. "Lancelot said he had new abilities when he left Avalon — that the magic there had affected him. Being trapped in a magic crystal has to have changed you, Galahad."

"Why don't you guys go up to the roof and test your theory," Aliana suggested. "It's private, and Wade and I have a practice area set up that you can use."

Following her to the roof, the three men looked around at the amazing view of the modern city while Aliana unrolled her sparring mat and pulled out some clean towels from a small storage closet. They decided to let Percy be the first to test Galahad's new talents.

The two men circled each other, and then Galahad just *moved*. Suddenly, he was behind Percy with the big man trapped in a headlock and falling to his knees. Percy tried to break the hold, but nothing he tried worked. Reluctantly, he tapped Galahad's arm to be released.

"Hot damn, that was amazing!" Percy said, taking a few deep breaths and pulling himself up with Galahad's offered hand. "Your grip was like iron! I could barely move."

"How about you, Arthur?" Aliana suggested. "Let's see if the magic that trapped you had the same effect."

Several minutes later, it was clear that Arthur hadn't developed the same abilities, but he did seem to have a way of predicting Galahad's moves. Maybe that was because the two had fought together for so long. Then Arthur went against Percy, proving that just because he couldn't beat Galahad didn't mean he couldn't fight. He managed to defeat Percy three times with an impressive and aggressive style. The guys continued changing partners, testing each other and testing the limits of Galahad's and Arthur's abilities.

"Damn," Aliana muttered, looking down at her watch.

"What's wrong?" Galahad asked as he and the others came to her side.

"I need to start getting ready for tonight."

Percy laid a hand on Arthur's shoulder and gave him his first lesson about modern girls. "Women need excessive amounts of time to get ready for these things. It takes them hours to get it together."

Rolling her eyes, Aliana turned to Dagg. "You stay here with the guys."

The Dragon shook his head. "You are my charge. I'm supposed to stay by your side."

"Maybe when we're in a dangerous situation, but not while we're home. Besides, you remember my rules. You disappear when I'm getting changed."

Grudgingly, Dagg agreed, but he still had the last word. "You can't keep shutting people out," he said softly so the others couldn't hear. "Burdens are meant to be shared, not bottled up inside."

"I'm just getting ready for a party, Dagg." She wasn't shutting people out; she just didn't want an audience. And besides, what was wrong with not wanting to drag others into her problems?

Locking her bedroom door, Aliana hooked up her iPod, blasting pop music while she took a quick shower and then got to work on her hair. Swaying with the music, she wrapped her long locks into hot curlers. By the time she finished, it was nearly three o'clock and she was starving. Wrapping a scarf around her head, she made her way to the kitchen, thinking the boys would still be up on the roof. Instead, she found the three warriors and her Dragon gathered around the kitchen island, eating cold sandwiches.

"I hope you guys saved some for me," she teased.

"Already have one ready for ya, darlin'," Percy said, pulling another sandwich from the refrigerator.

Standing next to Dagg, Aliana happily dove into her sandwich and their conversation. They had tested the limits of Galahad's strength and speed only to find that it was nearly limitless. They'd also discovered that Arthur was able to consistently predict his opponents' attacks. Percy even commented on how quickly the king had learned some new fighting moves.

"So, we have brains and brawn," Aliana said, finishing her sandwich. "Lancelot said last night that he'd become skilled at tracking magical signatures. Was he always a good tracker?"

Arthur nodded, smiling, as he picked up on her line of thought. "You're thinking that our new abilities are an extension of the skills we already had?"

"Yep." Aliana looked over at Galahad. "Were you always faster and stronger than the others?"

"Speed and strength were always my strongest abilities, and Lancelot could track a snow flake in a snow storm," Galahad answered.

"And I was always better with strategies and planning," Arthur added.

"Not to mention you could convince almost everyone to do whatever you asked of them," Lancelot threw in as he and Owen joined the group. "But why are we talking about this?"

"Galahad and I have discovered some interesting abilities, and we think the magic from Avalon could have enhanced the skills we already had," Arthur answered, studying the suits the raven-haired knight laid across the kitchen table.

"What abilities?" Lancelot's brow furrowed. Minutes later, they were all heading out of the kitchen and back to the roof.

"Just make sure y'all are ready by six. We can't be late for the party," Aliana called after them.

"Tell the others I'll be up in moment," Galahad said to Dagg after the others left.

The Dragon studied the pair, closing the door and leaving Aliana and her knight alone in the apartment. Her heart raced as he crossed the room to her side. Being alone with Galahad could prove dangerous to her heart.

"Are those your parents?" he asked, nodding at a picture just over her shoulder.

Aliana knew without looking which picture he was asking about. "Yeah." She turned to stare at the photo. "I took that six years ago at their anniversary party in New York."

The image was a beautiful one, taken at a rooftop restaurant in the city. Her mother's auburn hair glowed with the sun's setting light as she gazed up at her husband's hazel eyes. Her mother was stunning with her olive complexion, high cheekbones, and curvy body. Her dad had short black hair peppered with gray, a rounded face, and nearly gray eyes. The pair's hands were cupped together, holding a beautiful oval box almost the size of her mother's palm with a smaller, heart-shaped lid at the center.

"My dad gave her that music box for their anniversary. The heart flipped open and played their wedding song." Aliana had watched them dance to the soft music.

"They look happy together." Galahad's eyes seemed to drink in the detail of the picture. "You can see how much they were in love."

"They were everything to each other. I always hoped that one day I'd find someone to care about me that way," she said, accidentally letting the secret hope slip. "That probably sounds stupid to you." Her eyes darted around, looking everywhere but at Galahad.

"I do not think it a stupid hope." Galahad's words were soft as he drew closer, placing a comforting hand on her shoulder.

She smiled as she breathed in his wintery scent. "Thank you." She finally looked up at him. They stood still for a moment, his face so close she thought he might kiss her again. Her stomached flip-flopped, but she stepped back. "I need to finish getting ready," she said, her voice breathy, and escaped back into her room, leaning against the now closed door.

14

Sparring with Arthur and Galahad is damn cool, much more than I ever imagined. Already I feel a connection with them. But I can't help noticing the way they both watch Aliana. They're different when she's not around. Their sparring becomes more aggressive, like they're trying to prove something between them. Is this what they were like in Camelot? I wish I had my memories of that time. Lance is pissed at Aliana about this party tonight, though I think he's overreacting. But that's typical Lancelot.

— Percy

Pressing play on her music, Aliana pulled a stool into the bathroom and began the annoying task of styling her hair. She pulled the sides of her curly brown locks back and held them in place with small, glittering pins, letting a mass of hair fall down her back. A bottle of hair spray and an hour and a half later, she left the bathroom and pulled on the dress Lacy had made for her. There were three things Lacy had a passion for in life: fashion, parties, and boys.

Lacy was gifted with designing but not so much at subtlety. This dress had clearly been designed for ballroom dancing in a beautiful shade of lavender with sheer, glittery netting over the soft material. Its petal skirt fell just above her knees. Multiple strings were attached to the front of the dress by large, silver rings. Carefully, Aliana pulled the strings over her shoulders to lace them through the two loops on the back V of the dress. She was still struggling to get the darned things laced properly when claws scraped against her door.

"Can I come in?" Dagg called through the door.

Aliana wanted to tell him no but remembered his words from earlier. She opened the door, determined to show him that he had been wrong. She just wanted privacy, not to shut people out.

"Good timing," she said, closing the door behind him. "I need another pair of hands to lace up my dress. Or claws, as the case seems to be."

Laughing, Dagg laced the strings. Aliana let out a yelp when he tried to pull them too tight.

"What are you doing, Dagg?" She snatched the strings from his claws, loosening the dress.

"Is the dress not to pull together? Women do not show so much of their body."

"Dagg…" Aliana laughed as she sat down at her vanity. "Fashion has changed a lot in the last few decades. This dress is going to be prudish compared to what some of the other women will be wearing."

"I can't wait to see this," the Dragon said, his mouth curving up.

"You can't come tonight. Dragons are only in fairy-tale stories here. There's no way you could fly around the event and not cause a panic."

"I thought of that already." The Dragon crawled onto her vanity. "Magic makes many things possible." He shrank down to less than half his normal size. His flared wings curved back and his eyes turned into amethyst jewels. His entire body had hardened into a solid silver cuff bracelet.

"Now I can be with you and not cause a panic."

Aliana stared, half fascinated and half freaked out. It was almost too crazy to see an inanimate object move its mouth. "Unbelievable," she whispered, picking him up and stroking his curved wings. "This doesn't hurt you?"

The Dragon changed back instantly. "No, not at all."

"Wow."

"Indeed, but I do believe it's almost six."

Aliana shrieked, seeing she only had thirty minutes left to do her makeup. "Damn." She grabbed her eye shadow brush and set to work.

Twenty minutes later, Dagg announced, "Sire, gentlemen, I do believe Aliana is ready."

Aliana fidgeted nervously for a second, readjusting a tie on her strappy silver kitten heels, before stepping into the main room. She couldn't help gawking at the guys as she saw them all together. She had never been particularly fond of tuxes, but every single one of them looked like he had stepped off the cover of *GQ*. Arthur and Percy both wore charcoal tuxedos. Arthur's was paired with a red button shirt and Percy's with silver. Galahad and Lancelot had on black tuxes, with Galahad in a deep green shirt and Lancelot in royal blue. Owen stood out the most in a white tuxedo and black shirt.

How could she compare with them? For a moment, she felt so out of her league she wanted to run back into her room and hide. The guys stared at her, and she panicked. She *hated* being the center of attention. Then her eyes met Arthur's golden brown gaze and she started to relax.

"You are more beautiful than words can say," the king said, stepping forward and taking her hand, kissing it gently.

The last of her nerves slipped away. "Thank you, Arthur."

"You're going to be the hit of the party, Aliana!" Owen said with a cheerful smile on his face.

"Thanks, Owen, but I think you five are going to be getting all the attention. All of you look amazing." Her eyes fell on Galahad.

Dagg cleared his throat, and she held out a hand. The Dragon landed on her wrist, shrinking and hardening himself into his bracelet form.

"It's so he can go with us and not cause trouble," she explained.

As if he'd been doing it his whole life, Galahad helped Aliana into her coat. His hands rested on her shoulders for a moment before sliding slowly down her arms. She glanced at him as she picked up her clutch, which held her mask. She wondered if his mind was going back to the Sidhe's keep like hers was. The masked ball tonight almost seemed like it was a do-over for her and Galahad. Except this time they got to wear fancy clothes and she would finally get to dance with him without the threat of the evil Sidhe hanging over their heads.

"Lacy will have masks for all of you at the hotel," Aliana told them, checking for the bags of clothes and personal items she'd set out earlier since they'd be going to Lancelot's after the party.

"I already put your things in the car, Aliana," Percy said.

"Thanks." She smiled at the hot giant. *God, the women aren't going to know what to do with themselves.*

"And before you say it, yes, I know you're driving, Lancelot."

The others laughed at the unamused stare said knight leveled at Aliana. They all piled into the large vehicle with Owen and Aliana in the back seat, and Arthur and Galahad in the middle row. They'd offered Aliana shotgun, but she'd declined it to Percy. As they made their way through London, her stomach flipped-flopped. Whether it was because of the party or Arthur and Galahad, she wasn't sure. But sooner than she would have liked, Lancelot pulled up to the brightly lit, chic hotel.

She caught both Galahad and Arthur staring at her again as she texted Lacy that they'd arrived. A secret part of her loved the way they kept looking at her — like they were seeing her as a girl and not the key to their prophecy. Lancelot tossed the keys to the valet, and Galahad and Arthur each took one of her hands, helping her out of the tall SUV.

"Thank God you made it!"

Aliana glanced past the two to see her blond friend all but running to them. Lacy was fashionable as ever in a princess pink, Marilyn Monroe-style dress and white gladiator wedges. Her short hair was in a spiked pixie style.

Stepping past the guys, Aliana met Lacy halfway. Both girls giggled as they hugged. "Where did you find those sexy specimens of male figures?" Lacy whispered, looping her arm through Aliana's. "I call dibs on the tall one!"

"Lacy!" Aliana shushed her friend, unable to stop giggling. "They can hear you!"

"And your point?" she said saucily.

Aliana shook her head and said, "You know Owen."

"Nice to see you again, Lacy," Owen said.

"You too." Lacy looked him up and down. "I do love a Brit in a tux."

Owen laughed as Aliana introduced the others. "Lacy, this is Lancelot, Galahad, Arthur, and Percy." Aliana smirked as her friend's blue eyes kept going back to Percy. She and her friend shared a weakness for tall guys with broad shoulders.

"Nice to meet y'all," Lacy said. Flashing her frosted pink smile at Percy, her eyes widened in surprise. "Wait, Arthur, Galahad, and Lancelot?" She eyed the three skeptically before looking at Aliana. "Lia, what did you do, go rob a fairy-tale book without inviting me?"

"Of course not! I would never do such a thing without consulting you first." Aliana winked at the guys.

Lacy smiled as Aliana tried to keep a serious face. "It's time to head up," Lacy said, checking her cell phone. "The party kicks off in thirty minutes and we need to get masks for your fairy-tale friends over here. Which reminds me, where is your mask, Lia?"

"Right here," Aliana said, holding up her purse as they took the posh elevator up to the top floor.

"Here we go," Lacy said, ushering them down a bright hall. She grabbed a box from a young girl who gawked at the guys and pulled out several cat-eye masks for them to choose from.

Arthur, of course, grabbed the golden one, then Galahad grabbed the white, and Percy took the silver while Lancelot picked the blue, leaving the black for Owen.

"Perfect! Y'all look the part of the handsome, mysterious gentle-men. I love the silver, Percy," Lacy said, handing Aliana's coat to the girl who *still* couldn't take her eyes away from the guys. "Now, if you'll all excuse us, Lia and I need a moment of girl time." Without waiting, Lacy dragged Aliana down the hall and into the ladies room.

"Oh my gawd, are you serious?" Lacy said, fanning herself and leaning against the closed door. "Where did you find those men?"

"Avalon," Aliana said, wanting to see how her friend would react.

The blonde rolled her eyes. "Seriously, Lia!"

"I'm not sure you'd believe me if I told you the truth, Lace." Aliana dropped her purse onto the counter, pulling out her swirly, purple mask.

"Either way, you are so lucky! Did you even notice the way Arthur *and* Galahad were staring at you?"

Aliana's brow furrowed as she tied on the swirling mask, not wanting to admit out loud that she *had* noticed.

"Seriously, Lia, you need to open your eyes. They looked like..." Her friend searched for the right word. "Like they were enchanted with you."

Aliana shook her head in denial. "It's not like that, Lace. I'm help-ing them with a problem." *Understatement of the night.* "They just need my help, nothing else." But oh how she wished her friend were right.

"Lia, I swear sometimes it's unbelievable how blind you can be." Her friend sighed as she tied on her own silvery pink mask.

They returned to the guys, who cut off their hushed conversation as the girls walked up to them. Aliana wished she had her camera. All of the guys together in tuxes and masks would make a flutter-in-your-stomach, can't-stop-staring-because-you're-so-hot, amazing shot. With one glance at her friend, Aliana knew Lacy was thinking the exact same thing. They seemed almost too good to be true.

Another of the event planners approached, drawing Lacy's atten-tion. "Why don't y'all head into the exhibit room. I have to go check on a few things." She disappeared in a flutter of pink, and Aliana led the way through the French doors into the main room.

Rich, glittering balls of stained glass hung from the chandeliers. Rails of colored spotlights ran across the ceiling, shining brightly on the collection of artwork. Everything from the lighting to the soft music and exotic flowers made Aliana feel like she was walking through a fairy-tale gallery fit for a queen.

She stopped to admire a life-size bronze statue of a man sitting with his knees drawn up to his chest. The statue's eyes seemed to be staring at a nearby painting of a brightly-colored Paris street café.

"This is beautiful, Aliana," Arthur said into her ear. He was the only one of the guys who hadn't left her side. Owen and Percy had wandered across the room and were chatting with two women. Lance-lot and Galahad had stopped to examine a different painting near one of the fake columns.

"Lacy's company really outdid itself." She couldn't wait to tell her friend what an amazing job she had done.

"You said you had some work on display, Aliana," Lancelot said as he and Galahad joined her and the king.

"Yeah, they should be over by the stone lovers." She pointed to a small jade sculpture of a man and woman entwined on a bed of stone pillows.

Eager to see her work, they made their way over. Her photographic series was called *Myths*, all inspired by different stories she had heard growing up. All the photos were framed in glass, the edges filled with large bubbles to give the illusion of a cloud. Aliana's eyes widened when she saw a small "sold" sticker attached to four of her six photos.

"These are wonderful," Lancelot said, unmistakably surprised.

The first was the final battle between Zeus and Cronus. The second was a take on Beauty and the Beast with a handsome man covered not in fur but black and green dragon scales, holding a woman in a pale pink dress tightly to him. The third was a photo of Robin Hood aiming a bow. The fourth was a girl in Ancient Greece opening a small box that spilled golden light into the moonlit world.

The fifth was a photo of a sandy-blond-haired warrior dressed only in a pair of black *hakama* pants. He stood balanced on a small rock in the center of a turbulent river with a majestic waterfall framing him from behind. The warrior held a *katana* by his head, ready to strike at an unseen opponent. The serenity of the surrounding forest stood at odds with the fierce warrior.

The last photo was of a young girl dancing under water, a flowing train of colored scarves swirling around her like a mermaid's tail. Behind her were the eerie, glowing eyes and gaping mouth of a great white shark.

"It's like you can feel what each of these people feel. Each one tells its own, unique story," Arthur said, praising her.

"Thank you," Aliana said, unable to hide her blush from her king. Galahad whispered something to Lancelot as they studied the warrior photo. Galahad suddenly looked up like he could feel her watching him. He sent her a rakish smile as Lancelot walked away, leaving just the three of them.

"Who is the warrior in your photo?" Galahad asked as Arthur studied the picture again.

"That's my friend Wade, Lacy's brother," she said, beaming. "He's a crazy amazing martial artist."

Arthur turned back to her and asked, "Is this the friend you mentioned before we came to London? Will he be here tonight?"

Aliana grinned. "He's already here somewhere. He's working on some secret project for tonight."

Galahad and Arthur smiled.

"Your art is beautiful," Galahad said softly to her. "I understand now what you meant before and why you are so passionate about it. I particularly like the Mergirl."

"That one was really fun to do," Aliana said. "But it took me six nights at sea to get the right picture of the shark." She explained the photo process, and both men looked horrified as she told them about diving with the creatures in a steel cage at night. Avoiding a lecture, she pulled Arthur and Galahad to a life-size statue of a dancing girl.

"She looks so real," Arthur said, his arm brushing against Aliana's.

As her gaze wandered the room, Aliana spotted a man in a black jacket and bronze shirt watching them from behind a black and red phantom-style mask. She frowned as his familiarity pulled at her, filling her with an almost overwhelming need to go speak to him. She eyed the guys, but neither of them seemed to have noticed the man watching them. Just as she opened her mouth to say something, the lights flickered and went out. Just as quickly, spotlights came on over each of the six life-size statues that were spread out among the displays.

Aliana studied the statue in front of her, momentarily forgetting about the strange guy. She and the entire crowd gasped as the eyes of the statues snapped open, coming to life with a loud breath as sensual, electronica music spilled out of hidden speakers. Their bodies animated with the electronic beat as they all leaped from perches, dancing their way through the crowd. The six dancers all had different styles, but every move they made seemed to blend together like they were dancing as one. When one did a high kick, the others followed.

The lights flickered again and black lights came on, illuminating a new set of men and women dressed in white and black jester's costumes. These new dancers glowed in the purple-white light. The music changed to a slightly faster track with violins and drums joining the electronic beat. The joker dancers joined with the stone dancers as they made their way around the room, some brushing against the patrons. They came together as one, and like pied pipers, led the entire audience in an enchantingly beautiful dance through the main room and out onto the large, open roof deck. A stage was lit with electronic candles and soft, yellow spotlights. Aliana barely noticed all the guys surrounding her as she made her way to the edge of the dance floor in front of the stage, completely taken with the dancers as they all came together in a beautiful and ethereal choreographed routine.

The dancers glided together across the dance floor, pairing up and then dancing solo as bodies rolled off one another or twisted together in a play of hands and legs. The lights cast shadows over their moving bodies as they leaped, flipped, and kicked their way over the stage in a beautiful and strange dance of the night.

15

I was not sure I would sleep last night, but I did, and I dreamed of Aliana by my side in Camelot. But my ghost woman was also there. She seemed to almost blend with Aliana at times. Everything has changed so much, and the struggles of my men as they either try to adapt to this new world or cope with the loss of their memories worries me. I long for Camelot—a world I understand and belong to. These clothes, this party...the dancing, it is all so unusual, yet strangely beautiful. But it is nothing compared to Aliana's wonder-struck smile. She looks so jubilant. I can plainly see that there is something between her and Galahad, but there is a bond between the two of us as well. I am determined to win her. But I must to go slowly and gain her trust first.

— Arthur

A guy not much older than Aliana broke through the middle of the pack. Dressed in nothing but a white vest, gray slacks, and a fedora, he led the dancers in the final minutes of the performance. Aliana laughed as Wade danced his way toward her with Rat-Pack, Frank-Sinatra-smooth moves. He had a cool, bad boy swagger to him and a confidence that never failed to impress.

The music ended and the dancers struck their final poses. Thunderous applause rang out from the crowd as the lights came up. Wade bowed with the other dancers before they made a quick exit. Instead of following, Wade made his way to the edge of the dance floor, stopping in front of Aliana for a quick moment to drop his fedora onto her head before disappearing.

"That was Wade, was it not?" Arthur asked.

"Yeah. He's a big goofball. One of his many charms."

"I think he may also be Sir Gawain," Galahad said, his face drawn tight.

"What?" Aliana asked, looking at Lancelot and Arthur. Both men nodded. "But how could Wade be one of you?" Aliana removed the hat. "I've known him my whole life!"

"We—" Arthur was cut short by applause as a plump, balding man stepped onto the raised platform next to the DJ booth.

"Good evening and thank you all for coming to the Fagan Foundation's tenth annual Gala of the Arts," the man said in a wispy, aging voice.

"Oh boy," Aliana said, taking a step behind Galahad, hoping the man on stage wouldn't see her. "That's Mister Myers, the chairman of the board. He's a total bore and a weasel."

"You don't like him, then," Lancelot said as the boring man prattled on.

"You could say I'm not his biggest fan, and he's definitely not mine."

"Do you want to return to the gallery?" Galahad asked, but before Aliana could take a step away, the man on stage called her name.

"We are delighted to have the lovely Aliana Fagan back with us after a two-year absence. Aliana, dear, why don't you come up and say a few words."

Speaking in public, especially to a crowd as large as this one, terrified her, and Mr. Myers knew it. Aliana hated that her hands were already starting to shake. The crowd applauded, welcoming her as she crossed the large dance floor to the stage. As she reached the steps, Wade appeared on the stage, now wearing a powder blue horned mask. Before Weasel Man knew what was happening, Wade snatched the microphone from his hand and crossed over to Aliana.

"Sorry to interrupt folks, but we all know that Carrie Fagan preferred dancing to speeches." The crowd chuckled as he breezed down the stairs, stopping in front of Aliana, his hand held out to her.

"How about it, Lia? Wanna show 'em how it's done?" he asked, wiggling his eyebrows above his trademark devilish smile.

Relieved, Aliana took his hand. The two of them had been danc-ing together since they were eight. Their favorite style had always been a mash up of Latin and ballroom dancing styles. Aliana loved that she was comfortable enough with Wade to do such blatantly sensual moves with him in public without getting embarrassed. Because of their natural chemistry and passion, they'd often been mistaken for a couple, but they'd never been anything more than friends.

The crowd cheered as the couple took center stage. Wade signaled to the DJ with a twirl of his finger, and Aliana giggled, recognizing the pit-bull mix Wade had made a few months ago. They had put this dance together shortly after Aliana's last boyfriend had broken up with her because she wasn't "sexy enough." When Wade had heard that, he said they'd show the prick just how wrong he was. So they'd put together the sexiest routine they could think of and showed it off at their favorite club in Charleston during the jerk's birthday. The look on the ass's face had been priceless.

"You remember the steps, right, Lia?" Wade asked, twirling her around and pulling her tight to his body.

"Of course. I can't let my hero down," Aliana said in a seductive voice, wrapping her arm around his neck and staring into his laugh-ing, hazel eyes.

They swayed their hips to the slow beat as they moved in small circles, stepping between each other's legs. Wade's big hand slid up her side to her shoulder, and Aliana arched backward, gliding in a half circle before Wade pulled her back up just as the beat hit full speed. Aliana shook her hips as their feet moved lightning quick in a cha-cha step that would make Mary Murphy proud.

Wade's fingers twisted with hers as she pivoted out and back, out and back in a series of turns to match the electric beat. With her back to him, Wade took her hands, leading her in a set of lock steps, him going right when she went left. He pulled her against him, splaying one hand at her throat as the other pulled her arm around his neck. With a saucy glance over her shoulder, Aliana knocked Wade to one knee with a bump of her hip. Winking, she dance-stepped and kicked her way across the stage.

Wade was back on his feet and spun her again, pulling her back tightly to his front, one hand wrapped high around her torso, the other holding her hand out to the side. They circled their upper bodies together in an intimate Samba roll. She faced him again and locked a leg around his waist as he lifted her up, and they twirled across the stage, Aliana's skirt flaring like a cape of glittering purple. Her feet hit the ground and Wade spun her several times. The beat changed, and they rolled their bodies against one another from chest to hip, his hand in hers. He took her waist, lifting her high and then letting her drop, catching her thigh and dipping her low on the final beat of the song. With her arm around his neck and the other tracing lightly over his high cheekbone, it could easily look like she was inviting him in for a kiss.

They both started laughing, barely able to breathe. Wade set Aliana back on her feet, taking her hand, and turned to face the audience. They took their bows as the audience clapped. Even Arthur and Galahad, who appeared to be a bit in shock, cheered for them. Aliana paused, her endorphin rush ebbing. She was going to have to talk to Wade about the knights and everything that had happened the last two days. *Can he really be one of them?*

"I think our little show had a similar effect as last time," Wade said, pulling her out of her mini freak-out. He nodded toward Arthur and Galahad. "Your fairy-tale friends look like they want to beat me." Apparently his sister had filled him in on her new friends.

She glanced at the guys as she wound an arm around Wade. Galahad's eyes flicked to hers, and she realized he'd been staring at Wade. A peek at Arthur told the same story.

"Oh boy…" Aliana whispered to Wade as he kissed her on the forehead, laughing. "And what exactly did your sister tell you?"

Wade just winked, his devilish grin back. They joined the others away from the stage while people filled the dance floor.

"I wasn't expecting that from you, Aliana," Lancelot said.

"Thanks?" she responded, not sure it was a compliment.

Owen snatched her up into a bear hug. "You were spectacular! I knew you could dance, but that was smashing!" Owen turned to Wade. "And you didn't do too bad either." Everyone laughed except Arthur and Galahad.

"Big brother, Lia, you two were so hot out there!" Lacy said, pushing her way in between them to hug Wade and then Aliana.

"Lacy, you and Wade have done so much more tonight than I could ever imagined. Mom and Dad would have loved it!" Aliana hugged Lacy tighter, and her misty eyes met Wade's. "Thank you," she whispered. Gawd she had missed her best friends, her rocks, these last couple of days!

With a whispered "I'll catch up with you later" and a long glance at Percy, Lacy turned to leave. As soon as she disappeared into the crowd, Aliana pulled Wade and the others over to a deserted corner of the roof.

"Lia, what's going on?" Wade asked.

Gazing between him and the knights, a realization hit her, a feeling of rightness and certainty. Even while her friend sized up the others, he *looked* like he fit, like he *was* a part of the knights. He'd certainly always been as protective of her as they were. Now all she needed to do was find a way to convince *him* that he was one of them. "Wade, there's something I gotta tell you. It's going to sound crazy, but I need you to hear me—" Aliana sighed "—*us* out."

Wade's nervous gaze flicked from her to the guys. "Who are these guys really?"

"I don't know how to say this so I'm gonna just say it. Wade, meet King Arthur, Galahad, Lancelot and Percy. They're the Knights of the Round Table. Apparently they think you are one of them too—reborn like Owen and Percy."

Wade's brow shot up before he broke into a roaring laugh. "That's a good one, Lia!" He regarded her and the guys, sobering when he saw that none of them were laughing, not even Owen.

"What she says is true," Lancelot said, holding out a hand to her slack-jawed friend.

"Bullshit," Wade said, staring at Lancelot's hand like it was from outer space.

"Not bullshit." Dagg unwrapped himself from Aliana's wrist, returning to his normal size.

"Dagg!" Aliana hissed, grabbing the dumb Dragon and looking around to see if any of the other guests had caught sight of the mythical creature.

"What is that?" Wade asked, going pale.

"I am Daggerhorne, guardian to the Destined One—Aliana. What she has told you is the truth."

"You've made your point, Dagg! Now shrink your Dragon butt back into a bracelet before someone sees you!" Without another word, the Dragon did as asked.

Wade's jaw twitched, his tell when he was stressed. Uncertainty and disbelief swam in his eyes, silently begging Aliana to tell him this was all a joke. "Aliana, can I talk to you for a moment? Over there." He pointed to an empty spot several feet away. "Without the…*bracelet*."

Nodding, she handed Dagg to Galahad and asked Owen to join them.

"Aliana, do not go too far," Arthur cautioned.

She sighed. "We're just going over there." She pulled her cousin and best friend behind her, trying to think of a way to make Wade understand. It was selfish, but she didn't think she could do this without him, and now that she'd believed in who he really was, she was relieved.

"Owen, what kind of joke is this?" Wade demanded as soon as they were out of the others' hearing. "You can't seriously be buyin' this story!" His slight twang slipped. Another of his tells.

"I know how you feel, mate." Owen placed a mollifying hand on Wade's shoulder. "I just found out last night after she got back from Avalon with all her — *our* new friends in tow." Owen still sounded a little bit unbelieving, and Aliana couldn't blame him. She still half expected to wake up and find all of this to be a crazy dream.

"Wade, just let me explain, please," she pleaded, making her eyes big and hopeful with just a touch of tears.

"Not the sad kitten eyes!" Wade tried to look away, but he couldn't escape them. "All right, I give. I'll *listen*."

"Thank you." As quickly as she could, she explained everything that had happened during the last forty-eight hours, letting Owen add in his own knowledge.

Wade held up his hand, stopping them. "Let's say I actually believe you — you've certainly told me crazy stories before — the difference between then and now is that those were all make-believe." His jaw twitched again. "Lia, don't go all wrath-of-the-southern-spitfire on me for asking this, but are you *really sure* about this?"

Aliana snuck a quick glance at the guys, who cautiously watched the trio. She was scared that she wouldn't live up to what they expected of her, but this *was* real. She couldn't have felt the things she had if all of this was fake. Wade would believe too, eventually. "Yeah, I do."

"What did that…bracelet…mean when he called you the Destined One, Lia?"

She paused and hoped Wade wouldn't freak out. "According to their prophecy, I would wake Arthur — which I did yesterday — help reunite everyone — which I appear to be doing right now — and help them find the items they've lost. And apparently, I'll be 'the key' to stopping the evil sorcerer Mordrid."

Wade's frown deepened. He looked again to the other knights. "*The key?* Lia…"

"Please, Wade, you saw Dagg, and I have pictures from Avalon I can show you. You have to admit, it all kinda feels…right," Aliana said, taking his hand. "It can't be an accident that you and I have been best friends forever and that we found Owen."

"Now they have you thinking that we're only friends because you were supposed to 'reunite' us?" Wade snapped, his anger evident in his narrowed eyes.

"No, of course not!" she insisted, and saw him relax a fraction. "You're my family, both you and Owen, no matter what anyone else may think or say."

Wade sighed heavily, running his hand through his brown locks.

"Talk to them, mate," Owen said, encouraging him. "It will help. I know exactly how you feel, and you just need to give this a chance to settle."

Wade gazed out at the cityscape. He closed his eyes and let out a deep breath as he shook his head. "Okay, Lia, I'll admit, there is something about all this that does seem right, so I'll give them a chance. But I'm still half sure they're pulling one over on you."

Scowling, she smacked him in the arm before giving him a big hug. "Thanks, I really need my best friend."

The rejoined the others, and as soon as they got there, Wade said, "So, Aliana has filled me on her side of things, what do you all have to say about it?"

"If Aliana hasn't convinced you this is true, then why would you believe me?" Arthur asked. "As I see it, Percy, Aliana, and Owen have all gone on faith and trust. I wouldn't think you any different. The Knights of the Round Table stand for justice, truth, loyalty, and honor. Those are things we gave to the people we protected and to each other. Now, here in this world, I ask for no different. But it is *your* choice."

He held Wade's gaze for a long, tense moment. Aliana watched Wade's jaw twitch.

"All right, but I have a condition. We do not under any circumstances tell Lacy! I may not be able to keep Aliana out of danger's way, but I don't want my sister in any kind of danger."

Aliana bit her tongue to keep from arguing. She didn't like the idea of lying to her best friend, but at the same time, she didn't want Lacy in the line of trouble either.

Arthur nodded, accepting her friend's condition, and Wade's shoulders relaxed. "I swear, if I find out any of this is crap, I'm taking Aliana away and none of you will be able to find us."

"Try it," Galahad challenged in a low voice.

"Galahad." Aliana touched his shoulder briefly, taking Dagg's bracelet form from his hand.

"Everyone better put on their happy faces," Percy warned, looking over his shoulder. "Your very hot friend is on her way over here."

"Watch it, Tiny. That's my sister," Wade growled before putting on a smile.

"Everything okay over here?" Lacy asked, sliding next to Percy. "I'm thinking something has to be seriously wrong if you're all over here missing the party of the century."

"We're good here, sis. No worries. Just getting to know Aliana's fairy-tale friends a bit better."

"Wade," Aliana hissed, elbowing him in his side. "I blame you for this, Lace."

"Blame away, darling. I have a donor who insists on meeting you." Lacy pulled her friend to her side and whispered loudly, "He's kinda hot too." She glanced at Arthur and Galahad.

"Instigator! My point is proven," Aliana said accusingly but with a half-smile.

"So, if you'll excuse us, gentlemen," Lacy said, and the girls turned, walking away from the guys.

"Aliana," Arthur called, stopping them. "Maybe one of us should go with you."

"I'll be fine. Crowded party, remember?" Before the guys could object, she and Lacy continued away from them.

"What was that about?" Lacy asked. "And you should have seen those two's faces when you were dancing with Wade. I almost thought your Galahad was going to go out there and beat up my bro."

"He's not *my* Galahad," Aliana denied again. "Did he really, though?"

Lacy nodded with a vivacious smile. "Donation guy's just over there." She pointed to the man Aliana had seen watching her earlier.

"Who is he?" Aliana asked, studying him as if she could somehow see beneath his red and black phantom mask. She was fascinated by the guy all over again. There was something familiar about him.

"His name is Thomas Wylit. He's already bought three pieces tonight, one of them yours," Lacy whispered as they approached him. "Aliana Fagan this is Thomas Wylit. Mister Wylit, Aliana Fagan."

"Nice to meet you." Aliana held out her hand to him and he took it.

"It is a pleasure to meet you properly, Miss Fagan." He had a very cultured, tenor voice and an exaggerated pronunciation of his As. "I am a fan of your work." His tone and the way he said "work" made Aliana think he was referring to something other than her photos.

"Well, I'll leave you two to chat. I need to go check on the bar." Lacy again disappeared into the crowd.

"You are quite the talented dancer," Thomas said. "Your mother seems to have taught you well. I wonder, did she teach you the waltz from her first movie?"

"Um…yeah, she did. I'm sorry, but have we met before?"

"Dance with me," he said. "Then I will answer your questions."

Aliana shifted back to examine him. His red and black phantom mask accented his sharp cheekbones, hard jaw, and gray-blue eyes. Something lurked below his polished surface, though, a kind of dangerous mystery.

"I don't bite, Miss Fagan."

"Call me Aliana," she said, deciding to take a chance, knowing that the guys were probably keeping watch. She looked at the dance floor. At some point a live band had taken the stage, and it was playing a song from one of her mother's movies. The singer ended the song, inviting anyone who knew Carrie Fagan's movie waltz to the dance floor.

"So, will you join me?" Thomas asked again.

"Did you know this was going to happen?" she asked, taking his hand.

The man chuckled. "I confess, your friend did tell me in advance." They joined four other couples on the dance floor, including a pair of the stone dancers from earlier.

The ladies formed a line facing their partners. As the soft guitar and piano started to play, the men bowed and the ladies curtsied. The dance started off in a set of turns and near touches as the ladies did a box step around the men, coming back to face them, stepping close and locking gazes.

Still not touching, they circled each other, Aliana's right shoulder lined up with Thomas's. Stepping back again, they bowed and came together. His hand was gentle against her waist as he effortlessly led her in a classic four-corner waltz.

"Earlier it sounded like you knew my mother," Aliana said as he spun her in a circle.

"I did. I knew both your mother and father, actually."

Aliana gasped. "Did your parents know mine? Or were you one of my dad's students?"

"Why would you jump to those conclusions?"

"Well, how else would you have known them? You're not much older than me."

Both his hands went to her waist, lifting her in a spinning circle with the other dancing pairs. "I'm twenty-two, thanks. And I would think with all you've recently discovered, that your view of things would have *broadened*."

Aliana tensed, nearly forgetting the next step, but as if he expected her reaction, Thomas kept her on pace.

"I don't know what you're talking about," she denied as he spun her again.

"Don't be coy, Aliana. You know what I'm talking about."

Wrapping his arm around her waist, he lifted her against him. Automatically, Aliana flared her legs as he spun her around. Who was he? Was he a threat to her and the knights? She considered walking away from him, but his arm went around her again and they fell back into the waltz steps.

"I don't know who you really are, but if you know all you hint at, then you should know not to mess with me or my friends."

"They wouldn't hurt me." He sounded so superior that Aliana's teeth clenched as she pushed aside the urge to hit him.

She wanted to leave him on the floor, but if she did, she'd only create a scene, and who knew how the guys would react. She danced the final moments of the song with him, lining up with the others in their original position. Out of habit, she curtsied to him, sending a glare in his direction as she escaped the dance floor to find her knights.

16

I don't like the way Lacy looked at this Percy guy, and I'm worried about my best friend. Aliana's done nothing but run from place to place, taking stupid risks since her parents died. I can't help thinking these fairy-tale friends are bad news, but at the same time, these guys and their story feel right — like it's the truth. I just don't know — and I hate doubting myself. Lia's the one who dreamed of adventure; I wanted the normal life. If this is all true, looks like that's out the door.

— Wade

Aliana saw her friends by the other side of the dance floor. She quickened her pace, wanting to tell them about the mystery guy, but before she could get to them, another man in a mask stepped into her path.

"Miss Fagan," he said. The brown eyes that peered through his leather mask were so dark they almost looked black. "Would you care to dance with me?" His smile reminded her of a viper.

Panic bloomed in her chest. Thomas Wylit had fascinated and confused her, but this guy terrified her. "No, I need to get back to my friends." She moved to step around him, but again he blocked her way.

"I would like to dance with you, Aliana," he said again.

"And I said no!"

Stepping to the side, he let her pass, but as she moved alongside him, his fingers brushed against her bare shoulder, and he whispered, "I would take the time to get know your friends better. They are more treacherous than you realize."

Her eyes grew large as unpleasant prickles shot through her body. She snapped her head around, but the guy had disappeared.

"Aliana." She slowly turned to see Arthur and the others.

"Who were you dancing with?" Wade asked.

She stepped between Arthur and Galahad. No matter what that creeper had said, being surrounded by them made her feel safe, and she had to trust that. "He said his name was Thomas Wylit."

Lancelot's eyebrows shot up before he whispered something to Percy and nodded to Arthur. When Arthur nodded back, Lancelot disappeared into the crowd.

Aliana looked between Arthur and Galahad, confused. "He's going to find the guy," Galahad explained. "You seemed upset on the dance floor. What did he say to you?"

"I wasn't really upset, but he hinted that he knows who all of you are and what I've done." She shook her head. "I swear I've met him before, but I can't remember from where."

"Lancelot will discover who he is, Aliana. Do not worry," Arthur said, laying a gentle hand on her shoulder.

"Are you going to tell them about the other one?" Dagg asked from around her wrist.

"Dagg, you're going to draw attention!" Aliana scolded.

"What does he mean?" Galahad asked, his eyes darkening a shade.

"Some guy stopped me when I was leaving the dance floor. He asked me to dance, but he totally creeped me out. He didn't seem to want to take no for an answer, but he let me go."

"Who was he?" Arthur asked, scanning the crowd.

"Don't know, but he was wearing a brown leather leaf mask."

"We'll keep watch for him," Galahad promised. "He won't bother you again."

"It's no big deal, really. There are always strange guys around events like these."

"Either way," Arthur said.

"Why don't we all try to enjoy the rest of the party," Wade suggested, breaking the tense mood. "We can't leave any time soon without incurring the wrath of Lacy, so let's just relax and have fun. To be honest, I want to enjoy this 'normal' party before you all drag me into…whatever it is you're going to drag me into."

Aliana peeked at Arthur, hoping he would agree. She wanted a little more "normal" too.

"All right," Arthur said. "But, Aliana, one of us *will* remain close to you for the rest of the night." He waited until she nodded, and then a smile twitched the corners of his mouth. "And if you would still like to dance, perhaps you can show me how."

"Sure." Aliana smiled brightly. "We'll start with something simple."

"Then I would like your next dance." Galahad's eyes captured hers.

Aliana couldn't seem to make her voice work, so she just nodded, letting Arthur pull her onto the dance floor.

"I think I understand the basic steps," Arthur said, taking her hand and placing his hand at her waist. "They seemed easy enough when I was watching you earlier. You are a beautiful dancer."

Aliana blushed and smiled at the floor. "Thank you." The band was playing a slower song from the mid-nineties that told the story of a heartbroken man. His lady had left him with nothing but the ghost of their love haunting him like a ship lost at sea. Aliana guided the king in the first few steps, but he quickly took the lead. "I'm impressed, Arthur."

"One benefit of my new abilities is that I seem to be able to learn things, even from just watching. It's nearly effortless." He spun Aliana out and pulled her back in, their bodies settling against each other as they continued to dance to the haunting music. "This song seems so sad," Arthur said softly. "Losing someone you care about is a hard thing to do."

"Yeah it is, but a lot of musicians and artists form their songs and art around what they feel—both the good and the bad."

"The music now is much changed from what we had in Camelot. Most of the songs we heard were tales of warriors and battles."

"You must really miss your home." Aliana hated hearing the almost painful longing in the great king's voice. Moving closer, she laid her head against his shoulder, hoping to give him some sort of comfort.

"I do miss Camelot, but there are times, like this, when it doesn't seem so bad." He rested his head against hers and they danced the rest of the song in comfortable silence.

Aliana fell into the security of Arthur's arms, wondering why it was so easy to relax with someone she had only just met. She blushed, remembering the kiss that had awakened him. Something had formed between them in that moment. It was nothing like the bond she shared with Galahad. The bond she had with Arthur didn't have the intensity she felt for his knight. Arthur was like a favorite pillow or blanket—easy to curl up in with its comforting warmth. Aliana realized that Arthur could quickly become a great friend and confidant.

The music ended and Arthur tucked Aliana's hand into the bend of his arm as they walked back to their group.

"Where did Wade go?" Aliana glanced around, searching for him.

"He went to see if he could find that guy who was bothering you before you went to dance with our fearless leader," Owen said.

Aliana scowled at her dragon. She didn't want the guys to worry about the creeper and miss out on the party.

"I do believe you promised me your next dance," Galahad reminded her.

The calm from a moment ago disappeared in a flutter of rapid heartbeats as she took his hand. Galahad pulled her to an open corner, and she saw that Percy and Lacy had followed them. Aliana met her friend's glittering eyes just as Lacy stepped into Percy's arms. Lacy wiggled her eyebrows, and Aliana suppressed a giggle that died in her throat when the band changed to an older Adele song and Galahad wrapped his arms around her.

"I am afraid I won't be as good at this as your other partners," he admitted.

"Then let's try another way." Aliana placed both his hands at her waist and wrapped hers around his neck, gazing into his eyes as he pulled her close. They moved together in a slow circle to the sweet melody. They didn't talk. Aliana didn't know what to say, and she couldn't find it in her to look away from his beautiful blue eyes. His wintery scent wrapped around her. The band around her heart tightened as he pulled her even closer against his body.

A small part of her brain whispered that he would eventually break her heart, but even with that thought, she couldn't pull away from him. Everything else faded away except for their swaying bodies. His fingers brushed against her bare skin, sending sparks up her spine. Aliana gasped softly. *Did he feel it too?*

"Are you all right?" he asked in a soft voice.

"Yes," she said breathlessly, lost to whatever magic was weaving around her. She was caught in the spell that was his blue eyes.

Galahad smiled then, his fingers still against her skin.

"Aliana," he whispered, watching her with eyes so dark they looked like liquid midnight.

The song ended, and their fairy-tale world fell away, but the afterglow bliss remained. Galahad kept his large hand at the small of her back when they joined Percy and Lacy near the gallery doors.

"So, are we all having fun?" Lacy asked, winking at her blushing friend.

"You throw a great party, Lacy," Percy said, smiling down at her.

"Well, thank you, but I didn't do it alone, and I need to go check in with the others to make sure everything's set for the rest of the night." She pivoted away and then peeked back at Percy. "Will you still be here later?"

The giant smiled, nodding. Lacy flashed him a bright but slightly shy smile.

Interesting, Aliana thought. She had never seen her friend be shy with a guy before, and she couldn't hide her delighted smirk as Percy watched the pink lady disappear.

"Lacy's amazing," Percy said. "Does she have a boyfriend?"

"Nope," Aliana said with a little pop on the P.

Percy was silent for a moment and then followed the path her friend had taken.

"Well, that was unexpected," Galahad said.

"I love it!" Aliana giggled, wanting to do a little happy dance for her friend. "I just hope Percy is as tough as he appears. Lacy is a firecracker."

"Do you want to rejoin the others or would you like to walk around?" Galahad asked.

"Honestly, I think I'd like to get away from the crowd for a bit." Her mind screamed that this was a bad idea. Maybe she was still caught up in the magic of their dance. Either way, she tuned the voice out. With his hand still at the small of her back, he guided her through the richly decorated room to a long curtain, which he pulled aside to reveal a small balcony. "I didn't even notice this earlier." Aliana walked outside and leaned her back against the stone railing, looking up at the cloudy London sky, wishing she could see the stars.

"I noticed it before the dancers came to life earlier."

Aliana followed Galahad's eyes, twisting to stare out at the brightly lit city. She couldn't help worrying about everything that was to come in this adventure she found herself tangled in.

"What are you thinking about?" Galahad asked, drawing her attention back to him. He stood only a few inches from her with both his arms coming to rest on either side of her on the railing.

"I was just wondering what's next," she said, enjoying the feeling of being wrapped up in him. "I didn't expect to find another knight here tonight. Much less that it would be Wade."

"You are unhappy that your friend is one of us?"

"Of course not! It would have been so much harder if I had to keep him in the dark on this."

"Then what is wrong?"

"It's just still hard to accept. I need a little more time to adjust."

Galahad brushed her hair over her shoulder, his eyes tracing its curve. "We have come this far already, Aliana. In only two days we are almost whole again. I believe that everything will be all right. You must understand by now that we...that *I* would never allow anything to happen to you."

Aliana saw the conviction in his eyes and, God help her, she believed him. "Lacy wasn't far off when she called you a fairy tale. That's what all of this has been. You, everyone. It's like you're all straight off the pages of a book. Every girl dreams of finding her knight in shining armor or her Prince Charming."

"And which are you looking for?" His head dipped closer to hers.

Her heart raced, and she struggled to take a breath. All she could think about was his kiss. Would he kiss her now? She wasn't in any danger, so why would he want to, unless...

"Galahad," she breathed, her hands rising to rest against his firm chest, his arms still caging her against the railing.

His lips hovered over hers, his breath sweet on her lips from the wine he had been drinking earlier. Their gazes locked together, and Aliana realized she wanted this more than she wanted her next breath, but her body stood immobile. His eyes dropped to her lips, and her heart jumped, beating so rapidly she was afraid it would escape. Slowly, his lips touched hers, featherlight. His eyes met hers again before his mouth fully took hers.

Aliana's eyes closed. A fire burned through her as she gripped his shoulders. His arms closed around her waist, pulling her against him, his kiss consuming her. They were the only people in the world. She heard herself sigh, and felt Galahad's arms tighten as he nipped at her lower lip.

He pulled away, leaving both of them breathing heavily, and rested his forehead against hers, his eyes still shut with an expression of bliss on his face. Her heart ached and soared at the same time. *She* had put that look on his face. Her, Aliana.

"Have I told you how beautiful you are tonight?" he whispered, brushing his lips against hers for another long moment.

"Thank you," she said through the fiery haze in her mind. "You are so handsome in that tux. I'm surprised the other women here haven't snatched you up."

"I don't care about any of them, Aliana." He pulled her gaze to his with two fingers under her chin and kissed her again, softly and sweetly.

"Lia, you out here?"

Aliana pulled back, bumping into the railing as Lacy walked onto the balcony. Her friend's eyes grew huge with shock before she smiled like an imp.

"I'm sorry to interrupt," Lacy said. "Your friends are searching for you two. They say it's important."

Aliana glanced at Galahad, seeing the unkind glare he was throwing toward Lacy.

"We'll be right in," Aliana said, clearing her throat.

"I'll just wait for you two in here. Continue, by all means." Lacy flashed a triumphant smile and disappeared through the drapes.

"We should go find them," Aliana said a moment later when Galahad still hadn't made any move to let her free.

He sighed, nodding, but he still didn't move.

"Galahad." Aliana placed her hands on his tense arms, and he finally dropped one arm, letting her slip past him. He followed closely as they met Lacy on the other side of the curtain.

"So?" Lacy whispered. "Was it as hot as it looked?"

"Lacy!" Aliana hissed, smacking her friend on the arm and smirking. "I don't know, but it couldn't have been as good as yours. Your lipstick's smudged. Will I find some on Percy?"

Lacy flushed bright red all the way to her hair. "Um…they're waiting for you both by your photo display." Lacy said, disappearing.

Aliana heard Galahad chuckle behind her. "It serves her right," Aliana said, defending herself.

They found the others right where Lacy had said they would be. Thomas Wylit was with them.

"Who is this?" Galahad asked, stepping in front of Aliana.

"I'm hurt, Galahad," the cultured voice said. "I would have thought my old friend would recognize me." Thomas removed his mask.

"Merlin?" Galahad gasped.

"Who else, my friend?" The two men shared a warrior's greeting.

"You're Merlin?" Aliana asked.

The dark-haired Druid nodded to her. There it was again, that familiarity she couldn't place. "And you're the Destined One." Merlin smirked. He wasn't as tall as the others, just a bit shorter than Lancelot, but what he lacked in size he made up for with an air of power so thick it was a wonder none of them had felt it earlier.

"Why didn't you just say who you were from the start? Why the game?" Aliana asked.

"Merlin is a fan of games, I'm afraid," Lancelot said. "He's always had a flare for the dramatic."

"My methods aside, it is good to be with all of you again." Merlin rested a hand on Arthur's shoulder.

"So now what?" Aliana asked the group, too stunned to think properly.

Less than two hours later, Aliana stood in the middle of a beautiful plum- and peach-colored bedroom in Merlin's sprawling, three-story, palatial home that had been built in the early fifteenth century. His "house" was hidden deep in the English countryside, well out of the city, surrounded by thick trees, a gothic-looking iron gate, and layers of magical protection.

After Merlin had revealed himself, they had all agreed they'd be safest at his home. After that, the eight of them had piled into Lancelot's blessedly large SUV. During the drive they'd agreed that their next move would be to find Leyon. But what would come after that? Would they try to find the Grail of Power or reclaim Excalibur first?

Merlin and Lancelot had definite ideas about the matter, and Arthur and Galahad had quietly agreed with most what the two enigmas said. Percy added small tidbits when he could while Owen and Wade exchanged half amused, half confused-and-in-over-our-heads glances. Aliana had tried to focus on the plans, but her eyes kept drooping until all their voices faded as she'd fallen asleep against Wade for the rest of the car ride.

After a quick tour of the main house — decorated with elaborate fifteenth-century flare and filled with priceless paintings and artifacts — Merlin had suggested everyone turn in and get rested before they tackled their next challenge. Aliana had tried to convince them they should get things figured out tonight, but Arthur had insisted that they all get some sleep.

Placing his hands on her shoulders, he'd told her, "Tomorrow morning will be soon enough to get everything sorted." When she had tried to protest he'd assured her that everything would be all right and walked her to her designated bedroom, which was tucked between his and Galahad's.

Aliana sank onto the small bench in her large bathroom, suddenly realizing how exhausted she was. Sighing, she changed into a pair of blue and gray plaid shorts and a black tank top. Washing away her makeup and brushing her wild hair, her thoughts turned to her confused feelings about Galahad and their kiss. As much as she debated the why of it, she couldn't bring herself to regret the kiss. Maybe she was going to regret it later but not right now. Going through her nightly ritual helped calm her and let her get her mind sorted and calmed. She crawled onto the luxurious four-poster bed, curling up under the soft covers as Dagg settled onto the pillow next to hers.

"How can Arthur and the others wait so long to find out what happened to Merlin after he left Avalon?" Aliana asked. "Something about Merlin's *supposed* reason for leaving feels hinky to me. There's more to it — there has to be. And he said he knew my parents."

"Merlin and Arthur were right to suggest we all rest tonight. Everyone is struggling to deal with all of the sudden changes, just as you are." Dagg's clawed hand stretched out to lie against hers. "Everything will look clearer after some rest."

Aliana nodded, clicking off the bedside lamp. Her eyes were already drooping with sleep.

She found herself once again on the bloody battlefield, surrounded by rotting black knights and mutilated Goblins. Horrified, she watched as Mordrid plunged his dagger into Arthur's side over and over. His evil gaze found hers, his sick smile and eerie black eyes trying to devour her.

Aliana's stomach revolted. She'd rather be trapped in the cave that had terrified her as a child than helplessly watch Arthur die. Just like that, she was lying in a pile of jagged rock, her leg pinned as she tried to not choke on the foul air. Eyes wide, she tried twisting her way free, but the rock pinned her too tightly. Gasping in the poisoned air, she searched the forgotten chamber. It was old, way older than anything her father had found so far. Her eyes fell onto the darkest corner.

There, in the darkest black, the sound of a thumping pulse disturbed the silence. She heard a loud hiss, then the scraping of nails, louder and louder as the pulse seemed to beat stronger and stronger.

A monster was trying to escape the blackness—trying to get her!

The darkness touched her. It was like an evil coldness trying to cling to her, to pull her into the blackness. She screamed, desperate to be free, smacking at the evil, trying to fight it away.

"Aliana!" someone called to her from above. Tears blurred her vision as she looked up. Her father's worried face and the dark, intimidating face of another man peered down at her. Her father told her to hold tight—they were coming.

She watched the monster in the dark, afraid it might try to get her papa, but another force pushed the dark monster back, forcing it into its hole. Her papa pushed the stones away, freeing her trapped leg, and gathered her in his arms. He barked out an order to pull them up. As soon as they escaped the chamber, more of the roof started to collapse. They all ran. Aliana clung tightly to her papa, watching the demonic hole crumble in on itself.

Her father set her down and checked for injuries. Too shocked to speak, she stared at the other man who'd helped to save her. She recognized him instantly.

"Merlin?"

She shot up in bed, gasping in the clean air.

"Thank Oberon! I've been trying to wake you!" Dagg exclaimed. "Are you all right? You were tossing and moaning."

"Merlin," she said, clearing her dry throat. "I need to talk to him — now!" She threw off the covers, stumbling out of the cushy bed.

"I can hear him and Lancelot in the kitchen with the king," Dagg said, opening the door to reveal Galahad with his hand raised to knock.

"What's going on? I heard raised voices." His deep blue eyes searched Aliana's.

"Come on," she said, dashing down the stairs, the two guys right behind her. She burst through the kitchen doors.

"What are you doing awake?" Lancelot asked.

But Aliana ignored him. "What was in that chamber?" she demanded of Merlin, her eyes boring into his.

"Which one?" the wizard asked softly. His face held traces of the dark intimidation that she remembered from her dream.

"You know which one! You were there when I got trapped as a child. You helped my father get me out of that horrible place."

"I was wondering how long it would take you to remember." His eyes darkened, and he smiled, but there was no humor in the gesture.

"Stow the mysterious veneer, Merlin!" Aliana shouted. "What or *who* was in that darkness?"

"Merlin?" Arthur looked between the two of them. "What is she talking about?"

Merlin hesitated. "That chamber held a gateway. One of a few points on the realm's magical grid where a gate can be opened to another realm." Merlin lips pulled into a tight frown. "That particular point was a direct gateway to the pocket dimension I trapped Mordrid in centuries ago."

"What?" Lancelot and Arthur cried, jumping from their stools. "Explain all of this," Arthur ordered Merlin and Aliana.

"We need to get the others up," Aliana told them. "It gets worse."

Dagg flew from the kitchen to wake the others, and Galahad crowded in close, as if to protect her. "How?"

"I think Mordrid was at the gallery party," she said, remembering the creepy stranger's near black eyes and cold, terrifying touch. "I think he was that guy who cornered me after I met Merlin."

17

Arthur knows — so does Merlin. They know there is more than what I told the others. It's so hard to explain the centuries, how they've changed me. I don't think even I had realized how much I've changed since I left. Can I still be the man I once was? I can't dwell on that doubt. I need to be sure the Destined One does all she needs to do in order to end our curse. If only she'd focus on this quest instead of on coming between Arthur and Galahad.

Lancelot

Everyone stood in tense silence as Dagg returned with Owen and Wade. The men were in different states of partial dress and sleepy awareness, and all eyes were fixed on Aliana. The scene would have been more distracting if she hadn't been wound so tight.

"What do you mean you think Mordrid was at the party?" Lancelot asked.

"Exactly what I said." She plopped down at the large kitchen table.

After exchanging looks, the others followed suit, with Galahad and Arthur taking up either side of her.

"Merlin, you did know my father. I remember you now." She turned her attention to the others to explain. "He accompanied my father on a dig in the eastern part of England. I had wandered off when the ground beneath me crumbled and dumped me into a hidden chamber. I was trapped and there was some kind of power…a monster trying to break free. My dad told me I had been down there for an hour, and during that whole time, that *essence* kept touching me. It wasn't until my dad found me that it started to retreat. Merlin was there too."

"Yes," the wizard confirmed. "I purposely kept your father from that part of the ruin, hoping to keep the chamber hidden, but then you fell in." Merlin ran a hand through his tidy locks, the first show of frustration she'd seen from him.

"I didn't put it all together until now," Aliana said, "but after we left Titania, I had a dream about your last battle with Mordrid. It was like I was there, and I *felt* that same dark power I'd felt in the chamber."

"But what makes you think it was Mordrid? Why do you think he was at the party?" Owen interrupted.

"Because that chamber she fell into is the grid point connecting directly to Mordrid's prison," Merlin explained again. "That darkness she felt was him trying to break free. When we got there and I felt his power, I pushed him back with my own magic and resealed the gate."

"I think it was more than that." Aliana twisted her hands together under the table. "When I had that dream about the battle, Mordrid saw me. His eyes focused on me and he somehow…realized I was there."

"And the party?" Galahad asked, his voice tight with leashed frustration.

"The guy who tried to dance with me touched me, and I felt that same power. His eyes were that same almost black color from the dream." She closed her eyes, not wanting to remember.

"So he has escaped," Arthur said to Merlin.

"Yes, but only recently." Merlin's jaw clenched tight. "I checked on the grid point not a day before Aliana awoke you."

"It can't be a coincidence," Lancelot said, his eyes far off. "The day Aliana brings Arthur back, Mordrid escapes."

"That worries me too," Merlin said. "But he'll be weak. It would explain why the black knights were so easily defeated in the woods. His power was drained after the last battle, and he's been cut off from his sources of magic for many centuries."

"You still need to tell us what happened to you after you left Avalon, Merlin," Aliana sternly reminded him.

The Druid sighed. "After I left, I spent years searching for Morgana, but she was always one step ahead of me. I traveled most of Europe and through most of the other realms but I never found *her*, just traces of her magic."

"Other realms?" Aliana, Wade, and Owen asked.

"There are seven realms of existence here on Earth: the mortal realm, Avalon, Isle of the Blessed, Olympus, Atlantis, Tir Na Nog, and the Underworld," Dagg explained.

"Horse honkey!" The words slipped involuntarily from Aliana's lips.

"Not at all, but a colorful choice of words," Dagg said.

Merlin cleared his throat. "I have already told Arthur, but like Lancelot, I was banished from Titania's realms—Avalon and the Isle of the Blessed. However, unlike Lancelot, I am unable to die. I've had to use my powers over the years to keep myself from aging, but it takes more and more power each time I restore my youth."

"That's rough, mate," Owen said with a wince.

Aliana agreed with her cousin but felt unsatisfied with Merlin's story, like it had been missing a detail—much like she'd felt about Lancelot's. She glanced over at Arthur then Galahad. Both of them seemed satisfied with the explanations, so why did she still have doubts?

"So, how do we find Mordrid? Will he be able to find Morgana?" Percy spoke for the first time since waking.

"I imagine she's already found him," Merlin said softly. "Several times I found traces of her magic near Mordrid's prison."

"Then she is going to help him regain his powers." Galahad shoved back from his seat, pacing behind Aliana's chair. "We need to find both of them before they get too powerful."

"Here's another question," Aliana said, looking away from her worried knight. "Mordrid's goal is to gain dominion over all the realms, right? So *how* exactly does he plan to do this?"

Dagg sighed, his ageless voice strained. "Every fifteen hundred years the planets form two very unique alignments. In the first, all the outer planets align with Earth, pointing to a certain point on Earth's magical grid. That grid point's power will be increased a thousandfold, and anyone strong enough can harness the power. Then, twelve hours later, Mercury, Venus, and the moon will join in alignment with the sun, causing a complete solar eclipse. The gates to all seven realms will open wide until the planets pass out of alignment."

Aliana took in the expressions of utter shock and fear on everyone's faces.

"So when those gates open, Mordrid could send his armies through and conquer the other realms." Arthur sat back in his chair.

"With the power gained from the first alignment, his magic would be too strong for any army to stand against. He'd be utterly invincible." Merlin's smooth voice was somber.

"An apocalypse," Aliana breathed, her chest tight, her heart beating loudly in her ears. "When will these alignments happen?"

"On the first full moon after the spring equinox, just before Beltane," Merlin said softly. "We have ten months."

"How do we stop them?" Galahad gripped the back of Aliana's chair, his shoulders squared like he was ready to fight right now.

"We train," Arthur said, rising from his chair. "And we find Sir Leyon. Then, like the prophecy says, we find Excalibur and the Grail of Power."

"And," Merlin added, coming to stand next to the king, "Lord Daggerhorne and I will train Aliana to use her magic. She will need to have full control of her powers to help defeat Mordrid."

"Now wait just a darn minute!" Wade jumped up. "What exactly are you expecting Lia to do? No way is she going to face a power crazy sorcerer!"

"Wade..." Aliana tried to calm her friend, but no one was listening to her.

"It's her destiny to face him with King Arthur and *all* the Knights of the Round Table by her side to defend her," Merlin shot back, his fists balled against the table as he stared down a livid Wade.

"Who are you to decide her destiny and say what she's supposed to do?" Owen growled, standing shoulder to shoulder with Wade.

"Guys, stop!" Aliana said, trying to stand, but Galahad's large hand on her shoulder held her in her seat.

"Enough!" Galahad shouted. "The prophecy doesn't say *what* role Aliana will play in the final battle. I suggest we worry about it when we have a better idea of what is coming."

Aliana looked up. His jaw was set and his amazing blue eyes were tight.

"Galahad is right," Arthur said, drawing all gazes back to him. "For now we need to focus on training and on finding Sir Leyon. Aliana needs to be trained to defend herself with her magic." Wade opened his mouth again but Arthur cut him off. "No matter what her role will be, it would be foolish and deadly for her to not be prepared."

Wade and Owen regarded her then nodded.

"I can help Aliana with a summoning spell to bring Leyon to us," Merlin said, back in know-it-all-Druid mode. "I would also like to restore your memories of your lives in Camelot. It would do all of us good for Owaine, Percival, and Gawain to have their original fighting skills in addition to whatever they know now." The three knights glanced at each other, agreeing.

"Then I can see no better time to do it." Merlin led them out to a sprawling patio that opened to a large garden bordered by forest. "Kneel," he instructed, and Owen, Percy, and Wade complied. The wizard held his hands out and they started to glow. Unlike Titania's magic, Merlin's looked like bright rays of golden sunlight. Those rays cut toward Aliana's friends, violently snapping their heads back.

She moved to stop Merlin, but Galahad grabbed her. "They're all right," he whispered into her ear, pulling her back.

The light faded after an intense, endless moment. All three guys fell forward, barely catching themselves. Wade sat up, rubbing his forehead with his palm like he was fighting a brain freeze. Owen scrubbed his hands over his face, taking deep breaths, while Percy shook his head as if trying to clear a fog.

"Are you guys all right?" Aliana pulled away from Galahad.

"What a rush!" Wade said, his hazel eyes finding Arthur's. He grinned brightly, stepping past her. "My king."

Wade bowed to Arthur, and Percy and Owen followed suit. Arthur couldn't have looked happier as he hugged each of them. "It is good to have all of you back again." He laughed. "Just one more and the Round Table will be complete again." Merlin, Lancelot, and Galahad all gathered around their friends.

Aliana hugged Dagg close while standing off to the side, wishing she didn't feel like an outsider. She couldn't help thinking that she was going to be left behind by her best friend and cousin now that they had their memories and their king. Now they were only going to see her as the damned *key* to their prophecy. She had just possibly lost two of the only people in the world who really cared for her.

"So what do you think, Lia?" Wade asked, reaching out for her to join them and drawing her close to his side. Just like that, her doubts vanished. She smiled, grateful that her self-pity moment seemed to have been just that—a moment. How could she have thought Wade would abandon her?

"I can honestly say I never thought anything like this would happen," she said, laughing.

"I suggest we all get changed into appropriate attire for training," Merlin said, his eyes drifting over Aliana's pajama shorts, thin top, and bare feet. Several chuckles were met by her glare.

With a harrumph, Aliana marched back inside and up to her room. Door firmly shut, she vented to her Dragon. "Why did he have to be an ass about my clothes? Percy, Wade, and Lancelot didn't even have on *shirts* for crying out loud."

"You're blushing, Aliana," Dagg pointed out almost gleefully.

Pursing her lips, she rummaged through her bags, grabbing a pair of hot pink jeans and an old Harry Potter shirt. The front read "Believe In Magic, Muggles" with a picture of Harry's wand. Aliana laughed.

Slipping on a pair of flip-flops, she found the knights gathered on the patio. They'd all changed into jeans. Merlin frowned at her shirt while Wade, Percy, Owen, and even Lancelot burst out laughing.

"I don't understand," Arthur said.

"We need to have a *Harry Potter* marathon soon." She smiled wickedly. "I think you'd love it!"

Nodding, but still looking mildly confused, Arthur led his men out to the open space of the backyard. Aliana watched as the warriors spread out and attached sword belts around their waists.

"Where did Wade and Owen get swords?" she asked Merlin.

"I've collected many things for them over the centuries. I've even created identities for each of the knights, complete with bank accounts and properties in their false names."

Aliana's brows scrunched together, questioning him.

"I didn't know how we would all come together," Merlin said. "I decided that being prepared for any circumstance was the best thing for all of us."

Merlin led her away from the guys and into a small, cream-colored room. The antique furniture was pushed against the walls, leaving an open space in the middle. The room would have been almost suffocating if not for the large bay window that showed the backyard, where she could see the guys practicing.

"We will train in here," Merlin said. "But before we start testing your powers, I need to teach you how magic works." They sat down on the soft, beige carpet.

Wanting to nettle the Druid and push aside some of her own anxiety, she asked, "Will I be learning potions and spells?" Merlin's eye twitched, and she had to bite back her laughter as he started her lesson.

"The first thing you need to know is that magic does not work the same for everyone. Potions and spells are used only by those not born to magic."

"So anyone can do magic?"

"Not exactly. A normal person would need to have a true spell and be connected to a point on the magic grid. If they have those things, then yes, they could do magic, but it would be weak, nothing compared to even a simple bit of magic that you or I can do."

"So I was born to magic?" Aliana said.

"Yes. Your magical ability means that one of your parents had to have had magic in their blood."

She looked away, trying to absorb this new bit of news about her birth parents. "What would happen if a normal person tried to get the power that Mordrid is after?"

"It would kill them," he said matter-of-factly. "Even Mordrid will need a conduit, an object to contain the power."

Aliana repressed a shudder, gazing outside again. Seeing the knights practicing with their swords made her feel safer. "So how does magic work for those born to it?" she asked, excited and terrified at the same time. Arthur, Camelot, and his men had been nothing like what she'd imagined all her life, so it was safe to assume magic would also be different.

"We draw power from within ourselves, and sometimes from the grid points and elements, if necessary." Merlin opened his hands, and his eyes closed in concentration. A large, almost holographic map of the world appeared between them. Amazed, Aliana watched as different colored stars blazed to life across the slowly rotating globe. Some were brighter than others.

"What do you see?" Merlin asked.

"Hundreds of lights. Some of them are closer together than others." She frowned, looking harder. "And there are thin, white lines that connect certain dots, dots of the same color."

"Excellent! Those connected points are places that someone can use to enter into a certain realm. Each shade corresponds to one realm."

"And the ones that aren't connected?" she asked, trying to count but losing track after the first thirty.

"Places to draw power, and as you can see, there are hundreds all over the world."

"And anyone born to magic can use them?"

"Only if they know how to find one," Merlin added. "For those who are trained, it's one of the first things they are taught."

Aliana leaned forward, resting her arms on her knees. "How do you find a portal?"

"Portals have an energy signature unique to the realm it connects to. We can use our magic like a homing device to find the signature."

Aliana's eyes drifted over the holographic map.

"Once you've been exposed to the signatures of the different realms, you can learn how to separate and identify them."

Aliana lifted her gaze to his face. "So what are the copper-colored ones near us here in London?"

"Those are gates to Avalon. Gates don't necessarily need to be in the same area. After all, the other realms are large places, worlds unto themselves."

"So you're going to show me how to find these today?"

Merlin shook his head, letting the map fade away. "No, first you need to understand more about how magic functions, and I want to test how strong your powers are."

"Well, teach away."

Merlin and Dagg regarded one another, shaking their heads. "We shape the power inside of us to do our will," Merlin said. "We can heal, move objects, control the elements, and so on. But because the magic comes from ourselves, we have to be careful. The stronger the magic, the greater the cost."

"Like when I was so weak after awakening Arthur?"

"Exactly. But to do magic that strong with less of a cost, you can draw on other powers—such as the elements or a grid point. You just have to form a connection."

Aliana nodded, letting the information soak in. Her eyes flicked out to the guys again. They had moved on to hand-to-hand combat.

"You said earlier that Titania cut you off from Avalon's magic. What did you mean?" she asked, turning back to the Druid.

"Clever girl," he said softly. "I'm known as one of the strongest Druids because I have the rare ability to tap into the magic...core, if you will, of an entire realm. My connection was especially strong with Avalon because my father was of there, and when my mother gave birth, I was blessed with his connection to the realm. My powers were strong enough to rival even Queen Titania's, but when I left Arthur's guard, she cut me off entirely from the connection." Bitterness colored his words.

"I'm sorry."

Merlin shook off her sympathy with a tight smile. "I knew her punishment for leaving would be harsh. As I was saying, you need to feel the magic so you can shape it."

Merlin and Dagg spent the next few hours explaining and demonstrating how to do simple magic. Aliana focused, but her eyes would stray to the guys every now and then. More specifically to Galahad. He and Lancelot were currently facing off against each other. Sweat rolled down their bare chests and shoulders, glistening in the early summer sun.

Aliana thought of how she'd felt after they'd left Arthur's hollow. She hated feeling that powerless, that weak. Everyone said it was crazy powerful magic that she'd used to wake Arthur, so the exhaustion made sense, but she wondered how draining *average* magic would be. She feared being that weak again and worried that if she did something wrong with her magic, she could put the others in danger. The warriors training just beyond the window were sure to return to being the elite fighting brotherhood they'd been in the days of Camelot, and she'd be the twenty-first century magical neophyte following them around. She didn't want that. She wanted them to see her as an equal, not just the key to destroying Mordrid and giving them their lives back. *How is that going to work anyway? Will they just go back to the past or will Camelot be reborn somehow with Arthur on the throne?*

The blinds fell with a loud snap.

"Pay attention, Aliana. What was the last thing I said?" Merlin glowered at her.

"Sorry." She ducked her head, her face blazing with embarrassment, feeling like an eight-year-old girl getting scolded by the teacher.

"I think it's time we took a break," Dagg spoke up. "We can test her strength after we have some lunch."

"Can I get some fresh air first?" she asked, and when Merlin nodded, she rose to her feet, grateful to stretch her tight muscles as she made her way out to the practice area.

"So, how are things going?" she asked Wade, coming to stand next to him as he waited on the sidelines. Galahad currently circled Arthur and Lancelot.

"It's been interesting," Wade said faintly. "Having these memories is like seeing flashes of a movie in my head. They don't even seem real, but fighting with a sword feels like second nature now. I don't need to think about it like I used to."

"You've always been amazing with weapons," Aliana pointed out.

"Yeah, but I was never in a life or death situation before." Wade shook his head, dropping his gaze to the ground. "I have memories of killing people, men in battle and…" Wade gulped. "Maybe I need time to let these memories settle, but I kinda feel like two different people. There's me—but then there's also him." He looked up at her, anguish and doubt in his hazel eyes. "At least Lacy isn't part of this. I wondered if my memories would reveal her in my past at all, but they don't."

Aliana took his hand as Arthur and Lancelot charged Galahad. He slammed Lancelot to the ground while Arthur managed to wrap an arm around his neck, trying to throw him off balance. He succeeded, bearing Galahad down to one knee, but the knight pried Arthur's arm away, twisting it behind the king's back. Lancelot kicked out a foot, knocking Galahad to the ground and freeing Arthur to pin him.

Wade cleared his throat, shaking away his raw emotions. "So, how is *your* training going?" He glanced at the stone-faced Druid, who had also come outside and now watched the match with a calculating gaze. The three men on the field got to their feet, smiling.

"Annoying and hard to focus on," she mumbled. "I tried, but I kept getting distracted."

"I bet you did." Wade laughed low. "I can't imagine Grumpy over there taking it too well."

"Understatement," she said, rolling her eyes.

"Are you three done for today?"

"He wants to test my powers next. It's silly really, I don't even understand how I used magic in Avalon!" She ran a hand through her hair.

"You'll figure it out, Lia," Wade assured her, wrapping an arm around her. "You always do."

Fighting a smile, she elbowed him lightly. "Sweet talker."

"Darn straight. Now watch me beat the arrogance out of Lancelot." Wade picked up his sword, squaring off against the raven-haired knight.

"How are you?" Galahad asked, taking Wade's spot as he wiped a towel over his sweaty face and body.

"Good, I guess," she mumbled as she tried not to ogle him. "How about you?"

"Better now," he answered, smiling down at her.

Aliana dropped her gaze, trying to hide her smile. She looked up at the sound of a sword hitting the ground. Wade flipped Lancelot over his shoulder, fist raised to strike as he pinned Lancelot. Aliana cheered for her friend as he helped Lancelot to his feet.

"Sabine has laid out lunch in the kitchen," Merlin announced.

"Who is Sabine?" Galahad asked, pulling on his shirt.

"She is one of the Pixies who helps me with my home."

"Still not making sense, mate," Owen said, following them through the door.

"Several decades ago, I saved her and several of her sisters from the Sidhe while I was in Olympus. By their law, they owed me their lives, so they decided to serve me here in my home. They have a small dwelling nearby, on the edge of the forest."

"They're servants? Pixies?" Aliana asked, incredulous.

"By their own choice," Merlin said sternly.

The kitchen counter was covered with a spread of meats, vegetables, fruits, steaming bread, and various butters and dressings. Arthur filled his plate, and the others followed right behind their king.

Aliana only took a little bit of food. She was too anxious to eat. "Where is Sabine now?" She leaned against the counter, taking a bite of her honey-buttered roll. The soft, savory delight practically melted in her mouth.

"She and her sisters are probably at their houses," Merlin answered, taking a large bite of his roast beef sandwich.

"I'd like to thank her at some point," Aliana said, hoping she'd get a chance to meet a Pixie.

"Aliana, come sit," Galahad said, nodding to the empty chair between him and Arthur.

"Leave it, Galahad," Wade told him. "She's got a thing about eating at counters instead of sitting down like a civilized human being."

"Shut it, smart ass," she said, throwing a grape at him. Just to prove him wrong, she walked over and plunked down in the seat, her plate next to Dagg's overflowing one.

Percy and Owen got into a heated conversation about which weapon would be better for certain situations. Lancelot, Merlin, and Arthur talked over different strategies, and Wade and Galahad had a hushed conversation. She was the only one left out, but it gave her a chance to study them all closer. The men's friendships were returning. Wade and Owen were the greatest proof of that. They had both been struggling just this morning, now they actively engaged the others. Aliana shoved a piece of fruit into her mouth, trying not to feel left out when she heard Merlin whisper a comment about a key.

Great. He still only sees me as their key. It wasn't like they had bonded over their training that morning, but she'd hoped he would have thawed to her just a little.

After everyone had eaten, the guys retreated back outside under the gray clouds that threatened to pour down rain. Aliana scraped the food into the trash, stacking all the plates and stalling her return to her training.

"We need to get back to your lessons, Aliana. Sabine will finish cleaning," Merlin told her, leaning against the doorway with his arms crossed over his chest.

Her stomach flipped as she followed him and Dagg back to the white room.

18

Aliana's magic is frustrating, just like trying to teach her when she won't focus on anything other than the knights. I worry Lancelot maybe right — there's something strange between her, Arthur, and Galahad. I need to find out more about this before she becomes a distraction to them, like Morgana was for me. No, I can't think about that woman. Loving her has already cost me too much.
Merlin

"Take my hands," Merlin said, holding them out to Aliana. He had small hands, not at all like Galahad's or Arthur's. "I need to maintain a physical connection to properly assess your abilities."

Biting the inside of her cheek, she placed her clammy hands lightly in his. Merlin gripped them hard.

"Relax," Dagg said from his perch on the nearest chair. "Breathe and focus on the magic you used to awaken the king. Remember how it felt."

Closing her eyes, she recalled the explosive energy. She thought about how it had grown as she freed Galahad and passed each of the challenges. She remembered the searing pain as it tried to escape when she crossed the bridge, all of it so clear in her mind.

The words she'd said and her overwhelming feelings for Arthur returned. She saw herself in the cave, the glowing light spilling from her mouth to Arthur's before her lips touched his. She watched a barely-there golden web wrap around them, sealing them together everywhere they touched.

"Stop!" Her heart raced as she struggled to pull away from the memory, not wanting Merlin to witness such a private moment. But then she could feel Arthur's lips against hers again, the gentle touch of his hand. She could see the happiness in his golden brown eyes as he whispered to her. *"It is you."*

"Get out!" she cried, pushing as hard as she could against Merlin's presence. Another spark leaped to life in her chest. It rose like an angry spirit, forcing Merlin's connection to snap.

Gasping for air, she yanked her hands from his. Her shaky legs buckled, sending her to the carpeted floor. Looking down at her shaking hand, she saw faint stars of pink fading away, taking more of her energy with them.

"Unusual," Merlin said to himself, stroking his chin.

Aliana smacked away his hands when he tried to help her stand. "Don't touch me! What were you doing?"

"What's going on?" Galahad's voice boomed. The door swung open with a surprising strength. The knight rushed to Aliana's side at his super speed. Arthur and Wade followed while the others peered in from the hall.

"Sire," Merlin said as Arthur lowered himself next to Aliana.

"Are you hurt, Aliana?" the king asked, tucking a few strands of hair behind her ear.

"I was trying to gauge her abilities." Merlin studied Arthur, Galahad, and Aliana. "I did not realize that she doesn't have even the most basic of shields. I saw more than just her magic."

"Why was she shouting?" Galahad asked, calmer now.

"I wanted him out of my head." She clenched her jaw. Her memories and feelings were hers. Beyond embarrassed, she pulled herself to her feet, wanting nothing more than to escape all the eyes watching her.

"She used a small bit of her magic to push me out, but it seems to have had a draining effect. I have never seen such a weak spell affect anyone like this before." Merlin frowned.

Dagg's warm body circled around Aliana's shoulders, relaxing her in moments. She smiled, feeling her strength returning.

"You are better now?" Galahad asked, his eyes finding hers.

"Why did such a small spell drain her so much?" Lancelot asked. He sounded almost concerned for her.

"I do not know yet. I'll need to have her try another spell."

"Aliana?" Arthur asked, his body curving closer to hers, protecting her from having to do something she might not want to do.

"I'm okay. We need to figure this out." She met Arthur's gaze, then Galahad's, trying to reassure them that she was okay to continue. Her eyes zeroed in on Merlin's icy gaze. "But my memories and my *thoughts* are off limits!"

"Fair enough," he agreed. Reluctantly, all the others filed out of the room, leaving Aliana alone with her Dragon and Merlin.

"Aliana, I'd like you to try summoning a small bit of magic to your hands." Merlin opened his palm and a gold ball of rays blazed to life upon it. "Find your magic inside you and bring it to your hand."

Still a bit leery, she repeated his actions, but nothing happened. She tried again, but no magic came to life.

"Concentrate, Aliana," Dagg told her, jumping from his perch to hover next to Merlin. "Find the magic inside again. Imagine just a small flicker in your hands."

She cupped her hands, imagining the pink lights from days ago. Warmth trickled into her palms. Opening one eye, she gasped, amazed at the small ball of pink sparks jumping in her hands.

"Dagg!" she cried. "I did it!" She laughed, her smile bright as the sun.

"A nice first step, Aliana, but don't lose focus," the Dragon warned.

"Try to guide it around the room," Merlin instructed.

She imagined the sparks moving in loops around Dagg, and they leaped to do as she wished. "So cool! I can't wait to photograph this." Next, she imagined them zooming off the walls before bringing them back.

"Well done!" Merlin praised her. "How do you feel?"

"Fine. I don't get why I was so weak a few minutes ago."

Merlin nodded, his fingers rubbing across his chin again.

Aliana's insecurities nagged at her. What if Merlin couldn't figure out the problem with her magic? She could put everyone in danger if she wasn't able to use it to defend them.

"We will figure it out," he assured her, like he could still read her feelings.

"Pardon me." A small, high-pitched voice interrupted them. A girl no more than two feet tall was half hidden by the door.

"Estrelle, come in. How are you?" Merlin smiled kindly at the small girl, surprising Aliana with his tenderness.

The redhead was dressed in a soft, brown, dress-like top and a pair of green bell pants. On her back was a pair of wings like a dragonfly's, shimmering with color as the light hit them. "I'm sorry to interrupt. Sabine says dinner will be ready soon. She wanted to know whether your guests would prefer wine or ale tonight."

"Ale." Merlin motioned her closer. He towered over her tiny frame. "Estrelle, allow me to introduce Aliana Fagan."

"The Destined One." The Pixie smiled and curtsied.

"Nice to meet you." Aliana held out her hand to the Pixie. After a slight nod from Merlin, the Pixie took her hand.

"I will let Sabine know your choice." The Pixie peeked shyly at Aliana and added, "It will be an honor to serve the Destined One. If you need anything, my sisters and I would be more than happy to help." She curtsied again. Her wings fluttered, lifting her in the air as she zoomed out of the room.

"Well, that was unexpected," Aliana said, her eyes still on the door. "But so totally cool! Do you think she would mind being a model for me?"

Merlin chuckled. "Estrelle is very shy, but her sisters, I'm sure, would love to." The Druid cleared his throat. "Before we go to dinner, I want you to try the summoning spell for Sir Leyon."

"What do I do?"

"You said you dreamed of us. You saw all of us as we were, correct?"

Aliana nodded.

"Can you remember what Leyon looked like?"

She shook her head. "I didn't really see everyone in clear detail. It's more like I saw certain features, bits of what you all looked like, but not the full picture. But I think he had really short, blond hair and was kind of tall."

"Yes, that's him. For the spell to work, you need to see him and draw him to you."

Aliana frowned. "Isn't that manipulating a person's free will? What if he doesn't want to be a part of all this?"

Merlin studied her carefully. "You have heard the others say they believed a part of their lives had been missing. Leyon could be feeling that loss too. Wouldn't it be cruel to leave him missing a part of himself?"

"Okay," she whispered. Pushing her doubts aside, she tried to remember more details of the dream. She saw the missing knight again trying to avenge Owen, the first of Arthur's men to have fallen. Leyon was less than six feet tall with dove gray eyes. He was amazing to watch in a fight. All of them were.

"I see him," she said, hating that she was going to have to watch him die again.

"Focus on him until everything else falls away," Dagg instructed, resting his small claw on her hand.

She could feel the magic sparks rushing to life as she paused the vision, blurring out everyone but Leyon. The blurriness cleared, revealing a historic-looking street filled with shops and cafes. She spotted Leyon sitting in the window of a used bookstore, working on his laptop.

"Leyon," she murmured, approaching the shop.

His head snapped up, his eyes searching.

"Leyon?" she asked, louder this time.

"Who's there?" His voice was lightly tinted with a Scottish brogue.

"I'm Aliana Fagan." His eyes met hers through the shop window. "We need you. The Knights of the Round Table won't be whole again till you join them. If you want to," she added.

She conjured a picture of all the guys in the clear shop window, hoping he would see them and understand. The magic inside her grew hotter and her energy quickly started draining away.

"Hurry!" She lost the vision. Aliana rubbed her temples, hoping to soothe the headache building there.

"What did you see?" Merlin kneeled next to her, offering a glass of water.

"I saw him, but I have no idea where he was," she said after gulping down half the glass.

"Did he hear you?"

"Yeah, I tried to show him who y'all are, but I started to feel weak and I lost the connection."

"But he heard you. That's the important part. You've established the connection. The magic will do the rest." Merlin watched her carefully, as if searching for any side effects of the magic. "Do you have enough strength to stand?"

Nodding, she got to her feet.

"The others are waiting on us for dinner," Merlin said.

"Do you mind if I skip it? I'm super tired and I really just want to take a bath."

"Are you sure, Aliana?" Dagg asked, crawling across her shoulders.

"Positive. I'm just really tired. I'll come down later and get some food," she promised. But right now her insides felt like they were twirling, and she knew she wouldn't be able to eat anything.

"I will have one of the Pixies bring you a plate." Merlin nodded to her, leaving for the kitchen. Hesitantly, Dagg followed him.

Trudging up the stairs, Aliana pushed open her door, shocked when a white blond Pixie flew out of her bathroom.

"Hi!" the little Pixie said vibrantly. She had on a bright pink dress and black, lacy slippers. Her wings buzzed behind her with a purple hue. "I'm Flora."

"I'm Aliana." She couldn't help smiling at the Pixie's lively face.

"Oh, I know. Stella told us all about you! I heard you were coming up, and I thought you might want a bath, so I prepared it for you." The Pixie flew up to Aliana, leaning in as if to tell her a secret. "Don't tell the others, but I added a bit of flower root and Pixie dust to help rejuvenate you."

"No one will hear it from me," Aliana promised. "But why is it a secret?"

"Pixie flowers are rare and hard to harvest into Pixie dust. We try to only use it when we have to."

"Oh, I see. Thank you for your kindness, then."

"Think nothing of it." The Pixie looked down at Aliana's shirt and busted out laughing. "I bet you drove Merlin crazy with that all day! He hates Harry Potter."

"I didn't expect you to know pop culture," Aliana said, kicking off her shoes.

"Are you kidding? This is the twenty-first century! Who isn't connected?" Aliana laughed at Flora's duh-you-idiot expression. "Besides, I like to dress in the latest fashions. Sometimes I can even convince the others to wear the clothes I make."

"Well, I think you have great taste. Would you like to model for me sometime?"

The girl squealed in delight. "I've always wanted to be a model!"

"Then it's a date, but first I should get in there before the water gets cold."

"Of course. I'll make you a plate for dinner." The Pixie fled and the door closed behind her.

"Unbelievable," Aliana laughed, laying her clothes on the bench next to a fluffy white robe. She sank into the tub. The water tingled, tickling her skin. She inhaled the fresh floral scent and something else she couldn't describe. It kind of smelled like Deidre's valley, but not quite the same.

She thought about how much everything in her life had changed in only a matter of days. A small part of her still thought this could all be a dream, but she also knew she couldn't have dreamed up all of this. She drifted off to sleep, not waking until Flora knocked on the side of the tub.

"Sorry to wake you, but I didn't think you wanted to spend the night in there." Flora grinned like she had a secret, turning her back as Aliana got out of the tub and wrapped herself in the soft robe.

"Whatever is in that Pixie dust of yours is amazing! I feel better than I have in weeks."

"I can bring you a small bottle if you want," Flora offered.

"Thanks, but I don't want you getting into trouble, Flora."

The Pixie shrugged. "Just let me know if you want some more. I can bring you a pinch or two."

"What time is it?" Aliana asked, slipping on fresh clothes.

"It's almost nine. You've been asleep for almost two hours." Aliana looked at Flora unbelievingly. "Don't worry. Your food is being heated for you right now. I should also tell you the really tall, hot guy, Galahad, has been asking about you, like, every ten minutes."

Aliana flushed bright pink.

The Pixie giggled in delight. "I love having a mortal girl around!" She zoomed out of the room, giggling the whole way.

Aliana finished dressing and made her way to the kitchen, waving at Percy, Lancelot, Owen, and Wade when she passed the media room. Her stomach growled loudly as she walked into the kitchen, and she salivated at the smell of hot chicken and a distinct wintery scent. Galahad sat at the counter next to a plate piled with Parmesan-crusted chicken and vegetable risotto.

"Hey." Her green eyes met his and she thought of the last time they'd been alone in a kitchen.

"Are you feeling better?" he asked as she took a seat, passing a glass of rose-colored wine to her.

"I am. I didn't realize how much magic drains a person." She took a bite of the juicy chicken and a sip of the wine, surprised by its sweet taste. "Wow, that tasted just like fruit punch!"

"What is fruit punch?" Galahad asked.

"It's just a blend of fruit juices. I'll see if Merlin can get you some."

"I'd like that," he said, taking a drink of ale from his pint.

Taking another bite of risotto, Aliana wondered if Galahad would bring up their kiss, half dreading the idea of talking about it. But as she finished her dinner, he only asked questions about modern devices. Apparently Wade had tried to show him how to use a cell phone. Aliana tried to hide her laugh when he told her about almost crushing it. But why didn't he ask her about the kiss? Was he regretting it, like he had when he'd kissed her for the first time to free her from the Sidhe? Disappointment soared in her chest, and a very small part of her was starting to regret the mind-blowing kiss. *Both* of them.

"Good. You're here."

The pair turned to see Dagg and Wade enter the kitchen. Dagg jumped from the knight's shoulder to the counter.

"You look better," the Dragon said, sniffing at the small bit of risotto still on Aliana's plate.

"Thanks?"

"What I think he means is, we're glad to see you looking more like yourself again." Wade wrapped an arm around her shoulders in a half hug.

"Don't you dare!" Aliana warned Dagg when he tried to eat the last of her dinner. Pouting, he backed away.

"So what were you kids chatting about?" Wade asked, leaning against the counter.

"Galahad nearly breaking your phone," Aliana said, taking another sip of her wine. Out of the corner of her eye, she saw Galahad frown. "Don't worry," she said, patting his hand. "Wade has broken his phone so many times that people have started to refuse to give him a new one."

Galahad smiled at Wade's glare.

"Not nice, Aliana. The rest of us are going outside. Apparently the Pixies have set up a nighttime obstacle course for us. Care to make a wager on who wins?" Wade winked at Aliana.

"Sure, I bet on Galahad," she said and smiled at her best friend's look of disbelief.

"Then win I shall," Galahad vowed, standing.

"You're not so tough," Wade joked. "I'll take your bet, Lia. The usual wager?"

She nodded. "Have fun boys!"

"You are not joining us?" Galahad stopped in the doorway, glancing back at her.

She shook her head. "No, I need to ask Dagg a few questions and I have some stuff I need to get done." She smiled at him as she put her dishes in the sink and ran water over them.

"Come on, G," Wade said, pulling her knight toward the backyard.

"What do you want to know?" Dagg asked once they were alone.

"Why did the magic exhaust me?"

"I have a suspicion, but until we test you further, I will keep my theories to myself."

"Come on, Dagg!" *Why is he holding out on me?*

"The truth is, you are nothing like either of us have ever seen before. I am not sure how to compare you to others."

"How am I different?"

"The way your powers react to your emotions, how you described the summoning spell and waking King Arthur, and your lack of natural shields. It's all unheard of." Dagg frowned. "You were born to complete a purpose, and that apparently has changed much in your handling of magic."

"So, I'm a freak." She looked away, not wanting Dagg to see her misery. Why was she always being told she wasn't like everyone else?

"Our bond allows me to feel your emotions, Aliana," Dagg reminded her a bit reluctantly.

Aliana couldn't help but notice that he didn't correct her for calling herself a freak.

"You do not wish for me to know them, but they are there for me to feel."

"Well, stop peeking then!" Her anger flared. "What I feel is my business, not yours or Merlin's or anyone else's!" She moved to leave the kitchen, but Dagg flew into her escape path.

"Merlin and I both agree that you need to learn how to create shields in tomorrow's lessons. That will solve many problems."

"Great, now get out of my way. I still have to process all the pictures I took in Avalon." She side-stepped the Dragon and fled to her room, grateful that he didn't try to follow her.

She threw herself onto her bed, opening her laptop and pulling up her photos of Avalon. But she couldn't focus as she scrolled through. With a frustrated growl, she flipped onto her back, throwing a pillow over face. Her temper was starting to fade, but the hurt remained. "Why can't a single one of them see me as more than their stupid Destined One?" She threw the pillow at the window with a huff.

Sulking wasn't going to do her any good, so she grabbed her iPhone and earbuds and decided to explore Merlin's home instead, thinking she needed the distraction. She wandered through the halls, studying the paintings and artifacts that lined the wood-paneled walls. Everything about the place screamed old English sophistication and money. She could almost imagine she was back in the fifteenth century as she wandered past the sitting room toward a wing of the house Merlin hadn't shown them. Most of the doors there were locked, but a light shined toward the end of the hall.

She peeked inside the lit room, surprised to see Arthur sitting on the floor, leaning against an antique couch. It was one of the few pieces of furniture in the nearly empty room. He rested his arm on his bent leg and stared out the floor-to-ceiling windows. The wall opposite him was covered in mirrors, making the room look like it was outside rather than inside.

"Arthur, are you okay?" She hesitated in the doorway.

His gaze twisted around to find hers, and he smiled, morphing his hard expression into a something much more striking. "Aliana, I did not expect to see you here. I was just thinking."

"I didn't mean to disturb you. I'll go." She turned to leave.

"No," he said quickly, causing her to turn back. "Your company is always welcome."

Biting back a smile, she closed the door, joining him against the couch. "I thought you would be out with the others."

"I was, but I wanted time to think."

"I can understand that." She set her iPhone down between them.

"Lancelot was showing me that yesterday, but what are those things?" He pointed to the earbuds.

"They let me listen to music without anyone else hearing it."

"Can you show me?"

She turned on her music and held the earbud up to his ear.

Arthur smiled brightly. "Outstanding," he said, nodding his head along with the Hunter Hayes song.

"Yeah, it is pretty cool." She smiled, shutting off the music. He handed her the earbuds. "Would you tell me about Camelot?"

"Camelot was the greatest kingdom in Albion," Arthur said, his eyes glittering like gold. "My father and grandfather built it from the scraps left behind when the Empire fled back to Rome. We were the envy of the other kingdoms. Our people had plentiful food, good homes, and bustling trade." He smiled, his gaze seeming to travel to the distant past.

"You miss it. I can't blame you."

"Yes, but I can't help thinking of all the lives lost because I failed." He glanced down, gripping his wrist. The twinkle in his eyes faded.

"Arthur, you can't think that! You couldn't have known what Mordrid had planned."

"I was king. My people's safety rested with me. It was my duty to protect them." His voice was firm and angry. His hand gripped his wrist so tightly that his knuckles turned white.

"Don't blame yourself," Aliana said softly, placing her hand on his. "Your people couldn't have asked for any more from their king. You served them honorably. And if it will help, think of defeating Mordrid this time as recompense and justice for your people and your kingdom."

His hand relaxed under hers as he let out a breath. "I hope that will be enough. I want to avenge my people."

19

I beat the others on the obstacle course, just like I promised Aliana I would. Dagg and I joked with Owen and Percy about their landing in the mud pit — it is good to laugh with them again, like we did in Camelot. At first it was difficult to reconcile my brothers with these new friends before me, but we are slowly rebuilding the bond we all shared once. I look around, hoping to see Aliana, but she's not here. Neither is Arthur.

Galahad

"So, were you married after you broke from Guinevere?" Aliana asked after a short silence.

"No. Not for lack of effort on my father's behalf." He laughed softly. "He was furious when I broke my engagement. Only my mother had been able to temper his wrath. But he made it his mission to find another union for me."

"Surely you had women who were interested in you." Aliana wasn't sure why she was pushing, but she wanted to know.

"Many, I'm afraid." He told her about a few of the noble women and princesses who had been paraded in front of him. Aliana laughed when he spoke of two ladies who had shredded each other's clothes in jealousy. One princess had even gone as far as to accuse another lady of theft just to get her away from Arthur.

"Wow, Arthur, you seem to have had some bad luck with women!" Aliana joked.

"How did Lancelot put it? I'm a glutton for punishment." Arthur gave a small chuckle as he looked out at the forest surrounding Merlin's home. "Every woman who came along wanted only my title and money. They didn't care for my people or me. Even the few who I tried to care for only managed to keep my attention for a couple days. I had watched Lancelot and Guinevere fall in love, as well as my other knights, but I was never free to find that same love."

For just a moment, Aliana caught a flash of sadness before it fell away, hidden behind the controlled mask he wore like a shield. But she caught the faint sound of his sigh. Gently, she laid her hand on his muscular arm, left bare by his T-shirt, and softly rubbed slow circles on his skin with her thumb. Though he'd been a sixth century warrior, only a few faded scars marred his skin. Aliana wondered about how they'd gotten there. Looking back up, she caught him staring at her hand.

His golden brown eyes lifted to meet her green ones, boring into them like he was trying to see into her very soul.

Embarrassed that she'd been caught staring, she glanced away, pulling her hand from his arm. But Arthur's hand quickly covered hers, holding it to him, and Aliana's eyes jumped back to his face, surprised. For several long moments they just gazed into each other's eyes.

Arthur finally broke the silence. "There are times when I feel there may have been someone in my life, but I have no memory of her. Just ghosts of a thought, a feeling of rightness and love, but I can't remember such a woman in my life," he whispered in a tortured voice.

"How could you feel what you do but not remember the woman who inspired those feelings?" Her voice was gentle and sad.

"I…when you awoke me in that cave…" He let out a hard breath and shook his head. "I do not know."

Aliana looked out the window at the dark forest. She could almost feel Arthur's frustration and loneliness. She remembered his comments about the sadness of the song they'd danced to at the party and understood how well he must have related to it.

He didn't deserve to have those feelings. She wanted to see him smile. "This is my favorite part of the day," she said. "During the summer, Papa would take me and my mother out to the beach behind our house, and we would have midnight picnics." Aliana smiled. Those memories were priceless for her. "One night we saw a pod of dolphins just off the shore, playing and leaping out of the water. I thought it was the most magical thing I'd ever seen. My papa told me the story of Atlantis and how dolphins were supposed to be one of the creatures guarding the gates to the sunken kingdom." She laughed, remembering how her mother nearly had a heart attack when Aliana started running toward the water to join the magical creatures. "My mother lectured me for a half hour about the dangers of being in the ocean after dark before my father started laughing at us."

"I envy you," Arthur admitted, a bit of heartbreak leaking into his words. "All my life I was trained to fight and protect. The lessons and stories I was told were all to teach me how to rule and how to be the strongest warrior. There is nothing I would not have sacrificed to share what you had with your father."

"It couldn't have been that bad, Arthur. You were surrounded by friends."

"It was not the same. The men here were the only ones I called friends. Even then, I only shared parts of myself with Merlin, Galahad, and Gawain. I trusted them, but back then there were many things that were not talked about."

Aliana frowned. "That couldn't have been easy." God knew keeping her own feelings bottled up for so long was starting to tear at her.

"I never knew any different. It was normal for us." Arthur shook his head. He leaned back against the couch, and the pair sat in pleasant silence for a few moments. "Aliana, would you consider teaching me more of your dances?"

Surprised by the abrupt change in subject, Aliana's brows shot up. "Sure, but why do you want to know?"

"You seem to enjoy it. I figure something that makes you smile so brightly must be worth the effort."

She looked away, smiling through her blush, and nodded. What was she supposed to say to that?

While they pushed the couch back, she suggested they start with the waltz. She demonstrated the basics of the dance, showing Arthur proper posture, arm placement, and the steps, giggling when a turn or a step would trip him up — it was so unusual that he didn't pick it up immediately. They spent the next hour laughing and practicing, and by the end of the hour, Arthur had the basic motions down.

"Will you meet me tomorrow night?" he asked, walking her to her room. "I would like to continue with our dance lessons." He paused for a brief moment before continuing. "I find your company very enjoyable, and I would like to know more about you."

Aliana's face heated. "Sure. I like hanging out with you too."

"Good night, Aliana," Arthur said, taking her hand in his and brushing a kiss across her knuckles.

"G-G-Good night, Arthur," she said with a stammer. Stepping into her room, she felt the dumb smile on her face. Just like she'd thought, Arthur was already becoming a close friend.

"Glad to see you're back," Dagg said from the edge of her bed, jolting her out of her haze. "I'm sorry about earlier, Aliana. I should have found a better way to explain your magic."

Aliana stared, astounded by his apology. "Thanks, Dagg, but you weren't the only one at fault. I'm sorry for going off on you. I overreacted."

He smiled and she smiled back. "I think we can both agree to put this behind us."

Aliana nodded, disappearing into the bathroom.

"You should get some rest," he said when she emerged. "We have a lot of training to do and you need to practice with the others to sharpen your fighting skills."

And that's how the next two weeks went. They'd have breakfast at sunrise, then Wade and the others would work with Aliana on her fighting skills, teaching her how to handle a bow and staff. She'd flat out refused to touch a sword. When she was a child, she'd come across one of her papa's men cleaning the blood of a slaughtered boar from a blade. She'd hated bladed weapons ever since. All of the guys, even Galahad, had objected to this hole in her training, but she eventually won the argument.

They all went easy on her at first—all of them except Wade, who knew what she could do better than the others. Percy got quite a surprise the first time he worked with Aliana and treated her like a child rather than a female who could fight. But he found out that she was better than he'd assumed after she knocked him flat on his chauvinistic butt. The guys were patient with her, encouraging her when she did well and gently correcting her when she got something wrong. It was bone-wrenching work, at times, but the guys were starting to see she wasn't a damsel-in-distress who couldn't be counted on to free them. It wasn't just the knights who were growing closer—they were *all* growing together as a family. She now had more "big brothers" than any girl should ever have to deal with.

The bulk of her days were spent with Merlin and Dagg—building her shields, discovering new ways to use her magic, and learning how to locate portals. Galahad was always present to spend time with Aliana during her breaks, and occasionally they hung out, just the two of them, in the evenings. They listened to music, she taught him about photography, and he told her stories from Camelot. Every few days, he'd even join her magic lessons. One of her favorite moments was during a spur of the moment sparring match between them. She came close to beating him, but he eventually won, pinning her to the soft grass. They were pressed so close and she thought for sure he was going to kiss her again, but he pulled back just before Flora came to get them for lunch. Someone was always interrupting them, and it was both frustrating and disheartening.

The knights, Aliana, and Dagg ate all their meals together as a group, and each one was a production of "family" bonding and outrageous jokes at each other's expense. Everyone was falling into a comfortable rhythm, their friendships growing. At night they often watched movies together or planned different strategies for finding and facing Mordrid and Morgana.

Every few nights, Aliana and Arthur met in the room with the mirrored wall. When they were together, Aliana could relax and not worry about whether or not she was good enough. She felt safe with him, like she could trust him with anything. They both opened up, sharing stories about their past—good and bad. She continued to teach him dances and sometimes told him stories and fairy tales she'd learned growing up.

Everyone deemed to notice the growing closeness of the two, and one night, Lancelot cornered Aliana in Merlin's *Beauty-and-the-Beast-*worthy library to confront her about it. "You need to stop whatever is going on between you, Galahad, and the king."

"I don't know what you're talking about," she said, confused. She was growing emotionally closer to Galahad, and Arthur and she were becoming good friends, but she didn't understand why that would upset Lancelot.

"You are a distraction for them. You need to back off so they can focus on completing this quest."

"You don't know anything about me, Lancelot. Arthur and I are friends. And Galahad and I…" She hesitated, not sure what they were. "He's also my friend. All of you are. What's happened to make you such a judgmental, cold-hearted jerk?"

"I've seen what happens when a man lets his infatuation with a girl cloud his judgment. I've seen the deadly consequences of it. You need to step back and let Galahad and Arthur focus on the quest. You are the Destined One—a path *you chose*—so you need to start acting like it instead of like a love sick teenager."

Aliana's temper flared, and she took a step closer to the arrogant knight. "You're a great teacher, Lancelot, and I even consider you a friend on most occasions, but you're out of line! I care about Galahad and Arthur, and I won't stop hanging around with my *friends*. Whatever it is that's destroyed the Lancelot of legend, you need to deal with it and stop projecting it onto me."

She stormed out of the library to the backyard, trying to cool her temper. Lancelot made no sense! She tried to forget the argument, but a few days later, Wade found her after her magic lesson and asked what was going on between her and the king. Sighing, she explained that they were just friends and she didn't understand why certain people seemed to have a problem with that. Wade let the subject drop.

Aliana's fiery nightmares had relented since that first night back in London. They'd been replaced by dreams about Leyon. She and the lost knight never talked, and it seemed like he couldn't see her, but she knew he was trying to find them, and it gave her hope.

Aliana followed Merlin into the candle-filled training room. She was still sore from the beating she'd taken at Lancelot's hands earlier that day. He was a hard instructor, but she couldn't deny the progress he'd brought about in her skills.

"We'll pick up where we left off yesterday," Merlin droned. The last few days had been spent on her external shields, learning to deflect magical attacks. The magic felt different depending on what she was doing with it. When she was defending herself, it felt fizzy, like soda pop. Her shield magic had a spongy feel to it, not heavy or taxing but just bubbling around her. When she tried to attack, the magic sizzled and pulsed in her muscles, like a crazy, out of control adrenaline rush.

Developing connections with the elements was a part of her training she liked. Already she had tried water and earth, but only the latter had responded to her. For all their practicing, they had yet to figure out Aliana's strange connection to her magic. She was frustrated with both Dagg and Merlin because they refused to share any of their speculations. It may have been petty, but she had decided to keep her own ideas about it to herself too. Not that it mattered—surely Merlin and Dagg would have already thought of anything she noticed. What she had realized days earlier was that it was easier to do large spells when Dagg was close by or touching her.

"Focus your mind," Merlin said.

The blinds snapped shut as the lights went out. He placed a small, lit candle in front of her, and she zeroed in on the flame until she saw nothing else. Her eyes closed, but the image of the single flame remained in the emptiness. She felt the gentle heat swirling around her, growing. Faster and faster the flame grew, multiplying, each new flame brighter and hotter.

Her nightmare resurfaced. The roaring fire greedily consumed everything, exploding outward and trying to claim her—the prize it had been denied years ago.

Her control snapped and the fires raged. She couldn't breathe. Like a shadow monster, the smoke tried to choke her as she desperately searched for an escape. She couldn't do this! The flames were too strong.

"Aliana," they called to her.

"No!" With everything she had, she pushed against the fire, clinging to the darkness until it consumed the flames. Gasping for breath, her eyes snapped open. She trembled, reeling from the flames that haunted her.

"What happened?" Merlin kneeled down, his eyes level with hers. "You were fighting the connection."

"Aliana?" Dagg asked, curling in her lap. She felt him pushing against the barriers she had erected around her mind. Thank God she'd been able to create them, but she had to be on constant guard to keep them up. She felt Dagg push again.

"Stop, Dagg!" she ordered. The Dragon backed away.

"Why did you fight the connection?" Merlin asked, his voice strained like it always was when he was trying to control his temper with her.

"The fire wasn't trying to connect!" she hissed, getting to her feet.

"We could see your magic blending with the fire. Like it or not, you have a connection to it." Merlin stood, raking a hand through his perfectly combed locks.

"I can't, Merlin!" Maybe she did have a connection, but whatever that connection might be, it was nothing good. "I need to take a break." Without waiting for permission, she fled the room, seeking out the knights.

She found them sparring in the muddy clearing. Galahad and Percy stood on the sideline, watching Lancelot go against Arthur while Owen battled Wade.

Galahad's eyes found her immediately. "Bad morning?" He frowned, looking past her to what was no doubt a scowling Merlin. That expression had become the Druid's trademark when it came to her and her magic.

"You could say that." She sighed, trying to dispel the last of the fire from her mind. She glanced out of the corner of her eye at Merlin, who watched the sparring matches, but she could almost hear his disapproval of her choice to go running to Galahad. They both knew her knight would defend her no matter what. Her anger started to deflate.

Guilt crept into her mind. It was childish of her to keep running to Galahad every time she got stressed out with Merlin.

"Aliana, we should return to your lessons," Merlin said, sounding like a bored, annoyed schoolteacher.

She saw Galahad about to protest, so she cut him off. "I know, I just wanted some air for a moment." She glanced sideways at the Druid and added, "Sorry."

The back of Galahad's hand brushed hers, his eyes asking if she was sure. She took his hand, squeezing it gently. The familiar sparks shot up her arm, and she couldn't help smiling. They heard a heavy thud as Lancelot knocked Arthur's sword to the ground.

"I guess that's my cue to go." Aliana waved at the guys as she followed Merlin back inside.

"I think it would be best if we focused on your defensive magic for now." The Druid leveled her with a hard gaze. "But after lunch we *will* go back to establishing your elemental connections."

Aliana gulped but nodded. There was no point in arguing. Merlin set his magical barrier around her. He launched different spells into the sphere, and she tried to defeat them. Focusing, she called forth her magic, creating a barrier shield on her arm much like a physical shield the knights would have used. Merlin and Dagg's magic hit her barrier, and most spells bounced off, fizzling out. But a few seemed to absorb into her shield, their magic becoming hers, making her strong enough to launch a bit of her own magic at the attacks. Aliana deflected one of Merlin's attacks just as Galahad and Arthur opened the door.

"Are the three of you about done? Sabine has lunch waiting," Arthur said, looking her over as the magic faded from around her.

"Please, I'm starving," she said, walking between the two new arrivals and toward the kitchen. They all stopped at the kitchen door, hearing angry voices. Lancelot and Wade stood toe to toe, bodies tight, ready to start throwing punches.

"Shut the hell up, Lancelot! You don't know anything about it! It's none of your business!" Wade ordered, his tan skin flushed with anger.

"It's all of our business if it's going to affect us when we face Mordrid and Morgana!" Lancelot raged in a quiet, menacing voice.

"What's going on?" Arthur demanded, separating the two warriors.

Lancelot's eyes cut to Aliana. They were hard and bitter, telling her all she needed to know. They were fighting about her.

"One of you *will* answer me, now!" Arthur's voice was hard and commanding.

"It was just a misunderstanding," Wade said, flicking his gaze to her before dropping it to the floor.

"Not good enough." Arthur fixed his I'm-the-king-and-you'll-answer-me-now look on both of them.

"It was nothing. Just a difference of opinion, Sire," Lancelot insisted, his voice cold.

"Why don't we have some lunch?" Aliana said, attempting to break the tension. "We're all hungry. Tempers will cool after everyone's eaten."

Arthur reluctantly backed down, but his glare promised to get answers soon.

Suddenly not hungry, Aliana grabbed a few pieces of fruit. She managed to choke down a couple of bites before her stomach started to protest. Why was she screwing everything up?

Everyone ate quietly. They'd all been getting short-tempered lately. They needed a break, but when she'd suggested that to Merlin a few days earlier, he'd shot her down.

After finishing, they returned to training. Merlin's damned candles had already filled the room by the time Aliana reentered the room.

"We'll try again. This time keep focused." His order was short and sharp.

She sat down again, and this time Merlin left the candle in front of her unlit. She called on her magic, lighting the small wick, but none of the other flames responded when she tried to spread out her magic.

"Give it another try, Aliana," Dagg said supportively. She tried and tried but kept failing.

She couldn't focus, wondering why Lancelot and Wade had been arguing about her. Was it about her hiding behind Galahad and Arthur when she got upset with Merlin? Or maybe they were angry she had yet to bring Leyon to them—her recent dreams told her he was close, but he seemed to be unable to find them. Either way, it hit home again how much was riding on her being the Destined One.

"I can't do this, Merlin. It's not going to work. Can't we just try air or energy?"

"You react to the fire, Aliana. You have a connection," he insisted.

"But I can connect to more than one element, right? Let's just try another." She couldn't face the fire again.

Merlin shook his head. "The power is inside. You have to control it and make the connection bend to your will."

Aliana sighed, dropping her head in her hands. "Merlin, maybe I'm not as powerful as y'all seem to think I should be. These abilities you say I have aren't normal, even by your standards!"

"Aliana, you have a great capacity for magic. I can feel it even thirty feet away. You were born to do this. It's your destiny, your purpose in life."

Her *only* purpose in life?

She felt her heart crack and tried to take a deep breath, but all she could manage was little gasps. Mortified that she was hyperventilating in front of Merlin, she tried to calm down but nothing helped.

He's wrong! I am more than this stupid prophecy.

Suddenly, the despair vanished and she could breathe again. She looked down at the Dragon in her lap. He was the one cooling the emotional storm inside her.

"I told you to stop that, Dagg!" She pushed the Dragon from her lap and scrambled to her feet. "I told you to stop manipulating my feelings!"

The candles flashed to life all around the room. Stunned, she looked down. Tiny bits of pink fell from her hand. Her jaw dropped, eyes zooming back and forth between the candles and her hands.

"Well done, Aliana! You're starting to tap into the connection," Merlin praised.

Merlin's right. This is all you're meant for, her mind whispered. How could she have been stupid enough to start feeling like she was one of them, like more than their key? Biting back a whimper, she forced down the lump in her throat. Merlin said something, but she hadn't been paying attention.

"I'm sorry, what?" she asked, her voice barely there.

"I understand this is all hard for you." He tried to place a hand on her shoulder, but she flinched back. She was afraid her magic would spring to life again or worse, that he would try to read her. "It's hard on all of us at first, but this is good progress. Fire is a powerful element to have at your command. Do you want to try it again?"

"No." She rubbed her temples, trying to buy some time to get her voice even again.

"Are you all right, Aliana?" Merlin asked, stepping closer.

"I'm a bit light-headed." Not a total lie, but she would use anything she could to make an escape. "I think I just need to go lie down." Hoping he wouldn't follow, Aliana escaped the room, heading straight for her own room before her powder keg of emotions exploded.

"Aliana?" She wheeled around on the bottom stair as Arthur called her name. "You're upset." His brow furrowed as he stepped out from the library.

"I'm fine, Arthur."

His full lips thinned. He knew she was lying. *Son of a biscuit!* Damn him for reading her so well.

"Okay, I'm not fine, but I'm just tired," she said, knowing he wouldn't give up until he was satisfied. "This magic stuff is just… taking more out of me than I thought it would."

"Merlin's pushing you too hard. I'll speak to him."

"No!" she said quickly. "You don't need to do that. I just really need a nap. Please don't make a fuss about this." That was the last thing she wanted. But then, if her only purpose in life was to fulfill this prophecy, did what she want really matter?

"Can you tell the others I went to bed early, please?" she asked, taking a few steps up.

"What about dinner?"

"I honestly don't think I could eat anything. I'll come down later if I get hungry," she promised, knowing she probably wouldn't.

Arthur grabbed her hand before she could climb any more steps. She gulped, frozen in place as his thumb gently brushed against the inside of her wrist. "Only if you are sure you're all right." His golden eyes refused to let her eyes leave his.

She nodded slightly. "I will be." Without giving him a chance to say more, she rushed the rest of the way to her room and had barely turned on her music before the first body-shaking sob broke free. Still in her jeans and She-Ra T-shirt, she collapsed onto the bed, burying her face in her pillow to muffle her crying.

How could everything in her life not mean anything? If the only reason she'd been born was to fulfill this stupid prophecy, what was the point of the life she'd lived—her friends, her family, and her art?

And what about her feelings for Galahad? Maybe she'd been right from the start. All she was to him was a way to stop Mordrid and get their lives back. That was all she was good for, and she was even screwing that up. She sobbed harder. Her heart cracked again as she lay there, crying out all her frustration and heartache.

Aliana ignored the repeated knocks on her door and Owen's offer to bring her dinner. As far as they needed to know, she was asleep. Right now, she needed to get all her inner turmoil out so she could put on her happy face in the morning. The guys had enough to deal with and didn't need to be bothered with her problems. The only thing they needed from her was their freedom.

Freeing the knights, saving the realms, and stopping Mordrid were the only things that mattered. The sooner she could accept that hard truth, the sooner she could pretend to the world that that knowledge didn't threaten to break her completely.

2₀

I have to force myself to not confront Merlin because that is what Aliana wants. But I made it clear to Lord Daggerhorne that Merlin is not to upset her again, and he needs to be sure Merlin understands that. I want to see her smile, like she did last night when telling me about her parents. She doesn't know that I saw Galahad kiss her at the party, and I can't tell her. First Guinevere, now Aliana. I'm done holding back because of my ghost woman. Aliana's not his yet—I won't stop until she tells me she is. Even then I'm not sure I'll give up.

— Arthur

Aliana struggled to open her tear-swollen eyes. It wasn't even one a.m. She rolled onto her back, moaning in pain as her shoulders and neck protested the movement. Groggy, she traded her jeans and T-shirt for her PJs, then washed her face and swallowed some aspirin before falling back into bed.

She tossed for a few minutes, unable to get comfortable, and her thoughts from earlier returned. Disgusted with herself, she rolled out of bed, grabbing her quilt and sandals. Quietly, she crept out of her room and down the hall toward Merlin's rooftop terrace. She inhaled the crisp night air, wrapping the quilt around her shoulders. Everything always seemed a bit better when she could breathe in fresh air under the moonlight.

Plopping down onto a wooden chair, she curled up, staring at the crescent moon playing peek-a-boo from behind the clouds. Taking another deep breath, she finally relaxed, wishing that Merlin wasn't right about her "destiny" but knowing she would have to accept it. Maybe there was a way to accept it on her own terms, she thought as she drifted back to sleep.

Aliana shot awake on the hard wood chair. Gasping, she fanned herself, trying to cool the burning skin her nightmare always left in its wake. The fiery dream had returned, and she couldn't get her parents' screams out of her head.

She watched fog roll over the roof. Her eyes were still glazed from sleep, and through the mist she could barely made out a small shape on the roof ledge. A small fox with dark eyes and three tails sat on its haunches, staring at her. She wiped her eyes and looked again. Nothing was there except more fog where the imagined animal had been.

"Get a grip," she scolded herself, grabbing the quilt. "The guys' paranoia is starting to rub off on you." Shaking her head, she snuck back downstairs.

"You shouldn't fall asleep outside," Dagg said, surprising her at the bottom of the steps.

"Shh," she hissed. "Don't wake the guys. Why are you here?"

"Your shield slipped, and I felt your anxiety. I was coming to wake you."

"How many times do I have to ask you to stop reading my feelings? I need to have some sort of privacy here."

"You already shut yourself off too much, Aliana."

Beyond fed up with all these *boys* telling her what to do, she glared at the Dragon as she passed him. "I don't need a know-it-all, nosy Dragon telling me what I should and shouldn't do with *my* feelings."

Galahad opened his door as she walked by. "What's going on?" He wore only a pair of low-hanging sweatpants.

"Nothing," she said, clearing her throat, and letting her eyes wander over his body. "I fell asleep upstairs." She counted back from three, waiting for his lecture. He opened his mouth right on cue, but she held up her hand before he could speak. "Dagg already scolded me. I don't need to hear it from you too."

"What makes you think that was my intention?" he asked, crossing his arms across his broad, bare chest.

Aliana stared at him. "That's all any of you seem to do. Even Percy and Owen are lecturing me now."

"Aliana…"

"Please don't, Galahad." She didn't having the energy to fight with him. "I just want to take a shower." She escaped into her room.

Dropping the quilt, she flipped on the shower and discarded her pajamas. Standing under the barely warm water, she worked to get her combustible emotions pushed away into the hidey-hole in the back of her mind. When she felt more in control, she shut off the water. Wade would be knocking on her door soon for their early morning training. She quickly pulled on black riding shorts and a yoga top.

As she brushed the tangles out of her hair, she sighed, realizing she owed Galahad and Dagg another apology. It wasn't their fault her magic-freak self was only good for this one thing. They were both victims of this whole curse too. Merlin's words tried to surface again, but she pushed them down. The sky lightened, spilling gray morning light into her room.

Then Aliana got an idea. She opened the calendar in her phone, just remembering an appointment she'd totally forgotten about. It was with a potential client and was set for the next day. "Perfect! If I can get Arthur on my side, maybe I can convince Merlin that a field trip to get a break from this place is what we all need." Maybe her purpose was to fulfill this prophecy, but she couldn't let that rob her entirely of her life and the things that made her happy.

Her thoughts were interrupted by a knock at her door.

"Morning, Wade," she said, swinging the door open.

"Morning, Lia." He wrinkled an eyebrow, taking in her light-hearted mood. "You good? You had me worried last night when you didn't come down for dinner."

"Sorry 'bout that. I was just exhausted and trying to deal with things—badly. I didn't want to worry you guys."

Wade studied her for a moment before she patted him on the arm and closed her door, stepping into the hall. "Can we get a quick breakfast before we start today? You still owe me my winnings from Galahad kicking your butt in the obstacle course." Their wager was always to prepare and serve a delicious meal.

"Sure," Wade said, following her to the kitchen. "I was actually thinking we'd skip practice altogether today."

"Why?"

"Because, like I said, you had me worried last night, and I know you a lot better than any of the others. I think you could use a day off, and frankly, so could I."

"Oh." Leave it to Wade to say just the right thing. "If you're okay with it, then I'm not going to argue. I need to talk to Arthur, anyway."

"It's settled," Wade said, grabbing eggs and vegetables from the refrigerator while he muttered about how unfair it was that Galahad had super speed and strength.

Laughing, Aliana poured them both a glass of juice and took a seat at the counter while he created an omelet masterpiece. Dagg flew in a few minutes later, landing on the seat next to her. She offered him an apologetic smile. "I'm sorry for yesterday and last night. You were just trying to help me and I overreacted again."

"Thank you for that, but please understand I only do what I do because I worry for you." He hopped up onto the counter and whispered, "Things aren't always what we think they are. Purposes and destinies in life are not always clear to us. Very rarely do they have only one purpose."

"I think Merlin made mine pretty clear. I understand now what I have to do."

Dagg opened his mouth to say more, but Wade placed a steaming hot pepper and onion omelet in front of Aliana with a bow and a devilish smirk.

"For you, m'lady."

"Don't start, Wade! Make one for Dagg too."

"Will Wade be cooking for me as well?" Galahad asked, leaning against the doorframe. He was gorgeous in a pair of fitted jeans and a green T-shirt that clung to his broad shoulders and chest.

"You're on your own, pretty boy," Wade muttered, cracking more eggs.

"Ignore him." Aliana smiled as he took the stool next to her. "You can have mine and he can make me another."

"Don't you dare!" Wade said, spinning around and shaking his spatula at her. "You didn't eat last night. He did."

"He's right. This one is yours," Galahad said, pouring himself a glass of juice.

Nodding, Aliana took a bite of the heavenly creation. "Great as always, Wade."

He placed another omelet in front of Dagg, and the Dragon, of course, promptly attacked his breakfast.

"I'm sorry. I didn't mean to be such a brat in the hallway this morning," she said softly to Galahad.

"You weren't completely wrong. We do tend to lecture you more than we probably should." He tucked a stray piece of hair behind her ear.

"Still." She blushed, pulling away from his touch and taking another bite of her breakfast, but the eggs had lost their flavor.

"I understand that this is harder on you than it is us. If you have need, you can talk to me about it," he offered almost shyly.

Aliana was touched, even though she knew she shouldn't be—he was only trying to preserve the sanity of *the key*. She nodded as she took another flavorless bite.

One by one the others filed into the kitchen. Sabine came in and took over the cooking. The purple-haired Pixie was terribly efficient and ran her kitchen like a drill sergeant. She'd even scolded Merlin a few nights earlier when he'd almost ruined dessert.

"Lia and I are going to take the morning off," Wade announced. "Honestly, we all could use a break."

Percy, Owen, and even Galahad voiced their agreement.

"I think that would be wise," Merlin said, surprising the group.

"Then I suggest we make use of that great pool Merlin has!" Owen said, smiling brightly.

Not long after breakfast, Aliana took a seat on one of the deck chairs, her laptop in hand. For this Southern belle, the sunny day was just a bit too cold for swimming. Wade and Percy roped the guys into an overly aggressive game of water volleyball. Aliana burst out laughing when even Merlin joined the fun, using magic to screw with Owen's serve. Who knew the stoic Druid had a playful side?

She finally started sorting the pictures from Avalon while she tried to figure out the best way to approach Arthur about her plan. Looking up again, she watched the water cascade down his body as he pulled himself out of the pool. She couldn't take her eyes off the king as he dried himself off and walked toward her, nodding toward her laptop.

"What are you working on?" he asked.

"I'm going through the photos I told you about from Avalon." She shut her laptop and set it aside. "Arthur, can I talk to you about something?"

"Anything."

"I was thinking. We've all been training for two weeks without a break from each other or this place." She paused, watching his reaction, and he nodded for her to continue. "Well, I'm supposed to have a meeting with a potential client tomorrow in London and…"

"Aliana…"

"No, Arthur, hear me out please. I was thinking we all could go into the city. Percy and Owen can come with me while Merlin and Lancelot show you and Galahad more of the city. You can search for Leyon. My dreams all show him there. And I can send Wade to get some more of my clothes from my home." She bit the inside of her cheek as Arthur took a seat next to her.

He looked skeptical. "What has Merlin said about this venture?"

"I haven't asked him yet, but last time I suggested leaving the grounds he said it was a bad idea," she admitted, not wanting to lie to Arthur. "I'll be plenty protected with Percy and Owen, and I think we'll have a better chance of finding Sir Leyon in the city."

The king shook his head. "I am inclined to agree with Merlin. Morgana and Mordrid have been too silent. Even J'alel reported there have been no sightings anywhere."

"You've talked to J'alel?" Why hadn't anyone told her?

"He came to us a few days ago. We thought it best to not disturb your training." His eyes flicked over her hurt expression. "I can see that was a mistake."

Aliana bit her cheek again, holding back some choice words. What was important now was getting to London. Yelling at Arthur wouldn't help to accomplish that, but maybe laying on the guilt would. "Honestly, I need a break from all of this. I need to do something *normal*. All of this isn't my life like it is yours."

"If I agree to this, how do you propose we find Sir Leyon?"

Aliana shifted, trying not to get too excited. "I know where he was in my last dream. You guys can start there while I go to my meeting." The trick with Arthur, she'd learned, was to push just a bit and lay on a dose of guilt or big eyes.

"I have two conditions," he said, caving.

Got ya, she thought, trying to contain her smile.

"Lancelot and Wade go with you." Aliana tried to object, but Arthur cut her off. "Lancelot will not give in to you as Owen and Percy would."

Busted.

"You will have one hour to meet with this person, and then you *will* meet us back at the hotel. And I should not have to tell you that Lord Daggerhorne, Lancelot, and Wade are to never leave your side."

"Agreed." She smiled.

"What's agreed?" Merlin asked as he and Galahad toweled themselves off. Aliana's mouth went dry.

"Aliana has proposed a trip to the city tomorrow." Both guys eyed her, surprised. Well, with Merlin it was more of a glare.

"Is that wise, my king?" Galahad asked.

"If we take protective measures and remain vigilant, yes, I think this a good idea." Arthur called the others from the pool and told them the plans. Lancelot didn't appear particularly happy, but he didn't object.

The rest of the day passed in a marathon of action movies and Pixie-made pizza. It was almost midnight when Aliana finally crawled into bed, slipping into another dream of Leyon.

They were in a maze with towering bush walls and vines.

"Where are you?" he asked. "You said they needed me." His Scottish accent was faint.

"I'm here!" She summoned her magic. "We're coming to the city."

The dream faded before she knew if he'd heard her. She groaned as the bright sun hit her face. Rolling out of bed, she showered and dressed in a pair of brown jeans and a long, bright pink tube top. For the first time that week, she sat down and took the time to apply makeup, even going so far as to give her eyes a pink, smoky look. Slipping on a pair of golden gladiator wedges, she took a second to admire her handiwork.

"I see this is a casual meeting," Dagg said as she walked into the room, pinning part of her hair up with a gold clip.

"Great thing about my job—no dress code." She reached into her closet and pulled out a white, cropped jacket. "Better?"

"Wow, Aliana, you look smashing!" Owen said when she joined the knights on the pebbled driveway.

"Thanks." She checked her camera case to make sure she had the lenses she'd need.

"I do not think this wise. I have an ill feeling," Galahad whispered from behind her.

She turned and smiled. "My meeting won't take more than an hour, and I'll do as Arthur said and keep the guys with me. You have the chance to find Leyon and complete the knights."

He frowned.

"Everything will be fine." She gave him a small smile and climbed into the back of Lancelot's car.

When they arrived at the edge of the city, Lancelot drove to the Covent Garden district while Merlin veered his car in a different direction to go to another part of the city. Lancelot's car stopped outside a beautiful, old, brick house with black gates.

"Who are you meeting?" the knight asked.

"Her name is Vivian Farris. She called me with her proposal a few weeks ago, before any of this happened. She's from old money and wants a fantasy portrait."

A petite, redheaded girl greeted them in the foyer. "She's waiting for you out back, Miss Fagan." The guys moved to follow, but the girl stopped them. "I'm sorry, but Miss Farris's orders are clear. Only Miss Fagan is to meet her. You will have to wait here."

Lancelot shot Aliana a hard look. Holding back a groan, she told the girl they were her assistants and that she needed them. She had promised Arthur, after all.

"She won't be happy," the girl whined, seeming nervous. "Very well." Silently, she led them out back to a tall garden maze.

"What do you think, Miss Fagan?"

Aliana and the knights turned toward the light, airy voice. Vivian was medium height with a woman's soft curves. Her shoulder-length, blond ringlets complemented her dark brown eyes. She wore a short, black and red dress with a pair of studded kitten heels. No one would have suspected the girl was only eighteen.

"I think it's brilliant," Aliana said, feeling a spark of jealousy at Vivian's effortless beauty. Lancelot and Wade had yet to look anywhere else but at her.

"Wonderful!" the girl said, breaking the boys from her spell. "I want to take you to the heart of the maze. I'd like that to be the location for what's to be done." She led them through the vine-covered archway.

"What's at the center?" Wade asked, following the two ladies.

"A statue of the goddess Hera, but I would like to show Aliana first. You gentlemen can remain here." Her voice was airy but her words firm. She was clearly used to getting her way.

"We are her assistants. We go where she does," Lancelot said in a bored voice.

Aliana didn't argue. If she didn't follow Arthur's orders, they'd never give her any freedom again.

"Very well," Vivian said, turning her back and leading them deeper into the maze. They soon reached the center courtyard. It was small but beautiful. Everything was centered around the statue of the Greek goddess.

"What were your thoughts?" Aliana asked, taking in the different angles and light.

"I was thinking this is where I would put an end to the Destined One." Vivian shoved Aliana forward to her knees.

"Aliana!" Lancelot and Wade jumped to defend her, but Vivian shot out her hand, blasting them back with magic.

"Sir Lancelot, always so gallant."

Aliana got to her feet, searching for a way past Vivian, but the blonde's magic pulsed through the air, keeping Aliana still.

"Morgana?" Lancelot asked, his eyes wide, just as Wade also seemed to recognize her.

"Who else?" The air around the witch shimmered with ice blue magic, morphing her appearance. Her hair was now a darker blond, her eyes a raging hazel, and her nose just a tad too big for her face. She was striking, but the hatred and evil rolling off her was terrible.

"And the brave Sir Gawain, too. Or is it Wade now? I believe that's the name your sister has been crying out since my black knights took her."

"What? You're lying!" Wade roared, trying to attack, but he was blocked from reentering the center.

"Wade, help me, please!" Lacy's terror-filled cries stained the air.

"Lacy!" he cried, looking around frantically. "Where is she, you witch?"

Aliana had never seen such hatred and outrage in her best friend.

"Oh dear, what to do? Save your sister or the Destined One? Choices, choices," Morgana taunted with a wicked laugh.

"Let her go!" Aliana ordered. "She has nothing to do with this!" Her magic rose inside her, diffusing some of the surrounding power.

"I'll make the choice for you, then." Vines shot out of the walls, sealing off the entrance to the heart of the maze.

Aliana heard Lancelot and Wade trying to rip through the vines as Dagg leaped from her wrist.

"Where is Lacy?" Aliana demanded, finally able to move as Morgana pulled back her power.

Dagg hovered at Aliana's side, waiting to attack. Lacy cried out again.

"Damn you, Morgana!" Wade cried out.

"Go save Lacy! Dagg and I can handle this!" Aliana yelled through the greenery.

"No, Aliana!" Lancelot protested.

"Go! You can't help me, but you can help Lacy. Go!" she ordered.

Morgana cackled as the guys left. "How amusing! The Destined One fancies herself a hero. Do you really think you and your *pet* can stop me? I've walked this earth for over a millennium. I control magic stronger than any you could ever hope to."

"We'll just have to see." Aliana slid into a fighting stance, her hands raised. If Merlin and Dagg were right about her odd, unpredictable magic, she just might have an advantage over Morgana.

"Very well." Morgana twisted her hand, and a blue ball of flame leaped in her palm. "Let's see how you like this." The witch forced the ball at Aliana.

Throwing up her arm, Aliana's shield of light appeared. The fire hit it and fizzled.

"I see Merlin is up to his old tricks. Did he tell you that he trained me in magic as well? Let's see if he taught you how to fight this."

Morgana shot a stream of solid magic straight at her, but the moment it hit her shield, power shot through Aliana's veins like wildfire.

Using the magic to boost her speed, Aliana leaped at Morgana, throwing a series of punches and kicks at the witch. Morgana was caught off guard, but only for a split second and managed to avoid most of the rapid attacks.

"A fighter! This'll be more entertaining than I thought," Morgana taunted, throwing a few of her own punches. She was an alarmingly superior fighter, yet Aliana got the uneasy feeling that Morgana was toying with her.

Aliana struggled to keep up as the witch mixed magic attacks with her strikes. But Aliana's magic lent its own strength, letting her hit harder than usual as they traded blows. "Entertain this!" she screamed, landing a side kick to Morgana's face, her heel cutting into the perfect skin.

"Enough of this child's play! It's time I showed you who is the superior sorceress," Morgana hissed, eyeing the blood on her fingers. She shot another bolt of magic, but Aliana blocked it with her shield.

Dagg swooped down, using his magic fire to attack.

"Pest, I'll be rid of you!" Vines shot out at Dagg, but the Dragon burned them all to ash. That turned out to be all the distraction Morgana needed. She let loose another gust of magic, hitting Dagg before Aliana could scream out a warning.

He collided with the Hera statue, and it crumbled onto the silver Dragon, trapping him.

"Dagg!" Aliana ran to her friend, but Morgana struck her from behind with her bolt of magic. The evil magic wrapped around her, vaulting her into the thorn-ridden wall, which cut through her thin jacket and scraped her skin raw.

"You're weak. Why Mordrid wants you alive, I do not know, but…he never said you had to be in one piece." A deadly calm smile graced Morgana's mouth as power crackled all around her. Aliana paled, realizing just how much Morgana had been holding back. There was no way she could win.

Morgana shot another bolt of magic, and Aliana barely managed to block it with her barrier shield. The magic pushed her deeper into the thorns, and she couldn't find the leverage to fight back. Instead, she opened herself to the magic and absorbed everything Morgana threw at her. The cold fire seared her insides, coming too quickly for her to take command of the power. She struggled to her feet, her vision blurred with blue as the opposing magic struggled with her own. She saw Morgana's attack too late to move.

"Get away from her!" a Scottish voice cried. Morgana turned, unable to avoid the man that slammed her to the ground.

"Sir Leyon?" Morgana asked, unbelieving.

Aliana ran to him as he rolled to his feet, pulling a *katana* from beneath his duster. Chopping sounds came from behind Morgana. Lancelot and Wade had cut through the plants.

Lacy, pale and bleeding, was tucked tightly to Wade's side while the two knights wielded swords they must have taken from the black knights. Morgana jerked to the side as Lancelot charged her, his sword only just missing her neck.

Dagg shot out from beneath the stone rubble, hissing fire at Morgana. She deflected most of it, but some of the flames singed her hair and dress. She turned her rage toward the injured Lacy. Aliana panicked, grabbing at the blue power inside of her and forcing it out toward Morgana. The witch was blasted back into the vine walls, hitting the ground with a jarring thud.

The evil blonde struggled to her feet, her rage burning the air all around them. "You'll pay for that, you insolent girl!" she screeched, but as she moved to attack, Leyon blocked the witch's path, nearly taking Morgana's head off with a swipe of his *katana*. She jumped back, looking around at all of them. "I can see the odds are no longer in my favor, but mark my words: I'll be back to finish this." Her burning, evil eyes swept over them as she disappeared in a shimmer of blue.

"You are Aliana?" Leyon asked, checking her for injuries.

"Yes, but how did you find us?"

"Lia!" Lacy sobbed, throwing her arms around Aliana so tightly that they both nearly fell over. "What's going on?" she asked, her usually perky voice wobbly.

"How badly are you hurt, Lace?" Aliana asked as she fought her tears. This wasn't supposed to touch her friend. "I'm so sorry."

Lacy pulled back, wiping her tears as Wade took her in his arms again, kissing the top of her tangled hair. "I got you, little sis. They won't hurt you again."

"How badly are you hurt?" Lancelot asked Aliana, tossing aside the rusted swords.

"Just a few scratches." Aliana nearly sobbed again when Dagg wrapped himself around her shoulders. For a moment, she let her shields slip so that his calming magic could take the edge off of her adrenaline rush. She let him feel how grateful she was to have him.

"Aliana, what is *that?*" Lacy panicked, trying to get to her friend, but Wade held her firmly, telling his sister to calm down.

"Let's get out of here," Wade said, pulling his sister toward the exit. "We'll explain everything, Lace, just as soon as we join the others."

"Thank you," Aliana said to Leyon as they followed Wade. She was tucked between the newbie and Lancelot as they rushed to the car.

"I'm just glad I found you when I did." He hid his *katana* under his jacket before stepping out onto the street.

"I know you don't remember me, but it is good to see you again, Sir Leyon," Lancelot said as Leyon climbed into the front seat.

"Thank you, and you can call me Leo. Leo Kell."

"That's lovely. Now will someone please tell me what the bloody hell is going on here?" Lacy seethed, her choice of British curse word coming out in her thickest Southern accent as she sat sandwiched between Aliana and Wade in the back seat.

"It's a *very* long story, Lace."

21

All these new…old memories are overwhelming, but my life is starting to make sense. I thought I was going daft after I saw Aliana in the window. Try as I might, I couldn't think about anything else for weeks. I kept seeing her, but it was impossible to find her. It baffles me how I knew to be at that garden, but I'm glad I was there. I was in the right place for the first time in my life.

—Leo

Aliana stretched out on her bed at Merlin's palatial home with her still shell-shocked best friend. Lacy had been silent for almost thirty minutes. Very unusual for the high-energy blonde. Wade and Lancelot had found her trapped by Morgana's vines with two terrifying black knights circling her like sharks, their weapons drawn.

"They kept scraping their swords against me, Lia," Lacy whispered, fighting her tears and trembling hands.

"I'm so sorry, Lacy. I never thought any of this would touch you." A new wave of guilt washed over Aliana.

"I don't blame you, Lia, but what on earth are you thinking, being mixed up in all this?"

"It's not like I had much of a choice. It's my *destiny* according to Merlin. Besides, how could I have just turned my back on people who have been trapped for hundreds of years?"

"I get that, but judging by what you alone have told me, you're not handling this very well. Lia, how can any of it end happily?"

"Okay, maybe I'm struggling. Can you blame me?"

Lacy shook her head. "And you can't back out? Find someone else to be this Destined One?"

"I made my choice. I accepted this. I can't back out now."

Lacy frowned and stayed silent for a few moments. "So, Wade was a knight? That explains a lot about brother dearest."

"No kidding. What do you think about Percy being one of them?" Aliana wanted to see her friend smile again and boys were the best and quickest way.

"He's amazing." Lacy sighed, a dreamy smile replacing her fear. "I've never met anyone like him. God knows how I love a tall, hot guy with a chivalry complex!" Lacy laughed for the first time since they had fled Morgana's trap. Aliana was relieved, but she knew that once Lacy was back to her normal self, she'd have questions, lots of them.

"What about you and Galahad?" she asked, going right for the juicy one. She tapped her fingers on her chin with a thoughtful look. "You know, I thought you were joking about their names the other night. Have you done anything about Galahad? Last I saw, you two were in the middle of a pretty hot lip lock."

"Lacy, that's not…he's not…" Aliana shook her head. "Believe me when I say I wish this wasn't true, but he only sees me as a way to fulfill this prophecy. If he spent even ten minutes with another girl he'd forget me."

"Lia, you are not that blind or dumb. He didn't see anyone else but you at the party. Not to mention he has scarcely left you alone since we got back. I almost swooned when he went all protective, possessive-He-Man-knight on you!"

Aliana nibbled her lip. Her friend was a great judge of character, so maybe…

Lacy stretched out next to Aliana and reached out to cover her hand. "You're just scared to let him in."

"I let Josh in and he tried to rape me."

With a disgusted grunt, Lacy hit Aliana with a throw pillow. "And you got his ass dropped in jail! Josh was a pathetic-loser-attempted-rapist. He's nothing compared to Galahad! This time your heart has led you to the right place."

Aliana scrubbed her hands over her face, trying to fight her frustration. "I've been struggling with what I feel for him for weeks. I'm a coward!" She would never make such a revealing confession to anyone but Lacy.

A knock pulled the girls from their thoughts. "Aliana, Lacy—Merlin and the others want you in the library," Estrelle said, cracking open the door.

"Thanks. Can you tell them we'll be right there?" Aliana asked, sliding off the bed. The Pixie nodded and disappeared. "You sure you want to do this, Lace? You could stay up here. You don't have to get any more involved."

"You wouldn't leave me if our roles were reversed. Besides, my brother is part of this too."

Aliana hated the thought of Lacy in danger, but her friend was even more stubborn than she was. If she didn't include her, Lacy would just follow anyway—because once Lacy's mind was made up, the was game over. Aliana's stomach pitched as she led the way to Merlin's grand two-story library. Everything had changed today.

The talking stopped and papers were shuffled as they entered the room.

"What's going on?" Aliana asked, knowing she wasn't going to like the answer.

"Merlin was just explaining a few things to us," Arthur said, clearing his throat.

"He's traced the magic Morgana used today," Wade said, motioning for Lacy to sit between him and Percy on the brown leather couch. "He thinks he's found a portal that can lead us to her."

Aliana took the empty seat next to Galahad and said, "Morgana said you trained her, Merlin. Wouldn't she know you would track her?"

Merlin's cheek's reddened a degree. "I never taught her tracking. When she came to me, she had already been trained. I only helped her to develop certain skills." He kept his eyes focused on a bookshelf.

Wade, Percy, and Leo shared a look, arching their eyebrows. Percy's accompanying crooked smile screamed to Aliana that they knew Merlin's response was crap.

"I don't know anything about magic," Lacy said, "but I know that psycho, gives-blondes-a-bad-name witch is scary smart. I overheard her talking to some crazed-looking guy. She knew what to expect when she set her trap." She leaned against her brother for comfort.

"She wouldn't expect us to react so quickly now." Lancelot uncrossed his arms, pushing away from the shelf he had been leaning on.

"It should take me maybe another day to pinpoint an exact location. Once we have it, Lancelot can track her." Merlin turned to Arthur. "When we find them, I suggest we attack immediately."

"But the prophecy says we have to find Excalibur and the Grail of Power first," Aliana reminded them.

"Prophecies are made to be interpreted. Who's to say we aren't meant to stop Morgana, at least, before any of that?" Lancelot said.

"Sire, what do we do?" Leo asked. Unlike the others, after Merlin had restored his memories, the newest member of their clan only addressed the king by his title.

Arthur had been watching silently, listening to everything. "Any chance to strike a blow against Morgana and Mordrid is a good one, but we need a strategy. Morgana has been in this world longer than any of us. Who knows what she has learned."

Aliana sat back, crossing her arms.

"What exactly is your plan? And what will Lia have to do?" Lacy voiced Aliana's thoughts.

"Nothing. This is not a magical attack. She stays here, protected." Galahad's eyes met hers, his tone unyielding.

"Aliana needs more training. You've come along quickly, but you are not a match for either Mordrid or Morgana, let alone both at once." Merlin's gaze was hard.

"You can't leave me on the sideline! I was good enough to stand up to Morgana today!" She watched the others in the room. Lancelot quirked a brow while Percy and Leo looked away. Owen's eyes were apologetic, and Wade just shrugged. "Arthur?" she asked. Surely he wouldn't leave her out.

"I'm sorry, but it's too dangerous," the king said.

Her jaw fell open. She was too shocked to even form words.

"Aliana, if we reveal the extent of your magic now, we lose the element of surprise," Galahad said, his hand on her shoulder.

She wanted to argue with all of them, but there was no point when they had decided against her. And damn Galahad—he had a good point. She was going to have to make her own plan then. "What about Lacy?" She was going to need her partner in crime to pull anything off.

"We'll have to find a safe haven for her, away from here." Arthur smiled at Lacy, completely unprepared for the powder keg he had just opened.

"Not a chance, Kingie. Wade's my brother and Lia's the closest thing I have to a sister. If you think I'm going to stand aside while they put their lives in danger, y'all are a hell of a lot dumber than you look."

Wade groaned while Percy and several of the others hid their chuckles.

"I'm sorry, but that's—" Lancelot started, but Lacy cut him off.

"Not a choice for you to make. This is the twenty-first century; the choice is mine."

Aliana held her breath, hoping the others wouldn't force Lacy to leave. She really needed her friend, and Wade would feel better with his sister safe by his side.

"Wade?" Arthur said. "She's your sister. What do you say?"

Wade studied his sister, worry present in his expression. "I haven't had any control over her actions since we were kids, and if you think you can force her..." He eyed Merlin and Lancelot. "I'll warn you, she likes to hit below the belt."

Merlin grumbled a curse, shaking his head. "If we let you stay, you must follow the rules we set. They are for your safety as well as Aliana's and ours."

"Now that that's settled, what were you saying earlier about attacking that witch?" Lacy grinned wildly.

"Merlin, since y'all have decided my role, at least let me help you locate Morgana." Aliana was determined to find out as much as she could about their plans.

"No, I have what I need. I suggest you show Lacy around the grounds before dinner," Merlin said, dismissing them.

Lacy started to object, but Aliana caught her eye, tilting her head toward the door and winking.

"Well then," Lacy said as she and Aliana stood, "I guess us lowly girls will leave you *boys* to your secret planning." She grabbed Aliana's hand, pulling her out of the library and down the hall toward the backyard. "Please tell me you're not going to just sit back and take this?" she whispered furiously.

Aliana rolled her eyes. "You know me better than that. But with these guys, I have to be clever about how I approach things."

Lacy narrowed her eyes skeptically but nodded.

"So what's the plan?"

"I'll talk to Arthur and Galahad and see if I can get them to give up the goods about their plans. And I think you should see what information you can get from Percy. Batting those baby blues of yours and your best bedside manner should do the trick."

Aliana smiled at her friend's suddenly red ears. Lacy had it bad for the gentle giant. "I guess I can do that."

The two stayed outside, planning in quiet voices, until Flora flew out to get them for dinner.

"You two look like you're up to something," the Pixie probed. "Anything I can do to help?"

"Wow!" Lacy said, getting her first good look at a Pixie. "You are so totally awesome."

"And don't you forget it!" Flora giggled.

Dinner was as it usually was, full of talk about tactics, weapons, and strategic attack along with an occasional, well-placed joke. Aliana took her typical seat between Arthur and Galahad while Lacy pulled up a chair between Percy and Owen.

Lacy flirted with her usual shameless charm, gaining Percy's undivided attention and Wade's glares.

"You seem happier than I expected after the way things went earlier," Galahad said softly to Aliana. "I didn't think you would take our desire to keep you safe so—"

"I'm not stupid, Galahad. I hate to say it, but you had a point earlier. I just wish you would at least tell me the plan so I won't spend the whole day going crazy."

He leaned in closer whispering in to her ear. "Would you meet me on the roof after dinner?"

Aliana glanced up. His eyes were that intense blue they always got when he was focused on her. Her plans forgotten, she gulped and nodded.

"I am sorry your friend got pulled into this," Arthur said, drawing her attention from Galahad. "I know how much you care about her."

"Thanks, but if anyone can handle this, it's Lacy. She's the toughest girl I know and way braver than me."

"I will not deny her courage, but I don't think you give enough credit to yourself," Arthur encouraged her, as always.

When dinner was cleared, Arthur, Lancelot, and Merlin left to finalize their plans for the attack. Wade glared at Percy, who offered to take Lacy on a tour of the house.

"Leave them, mate." Owen clapped his hand on Wade's shoulder. "Let's get the neophyte here caught up."

The newest member of the Round Table had been mostly silent since Merlin had restored his memories that afternoon. Leo smiled at Aliana as he, Dagg, Wade, and Owen filed out of the kitchen, leaving only her and Galahad.

"Shall we?" he said, rising and offering her his hand.

Nerves rushed through her, but the moment she took his hand, sparks shot up her arm and went straight to her heart. She immediately relaxed, following him up the stairs to the rooftop retreat. The night air was warm with the lightest of breezes teasing Aliana's heated skin.

"Galahad—"

"Aliana—" They spoke at the same time.

Aliana laughed, biting her lip. "I wanted to…"

"Please, let me speak first, Aliana."

She nodded, feeling his eyes on her as she leaned against the railing. She looked up and saw worry clouding his blue gaze.

"I knew I shouldn't have let you go without me today. When Lancelot told us you had been attacked, I was so angry, so full of rage. Most of all, I was scared of losing you." Galahad's usual absolute confidence had vanished. He roughly shoved his hands through his tousled brown locks.

Aliana's heart hurt for him. "Galahad, I'm…" His fingers touched her lips, silencing her.

"Just the thought of you in danger drives me to madness. I want to lock you away where I can always protect you, but I know that is not something I can do," he growled, quietly letting his finger fall from her lips. "For centuries I waited for this faceless Destined One to appear and free us."

Aliana looked away from him, but his hand cupped her face, turning her emerald eyes back to his.

"Then you came along and freed me. A girl with big eyes and a beautiful, caring soul. I knew right away that you were the one I had been waiting for." He stepped closer until only a few inches separated them. It was as if magic had leaped to life around them, freezing time. "I have waited so long for you. We all have. Yet, I would gladly go back to being a prisoner of the Sidhe if it meant I could spare you all this danger and hardship."

Aliana gasped, her eyes wide with questioning surprise. His free hand settled lightly on her waist, and she let him pull her against him, scarcely daring to blink for fear she would wake up to find all this to be a dream.

"I wish it wasn't you that had this destiny," he said.

Aliana's heart raced, beating so loudly she feared Galahad would hear it. He truly cared for her! But was she ready to give him her heart?

"You have lost much in your life," he said. "I know how that feels. Losing the people you love, family and friends, it can make you wish to never feel such pain again. But no one should live their life like that, Aliana. Least of all you." His thumb stroked her cheek, and she leaned into his touch, her eyes fluttering closed.

"Give me your trust, Aliana, and I swear I will never willingly betray it. Give me your heart, and no one will care for it like I will," he promised in a gruff voice.

"And what about your heart, your trust?" she whispered, her gaze returning to his, begging for the truth.

"Don't you know Aliana? You had all of me the first time you touched me. My heart, my trust, my soul, and my loyalty." His face lowered to hers, stopping only inches from her lips. "And you have my love."

His sweet breath mingled with hers, and his wintery scent wrapped around her as the bond between them thumped, trying to pull them together. Yet, even if the band she'd felt around her heart since the first time he'd looked at her didn't exist, she still would have fallen in love with this knight.

Her eyes widened as she finally admitted to herself what she had been fighting from the beginning. His blazing eyes and soft promise wove their way around her heart, shattering the last of the walls she had built to protect herself. His lips were so close and she wanted so much for him to kiss her, but he waited. It had to be her choice.

"I want to be brave enough, Galahad." Her voice cracked, her eyes searching his. "It scares me how much I care for you. I have fought this. I want my life to be more than just fulfilling a prophecy! I've had my heart broken so many times, and I'm scared that if something happens between us to ruin this, I won't be strong enough to survive the heartbreak this time." She gave him a sad smile. "My mom used to tell me that love is trusting a person enough to know they'll always stand by you. She said that everyone has one person in the world meant for them—their soul mate. We just have to be strong enough to let them in when we find them."

Galahad's eyes filled with hope. "I want you to be mine, Aliana, only mine. But the decision is yours." His voice rasped against her lips.

Aliana closed her eyes, taking a leap that she hoped she'd survive. Softly, she brushed her lips against his like the caress of a butterfly's wing.

His hand tightened on her waist, his breathing speeding up. "Is this your choice?"

"Yes." She kissed him again.

Galahad's hand slid into her hair, his lips taking over. They were hot and demanding like the sparks that were building into an inferno inside her. Aliana gripped his shoulders as she rose to her tiptoes. She wrapped her arms around him, her fingers teasing the base of his neck as she deepened the kiss. Galahad groaned, pulling her tighter against him, tilting her head and nipping at her lip. Without hesitation, she opened her mouth to his command, and his tongue swept in, dancing with hers.

He was consuming her, laying claim to every part of her, and Aliana responded in kind. She was his, and he was hers!

Galahad's lips broke from hers, trailing kisses across her chin and down her neck. She gasped as his teeth nipped at her sensitive throat. Wanting to feel his lips against hers again, she pulled him back to her mouth. They stayed there for what seemed like ages, kissing and touching until they heard the others gathering in the backyard.

Aliana broke the kiss and rested her forehead against his, fighting to catch her breath and cool the raging inferno between them. "We should probably go down and join them," she said as Lacy's shrieks of laughter filled the night air.

His fingers ran across her cheek and down her neck before tangling in her long locks again. His lips claimed hers, strong and sure, leaving a searing brand on her heart. He pulled back a scant inch, whispering, "What if I said I wanted to keep you up here all to myself?"

Aliana giggled breathlessly. "I wouldn't object, but Dagg might. I can feel him waiting for us."

His lips brushed against hers once, twice, his fingers tangling with hers. "Your wish is my command."

Aliana laughed. Her heart felt so light. For the first time in over two years, she felt whole again.

Dagg was waiting for them at the base of the curving staircase. His purple eyes flicked to their entwined hands, and the Dragon smiled. "Glad to see that's sorted," he teased, circling the pair.

"What are the others doing?" Aliana asked, wanting the Dragon off the subject.

"Lacy has somehow convinced everyone it's a good idea to see who the better tracker is. She has managed to blindfold first Percy and now Wade to see if they can seek out everyone else."

"You're kidding! They're playing Marco Polo?" Aliana doubled over, laughing.

"Shall I go prove my dominance again, Aliana?" Galahad's mouth turned up in a smile as she pulled herself together.

"Go get 'em, tiger."

Galahad settled his hand on her back, leading her out to others.

Wade fumbled around the yard, a black scarf tied over his eyes as he called out to the others. Lacy couldn't contain her giggles when he charged toward her. But before her brother could grab her, Percy swooped in, wrapping his arm around her waist and pulling her against his body, out of Wade's path.

"Damn it!" Wade cursed, taking off after Leo.

Lacy and Arthur spotted Aliana and Galahad at the same time. Arthur studied them with a slight frown on his face.

"'Bout time you two joined us." Lacy winked at Aliana, giving her a big thumbs-up.

Wade untied the blindfold. "I think it's Galahad's turn. Don't you, boys?" He tossed Galahad the cloth.

"Don't be a sore loser, brother," Lacy teased.

Handing the scarf to Aliana, Galahad bowed so she could tie the black fabric around his eyes. "No peeking," Aliana warned, giggling.

As the others spread out, calling to Galahad from every direction, Wade came to Aliana's side. "I see Galahad finally made his move." Wade glanced from her to the tall knight, who was currently tracking down Owen and Lancelot. "But you know you'll need to explain this to the king."

"Why? I mean, I planned to tell him. He's my friend just like you and the others."

Wade shook his head. "You can't see that he's infatuated with you?"

Arthur approached, and Wade returned to the game, letting the king take his spot.

"This may be none of my affair, Aliana, but you and Galahad seem *closer*," Arthur said.

She blushed but smiled, watching Galahad as he tackled both Percy and Leo with his super speed. Only Merlin and Wade were left uncaught.

"Yeah, we…remember when I explained to you about girlfriends and boyfriends?"

Arthur nodded, his face set in the calm mask he only seemed to drop when they were alone.

"Well, I guess that's what Galahad and I are now."

Arthur was silent for a moment and Aliana frowned, worried, until she saw the corner of his mouth turn up. "I assume our chats and dance lessons won't be continuing."

"Why not?" she asked.

"I would think you'd be busy with Galahad." Arthur watched said warrior tackle Wade.

"Just because the relationship between me and Galahad has changed doesn't mean I don't want to spend time with you, Arthur." She looked up at the king, taking his hand. "I like spending time with you. It's fun and I feel like it's one of the only times I can just be myself. You're my friend. Galahad will understand."

Arthur appeared relieved but something in his expression still seemed troubled. She guessed that he was probably thinking about his mystery love again — the vague memory of her seemed to constantly plague him.

The night ended soon after that. Lacy followed Wade, Leo, Percy, and Owen to their wing of the house, where Flora and the other Pixies had prepared a room for her.

Dagg flew off to the kitchen, intent on grabbing a snack before bed, giving Aliana and Galahad privacy to say good night. Galahad followed Aliana into her bedroom. It was the first time he had been past the doorway, and he paused a moment to take in the lovely room. "I see you like flowers," he said, noticing the bouquets Flora had placed around the room.

"They smell nice." Aliana stood with her hands clasped, completely distracted by having the gorgeous knight taking up so much space in her room.

Galahad was suddenly in front of her, catching her startled gasp with his lips. The kiss was long and sweet, his hands brushing down her arms and circling around her waist. All too soon, he pulled back, his eyes still closed and a satisfied smile on his lips. "Good night, Aliana."

"Good night, Galahad," she whispered back, still out of breath. He leaned in, kissing her softly one last time before stepping into the hall and closing the door behind him.

"Wow," she said, falling back onto the soft covers of her bed.

22

I knew something had changed the moment they stepped out from the house. When Aliana told me that she and Galahad are dating I had to battle down my howl of anger, and I'm ashamed to say, my jealousy. Losing my chance with her hurts more than struggling to remember my ghost woman, yet I must accept it. Both women are a distraction from my duty to my friends, my kingdom, and to fulfilling the Fae queen's prophecy. Saving the realms must come first. Yet that knowledge doesn't make the decision to not wake the girls as we prepare to face Mordrid and Morgana any easier. But I agree with Merlin; it is for their safety.

— Arthur

"Lia, wake up!" Lacy demanded, pulling Aliana's pillow out from under her head.

"What the heck, Lacy!" Aliana whined, noticing Dagg perched on Lacy's shoulder.

"Get up! The guys are suiting up to leave!"

Those words banished Aliana's sleepiness. The brunette jumped from her bed, grabbing clothes from the floor and running into the bathroom to change. "When did this happen?" she asked, hopping on one foot, trying to get her jeans on.

"Merlin located Morgana early this morning. They want to attack before the rain clouds clear. Mordrid and Morgana won't be expecting an attack this soon," Dagg explained.

Aliana's temper flared, realizing that the guys weren't going to bother to wake her. Galahad hadn't come even after everything he'd said the night before. Thundering down the stairs, the trio stopped in the foyer, watching the eight men strap weapons onto their chain mail- and leather-covered bodies.

Leo had *katanas* strapped over his shoulders and was loading a crossbow, securing several bolts for reload. Percy, Owen, Lancelot, and Wade all had broadswords hanging from their right hips along with shorter, thinner swords on the left. Dagger handles peeked out from their boots.

At his waist, Arthur had attached the beautiful sword the fire Elves had forged for him. At his feet was an honest-to-God spiked mace. He was breathtaking, but this time it wasn't his good looks that made Aliana's heart race. It was the realization that they were actually doing this.

Galahad had his sword strapped across his back with several daggers and long knives at his waist. His eyes met hers as he kneeled down, hiding small knives in his boots. He rose, like a terrifying and strong warrior god ready to defeat his enemy using any means possible.

Worry and terror swamped her. This wasn't a good idea. They should wait, but what could she say to convince them? "Were any of you going to wake me before you went running off into a fight for your lives?"

She and Lacy hadn't even had time to pull together a decent plan to follow them. Lacy had come to her room late the night before to tell her she'd been successful in getting some information from Percy and Owen. But Wade had caught on to her snooping and cut her off.

"This is our best chance. We have to take it while we have the advantage," Lancelot said, straightening his vest.

"Aw, come on, don't look at me like that, sis," Wade said as Lacy went to his side, worry evident on her pale face. She had to be having a harder time with this than Aliana—at least Aliana had seen them fight before and knew what they were capable of.

"Do not fret, Aliana." Arthur smiled, coming over to kiss her hand. "Our plan is solid and the dark clouds will give us cover. We know what we're doing."

She wanted to believe him, but the little worrying voice in her head wouldn't be silenced. No sooner had he let her go than Merlin announced it was time to leave.

"How are you even getting there?" Alana asked, growing more frantic by the moment.

"I am taking us through a grid portal, and Lancelot will guide us the rest of the way," Merlin explained.

"Can I at least help?" Aliana tried one last time. They all shook their heads.

"You are learning fast, Aliana," Merlin said. "But you're not ready, and it's safer for you and us if you are here. If you were on the battlefield with us, we would be too worried about you. None of us would be able to focus on the enemy."

"You mean you want us hidden away while you *men* go off to battle," Lacy snapped.

"Lacy," Percy said, drawing the blonde to his side. "We're trying to protect both of you."

Lacy smiled sadly at the knight she was falling for. "Then you and Wade better come back in one whole piece or I'll kick your asses! That goes for all of you." She tried to glare at all the guys.

The guys chuckled, but Aliana couldn't even crack a smile. One by one they walked out the door, all offering smiles and reassurance that they would be back. Aliana, Arthur, and Galahad were the only ones left inside after Lacy and Dagg joined the others. Galahad wrapped his arm around Aliana's waist, tucking her against his side.

"Were either of you going to wake me before you left?" she whispered, holding back tears of frustration and worry.

"Yes," Arthur assured her. "But we wanted to be prepared first."

"So you could take off quickly if I tried to follow." She was livid, but she couldn't bring herself to separate from Galahad.

"We are sorry, Aliana," Galahad said, rubbing his hand over her waist.

Arthur bowed his head to Aliana and left.

"Galahad, please tell me where you're going!" she begged. They had just gotten together. She couldn't lose him so soon.

"Far enough away that you will be safe." His fingers traced the skin bared by her short tank top. But even the sparks that came with his touch couldn't calm her.

"Please be careful. I have a bad feeling about this," she whispered, wrapping her arms around his waist, not caring that the hilts of his daggers pressed into her sides.

Galahad tipped her face up to meet his, taking her mouth in a warm, deep kiss full of promise and love. Pulling back, he stroked his fingers across her cheek before claiming one last, intense kiss. Aliana clung tightly to him, her fingers gripping the thick leather he wore over his chainmail.

Galahad broke the kiss and rested his cheek against hers. "I will see that everyone comes back safely. Please promise me you will stay here. I cannot focus if I'm worried your friend will talk you into doing something foolish."

Aliana flushed. Wade must have ratted them out.

"I thought so." Galahad sighed, kissing her forehead.

"I'll stay safe," Aliana assured him. She would be safe with her magic and Dagg watching her back.

"They're waiting," Lacy said, her face somber as she poked her head inside. Dagg was on her shoulder.

Aliana and Galahad walked outside. He kissed her hand and then followed Merlin and the other Knights of the Round Table into the thick trees, toward battle. Here was another dream come to life before her, but Aliana couldn't feel any of the happiness or excitement that she had in Avalon. Maybe she would when they came back safe.

She and Lacy stood in the driveway, not willing to go inside until the guys were gone from their sight. A quick flash of yellow streaked into the woods.

"Is that —?" Aliana whispered to Lacy, not wanting to alert Dagg just yet.

"Yep. Flora's leaving us a trail," Lacy whispered before Dagg wrapped himself around Aliana's shoulders.

Wondering when Lacy had roped Flora into all this, Aliana took Lacy's hand, pulling her inside the house and toward Merlin's armory.

"And what do you two think you're doing?" Dagg asked.

"About that." Aliana picked up a curved bow — thanks to all her training, she was now a better shot than most of the knights. "You didn't really think we were just going to sit back and let this happen, did you?"

Dagg landed on the quiver she was about to pick up, glaring at her with disapproval. "I heard you make a promise to Galahad."

"I chose my words carefully. I promised him I'd be safe." She picked up the Dragon and set him aside. "And I will be—with you there to watch our backs." Dagg continued to argue, but both girls brushed his worries aside. "Like it or not, those guys are going to need me. I just know it!"

"That doesn't mean you should make the situation worse by doing the opposite of what they want you to do."

Lacy rolled her eyes. "If it were up to them, we wouldn't ever be allowed to leave the house."

"I could stop you with magic," Dagg threatened.

"But you won't," Aliana said softly, calling his bluff.

Slinging the bow across her back, she caught the staff Lacy tossed her way. Her friend buckled a sword around her waist. Unlike Aliana, Lacy had no problem handling a blade. Like Wade, Lacy had been in martial arts training since she was a young kid and knew how to handle a lot of weapons, including swords. Her brother hadn't been joking when he'd told the guys she fought dirty—he'd taught her almost every dirty defensive trick there was.

The trio whirled around as the heavy door blasted open with a bang. Flora plopped onto a table, hand on her chest. "They…used the portal…by the stream." She gasped, fighting to catch her breath.

"Now you've involved the Pixie?" Dagg growled, exasperated.

"Would you have followed them for us?" Lacy asked, shooting the Dragon a dirty look.

Aliana opened a cabinet filled with thick leathers designed for fighting. She had been surprised a week earlier when she'd discovered the battle suits made for women. When she'd asked Merlin about them, he'd simply said that was a tale for another day.

Suited up and with weapons secured, Aliana and Lacy left the protected house, following the golden-hued glow that Flora had left for them.

"This is not a wise plan!" Dagg insisted again, following the pair into the woods.

Drawing on her magic, Aliana reached out, connecting with the earth. Merlin's forest was lush and teeming with life. She felt the energy of the animals and the steady rush of power as the earth pushed toward her.

"Don't take in too much at once," Dagg reminded her, apparently deciding it was no use to argue anymore. "Your body can't handle the stress yet."

Aliana didn't need the reminder; she remembered what had happened in Avalon and against Morgana. She wouldn't be of any use if she couldn't control the magic, so she closed off her connection.

"Lady Aliana." She looked around for the familiar, silky voice. J'alel stepped out from behind a large tree, his friendly face a welcome sight.

"J'alel!" She walked toward him. "What are you doing here?"

"I heard the king was planning an attack. I came to offer my aid."

She returned his warm smile.

"They've already left. We were following them."

"They do not know you are joining them?" His questioning gaze wandered from Aliana to Lacy and then Dagg.

"Don't tell us we shouldn't go," Aliana implored the Elf.

Lacy coughed loudly. "Manners, Aliana."

As soon as Aliana turned from J'alel, black and gray magic shot past her, sending Lacy and Dagg sailing back.

"What?" Aliana wheeled around to face J'alel, but the Elf was gone.

In his place stood a tall, long-limbed man with raven black hair curling around his chin and neck. His thin, cruel mouth turned up in a smirk as she recognized him from her dream.

"Mordrid." She nocked an arrow, ready to fight.

Mordrid raised a hand, and his black-gray magic wrapped around her like snakes, binding her arms and feet. Her bow fell from her hands, the quiver on her back following. Aliana dropped to her knees, struggling against the magic. The harder she fought her bonds, the tighter they gripped, causing pain to tear through her.

Dagg roared, flying from behind her to attack the black wizard. He dodged blasts of the black magic, hissing streams of Dragon fire. An arrow flew through the air, hurtling toward the wizard, but he deflected it with a flick of his wrist, throwing Lacy violently against a tree.

"Lacy!" Aliana cried as her friend hit the ground. The snapping sound of breaking bones was unmistakable.

Black magic curled around Dagg like a demon cloud charged with electricity. The Dragon roared in pain.

"Leave them alone!" Aliana begged, trying to call on her magic, but the racing of her heart and the searing pain wouldn't let her concentrate.

The dark wizard's eerie, black eyes leered at her as he ran a finger across her cheek. Cold, evil magic flowed over her skin, much like the creepy power she'd felt in her dream weeks ago. "I knew you'd recognize me." His penetrating, nasally voice sounded pleased, as if he'd won some great victory because she remembered him.

"How were you in my dream?" she demanded, trying again to push against the bonds holding her, but they only tightened.

"You should have tried harder to stop them," he taunted. "Your knights are walking right into our trap, just like you and your friends."

Dagg roared again.

"Why are you doing this?" She struggled to take a full breath. She needed to calm down and focus her magic enough to fight back.

Mordrid sneered. "I must finish what I started over a millennium ago. Arthur and your friends have much pain coming to them." With a twist of his wrist, Aliana's bonds lifted her to her feet and then pulled her higher so that she hovered a few inches off the ground. Fear flooded her as she realized that she was completely at Mordrid's mercy.

He drew her close, much closer than she ever wanted to be to him. His eyes weren't black like she had thought. They were a dirty brown flecked with black. His hot breath fanned over her face as he whispered in her ear, "Everyone is waiting on us, my queen."

Fighting back the bile burning her throat, Aliana watched his magic lift Lacy's unconscious body off the ground, pulling her friend and Dagg along behind them. Aliana pushed her magic out again. The bonds loosened for an instant before snapping back, tighter than before. She could already feel the bruises forming, but she couldn't give up.

Mordrid smiled as she bit back her cries of pain. "Nice try, but your magic is nothing compared to mine...yet."

"Yet?" Aliana wheezed, trying to push past the pain and terror. Her friends needed her to hold it together.

"Yes, after I kill your knights I plan to train you and turn your magic to the dark. You'll be the jewel in my crown when I rule the realms."

Aliana fought back her tremor as his unblinking, lustful eyes raked her from head to toe. *I'm going to be sick,* she thought as his magic crackled around her, pulling all of them away. More pain layered on top of the agony already racking her body. Just when she thought she'd pass out, the crushing pressure disappeared. She heard the sounds of a fight raging close by and forced her eyes open. Battle cries filled the air. The clanging of metal rang loudly in the distance as sword clashed against sword.

"How did you know we planned to attack? Or that Lacy and I would be alone?" she demanded, hoping to buy herself some time to gather what little of her magic she could.

"You seem like an intelligent girl. You tell me." Mordrid smirked.

Aliana thought back, and then remembered the night she had fallen asleep on the roof. "The TreTale."

"Very good. Merlin's powers are not what they used to be. My little spy easily penetrated the defenses around his home." He laughed again, moving them toward the battle.

"You don't know what you're talking about. Merlin is the strongest Druid ever!" Aliana may not have always liked the guy, but facts were facts.

Mordrid chuckled. "Merlin has you all fooled. I know you have your doubts about him, and Lancelot for that matter. I warned you to be cautious of their treachery."

"You're trying to turn me against my friends! It won't work." But he was right about one thing—Lancelot and Merlin did have secrets.

"You can deny it all you want, but your mind tells you I am correct." He smirked. "Let's say that by some miracle you stop me, and what do you think will happen after? The only reason they want you is to gain their freedom from their pact. They will leave you and not look back. They don't really care for you, not like I do."

"You don't know what you're talking about!" But did *she?* Would they all leave her when this was over? No, Galahad had proved himself to her last night, and the warriors had all become her family. They wouldn't just leave her!

"Time to watch your heroes die, my dear Aliana."

Her head snapped up. "As soon as they see us, they will stop you and Morgana. And when I get free, I'll be by their side helping!"

Mordrid spun around, gripping her chin, roughly forcing her to meet his unrelenting gaze. "They won't know I have you until I want them to. You think all of those fools are so noble, that they've told you the truth about everything? You have no idea what you've been thrown into. But you will when you are by my side." Yanking her forward, he crushed his lips against hers.

Disgusted by him and his dark magic as it tried to consume her, Aliana fought back, wrenching her mouth from his hard, cruel lips. "Never!" she hissed. "I don't help monsters."

"Maybe I'm not the monster you think I am," he growled softly.

Battle sounds exploded when Mordrid pulled his prisoners into an enclosed valley. Carnage was all around them. Shattered pieces of black armor littered the field that was also flecked with the blood of her knights.

Morgana and Merlin were close, fighting furiously with his golden magic pitted against her cold blue.

"You'll die at my hands, *lover*," Morgana hissed.

"I already ended you once, Morgana. I will do it again." Merlin grunted, blocking a stream of her acid-like magic.

"You betrayed me! Left me for dead. You should have finished the deed," she spat back. "Rest assured, *I* won't make the same mistake."

Merlin's eyes flashed a brilliant gold. Rearing back, he threw a spell so strong it nearly blinded Aliana before she looked away.

With one powerful stroke from his fiery sword, Arthur decapitated two of the almost two dozen demon knights. Turning, he took down another as it snuck up from behind. Wade, Percy, and Leo fought on, their backs to each other, surrounded by enemies. They attacked hard, maiming black knights with nearly every stroke. Lancelot and Owen tried to fight off eight of the spirits, but they were losing quickly. Galahad came roaring from behind, his super speed keeping him a blur until he stopped long enough to chop off helmets and body parts. In seconds, a dozen more black knights fell in rotting pieces to the ground.

The enemy's numbers dwindled and the knights fell back, joining Arthur as the battle swung in their favor. Pulling out one of his daggers, Galahad launched it like a boomerang, cutting down two more black knights. Finally, the odds were even as Merlin joined the knights to form a magnificent battle line. Fearsome power rolled off them. It was no wonder Titania had said they were undefeatable side by side.

Aliana smirked, wanting to gloat at Mordrid, but the wizard just watched, waiting.

Tortured moans and cries of outrage filled the gray sky as ghostly streaks of gray surrounded the knights. The empty armor rose from the ground, consuming the spirits and restoring Mordrid's evil army.

"No!" Aliana cried, struggling to break free.

Merlin's head snapped to the side, to face her, and his eyes widened in disbelief and anger. Mordrid must have removed whatever power he had used to shield her, Lacy, and Dagg from view. The others chanced a glance away from the enemy line, outraged when they saw her.

Percy and Wade looked horrified when they saw Lacy's unconscious body.

"Aliana!" Galahad roared. Using his new speed, he moved around the black knights, but Morgana threw up a solid wall of magic, blasting him back as he crashed into the icy magic.

"I see this one thinks he has a claim on you, love. He'll be the first I kill," Mordrid promised, stroking a finger down her cheek.

23

My queen is absent again this evening. She must be deep into one of her schemes. Perhaps it is time I took a closer look at Titania's actions as of late. She has not been this secretive since I allowed her return from the exile she earned by helping that mortal king and his men.

Oberon, King of Avalon

"Don't touch her!" Arthur ordered, his face set in harsh lines, fury evident in the rigid set of his body.

Aliana's anger swirled and her magic jumped. She couldn't let Mordrid use her against the knights! She turned her head away from the evil sorcerer, glancing at her captured friends. Dagg growled and hissed, fighting to free himself from the black cloud that ensnared him. Flashes of his purple magic broke through.

"You see the prize I have won. Does it eat at you knowing that I have what's most important to you?" Mordrid's cold voice rang with a long-festering hatred.

Camelot's knights eyed the black knights, holding their weapons ready to destroy the reincarnated army. The power flowing through the small valley choked the air, promising death and pain.

"Let them go unharmed," Galahad challenged, his voice grave and vehement, "and we'll make your deaths quick."

"You're daft!" Morgana guffawed. "You can't win! Kill these black knights and more will come."

Their power isn't at full strength. Merlin's voice rang in Aliana's mind. Her eyes moved from Galahad to the Druid, and Merlin gave a slight nod.

I can't get free of his magic. Mordrid knows every time I try to break free, she whispered through the link.

Draw on the elements. Diffuse his magic like you do with your shield, Merlin instructed. *We'll distract him.*

Without warning, Merlin threw up his arms, calling down endless bolts of lightning, all directed at Morgana, Mordrid, and the black knights. Aliana's knights charged. Their fierce battle cries and the clanging of their swords were nearly deafening. Merlin succeeded in drawing Mordrid into the fight. He and Morgana battled the onslaught of crackling gold magic.

Taking a breath, Aliana shut out the aching pain.

Control.

Her friends needed her.

Mordrid would kill them all if she gave in to his dark magic.

Merlin and Dagg had already given her the tools to fight this evil! She focused on the magic that trapped her. It was burning cold, moving against her skin like a coiled snake. She wanted to fight against it, but she quelled the reaction. Instead she pulled the magic slowly into herself. The black power crawled through her veins like insects, but she kept absorbing it, little by little.

Daggerhorne is almost free. Merlin's thoughts pierced her calm.

Good, she thought, keeping her concentration. One slip and Mordrid would know what she was doing. She couldn't let that happen. The lives of the people she loved were at stake.

Gripping the gray with her own magic, Aliana tugged and beckoned the darkness. There! She had it. The magic was hers! She loosened the bonds binding her, but kept up the appearance of being confined. She needed a plan to get Lacy to safety before she broke free.

Dagg growled low behind her, but this time his rumble was strong and pain free. She looked back and saw the Dragon's glowing, purple eyes through the cloud. He had control just like she did. She flicked her eyes to Lacy, hoping the Dragon would understand and get her friend to safety. Returning her attention to the raging battle only a few feet from her, she saw Morgana and Mordrid teamed against Merlin, but the Druid fought them back with a deadly ferocity. Arthur and his knights cut down more black knights, but they couldn't seem to make any headway in the vicious battle. More spirits came as quickly as they fell.

Lacy moaned behind Aliana, who turned meet her friend's confused gaze. Aliana tilted her head toward Dagg, silently warning her friend to be ready. Lacy bit her lips, holding back a cry as she shifted her mangled arm. Praying Lacy would be all right, Aliana summoned her pink magic, pulling hard at the last of Mordrid's control and releasing his bonds from around the three of them. A nearly soundless void wrapped around her, and the battle slowed before her eyes.

"What?" Mordrid's outraged cries of surprise were muffled, like she had cotton in her ears.

Dagg shot out of his cloud prison like a demon from hell, attacking Mordrid and Morgana with an endless stream of Dragon fire. His devastating power burned their skin, consuming the evil duo, setting their clothes and bodies ablaze.

Aliana's feet hit the ground and she ran, grabbing Lacy's uninjured hand as her friend struggled to get to her feet. They dashed toward the others. Aliana summoned her magic, pushing the black knights aside so she and Lacy could break through the enemy line. Galahad's arms were there instantly, wrapping around her and Lacy, pulling the pair back behind the knights' defensive line.

"No!" Mordrid cried, extinguishing the Dragon fire. Morgana fell back to his side. Their clothes were covered in burn marks and ashes, and their skin bled and boiled with blisters.

"I will make you pay!" Morgana shrieked as the black knights attacked in brutal force. Galahad released the girls, taking up his sword and rejoining the fight. The stream of spirits kept coming as the knights severed black heads one after another. Arthur's men were beaten and bloodied, showing signs of fatigue. They couldn't keep up the battle at this pace for much longer.

The black magic crawled under Aliana's skin again, starting to fight against her own bright magic. Her head pounded and she fell to her knees as the pain tried to rip her in two. She had to get rid of this poison. Her body shuddered again, pitching her forward, her hands and arms hitting the hard ground and digging into the soil. The magic of the earth element surrounded her, whispering, offering itself to her. Aliana knew what to do.

Corralling the blackness with her pink magic, she forced the invading magic into the ground, giving the destructive power to the earth. Electric-charged vines shot out of the dirt, wrapping around and spearing through the black knights, ripping them apart, crushing their armor. The earth swallowed the foul decay that was left behind. With no physical object to return to, the black spirits wailed and vanished, leaving Morgana and Mordrid behind, bleeding and defeated. One of the spirits sailed by Aliana, brushing over her, but instead of darkness, she felt goodness, relief. The spirit almost seemed to be thanking her.

She looked up at Mordrid. Her sight was blurred, but she could see the rage and astonishment in his sick, black gaze. "We'll be back to finish this," he promised her with a twisting smile that made her want to gag.

Morgana raised her arms and the two evil sorcerers disappeared in a whirlwind.

Thanking the earth, Aliana released the element's power. An arm wrapped around her as Lacy pulled her up, and Dagg wrapped himself around her shoulders, pushing his healing energy into her body.

Sparks sizzled on her skin as Galahad cupped her face, his azure eyes frantically searching hers. "You brave, foolish girl. Don't ever do that again!" He pulled her from Lacy's hold, carefully cradling her in his arms. "What were you thinking?" he breathed against her ear, his arms tightening.

"Take us home, Merlin," Arthur ordered as everyone gathered around the couple.

Merlin slashed his hand down like the stroke of a sword ripping the air, causing a golden portal to open. Aliana wrapped her arm around Galahad's neck, bracing for the pain she'd felt when Mordrid had transported her earlier, but all she felt was a brush of cool energy soothing her abused skin. She turned her face into Galahad's neck, inhaling his wintery, spicy scent. Their bond burned away the last of the creeping blackness. She didn't even realize they were back at the house until Merlin started barking commands.

"Sit them on the couches," he ordered as Stella, Flora, and four other Pixies rushed into the room, bringing bottles of glittering powders.

Galahad sat down with Aliana still in his arms, his heated eyes telling them all that he wouldn't be separated from her. Her heart fluttered as his lips brushed her forehead.

"Drink this, Aliana," Flora said, her blue eyes big with worry and unshed tears.

Aliana smiled at the Pixie, taking the cup. Drinking the sweet nectar, she looked to Lacy. Percy and Wade were hunched over her fierce friend as Stella and Merlin healed the blonde's broken bones.

"How did this happen?" Arthur asked, kneeling next to Aliana. His hand gently brushed sweat-clumped locks of hair from her face.

"I was stupid," Aliana admitted, her voice weak. "You were right all along, Galahad. That TreTale was meant to find me. It followed us from Avalon." She looked up, fearing how angry Galahad, Arthur, and the others would be with her. She explained about her and Lacy's plan to follow them into battle and how Mordrid had tricked them, taking them prisoner.

All of the guys burst out in anger, demanding to know why the two of them would do something so stupid and reckless.

"Why did all of you?" Aliana said, trying to push out of Galahad's arms, but he refused to let her go. "I told y'all this was a trap!"

"We knew that was a possibility, but we had to make this move!" Merlin growled.

"You let your hatred and arrogance blind you," Aliana spat at him.

"Enough!" Arthur's voice silenced them. "Aliana, you ignored our orders, placing yourself and your friend in unneeded danger."

Aliana reeled back. Arthur had never yelled at her before. "You clearly didn't hear me. Mordrid's TreTale had already gotten past Merlin's shields. If we had stayed, Mordrid would have still gotten us."

"Fighting amongst ourselves won't change what's happened," Leo said, standing next to the king. "We need to move past this and plan our next move."

"Leo is right," Galahad said, standing with Aliana still cradled in his arms. "We won despite everything, thanks to Aliana's magic. But we also learned that Morgana and Mordrid have a weakness."

Galahad looked down at her, his face pained. "And we learned more of Mordrid's plan."

"We need to find another place to stay," Wade murmured, his arm around his sister. "The sooner the better."

"Merlin?" Arthur asked, turning to the fuming Druid.

"I'll arrange it," Merlin vowed, leaving the room.

"We all need to rest," Arthur said, staring at Aliana. "Thank you for saving us."

"We weren't trying to make things worse," Lacy whispered.

Before anyone else could speak, Galahad carried Aliana out of the library and up to her room, moving so fast that she didn't have a chance to protest until he had them shut up in her room. "I can take it from here, Galahad," she said when he set her on her feet.

Instead of answering, he claimed her mouth in a kiss just this side of bruising. Whimpering, Aliana clung to him, desperate to forget her terror and the pain of the day. He held her tight, his hands wandering up and down her back and into her hair. He couldn't seem to get enough, and neither could she.

She cried out as his hand rubbed across a bruise left by Mordrid.

"I'll kill him for touching you," Galahad swore, his voice as full of rage as his gaze. "He will not have you."

"Galahad, you can't let this get to you," she whispered, worried by the hatred in his voice.

His hands gripped her arms below her bruises, his thumb gently stroking over the bluish back marks. "No, Aliana. You don't know what he's capable of." He rested his forehead against hers.

Reluctantly, he stepped back. "You should take care of your wounds and rest. I'll go get us some food."

"What about you?" she asked, taking his hands in hers.

He brought their clasped hands to his lips, brushing feather light kisses across her fingers. "I will rest when you are taken care of."

Sighing, she nodded, kissing his cheek before disappearing into the bathroom. She heard the door shut softly. The sudden silence racked her almost as much as Mordrid's magic had. All she was left with were her own tortured thoughts. Tears leaked from her eyes as she filled the large tub. Her friends had come close to losing today. Lacy could have easily been killed, and Mordrid's sick obsession with

Aliana had put Galahad's life—all the knights' lives—in danger. Sinking into the water, she let loose a sobbing scream. She had already lost her parents because of her own stupid actions, something she still couldn't let herself think about. Today, she could have lost more people she loved. All because of her.

"Aliana?" Jerking up, she brushed away her tears to see Flora walk into the bathroom. "I thought you might want some Pixie dust." The tiny Pixie held out a vial of glittering magic.

"Thanks," Aliana said, her voice wobbling. "But can you give it to Lacy? She needs it more than me."

"Sure." The Pixie nodded solemnly. "Is there anything I can do for you?"

"No." Aliana tried to give the Pixie a small smile, but she was pretty sure she failed.

"Okay. Galahad is waiting out in the hall for you with some food."

"And the others?" Aliana asked, splashing water onto her face, trying to scrub away her tears and the haunting guilt.

"Percy and Wade are with Lacy. The others are in the library." With a nod, the Pixie left Aliana in the quiet of her bathroom.

She got out of the tub. Toweling off, she slipped on her favorite yoga pants and T-shirt and twisted her wet locks into a tight braid. Taking a breath, she opened her door. Just like Flora had said, Galahad waited in the hall with half of a pizza and glasses of Pixie juice. Stepping back, Aliana motioned for him to come in. He'd changed out of his battle clothes into a T-shirt and jeans, and his hair was still damp from a shower.

"Thanks," she said, moving aside her laptop to make room on the small coffee table at the end of her bed. Galahad set the tray down, taking a seat on the floor at her side. "I'm sorry, Galahad." She stared at the pizza, afraid to see the disappointment in his blue eyes.

"I'm still upset. You placed yourself in danger!" He sighed in frustration. "But we were wrong too. We needed you with us—we would have lost today without you."

Aliana snapped her head up, thinking she had heard him wrong.

His hand wrapped around the back of her neck, tracing small circles over her skin, and her anguish started to fade as their sparks flared. "Eat," he commanded, his voice rough.

Aliana's stomach growled.

Every now and then as they ate, Galahad would run his fingers down her arm or tuck an escaped piece of her hair behind her ear. With every touch, more sparks rushed through her, soothing her anxiety and tense muscles.

"Please don't ever scare me like that again, Aliana," Galahad pleaded softly, pushing aside his plate. "I can't stand the thought that Mordrid had you at his mercy."

"We knew this would be dangerous," Aliana said. But until that day, she hadn't realized how real the danger was. Beyond exhausted, emotionally and physically, Aliana took Galahad's hand and pulled him onto her bed.

"Aliana?" he asked, hesitating.

She smiled, scooting toward the middle of the bed to give him more room. "I'm so tired, Galahad, but I'm afraid to go to sleep. Please just hold me." It had taken every ounce of courage she had left to admit her fears and make the request.

His eyes never left hers as he stretched out on her bed, leaning against the headboard and mountain of pillows. Aliana curled against his side, resting her head on his warm chest and wrapping one arm around his waist, then closing her eyes. The knight's winter spice scent and strong arms wrapped around her, holding her in his warm, caring grasp.

"Sleep, Aliana, I'll protect you," he whispered into her hair, kissing her lightly, his thumb moving back and forth over her skin.

Surrendering to exhaustion and the comforting sparks of their bond, she slipped into a deep sleep.

Aliana looked around the familiar college professor's office. A large desk overflowing with piles of papers, colored files, and small artifacts took up most of the room. Two chairs faced her father's desk and the wall of books behind it.

When Aliana had turned fifteen, her parents had decided to give up their traveling lifestyle and settle down so Aliana could attend high school with her three best friends from home. They wanted her to experience school like any other teen. Allen Fagan had taken a prestigious teaching job at a private university just outside Charleston, South Carolina. Carrie Fagan had opened a private acting and dancing school for local children who dreamed of being famous someday.

Aliana remembered all the times she and her mother would bring dinner to her father at his office when he had late classes or had simply lost track of time. Even though he rarely went on excursions anymore, he was constantly asked to lend his opinion and help with research. He was the best in his field.

The office door opened and in walked a short, balding man wearing a charcoal blazer over a stained shirt and faded khakis. "Come now, Allen." Her godfather, Joe Riley, groaned.

Allen Fagan was not a tall man. He was of average height and build with dark chocolate hair and loving, gray eyes. His smile was big and friendly as he brushed past his oldest friend, carrying a stack of research books.

"You can't seriously think Camelot stood on the eastern shores of Britain. You know very well evidence has been found to support that it stood near Somerset," Joe insisted, rubbing at his graying beard.

"I know what they think, but their digs turned up nothing. I still believe it was along the boundary between Essex and Suffolk."

"Your digs didn't turn up anything either," Joe reminded him. Her father's face tightened as he set down the books. He'd never forgotten Aliana's fall into the hidden chamber.

Changing the topic, he opened the top book on his stack. "A student brought this to me today." He flipped through the pages. Handing the book to his friend, Allen pointed to an article. "He seems to think this poem is referring to Excalibur and its true resting place."

Her godfather laughed. "So now your student wants to propose a new location of the mythical sword?"

Allen smiled ruefully. "I'm just glad that he's interested enough to suggest it."

Studying the old book, Aliana caught sight of a small red emblem on the cracked spine. It looked like a shield with a Dragon taking flight.

The Pendragon Crest!

She rushed forward, trying to see the pages, but she couldn't move from her spot next to the windows. "Papa, what book is that?" she asked. But he couldn't hear her.

The dream started to fade, and Aliana struggled to hold on to it. She wanted more time with her father, but he soon drifted away, the sound of his rich laughter ringing in her ears.

Gasping, Aliana shot awake. Arms tightened around her when she tried to sit up.

"What's wrong?" Galahad's sleep-thick voice rolled over her.

Gazing out the window, she saw the red and pink sky colored by the setting sun. She was in Merlin's home, not her father's office.

"Aliana?" Dagg asked from the pillow next to her. She hadn't even realized the little Dragon was in the room with them.

Looking up at Galahad, she breathed out, "I think I know how to find Excalibur!"

EPILOGUE

"How can you smile at a time like this?" Morgana demanded, storming into Mordrid's private chamber. She glared down at her smug cousin, who lazily reclined in an overstuffed chair.

The dark wizard spared a glance at his seething ally before turning back to the mirror he had been studying.

"They are going to try to find Excalibur next." Mordrid guffawed. "They still have no idea what that bitch Titania has done. Or that my little spy can get past the new protection spells Merlin laid."

"What has Titania done?" Morgana leaned against the chair, her confused eyes meeting Mordrid's in the mirror.

"You haven't figured it out? You followed the bitch queen for half a century before she returned to Avalon." He tsked at her in mock chastisement.

His self-aggrandizing gloating grated against the witch's nerves. She glowered, hating it when Mordrid realized something she didn't. "I know much about her, and I don't need reminding of all the men she bedded in those five hundred years." Morgana choked back a gag.

"Jealous? Surely Merlin also had many lovers during his banishment. How many did you have?" Mordrid deflected Morgana's hand when she tried to slap him.

"Curse you, cousin! Just tell me," she raged, hazel eyes flashing a dark blue as her magic rose like a viper.

"Have you never wondered why the queen broke Oberon's laws and saved that waste of a pretender king?" Mordrid spat.

Morgana sneered, rolling her eyes. "She hates us. She knows you can destroy her and take Avalon."

"But what else?" Mordrid asked, raising his eyebrow.

Morgana looked away, thinking. Queen Titania was a power hungry woman. Not only did she rule the Isle of the Blessed, but when she had taken Lord Oberon as her husband, she had gained Avalon as part of her dominion. Camelot was a jewel she had always coveted, but it wasn't part of the magical realms. She could never have it.

The sorceress's eyes widened, realizing what Mordrid was implying. "She wants one of her blood to sit on Camelot's throne."

"Precisely," Mordrid sneered. "What's the surest way to accomplish that?"

"The Destined One." Morgana laughed at the irony.

Mordrid turned back to his mirror, and a vision of Aliana from the party weeks ago appeared. Titania would get what she wanted, but Aliana would be at his side, not Arthur's. She would be his once he killed King Arthur and his blasted Knights of the Round Table.

Mordrid smiled, thinking of when he would have Aliana for himself. He turned to Morgana. "Tell your puppet they're coming right to him," he ordered, dismissing the sorceress.

Morgana's smile was ice cold as she nodded to him. She had a trap to set. One that would break the spirit of the Destined One even more than the death of her parents had begun to.

She couldn't hold back her cackle. "This will be fun."

Acknowledgments

I owe a big thanks to my editor, Beverly, who worked tirelessly on this project for me and helped make *Legendary* the best it could be! Also big thanks to Jennifer for being a champion for me and my first series. We are having a very fun ride. And, of course, major thanks and gratitude to Omnific for taking a chance on me and my story

I also want to say thanks to all the authors who have given me such excellent advice and encouragement since I started this part of my life. Finally, a big thanks to my parents for supporting me and all my crazy adventures through the years—and those still to come. I love you!

About the Author

LH Nicole is a seasoned pastry chef in our nation's capitol and a lifelong fairy tale (Disney and Grimm) lover. She believes in love at first sight, is addicted to eighties and nineties cartoons, and anything that can capture her ADD-way-too-overactive imagination. Joan Lowery Nixon and L.J. Smith were the first authors she became addicted to, and they inspired her to steal away whenever she could to read and write. You can keep up with LH and all her news and adventures on:

Facebook: www.facebook.com/LHNicoleAuthor

Tumblr: LHNicoleLegendary.tumblr.com

Blogger: LHNicoleAuthor.blogspot.com

Legendary Saga website: LHNicoleLegendarySaga.com

check out these titles from
OMNIFIC PUBLISHING

◆—⋯⋯→Contemporary Romance←⋯⋯—◆

Boycotts & Barflies and *Trust in Advertising* by Victoria Michaels

Passion Fish by Alison Oburia and Jessica McQuinn

The Small Town Girl series: *Small Town Girl* & *Corporate Affair*
by Linda Cunningham

Stitches and Scars by Elizabeth A. Vincent

Take the Cake by Sandra Wright

Pieces of Us by Hannah Downing

The Way That You Play It by BJ Thornton

The Poughkeepsie Brotherhood series: *Poughkeepsie* & *Return to Poughkeepsie*
by Debra Anastasia

Cocktails & Dreams & *The Art of Appreciation* by Autumn Markus

Recaptured Dreams and *All-American Girl* and *Until Next Time* by Justine Dell

Once Upon a Second Chance by Marian Vere

The Englishman by Nina Lewis

16 Marsden Place by Rachel Brimble

Sleepers, Awake by Eden Barber

The Runaway Year by Shani Struthers

Hydraulic Level Five by Sarah Latchaw

Fix You by Beck Anderson

Just Once by Julianna Keyes

The WORDS series: *The Weight of Words* by Georgina Guthrie

Theatricks by Eleanor Gwyn-Jones

The Sacrificial Lamb by Elle Fiore

The Plan by Qwen Salsbury

◆—⋯⋯→New Adult←⋯⋯—◆

Three Daves by Nicki Elson

Streamline by Jennifer Lane

Shades of Atlantis by Carol Oates

The Heart series: *Beside Your Heart* & *Disclosure of the Heart*
by Mary Whitney

Romancing the Bookworm by Kate Evangelista

Fighting Fate by Linda Kage

Flirting with Chaos by Kenya Wright

The Vice, Virtue & Video series: *Revealed* (book 1) by Bianca Giovanni

Young Adult

The Ember series: *Ember* & *Iridescent* by Carol Oates
Breaking Point by Jess Bowen
Life, Liberty, and Pursuit by Susan Kaye Quinn
The Embrace series: *Embrace* & *Hold Tight* by Cherie Colyer
Destiny's Fire by Trisha Wolfe
The Reaper series: *Reaping Me Softly* & *UnReap My Heart* by Kate Evangelista
The Legendary Sage: *Legendary* by LH Nicole

Erotic Romance

The Keyhole series: *Becoming sage* (book one) by Kasi Alexander
The Keyhole series: *Saving sunni* (book two) by Kasi & Reggie Alexander
The Winemaker's Dinner: *Appetizers* & *Entrée* by Dr. Ivan Rusilko &
Everly Drummond
The Winemaker's Dinner: *Dessert* by Dr. Ivan Rusilko
Client N° 5 by Joy Fulcher

Paranormal Romance

The Light series: *Seers of Light, Whisper of Light* & *Circle of Light*
by Jennifer DeLucy
The Hanaford Park series: *Eve of Samhain* & *Pleasures Untold* by Lisa Sanchez
Immortal Awakening by KC Randall
The Seraphim series: *Crushed Seraphim* & *Bittersweet Seraphim*
by Debra Anastasia
The Guardian's Wild Child by Feather Stone
Grave Refrain by Sarah M. Glover
Divinity by Patricia Leever
Blood Vine series: *Blood Vine* & *Blood Entangled* & *Blood Reunited* by
Amber Belldene
Divine Temptation by Nicki Elson
Love in the Time of the Dead by Tera Shanley

Historical Romance

Cat O' Nine Tails by Patricia Leever
Burning Embers by Hannah Fielding
Good Ground by Tracy Winegar

CPSIA information can be obtained at www.ICGtesting.com
Printed in the USA
BVOW08s0154300715

411072BV00004B/8/P